REBELS

by

DAVE LLOYD

DEDICATION

This first book in the Montana Saga is dedicated to my long suffering wife of many years: Donna. She has helped me with all my books, giving me support, ideas, and even working with me to put the leather-bound editions together, one page at a time.

Here's to you, Honey!! Thanks for everything you do and have done.

This book is historical fiction, as accurate as I could make it, with the years of research and reading that I have done. However, there have been a few times when I had to tweak the chronology a little to get everything to fit properly in the plot line. I apologize in advance for this, should you pick up on it when reading. I also freely admit that there may be mistakes. I admit that I am fallible and stand ready to correct them in subsequent editions, if they are pointed out to me.

In the meantime, I hope you get some enjoyment from its pages.

Copyright ©2012 by Dave Lloyd

All rights reserved. No part of this book may be used or reproduced in any manner whatsoever without written permission of the publisher, except in the case of brief quotations embodied in critical articles and review.

    This is a work of fiction written in the vernacular of the day, sometimes politically incorrect by today's standards, but no disrespect is intended by the author to persons of any race, color or creed.

    Many of the photographs in this novel are by Courtesy of the Library of Congress.

Other novels and short stories by Dave Lloyd

Outlaw
The Pistol

The Montana Saga
The Rebels - book one
Pardners - book two
T.S. Grounds - book three
Home Ranch - book four

Riverboat Trilogy
Fort Sarpy - book one
Upriver - book two
Captains - book three

Books of Short Stories
Tales
Arikara and Lord Guest

Sharpshooter Trilogy
Sharpshooter
The Hunters
Legacy

Non-fiction

History of Early Rosebud

PART ONE

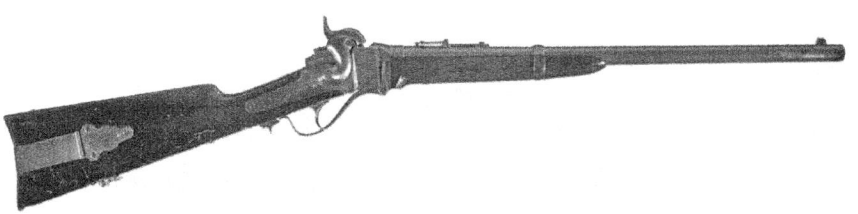

Chapter 1

Murphy's Station, 1864

Frank Shannon came awake with a jerk that raised him to a sitting position. He was in near darkness, but as sight returned, he dimly perceived objects scattered about him. For a panicky moment, he couldn't feel his legs. Then, as he squirmed, feeling came back with a rush—pain that made him grunt. His legs were pinned by his horse, lying stiff and cold across them. He managed to pull back somewhat, trying to scoot himself out from under the dead weight. As he started to put pressure on his upper arms, though, he felt the pain of a wound in his right shoulder, pain that made him dizzy. He'd been shot there, and the blood from it had brought flies that feasted on the red splotches that covered his front. He could feel them crawling and hear their buzzing as he waved his other hand, trying vainly to shoo them away. After arduous work and more pain, he managed to free himself from under Molly, his little Louisiana mare.

'What a great horse she was,' he thought. All heart and willingness—now reduced to a lump of fly covered meat.

Favoring the arm, he endeavored to raise himself to his feet, using Molly's rump to help him stand. He seemed all right otherwise. His legs held him up. He was lightheaded from his wound, the fall he taken, and the lack of food that had made his backbone think his stomach was trying to chew itself out of his body before the battle. *The battle*, he thought belatedly, *had they won—or lost it?*

He'd been through so many, it almost didn't matter anymore. He just wanted to get done with this war before it finally killed him. He sat on the mare's rump and checked the wound as best he could in the gathering darkness. The temperature was dropping, overhead, clouds obscured the waning moon, making the battlefield darker and more ominous.

The ball had gone nearly through the shoulder. Exploring gingerly, almost fainting from pain, he could just feel its roundness pushing from under the skin on his back. Touching it made it burn like fire. The damn thing needed to come out quick, before it and whatever had been driven in with it, clothing, dirt and such, festered and caused blood poisoning. But he couldn't reach it himself. He awkwardly pushed his handkerchief under his shirt and over the throbbing bleeding opening, hearing as he did so, a gargling breathy moan from nearby.

It sounded as if someone was strangling, and he realized he'd been hearing it for a little while. He pushed himself off the mare and went stumbling off to his left, abruptly nearly falling over an inert form he hadn't seen on the ground nearby. From the form came the awful sound. With his left hand, he felt around the unconscious man, trying to determine the extent of his injury. He'd evidently been shot in the face—through both cheeks, to be exact, and was now about to suffocate. Frank pried the shattered jaws open and pulled the man's slippery tongue back out of his throat. The poor soldier had been trying to swallow it. Using two fingers, Frank cleared his throat as best he could, of blood and shattered teeth and bone. How to keep the tongue from falling back and closing the throat was a problem, but he solved it by cutting a rein off Molly with his knife and tying it around the lower jaw to keep the tongue in place. With his own wound, and limited use of his right hand, this was not easily accomplished, but the man was now able to breathe, which he did with a peculiar whistle. Frank felt over the rest of the soldier's body, trying to determine if he had any other wounds. It appeared he did not. In the course of his inspection, he felt an empty holster.

He touched of his own side and his long pistol was gone, lost when he'd crashed to the ground. It was a real Colt .44 Army, not a poor Confederate copy, and along with his other pistol, also a .44, his horse and his Sharps rifle, a valued possession. He began a slow clumsy search for it, finding it finally in the grass not far away. He brushed it off and stuck it back in his holster, after swiveling the gunbelt around to his left side, to get at it with his good hand. His old Dad's short barreled gun was still in its holster at his back. Hearing a stirring and a moaning out a ways to his front, he went there and knelt by a man who, as he started feeling him over, died of a wound in his chest.

Now the battlefield was quiet except for a horse who kept slamming his head on the ground and trying to get up, on broken front legs. Frank went over and shot it with his pistol. The big animal lay back with a sigh which was echoed by Frank. He hated to see or hear any animal suffer, if he could help it. *God knows there's been enough horses killed and hurt in this war*, he thought. Each battle garnered a high number of dead animals, horses, even dogs, following their masters into the fury of combat. *It was a damn shame, to see the poor critters die. They hadn't declared war on each other, so why did they have to suffer And his Molly horse...* She had been a good one, though he preferred to ride a big gelding, like his Hank.

He'd taken her reins from a dead Yankee's hand at Chickamauga after losing Hank and she'd proven to be a greathearted animal—one that had soon come to recognize him when he'd come near. She would nicker and nuzzle his pockets, and of course, he always tried to have something for her—a stick of sorghum or cane, an apple or a peach, whatever he could find. Always staying close by and easy to catch.

He'd found out quickly that she could run like the wind. And she could jump. She was evidently used to jumping about anything in her path, as he'd found when they'd charged the guns at Antietam. They'd timed their charge from the woods as the guns were reloading and she'd jumped clean over an artillery piece, he taking the head nearly off a gunner who'd swiped at him with a rammer. For a moment, he'd felt like he was flying, as they soared in that wondrous leap.

Now she was gone and there was nothing worse than a cavalryman afoot. *Damn! The shoulder hurt.* He fell asleep, was cold when he woke. The moon was long down and the darkness was thick in the small valley.

He lay there, up against Molly, taking in the predawn light that was beginning to turn the tree tops to a rose pink, the shapes starting to take form as dead men and horses lying still around him. The cavalry battle had swirled and swept over the hill to the east, to come to some unknown conclusion.

He wondered about the wounded man he'd helped, if he'd survived the night. He hadn't heard the harsh breathing long after he'd cleaned his mouth of wound debris. Maybe he'd died. He looked that way and the man was sitting up, taking his ease against a dead horse, like him. He waved. The soldier gave a weak wave back.

Frank got up and took out his knife as he headed toward the other. He saw him tense as he glimpsed the knife and said,

"No cause to worry, just need you to help me like I helped you last night. You'da choked if I hadn't heard you and cleared your pipes for you. You must be as hungry as me, you was trying to swaller your tongue." He hunkered down in front of him and turned himself to present his back.

"Got a ball in my shoulder and wondered if you could cut it out of me."

Kneeling down before the man, a Johnny Reb like himself, he saw now, but an officer from the uniform, he gave him the knife. The man took the big blade and, with one trembling hand exposing the ball as it rested under bluish skin, used a quick twisting motion with the sharp tool that popped the lead out and down onto the ground. Frank fell forward, nearly fainting. He caught himself with his left hand and got his balance again.

"You're pretty handy with the toadsticker. Thanks. Can you see if you got whatever went in with it?"

He felt the manipulation keenly as the man worked the wound, working clotted blood and particles of clothing out of the wound channel. It hurt like a hot poker, but he stayed silent, though his head started spinning again. Presently the man grunted.

Frank turned then, and in the half-light, looked into gray eyes clouded with pain that stared out of a bloody broken swollen face. He shook his own head at the sight.

"Both of us need some doctorin', you specially. Can you get on your hind foots?"

Again the grunt. He reached down and took a hold on an arm and helped raise the man to his feet. He remembered this officer now, a captain on Hood's Divisional staff who had come along to get the lay of the land as they searched for a suitable ford across the Rapidan River. It was the back door to Grant's army they were seeking and it looked now like that back door was closed. The river here was wide, deep and fairly swift, swirling by the landing where the ferry docked on the southwest side of the river. There was no ford close or for miles, as far as the men knew. That was the reason for the ferry. But it had been a desperate hope, anyway. And this officer was needed back at Division headquarters to tell them so.

With his left arm around the man, he started them moving, when the man grunted again and going back to the horse lying there, he fumbled at them, trying to get something from his saddle bags. Frank helped him open them. A holstered pistol fell out, and a wrapped object that proved to be a bottle. Frank grabbed it up and unwound the set of light long-johns around it. It proved to be nearly full—of whiskey, to Frank's delight. The man grunted again and made a drinking motion to Frank, who didn't have to be asked twice. He uncorked it and took a deep swallow. The liquid was smooth and tasty going down and Frank savored it like a bee at the honey. He'd been a drinking man since he was twelve, sampling his daddy's home-stilled stock. This was superior stuff, charcoaled bourbon.

The officer twirled the cylinder on the Colt and put it in his holster, looking around for what proved to be the twin to it, lying close by on the ground, which he stuck in his belt. He dipped his hand in the bags again, taking something from them that Frank guessed might be money. Then he insisted on picking his saber off the ground where it lay by the horse's head.

Hell, no sense leaving anything valuable and easy to carry lying around. Scavengers would be looting the field as soon as they stumbled on it. In Frank's experience, the looting was quick and brutal in this war. Frank had seen them, both men and women, taking things from the wounded and dead, right down to the boots off their feet. But they would have to leave their horse gear. They'd be lucky to get themselves back, shot up as they were.

Damn it! That saddle had fitted him even better than the one he'd left on Hank.

They walked through the battlefield, away from the river, southwest. The first time they stopped, on a tree stump by the path, Frank took time to recharge his pistols and put a fresh load in his Sharps, while the other, though evidently in agony, did the same with his two weapons. Ingrained in them both after years of war was the need to be able to defend themselves at all times.

By midday, after many rest stops, they had stumbled back into the Confederate lines and been taken to the field hospital set up by the well in a farm yard. Frank sat and watched as the surgeon worked on the officer, cleaning bone and teeth from the wound and stitching the holes together, leaving room for drainage, as the captain twisted and strained against the pain on a bloody table. Then it was his turn, the fire of alcohol cleansing the wound and burning the tortured flesh. He passed out when the surgeon rammed in the wet cloth and pulled it through the hole in his back.

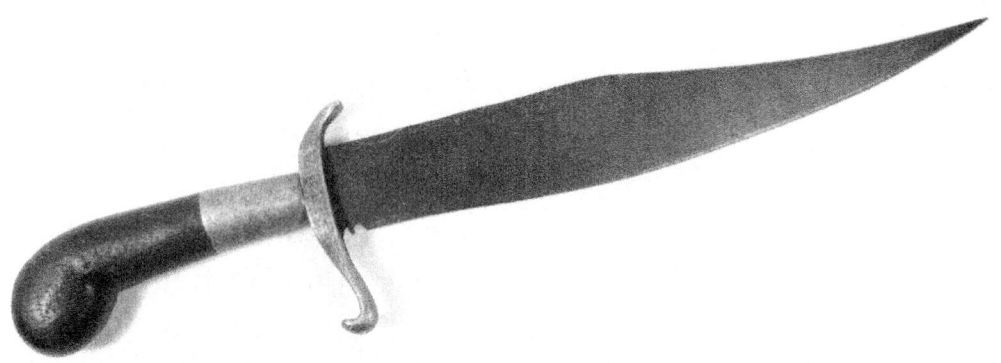

Chapter 2

Hood's Texas Brigade

Hood's Texas Brigade had been organized in Virginia in November of 1861, comprising the 1st, 4th and 5th Texas Infantry, along with the 18th Georgia Cavalry. This unit was then incorporated into the Army of northern Virginia and Colonel John B. Hood of the 4th Texas was elevated to the rank of Brigadier General and given the command. They first went into battle at Eltham's Landing in Virginia in May of 1862 and had gone on to fight in every action the northern Army of Virginia engaged in.

During the Seven Days Battle, the Brigade had distinguished itself by capturing the nearly impregnable Union position at Gaine's Mill. Later that summer, Hood was given command of the Division and Colonel Robertson of the 5th Texas assumed command, though the unit had kept Hood's name out of respect.

Under Robertson, the Texas Brigade had fought brilliantly at Manassas and at Antietam, where it had lost nearly 75 percent of its strength, the 1st Texas losing over 82 percent of its men, the highest loss in a single engagement of any Confederate regiment in the entire war. Heavy losses of the unit were also endured at Fredericksburg, Chancellorsville, Gettysburg, the Devil's Den, Chickamauga, Chattanooga, and Knoxville and many of the battles up to the present against Grant's Overland Campaign of 1864, on the eve of the terrible Battle of the Wilderness, in which wounded of both sides died horribly when the forest they were engaged in caught fire and burned much of the battleground.

    General Lee's Army of northern Virginia was like an old lion lying up in a thicket, waiting for the hunter. It was an ambush and Grant, like Hooker before him, had fallen into it. The Wilderness around Spotsylvania had been a mining district and nearly all the old growth timber had been cut down years before. The new growth had sprung up, covering the whole area for miles with tangled brushwood ravines, interspersed with little creeks that seemingly went nowhere. In this tangle, the Confederate veterans were already settled in their defensive lines. Grant was determined to throw them out, with a force that outnumbered them almost three to one.

* * *

    The struggle was to rage on for days, but Frank Shannon and Matthew Grounds, the disfigured officer, were out of the fighting, back with the wounded at the farmhouse, where injured men began piling up—first by the dozens, then the hundreds. There was no way that the surgeons could keep up and presently Frank decided he had to leave the area—the screaming of those being operated on mingled with the moaning and crying of those surrounding the hospital tents driving him away from the vicinity, away from all the pain and suffering.

He staggered erect, and as he left, he happened to glance over and saw his maimed acquaintance coming to his feet also. Their coming together seemed a natural thing and the two walked away to the rear, coming finally to a wagon park a mile away. A dozen teamsters were grouped around a fire and watched them approach silently. Frank helped the other drop wearily down by a tree a short distance away and went up to the men.

"Say, boys, I wonder if you-all have got some food and a couple blankets we might have—or buy?"

A gray haired one-armed teamster, evidently the spokesman and their leader, took a stubby pipe from his mouth and said,

"Sure do. Food's free." He gestured to an iron pot steaming beside the fire.

"And we could even come up with a couple cups for you boys, but blankets—guess we might have a couple we could sell you —if you-all had some hard cash."

Frank had a lone silver dollar and now pulled it from his pocket. He proffered it to the man, who took it and turning, rummaged in a nearby wagon, coming out with a pair of good heavy blankets. He handed them over and Frank went back to the tree and spread them both on the shivering officer. Then he went back and received two large tin cups full of stew, rabbit or possum from the looks of the whitish meat in them.

The others turned back to the fire, uninterested in two wounded men. They all had seen too many harrowing sights in this war to be curious any longer. Frank, for his part, was used to bartering or paying for what he got, though he knew, as they all did, that supplies were supposed to be dispensed to the units, not subject to purchase by individual troops. Food was another matter, as rationing was close and each mess supplied its own.

Though Grounds was ravenous, he had trouble getting the food through his shattered and swollen mouth and down his gullet. The meat was tough and stringy and Frank, watching him struggle, handed him his open clasp knife to cut it up in small pieces in the cup. The two settled down under their blankets then, and though the battle was roaring unceasingly little more than a mile away, they managed to sleep a little.

Twilight found them alone. The wagons had hitched up and pulled out, as the battlefield had started to shift and their supplies, chiefly ammunition for the guns, were needed. Frank started awkwardly rolling his blanket.

The officer scratched "Matthew Grounds, Captain, CSA." in the dirt and pointed to himself. He reached out a hand and they shook, Frank saying, "Sergeant Frank Shannon, 1st Texas." He didn't tell the officer that he couldn't read.

Chapter 3

Hood's Headquarters, The Wilderness

"Captain, with that wound, you're no good to us here. You cain't talk—you look like you're about to collapse! Go get yo'self healed up and come on back then. I hate to lose you, with the rest of the staff getting all shot to hell, but you need time to get back on your feet. Meantime, the Division is heavily engaged. Be gone, Sir!"

Hood turned in abrupt dismissal and began dictating orders to a harried colonel, leaving Matthew standing, swaying, at attention, taking in the words and realizing that the General was right. He'd written a terse account of the disastrous attempt to find a ford at the river. He had no further business here at Headquarters. Rather, he needed to get himself back in shape for duty.

He turned and left. From the porch of the farmhouse Hood was using as his command post, he could see down into the valley toward the site of the battle, where groves of trees were still burning, and lines of men were still bringing out wounded and dead bodies. Below him, an artillery battery had swept out of the smoke, unlimbered and were readying a salvo.

Once back in the fold, he and the sergeant had gone their separate ways to report in. Frank had found Company 'B', 1st

Texas, camped in a horse pasture down along a slow flowing creek, their guidon, bullet holed and faded, stuck in the rick of a hay wagon. They welcomed him back effusively, for Frank was a favorite in the ranks. Big Lars gave him a bear hug that cracked his back and hurt his arm, Jack Luther brought him a plate of beans, Corporal Luke Millett, deeply relieved to see him, found him a keg to sit on and Josh Batton, seeing his face whitening after the big man's hug, gave Lars a swat and shooed him away.

The giant had jumped ship in Galveston, Texas and starved on the streets until his vessel had sailed. A recruiter had gathered him up finally, promising him all he could eat and a life of adventure, if he signed up for the South. Slow of mind and body, yet he seemed to lead a charmed life, having gone all through the engagements so far without a scratch. Stolidly brave, he did what he was told, even under fire, and he seemed to have no temper, but his seamed back told of brutal treatment aboard ship and he never spoke of that period in his life. The men treated him like a trained pet bear and were protective of him. He idolized Frank and Millett and only reluctantly had stayed behind when Frank was picked by Captain Corder to go with him and a detachment to find a way to flank Grant's army on the west. Grounds and Frank were all of that group who returned. The others lay dead by the river, and the ensuing commitment of the Confederate forces had made the possibility of such a maneuver futile. Frank therefore had no one to report in to.

Frank's unit had not gone into battle with the rest of the 1st Texas, being designated to stay and protect the Headquarters. Now, their CO was missing and most likely the company, with its thinned ranks, would be incorporated into 'A'

Company, under an officer they had little use for: Captain Siderus.

The man was an arrogant southerner from Arkansas who cared little for the enlisted men, treating them little better than the slaves on his plantation. Shortly after he had joined the 1st Texas, his slaves back home had revolted, killing his brutal overseer, his brother and father before they took off for parts unknown. The two servants he had brought with him had disappeared soon after arriving in camp at Galveston. He had posted a heavy reward and enlisted the help of several bounty hunters but they had turned up nothing. The fleeing men had evidently headed west, into the land of the Comanche, rather than risking capture, a brutal flogging and return to his service. Stupidly brave and always willing to risk his men in any venture that might gain him personal glory, he was little liked by even fellow officers but so far had escaped being shot in the back by his own men through sheer luck. Frank, knowing his record and listening to his men berate him, wanted no part of him as his superior officer. But what to do?

The possible answer stumbled into his sight as he was shoveling beans into his mouth, the plate being held by a grinning Lars. Captain Grounds was walking aimlessly by, thinking deeply and trying to decide what to do and where to go. Go—but go where? Home was Georgia, many miles away. He had no idea where his striker, Sergeant Morley, and Spur, his servant, had gotten to and without being able to talk, was hard pressed to find them. He had been specifically asked for by Hood a month before, because of his demonstrated map-reading ability, and had joined the Headquarters group from the 18th Georgia, who like the other battle units of the Texas brigade, were now engaged on a wide front.

All his gear was with them, including his spare horse. His tack was gone. He'd had to leave it all with Atlas, his big gray gelding, dead on the field. However, he'd remembered to retrieve the money from his saddlebags, a heavy wallet that held more than $3000 in gold coin. THAT would have been a find for some looter! It was enough that he'd lost the expensive English saddle, the silver bridle and the expensive English carbine his father had given him. His hand went to his vest, where his gold watch, another gift from his mother, rested. He halted and pulled it out. It was stopped and he wound it, shook it to get it going again. He'd forgotten it, but it had survived the fight at the river intact. The watch, gold chain and fob itself was worth much—probably could be swapped for another good horse, if necessary. But he'd remembered the money, so that would be unnecessary.

But what to do now?

He turned at a step beside him. The sergeant who had saved his life at the river was there. He gave a half-salute with his left arm, more of a wave actually, since his right was in a sling. For the first time, Grounds was sufficiently in charge of his faculties to take a keen look at the man. He liked what he saw: a tall lean competent looking man of hawkish features, not young, maybe forty, though the war had aged them all, his legs bowed, evidently a horseman of the Texas stripe. His wide mouth was perpetually turned up in a half-grin, which seemed to reflect his cheerful disposition. But the steel was there in his eyes for a discerning man to see.

Frank for his part, saw a well-turned out officer who had fallen, with his wound and loss of equipage, on hard times. An officer with something about him that drew Frank to him like a magnet. Shorter than he, but not by much, he had a military bearing and gray eyes that looked calmly out of the bandaged ruined face. Clearly, the man had grit, which always impressed Frank, seeing as he had, the way he'd overcome the shock of his injury to retrieve his arms and load them, to be ready to defend himself. And there was something else. What it was, though, Frank would have been hard pressed to define. Some steel within the man.

"Sir," Frank said, realizing that it was the first time he had so addressed this officer, "Why don't you come over to the company here and I'll find you a plate of some beans and corn bread. You might could mash them and get 'em down. They's pretty good fixings. And while you're havin' a feed I'll send a man lookin' for your bivouac."

The man's eyes cast around him as if looking for alternatives and seeing none, he grunted assent. They walked back to the group by the hay wagon and after Frank had introduced him, he directed Lars to find a plate and dish up some grub for the officer. The act of courtesy surprised the others, who knew of Frank's general aversion to the officer corps. But sensing Frank's wishes, they hurried to make him welcome, one finding him a seat, the others showing respect—familiar, like the wagoneers, to the sight of injuries. Frank sent Amos Troyer, the gossipy little private who knew everybody's business, off to find out about the Captain's gear and presently the little man came back leading a short, thick corporal who stepped immediately to the Captain's side, saluting. He introduced himself to the others as the officer's striker. Morley, he said his name was. A talkative man, he told the group that the Captain had come from the 18th Georgia to the Headquarters Staff just a few weeks before the unit had been attached to the Texas Brigade.

Proud of his officer, he told the men that he didn't see how Hood would be able to do without him. This elicited a grunt from Grounds and Morley subsided. Matthew had painfully finished working the food into his mouth, emptying the plate, and he grunted and gestured to Frank standing near, who understood him rightly to mean he appreciated the food and the help. He rose and Morley bustled around, clearly flustered at seeing his charge so badly wounded. As they left the area, Frank walked away with them.

"Captain, if the Gen'ril can spare you, mebbe you'd consider attaching yourself to us. We need an officer now that we lost Captain Corder. There's talk of puttin' us together with 'A' and we don't want to be goin' in with them. Company 'B' wants to keep on as we've been. We're skirmishers, not regulars. I b'lieve the men'll go along with me on it, if you'd like to."

The little discourse earned him another grunt. They left it at that.

* * *

Back at his tent set up with the Headquarters group, Morley and Spur, his Negro servant, fussed around him, trying their best to make him comfortable. Spur, somewhat feeble minded, was distraught, on the verge of hysteria.

"Lawzy, Lawzy, Massa, what the Kunn'el goin' say when 'e 'ears yaw'ze got yahwr face blowed off!! An' Mistress Mawtha, she'll have a catawahlin' fit!! Yassir, she will!!"

He began snuffling, sneaking a peek now and then through the big flapping hands covering his face. The sight of the captain's bandaged head set him off again.

"Yore pore face!! How'se yaw'll goin'eat, wif no teefs ??"

The sniveling turned into low wails, threatening to get louder and Matthew was forced to get up and comfort the sobbing man, to Morley's disgust. (Though when Morley later heard of the loss of the big gray, the equipage and the prized carbine, he nearly started wailing himself. He'd had designs on that weapon since first being assigned to the captain and was deeply disgruntled over its loss.) A man whose concerns in life pretty much centered around himself, mainly his gut, he did have some fleeting feelings for this hurting officer, though he hadn't been with him long. The previous striker, Corporal Nestley, had been killed at Antietam. The Captain was a decent sort, he'd found, not like a lot of the primadonnas he saw around Headquarters or the staff area. And the man used his head.

He'd seen that when the Captain went into battle. He wasn't one to hold back but he was thinking all the time, not like a lot of the officers, who turned their brains off and rode their emotions into the strife and carnage. This man wasn't like that—and he could be quick, oh so quick, with that Colt he wore. The man picked his shots and made them count. Morley had seen him shoot some pigs the men ran out of a corn field, shot them by the men's request as the oinkers ran by, never missing a one from horseback, dropping them all, five of them, with neck or head shots from off a horse. Morley himself couldn't hit a barn with a pistol if he was inside it. Give him a musket, or better yet, an artillery piece.

He'd come from the 6th Virginia Artillery to the striker position because of a festering shrapnel arm wound he'd gotten in the fighting around the Devil's Den that kept him from working his gun. He still suffered from nightmares about that battle and was perfectly content for a while to do a striker's light duties in exchange for being on the line, though he dearly loved to fire a cannon. He supposed, after being released from light duty, that he'd go back to his battery and resume his duties there. Looked forward to it in a way. He missed the deep, pungent smell of powder burning and the sight of falling shot.

But in the meantime, he meant to make the most of his assignment back here around Headquarters, in officer country. That first meant the most and the best food he could find, and second, maybe some light fingered pilfering, when he could get away with it. His observation was that most enlisted men had little worth stealing. It was the officers, many of them rich, who had the possessions and money that he coveted. Like the one he was serving now.

* * *

The next day, after an agonizing night punctuated by the rumble and thunder of the battle, enough to keep anyone awake, Grounds lay exhausted in his cot. He was feverish and half in shock from the trauma of the throbbing wound, the broken teeth and bones all clamoring and sawing at his nerve ends.

Morley was off trying to find some tack for Albion, his spare horse, a rawboned sorrel he'd won at poker weeks ago from a major in the Signal battalion. Spur hovered near, anxious for his master but at a loss as to how to help him, his nervousness and continual jabber increasing the pain in Matthew's head, rather than allaying it. He turned at the sound of a voice he recognized outside the tent. "Hi, Darkie! Yore master hereabouts?"

Spur started his gabble, as he usually did when encountering a stranger.

"Oh, Lawzie!! Yahssir, yahssir, he's here in de tent jus' about to die, I believes! He sick to deaf, just to deaf, wif that face'a his blowed plumb awf. He cain't sleep, he cain't eat, he jus' lay and moan, like this!" He gave such an accurate imitation of Matthew's incoherent sounds that Grounds writhed on the cot from embarrassment. He grunted in exasperation and started to rise.

The tent flap went back and Frank appeared.

"Hello, Sir. Was hopin' you were feelin' better, but with that wound, I guessed not. I found you some Laudanum. Should help the pain and you might get some sleep."

He looked around, spied a glass and carefully measured a dose into it from a dark bottle. Then he helped Grounds raise up from the cot and saw that he choked down the medicine. Almost immediately the powerful opiate took hold of his senses, dulling the pain and sliding his consciousness off the tormented edge into a deep dark hole of blankness that he welcomed. The sounds of the battle faded. He slept.

* * *

The days passed and Frank's ministrations continued. It was he who brought a warm gruel each morning, sweetened with brown sorghum molasses, a mixture that Matthew was able get past his jaws and down his gullet. It was Frank who brought news of the battle. It was Frank again who found more Laudanum, when Morley had scoured the hospitals and come back empty-handed. The opiate was a lifesaver. Without it, he might well have died, from sheer exhaustion and pain. Certainly, his life was much easier because of it. Matthew never questioned how Frank had achieved the nearly impossible, just accepted it with grateful thanks. When he came, therefore, with a written request for Matthew's transfer from Headquarters to Company 'B', 1st Texas Brigade, he signed it without a question, content to try to repay the man with whatever coin he would accept. In his chemically clouded mind, Matthew didn't concern himself with the objections Hood might have to the scheme. The man had waved him away without a thought for his wound or his well-being. He felt no loyalty to the General, no more than he had given him. For a wonder, Frank triumphantly returned with a copy of an order making the transfer official. Company 'B' had a commanding officer!

Frank, for his part, had pulled strings and worked out an arrangement with the General's secretary, to get the transfer presented to the General in the proper way and persuade him to sign it. The cost was to be paid out in whiskey—and Frank already knew where to get it. The little ferret, Troyer, had told him that the Hospital Battalion had just gotten in a wagon load of premium sour mash grain alcohol. He had a sergeant in the Hospital outfit that owed him plenty and he intended to get his payback before it was gone.

Chapter 4

The Battle of the Wilderness

The news of the battle was not good. The Texas Brigade had gone forward after the now famous incident in which General Lee had attempted to lead an attack and the men had refused to follow their leaders until he consented to go to the rear, all afraid their revered General, like Stonewall, would be killed. They had suffered more than half of their fighting force dead or wounded, taking the ridge but having to later give it up under repeated counterattacks. Despite this, morale remained high in the ranks.

Matthew, meanwhile, was getting well. His wound had been examined by a German doctor, reputedly a good one, who was with the 18th Georgia, and he had reopened the pus pockets, cleaned them, removed some more bone and teeth shards, allowed some drainage to occur, done some additional stitching and given him some medicine to promote the healing. That, along with the Laudanum, had helped immensely and the pain was in abeyance for the moment. He could now gingerly work the jaw somewhat, but mastication of meat or solid food was out of the question.

Already lean, he was now a shadow of his former self. Frank's daily ration of gruel and molasses was about the most he could swallow, though he had found that soft bread dipped in soup was also something he could ease down his throat.

The outside of the wounds had healed pretty well, leaving a large indentation on each side of his face. That was the physical side of it.

Mentally, he was coming around, Frank could see. His greeting was more cheerful, he was trying some words, and was able to make himself understood. He was taking an interest in things around him, the Company, the war news, his tack replacement, getting another horse. He had even thought to ask Frank how his own wound was doing. The shoulder was healing but still very tender. The first few days, he'd taken some of the drug too, to get a decent night's sleep. Now, he was doing without it, making do instead with some of the sour mash he'd gotten from the Hospital Battalion. Pretty good stuff, really, but not up to what Grounds had had in his flask. Frank had been watering the Laudanum and was determined to wean his officer off the damn stuff. He'd seen what it could do if taken in excess for too long.

The Company, too, was gaining in strength. He'd managed to round up some malingerers off the sick rolls, get some AWOL soldiers surreptitiously back in the fold, and gather some recruits as they came into the Brigade, before the other sergeants got them. Now, they were getting their training from Corporal Millett, who always managed to do a good job with the new ones.

* * *

The regiment was operating now as dismounted cavalry, most of their horses having died of wounds or starvation. It was a terrific comedown for those Texans like Frank, who were born in the saddle and who wouldn't walk a hundred yards, usually, if they could straddle a horse. They made the best of it, though they were adamant that their officers rode. Frank therefore was ably aided by the men of his company to keep on the lookout for a saddle and tack for their new officer. As usual, it was Troyer who came to him with the news that he had heard that a Sharpshooter from the 10th had captured a beautiful black mare fully equipped, by the foolhardy expedient of passing himself off as a Federal scout and gaining access to the 3rd Pennsylvania's horse line. Once there, he had shown the sentry a hastily scribbled note that he had himself written, to the effect that he was supposed to bring the officer's horse over to Headquarters. Away from the line, he had boldly cinched up the saddle and rode it out of the camp and away in the night. He'd returned to the Confederate lines in triumph and the horse was presently picketed at the Quartermaster's. Troyer didn't know what was planned for its disposition. Immediately, Frank hustled himself to the Quartermaster's tent, to find several officers there already, vying with each other for the horse, which was indeed a beautiful animal. Frank listened to the arguments raging back and forth, then spoke up.

"I bid $100 in gold for 'er as she stands."

That quieted the crowd, who turned and looked at him. A major turned back and said,

"That is pure tripe. It's a spoil of war and should be reissued to the senior officer who needs it, not auctioned off like a -a-a- damn slave on the block."

The Quartermaster was an old hand at spoils of war, as Frank and the Sharpshooter knew who'd turned the horse in to him. He held up his hand.

"Not so fast, men. Money is needed for the Cause, too, to buy medicines and food. That's higher on my list than some ranker ridin' instead of walkin.' Now, I heard a hundred—who's goin' to bid $150 for this fine animal? Come on, get out yure wallets."

It didn't set well with the officers but was no more than they expected. The bidding quickly went up, and Frank waited until it stopped at $325, then spoke up again. "$400 in gold."

The officers turned and looked at this sergeant who presumed to get in the way of some ranker who needed a horse. Hell, sergeants weren't even riding, most of the time.

"$420." It was Captain Siderus, who'd come up to the proceedings and quickly seen what was going on.

Frank looked at him imperturbably. The company treasury was flush, mainly because of Troyer, who not only was an ace scrounger but was a ghoul, too, traversing the battlefields at night, rifling the pockets and wallets of the dead. It was mainly the Federal officers who were treated so. They were, like the Rebels, usually of wealthy background, and as such, targeted by every scavenger, both North and South. Frank, knowing of his propensity to prowl at night, periodically shook him down and halved the loot with him, putting the money in the company poke. In return, Frank covered for him when he was gone. It wasn't right, but Frank knew that someone else would end up with the loot, if it wasn't them. The grave diggers on both sides were lining their pockets, as were the hospital attendants, robbing the men as they came in, unless they were in good enough shape to defend their property. It hadn't been that way in the beginning of the war, but now, after four years, things had changed drastically.

Of course, the way the war was going, it was hardly worth plundering the Confederate dead. The bulk of their possessions were long since gone. But the company's coffers had close to $1200 in it, mostly gold and federal greenbacks, which spent better than Confederate. A major expenditure like this would take a vote of the men, but Frank knew he was on firm ground for up to half of it, because it wouldn't be there if not for him. The silence stretched and the Quartermaster, sensing the end of the auction, started cajoling the bidders, trying to milk a little more out of it. He extolled the qualities of the mare, her sleekness and beauty, the quality of the tack.

"$450." This from Frank in an offhand manner. He pulled a cigar out of his breast pocket and lit it, squinting through the smoke.

The ensuing silence told the auctioneer that the limit was reached and he hollered, "Sold!!" He himself had had dealings with Siderus before and was glad to sell the horse to Frank, if truth be told. The others turned away. Siderus, though, raged at the Quartermaster.

"Damn it, Sir!! What right has a mere sergeant to bid for such an animal, anyway!! I demand you take the bid I offered and turn it over to me."

He slapped his riding crop on his leg in distraction. He needed that horse! His big stallion, Trillyon, had gone down with the colic and was near death unless his groom could bring him out of it, with an ingestion of brandy and oats. He didn't expect that would happen, though. And he was presently a little short of funds, thanks to the cards not favoring him.

The Quartermaster, a big Swedish Captain whose skin by now was at least an inch thick, especially from dealing with arrogant officers like this one, merely shook his head and stated positively.

"Sorry. The horse goes to the man with the money to pay for him. You wanted him so bad, you should have topped the bid."

The other turned away in exasperation.

Frank led the horse back to the company area and all there exclaimed at the wonder of such a fine animal. They voted on the spot to allow the funds. It was unanimous, especially when they heard he had topped Captain Siderus in the bidding. Frank took the money back and paid off the Quartermaster, who sent his orderly off with $100 to pay the Sharpshooter. The company was repaid again when they led the horse up to their officer's tent and presented it to him. Frank grinned at his discomfiture. He actually tried first to refuse the gift, 'as being too grand'. Then, he wanted to pay the men back. They wouldn't hear of either one.

"Come on, Sir, mount up and let's see how you look."

The captain swung aboard and sat tall in the saddle. The men cheered. He made a grand sight on the beautiful mare.

When Morley led the horse to the line, he happened across Siderus' groom, Corporal Lang, who grinned all over his face when Morley told him the mare's story. As he ran his hands over the sleek mare, he laughed, though guardedly.

"What a horse this is!! I see now why the Captain was so blown 'bout losin' her to yore company. She's a regular darlin'!" Remembering his errand, he turned and picked up his bucket, then turned back.

"Say, don't happen to know anythin' 'bout what to do with a horse with a twisted bowel, does ye?"

"Twusted what?" If there was one thing Morley was not, it was a horse man. He'd been raised in the city.

"Twisted bowel—colic—it's when a horse gets a knot in its guts. Happens once in a while and most die of it, I guess. Come on, I'll show you."

The big bay was lying on its side, its belly clearly distended and its eyes rolling with pain and fear. It kept kicking its back legs against its stomach and groaning just like a man in its pain. Morley helped the man try to get some of the concoction in the bucket down its throat, but clearly the horse was too far gone to ingest much of the mess. They gave up presently and Morley, after talking a while longer, went off to get the day's rations from the Quartermaster. On the way, he bumped into Troyer and the men talked a little, Morley snickering as he told the other of Siderus' horse problem. The man was cordially disliked by everyone and Morley was no exception. Troyer went back to the company area and promptly told Frank what he'd heard.

"Hmmm." Frank went straightaway to the horse line to see for himself. He knelt down and ran his hands over the horse's gut, managing by touch to isolate the knot inside the poor animal as low down under its withers. "Hmmm."

"Corporal, run and tell yore Captain that someone wants to buy his stallion, that he'll give a hundred dollars for him, if he sells him within the hour."

The corporal ran off, mystified. *'Who'd want to buy a dying horse—maybe for the meat?'* he thought.

Frank meanwhile strode back and got Big Lars and Millett to help him, if they were needed. He also went to his pack sack and rummaged in its contents. Troyer tagged along. When he returned, Lang was there. The horse lay on its side yet, clearly in dire straits, throwing its head, sweating and still kicking at itself. Lang spoke up.

"He's in a card game. He asked who'd be dumb enuf to give hard money fur a dyin' horse. I just tole him there was a fool sergeant that thought he might cure 'im or would have his outfit eat 'im if he couldn't, I didn't tell 'im it was you boys." He ran an anxious hand over the distressed horse's head. It answered with a shudder.

"He said he guessed he would, if twas hard cash, no paper. Wisht you could fix him, he's a hummer of a horse, if he's not hurtin'."

Frank pulled the gold pieces from his pocket, handed them over to Lang. "Run, son, and be sure you get a bill of sale for me!" Lang took off like a scared rabbit. He was back in two minutes with the sale bill clutched in his hand. He gave it over to Frank, who looked at it, snorted and stuck it in a shirt pocket.

"Here, boys, catch hold heah and get him up standin'."

They did so, Big Lars taking most of the weight. The animal stood shaky and swaying. Frank twisted a set of hobbles on its back legs and secured them with a rope which he threw underneath to Lars.

"Here, hold back on 'im, keep him from kicking me." He dropped his sling and rolled up his left sleeve, showing a long, muscled arm. He wetted it from a bucket of water, took some bacon grease and rubbed it on, and then lifted the horse's tail and inserted it into its anus, working into the horse, who shook, trembled and, even in its far gone state, attempted to kick back. But it was thwarted by the hobbles and rope stoutly held by Lars. It threw its head back then and nearly fell, but the other men braced and held it up, while Frank burrowed his arm deep into the animal's insides. He grimaced at what he found there, working, working up to his shoulder, as if trying to crawl inside the poor beast. Abruptly, he withdrew his arm, the hand grasping a wad of undigested matter. He threw it down, plunged his arm again into the depths of the struggling creature and again pulled out a hard mass of undeterminable substance. Twice more he did this, then told the men to let loose, which they did, the horse promptly sitting on its haunches, as if to say, 'No more of that!! Frank washed himself off at the creek while the men looked at the matter he had brought forth from the horse's insides.

"Looks like he's been bin eatin' leather or such. It's all balled up in a black mess. Hard, too."

"Yeah, he was damn bound up, alright. We need to get this down 'im." He came up with a bucket that he had dropped some Laudanum and some ammonia in. Together, they forced a good draught down the horse. Then Frank had Troyer walk him a little. They stood and watched for a while as the mixture took hold and then the horse evacuated, some of the manure quite hard yet, some soft.

Next day the animal was solid on its feet and nickering for food. At Frank's direction, he was kept off his feed for another day. Siderus happened by in the afternoon and saw him being walked by Troyer and nearly had a fit. He was sure the horse was dead by now and long butchered out. First he berated Lang until that poor worthy was near to tears, then he went after Frank, who he accused of trickery to get his horse from him.

Frank was bland under the verbal abuse, saying merely that, "He could take it up with the General, if he wanted to carry the tale to him." Meantime, he had a bill of sale, signed before witnesses, that said the horse was his.

Siderus went off raving about what he'd do. Frank chuckled.

The next day he approached Frank, trying to buy Trillyon back. Frank was agreeable. "Sure thing, Sir. $500 will be 'bout right, I b'lieve."

The figure sent Siderus into another fit of cussing. Then he grew calm and said ominously, "Not a penny more than $200. That's doubling your money but paying you something for your effort to cure him. I'd advise you to take it."

"Sorry, Sir. I already have an offer of $450 from Captain Grounds."

"Grounds! What does he need another horse for? He's got two besides this one!"

"That's so. And say! I b'lieve I did hear him mention he'd sell the sorrel, come to think on it."

In the end, Siderus got a horse—Ground's sorrel gelding, a poor substitute for the big stallion. But he paid $300 for the animal. Grounds wouldn't budge on the figure.

Spare Cartridges
Courtesy of the Library of Congress

Chapter 5

Matthew Parker Grounds

Matthew Grounds was from a prosperous family whose ancestral plantation was located north of Savannah, on the banks of the river of the same name that formed the border between Georgia and South Carolina. The old main house was a grand confused jumble of added on wings that projected every which direction from the central structure in a way that was somehow yet pleasing to the eye.

The Grounds family mansion was ruled by a crusty old matriarch named Martha—Mistress Martha. She was Matthew's aunt from the London side of the family, who had come to visit after Matthew's mother's death, then saw just how the American side so needed her ministrations that she had never left for home, though she still maintained she had her luggage packed. At different times, not often, the male side of the family wished she would exercise their use.

In the main, they were happy to have her there, for she wrought a beneficial change in the household, ruling it with an iron hand, caring for Matthew's younger sister, Emmy, seeing that things such as meals were sumptuous and punctual, that the house darkies were kept at their duties, that the house was spotlessly clean at all times and the silverware accounted for and polished to a high shine. She reveled in entertaining the great families of the locality, but also mindfully kept within her allotted house budget, as set by Danforth Grounds, Matthew's father.

Danforth's overseer, Jacob Barlow, and Mistress Martha were bitter enemies but each grudgingly respected the other, as working towards a common cause. Barlow himself was a third generation employee of the Grounds', brought up on the estate under his father's tutelage. His wife, Sara, had thought to be the next mistress of the household after Margaret's death, in line of succession or seniority, so to speak. Since Danforth's wife had gotten the swamp fever and taken to her bed, Sara it was, who at first had control of the interior doings, only to be swept aside in imperious fashion by Mistress Martha when she arrived from England. The two women hadn't spoken for years.

When Matthew was twelve, Danforth had sent him off to Mistress Martha in London, with express instructions to send him on to Dover, where the Duke of York's Royal Military Academy was situated. This prestigious military school was open to male offspring of England's soldiers, providing the fathers had served for five or more years of duty. This stipulation applied also to those retired officers, of which Danforth was—having been invalided out of the Royal Dragoon Guards after a disastrous action in Afghanistan during the British war there. By sheer luck and his wound, he had escaped the massacre of Kabul Pass, where 15,000 British troops were killed, giving England a disastrous defeat.

It was a family tradition that the male Grounds heirs were all destined for the Duke's Academy, and Matthew was punctually put on board ship when the time came, and sent to the British Isles for his education. Danforth had high hopes for him, seeing him as a bright, athletic youngster of great potential—and the only heir. Emmy, being a female, didn't count in the line of progression.

The Grounds family had been Tories during the Revolution, and nearly lost their lands after America won its freedom from their mother country. Through judicious use of a fortune in gems looted by Danforth's grandfather from a Maharajah's coffers during Britain's early conquest of India, the plantation remained intact, though struggling to survive. After the revolution, Danforth's father, Sir Melville, had managed to heal the family finances by slaving along the west coast of Africa, a lucrative but highly ungentlemanly speculation. At heart a moral man, and having gained the knighthood in his early years through a heroic engagement in France, against Napoleon's armies, he felt his honor had been Stainted by his trafficking in slaves. Finally depression and guilt had ridden him down, and excessive drinking no longer assuaging the hurt, he committed suicide when Danforth was nineteen. At the time, Danforth was in Afghanistan fighting for his life with the British Expeditionary force there.

Jacob Barlow's father, Andy, ran the place until Danforth's leg wound forced him into separation from his regiment. Upon his return home, he found the plantation still running like a well-oiled machine. It remained so under his and Danforth's ministrations and Danforth had since tripled his holdings. The boy, Matthew, had a heavy burden to bear. Recognizing it, he was almost glad to get away for a time.

* * *

Mistress Martha Loring, lean and spare, plain featured and dressed in somewhat shabby black clothes that looked like mourning garb, though her husband had been dead for years, waited at the dock for the gangplank to come down. The little homesick sad-faced boy, gaunt from weeks of seasickness and little food, who stepped timidly down to the dock took her heart when she saw him. She had no children herself. They had died with their father in a Cholera outbreak in the city. At the time, she had wanted to die herself, had contemplated suicide, but it was against her religion, and she'd dismissed it as a heathen notion.

She lived alone in a small walkup not far from Piccadilly Square, a lonely widow of some means, as her husband had been well-to -do. Her days were spent reading, usually the Bible, though her one 'vice' as she called it, was the London Times Daily. Through it, she kept abreast of the city, the country and world doings. She usually did little cooking but wanted to make Matthew's stay memorable, so outdid herself in the culinary department, finding she enjoyed it immensely. Her cat, Alesia, a fat, black and white Persian, warmed to Matthew immediately when he entered the drab place and made a pest of itself while he was there. Somehow, Matthew felt at home with the aunt he had never seen, and they hit it off very well.

He was due at the school in a fortnight and they used the time in sightseeing. She was an excellent tour guide and they went to all the places of interest in the city. She found a new sense of excitement welling in her when she took him to Buckingham Palace and saw the changing of the Guard through the eyes of an impressionable young boy. The Tower of London was closed but they went back several times and were finally able to view it, even the upper cells where so many royal and famous figures had been incarcerated, including Sir Walter

Raleigh, a figure of note yet in the history of the American colonies. Canterbury Cathedral, The London Bridge, the British Museum—all consumed the better part of four days.

Matthew had brought a large denomination check with him that needed to be cashed and they went to her bank, the Bank of England, and receiving the funds, did as Danforth had directed, putting the money into her account for disbursement. At Bond Street, she took him to the haberdashery her late husband had frequented, Hawke's, and ordered his uniforms there, and then they went over to Peel's for his shoes and boots. After that, it was to Tautz's for the rest of his clothes. He'd brought a minimum of belongings with him, to make it easier to travel, and together, sitting at the little dining table, the cat purring in his lap, they had made a list of what he would require, working off the school's syllabus.

She'd adjusted her glasses and said, looking at the pamphlet,

"Hmm, I see that under the "Recommended Accoutrements" you might have use for some 'Sporting Arms,' in case you would have occasion to enjoy the shooting in the East Kent countryside." She looked at him.

"Do you like to shoot? I mean, is that something you would enjoy? I see from the "Sporting Section" in the Times that it is expected there will be goodly numbers of grouse on the downs this year. Grouse. . . Have you any familiarity with a shotgun?"

Her husband, Ben, had lived and breathed the sporting scene, especially bird hunting, and she had kept some of his favorite guns, selling the rest off because of lack of space when she had moved into her present apartment. Now she remembered them. They were far back in the large hall closet, where they had first been deposited, and lain in cases for years.

He looked at her and she saw a spark that had been absent before. "Oh yes, Ma'am!! I love to shoot! I hunted much as I could at home." He thought about the great hunting they had there on the plantation, the bird and rabbit hunting, the squirrels chattering at him in the trees, and experienced a sudden pang of homesickness that was evident to her.

She swept up and went to the closet, calling him to come help her. Together, they pulled leather-bound case after case out, and opening them, Matthew forgot his longing for home in the delight of handling fine weapons again that hadn't seen the light of day for many years. She exclaimed with dismay at the first one they opened. Nestled in the fine velvet was a matched pair of Manton dueling pistols, .56 caliber, the barrels showing a light patina of rust. Forthwith they embarked on a cleaning frenzy, for all of the cases opened showed the evidence of long neglect.

One of the cases contained a highly engraved Westley Richards side-by-side 20 gauge, with two sets of barrels. The beautiful little piece especially took Matthew's eye, and seeing that, Mistress Martha declared on the spot that he was to include that in his baggage when he left for school. The rest were shotguns and rifles of excellent quality, chiefly from the House of Westley Richards or Purdey, a small selection of what Ben had when alive.

Of the sightseeing places of interest in London, though, it was the National Gallery, in its new building, that so took his interest, with its corridors and huge rooms filled with works of the masters. Mistress Martha, taking note of his interest in art, queried him at length about his artistic endeavors and got out of him finally his great ambition—to be a famous painter, not a soldier, like all the males of the line of Grounds. This she knew he had never told anyone else in the family, for it was nearly a sacrilegious utterance, seeing how it went so far against tradition. They agreed it would be their secret.

* * *

School was at first a nightmare for the young American. He talked wrong, with his slow southern drawl and funny enunciation. He looked wrong, for his Aunt's choices of civilian dress had been sadly out-of-date, though his uniforms were appropriate. He even thought wrong—at least, that was how he at first came across to his English peers, who were still smarting over the upstart American colonies breaking away from Mother England.

It wasn't long, though, under the tutelage and expert direction of the staff and the umbrella-like protection of a sympathetic 'Old Boy' who was himself from the 'Colonies', that he became adjusted. It helped that he excelled at sports, where he more than held his own, and he shone in the classroom, displaying a canny ability at math that was the delight of his instructor and the envy of his friends. They soon began coming to him for help at their studies and he found himself in demand as a tutor in the subject. That led to a bond between himself and a schoolmate whose family was one of the most wealthy in the island nation and a local power in the county of Kent, where his father was Squire.

Though he went to Mistress Martha's for All Saint's Day vacation and Christmas that first year, thereafter, in the succeeding years, he spent many holiday vacations at Bertrand MacNeil's huge family estate, usually during a time when the boys were able to hunt. Bertrand, a stocky, athletic youngster, not too bright, loved to ride and fox hunt, and Danforth, on hearing of their friendship and knowing of the famed East Kent

Hunt, sent some funds for the purchase of a couple of good mounts, so that his son wouldn't have to ride borrowed or rented horses. Mistress Martha, who had ridden much when a child on the family estate, delighted in going with Matthew and Bertrand to a recommended Stratford breeder to purchase them. Her comments during the selection were listened to and soberly considered, because they recognized a fellow horse person. The result was a pair of premium animals, well bought, that Matthew kept at Bertrand's.

One was a five year old athletic tall sorrel with white stockings and a blazed face that the breeder asserted could 'jump o'er t' moon, could 'e get a runnin' st'rt'. The other, a small black with one white fetlock, that showed some arab blood, was fast and nimble on its feet, able to turn and quarter on itself so swiftly that Matthew, more than a half dozen times, found himself dislodged from the saddle and falling like a shot bird, the ground coming up to meet him with a thump. Mercury, a gentle animal, would stop and wait for him to mount again, sometimes nuzzling him anxiously if he lay for a while trying to regain his breath.

The sorrel was true to its name, Eolus, the Greek God of the winds. Though not as quick off the mark as Mercury, Eolus could run and jump with dash and speed that was more than satisfactory to the youngster. In addition, he was as gentle and affectionate as Mercury. Matthew loved his horses and rode whenever he could.

The East Kent Hunt's country covered (and still covers) the whole of the southeastern extremity of England, an area of over 1,400 square miles. The North Downs, a line of chalk hills running from west to east forms the spine of Kent County. North of this ridge the land falls to the marshy and low-lying shore of the Thames Estuary. To the south there is an area of clays and sands that form a rolling, wooded region known as the Weald that finally merges into the low-lying area of Romney Marsh. The long coastline of East Kent is alternately flat or cliff-lined. These are the white storm pounded cliffs of Dover and Thanet that face the rest of Europe over the English Channel.

This area was not the best section of the island for following the hounds, being as mentioned, hilly with thick woodlands, while many of the valleys were edged with thicket and the fields with wattle hedges. Over the whole of the county there was a spread of people: the intrusion of lower London, the city of Canterbury, and the towns of Deal, Folkstone, Aylesford, Sandwich and others, with a lot of plowed fields and market gardening close to them that had to be gotten over or around. The fences were also formidable, being stake and bound fences, with high stiles that tested the mettle of horse and rider.

It was also a military district, with consequent numbers of hard-riding English officers from Canterbury, Shorncliffe and Dover all continually wanting to be in the chase. Add to all, the fact that it was poor scenting country, usually with winds from the sea blowing across it, rain either coming or going, and it was hard to see the fun of it—but to the horse loving, outdoor people of England, it was.

The Hunt Master was Mr. F. Brockman, a superb sportsman and houndsman who had been the Master since 1832. Being a Kent man himself, and living in the country he hunted over, he was popular with the local farmers and covert owners, and took care to keep relations between the man on the ground and those on horseback cordial, seeing to it that a large portion of the membership funds went to charitable local offerings.

Due to several factors, including over-hunting, the local foxes were scarce when he took over the Hunt, and he had imported animals from France, a policy which was criticized by some, but not those who delighted in the Hunt. Hence, there were good numbers for the chase.

The school's more wealthy students all rode to the hounds when they could and Matthew had entered this fraternity as soon as he could as he loved to ride—the faster and better mounted, the better he liked it. This was dangerous in the chase but he was determined each time he rode to be as close to the hounds as he could possibly get, in part because he was American and wanted to show well against his English peers.

Consequently, he had some bad falls and once had to spend some time on crutches, with a broken leg that took quite a while to mend. His time off-horse was not wasted, as he went ever deeper into his favorite academic subject: math. To his secret disappointment, art was not delved into in the curriculum.

Brockman, seeing in Matthew and Bertrand ardent upcoming sportsmen, took pains to be sure they were included in the hunt as often as could be fairly done, to the boys great satisfaction. Their horses pounded behind the baying hounds through rain and sleet, fog and snow. both grew hard as their mounts from the constant exertion and Bertrand, at least, would have had much trouble keeping up with his studies, if it hadn't been for his friend's help. More than once during their time at the school, one or the other, sometimes, both, were in on the kill, and got to be toasted from the stirrup-cup, to their satisfaction, and the chagrin of the older men, who grumbled a little among themselves, but had to admit the boys were 'owing of it.'

As time went on, they got to be 'Old Boys' themselves, and Matthew's memories of Georgia and home were becoming dimmed, except when a frequent letter showed up. It was, in Matthew's mind to enlist in the same regiment his father had, and do a tour in India with Bertrand, who had already declared his intentions in that direction, his father having consented to buy him a commission upon their graduation. His urging of his American friend to do the same was swaying Matthew, and finally he wrote his father and asked for the funds to do the same. His father, proud but worried about his only son, wrote him back, enclosing with the letter, sufficient funds not only to purchase a position in the Dragoons, but to outfit himself well, too. A second draft was designated by his father as a graduation gift to do a few months tour of Europe. Clearly, cotton and tobacco were doing well in the 'Colonies.'

Accordingly, when the big day came for them, and they marched down the aisle in front of a large crowd of well-wishers, including an extremely proud Mistress Martha, it was already decided by the two school mates that they would travel to the continent together in the company and chaperonage of their friend, Mr. Brockman, who had finally consented to take them in charge and show them around Europe while his perennial quarry was denned up.

They had three months of intense travel and enjoyment, the highlight for Matthew being the Louvre, where he spent too little time entranced by the great paintings hung there, before his impatient comrades finally pried him away.

Mistress Martha received them back in London with an air of disdain and affected disinterest for their journey on the continent. She, like most of her English contemporaries, had strong feelings of distaste for the garlic eating 'Frogs' and their neighbors, carried forward from years of the Napoleonic wars. She was more interested in Matthew's descriptions of the wonderful paintings by the masters and Bertrand's depictions of the horses being raised on the French plains. She had three weeks of her young man's company before he boarded ship for India, and it took all her stoicism to keep from breaking down in tears as she saw him board ship at the same dock which he'd come into her life the few short years back. When she returned home, Alesia, that same old fat cat, now hoary with age and its whiskers drooping, had to meow at the door for minutes on end before its mistress came out of her depression long enough to let it out.

Sharpshooters – 18th Corps
Courtesy of the Library of Congress

Chapter 6
India, 1850

He had decided to sell his two beloved horses and remount himself in India, since the shippage for them would have been exorbitant. Bertrand had offered to board them for him at his home but Matthew had declined the offer, knowing how long they would probably be gone. Fortunately, he and Bertrand hooked up at the end of their journey in Cairo with several home-bound officers nearly as soon as they checked into their hotel there. These were anxious to sell their animals before boarding the returning ship and the boys found themselves facing a buyer's market and took advantage of it. One of the mounts Matthew bought was a young gray Arab stallion that he and Bertrand had flipped for and Matthew had won. He named the spirited horse 'Palukan'.

    Palukan carried him through much that Matthew experienced on that continent. There were long, exhausting treks across deserts and mountains and furious battles with the Pathan rebels along the Afghan and Punjabi borders. The last year of his tour, the horse saved his life and gave up its own in a race to the death with a rebel band when he was carrying messages to the regimental headquarters at Srinagar. The superbly mounted rebels had previously been successful in relaying down and killing the couriers and if it hadn't been for the stamina and speed of Palukan, he would have been caught. The horse, with a last trembling dash, took him through the gates and fell, its sides heaving. With shots from the parapet driving back the raging, swirling band, Matthew took its head in his lap. The dying shimmer of its luminous eyes, centered on him like those of a devoted spaniel, haunted his nights for months.

Another blow to the youngster came weeks later when Bertrand and his company were surrounded at an isolated dubya and wiped out after they ran out of ammunition and water. The corpses were mutilated beyond recognition.

The last months there were nearly a mirror of his father's, as he was in hospital at Cairo, recovering from multiple wounds suffered when he and his men caught up with and exterminated the band of Pathans that had done in Bertrand.

His company had spoken with awe of Matthew's courage and dogged persistence in the pursuit, his cunning use of the terrain they had traversed, and the way he had formed the ambush which caught the rebels by surprise, the furious way he had led the charge which culminated in the hand-to-hand struggle at the end, his fight with the indomitable rebel leader which had been such a near thing, their officer finally prevailing with his saber even after receiving a half dozen sword cuts that should have rendered him 'hor's de combat'.

The victors had cut off the heads of their dead enemies, and wearily gathering up their dead and wounded, managed to wend their way back to Srinagar, moving at night to ease the wounded and hiding during the day. Matthew and his sergeant were both honored at a medals ceremony weeks later, when he had recuperated from the battle. Then he had finished his tour and resigned his commission, having made his mind up during his convalescence to go home to America. But the ship, of course, was headed to England and he had a joyous reunion with Mistress Martha, who was beside herself at the return of her adopted son. Then the day that he most dreaded came and went like a nightmare: the telling of Bertrand's last days to his grieving parents in Kent. That scene, like the dying of Palukan, haunted him for months.

* * *

When it came time to leave England, Mistress Martha had taken him up on his invitation to accompany him back to America for a visit. Matthew knew by now that she had nothing left for her in her own country, with all her family there dead. Alesia had gone to cat heaven some years back. And the last letters from America had told them both of her sister's illness. She was needed there and went with Matthew gladly.

Chapter 7

Pendemere Oaks, Georgia
The Grounds Plantation

In England, Mistress Martha had been a neglected old maid of little consequence, either materially or socially, invisible in the stratified hierarchy of London. Suddenly, though, in Georgia, she found that she was an important part of an extremely rich and powerful family, whose lands extended for miles, not acres, whose house was grand, even by the standards of the Old South, whose influence went all the way to the Governor's mansion, where they were frequently invited to dine and take part in the social soirees given on there. The family lived in the stratified air of southern high society. As such, she was expected, as a mature matron of, if not aristocratic, at least well-born and genteel English blood, to take a place of substance and weight within the small family circle. Once she got her thoughts together and made an assessment of the situation, she took that place with undeviating determination.

Her sister, Maureen, was deathly ill. She had handed over her position as head of the house to the overseer's spouse, as there were no other adult women in the family, except for an aged grandmother whose mind usually was in the past, and who sometimes stayed up in her room for days. Emmy was a retiring young teenager, very timid. To have the great house run by a 'commoner' was not acceptable, now that Mistress Martha had arrived and she forthwith had taken charge. Inevitably there was friction but she brushed it aside and found that she had a real aptitude for the work. Even more, she enjoyed it. She came alive again, though she continually kept up the farce of being there only 'temporarily'.

At first, she would leave, she said, when her sister got well. Then, after her death, it was until Matthew should be married and his wife take her place. To perpetuate that sham, she kept some of her bags packed and ready—with old clothes that she never wore, anyway. She had seen, before leaving England, how shabby her wardrobe had gotten, and had indulged in an orgy of clothes buying, all put to excellent use when she arrived, as continental fashion was still the gauge by which the 'colonials' dressed themselves. Consequently, she was looked on with awe and respect by all who had come into contact with her, respect well placed, as she was above everything else, intelligent, well-spoken and very presentable for her age.

That she adored Matthew and catered to his every wish and whim was quickly noted and approved by the household, as they felt the same about the young man. His scars from the Indian engagements were superficial and didn't show and most people meeting him saw a handsome, bright young man barely into adulthood. They didn't know he had already seen mortal combat and more dead men than most of the older men in the community who were veterans of Indian battles and the War of 1812. College wasn't for him, either, though he did, for part of one year, attend Harvard. Coming home, he began his tutelage of cotton and tobacco growing and plantation running with his father and Jacob being his able instructors. Strangely, he missed soldiering and the thought of being a planter seemed dim and dull compared to what he'd already experienced.

* * *

What had saved him from dying of boredom was raising horses. This was something he deeply enjoyed: the sight and smell of a stable full of horses, their heads poking out of their stalls, each one a man could be proud of, each stall nearly filled with clean straw, each attended by a little darky whose sole mission in life (he thought) was to see that his horse was taken care of and healthy. That was satisfaction. That was fulfillment. Always he thought of his Arab stallion, its eyes haunted him at night, the race it had run and won coming back to his dreams.

Perhaps as a result of that race, one that encompassed a variety of terrain and long, grueling miles, he was not keen, as so many other young bucks, on raising horses to put on the short track, to win or lose in a distance measured in yards, rather than miles. He looked for horses that would give their all over a long distance, had exceptional bottom and endurance, and could form a bond of affection with their owner. Consequently, the stables gradually came to be a place where one would find the Arab strain predominating, a horse bred for power and vitality, a horse that looked as if it were in motion when it was standing still, a horse that combined the qualities of survival and strength and speed over the long haul.

It wasn't that he didn't like the long-backed Standardbreds that most of his peers were busily breeding and racing, or the dark colored Morgans, another horse of New England origins. They were represented in the stable, particularly because his father liked the Standardbreds, too, and had raised them since his youth. And Danforth's high standards had resulted in noted success. Acheron, his elderly stallion, figured in the bloodlines of many plantation's quality horses throughout the South. His mother, on the other hand, had been fond of the Morgans, as her family in Vermont had raised them. She had brought them from home and they had always been part of the Grounds plantation's scene since she had lived there. Danforth had brought her horses of the type for all the years she had ridden.

Matthew's father, though, had not been to the stables since his wife had died. Instead, he had his horse for the day's riding brought up to the house. Matthew knew it was because the Morgans down there missed his mother's attention and Danforth couldn't stand to see them pining for her. Emmy was scared of horses and declined to ride. Matthew had started to discreetly disperse them away to good homes as he could find them when his aunt, hearing of what he was doing, had entered on the scene and asked that he keep some of them back for her to ride. He'd done so and she had resumed her riding with relish, roaming far and wide on the estate and beyond, making the acquaintance of the surrounding neighbors' wives and families as she went. Both men got in the habit of deferring to her every wish, for she really had brought a large measure of English cheer and class to the household and they greatly loved her for it.

Matthew himself found little to interest him in the sighing, simpering women of the surrounding Georgia countryside, though there were some lovely belles who definitely craved and eagerly sought his attentions. Marriage was in his destiny, he knew, and at times he looked forward to it, but it was nothing he felt compelled to rush forward to meet. He privately thought, observing the deep-seated practicality that Mistress Martha brought to every problem and situation around the estate, that he might eventually go back to England and look there for a wife. Danforth didn't question him about it, but Matthew knew he wanted family about him and was distressed that his son wasn't pressing forward in that realm of their life. Danforth was young enough to think that he might sometime venture into marriage again, despite the nearly crippling injuries of his war years.

* * *

  The new decade, 1860, saw the highest prices for cotton ever, and European manufacturers clamoring for the South's "white gold". Danforth and Matthew conferred and decided on taking a step unprecedented by the plantation owners. For years, the cotton growers had seen their product bought cheaply by the foreign brokers and sold at sky-high prices abroad. Now several bolder, prosperous growers decided to charter a ship and see if transporting cotton and tobacco themselves would reap a whirlwind of profit or be a bust.

  Matthew, to his surprise, was chosen to accompany the cargo abroad. Cotton currently was selling for 17 cents a pound on the American market. Danforth and the others were sure that they could reap twice that, maybe more, on the shores of England. A large cargo ship was leased from a reputable New England firm, Masters and Sheehan, and soon loaded to maximum with fine Georgia cotton bales and barrels of tobacco. The ship captain, a Quaker named Carstairs, weighed anchor with a favorable wind and in five weeks' time, they saw the white cliffs of Dover, a sight that brought a nostalgic mist to Matthew's eyes, thinking of Bertrand and family.

The news of the ship's cargo had been carried ahead of them by faster sailing ships, and they were met at the London docks by a clamoring crowd of manufacturing representatives, who nearly swamped the ship, trying to get to Matthew first. He shortly sold the cargo for the unheard of price of 36.5 cents a pound for the cotton and what translated to 18 dollars a barrel for the tobacco.

Matthew and Carstairs were jubilant until they began to unload, then three very dour and stiff gentlemen came on board with an injunction to seal the cargo until the bills of lading should be examined and the "Weigh tax" paid at the dock.

After three days of fruitless waiting and arguing, Matthew finally realized that he needed to hire a law firm to help him wade though the red tape. He was fortunate in remembering Bertrand's father once having mentioned in his hearing something about his family's lawyers in London: The firm of Grant, Lever and Stockton. He told his cabby to take him hence and they, after he had dropped the name of MacNeil, welcomed him as a client.

They were able to cut through the maze of paper that the irate cotton brokers had thrown in their path and Matthew came away with a certified check from the sale of the goods that took his breath away. He deposited it in the Bank of England as advised by the law firm, and took a certificate of deposit home, cashable in any American establishment.

* * *

That was the start of their English venue and Matthew found himself abroad more than he was home, a circumstance he deplored, as he was away from his beloved South, the plantation and the horses he loved. That state of mind disappeared when he was taken one night upon arrival in London, to the home of Mr. Stockton, for a late supper. There he met his host's daughter, Melissa, and between them, sparks and shortly fire, seemed to flare. He spent much of that week and the next in her company. She was the youngest daughter, a willowy blonde whose blue eyes seemed to flash and change color when they rested on Matthew's strong face. They were married his next trip, a nice, but not too splendid, wedding, as befitted a city lawyer's daughter, and she went home with him to Georgia.

Danforth, having heard of her from his son already, and knowing his intentions, welcomed the newlyweds with open arms. Mistress Martha was ecstatic at the thought of a new female in the family and perhaps—could she hope?—the patter of little feet in the big old house. Melissa, for her part, loved the plantation and the slow, languid and elegant style of the South. But she had never seen so many bugs!!!

She came in July, the worst time for the miasma that crept in from the sloughs and swamps of the stagnant rivers of Georgia's bottom lands. Mosquitoes bred in dense swarms and avidly sought any skin that enclosed a living breathing body. Along with their blood sucking propensity, they carried disease. The locals merely called it "Swamp Fever." Later, it was known as Malaria. In whatever guise, and to one whose body had little previous immunity, it was a killer. By September, she was on her death bed and Matthew, who had known wedded bliss for a mere few weeks, was nearly crazy with grief. He slept by her grave for day and nights, never leaving it. If it hadn't been for the constant ministrations of Spur, Mistress Martha and

Danforth himself, he probably would have died of starvation and a broken heart. He came away from that time a changed man, a man who had little taste left for life. The war's coming brought him a measure of relief and he had gladly gone to join the 18th Georgia when it was formed.

    Now, years of war had hardened his heart and done little to change his outlook on the burden of life. Somehow, though, he had escaped death or injury until the battle at the river. There, receiving a wound that he thought for a while was going to kill him, he had found that he did want to live.

Chapter 8

Route March, May, 1864

Now the two armies, both grievously wounded, began circling movements designed to bring the other into a hoped-for vulnerability. Neither was successful and both eventually drew off to lick their wounds, regroup and resupply. This was not so hard for the now well-functioning northern Quartermaster corps. Wagon trains rumbled down the valley roads and fresh regiments of recruits came marching along with them. Lee's Grand Army of Virginia was not so fortunate: their supply lines were strung out and, because of the blockade, increasingly ill equipped, their recruits fewer and fewer.

Company 'B' of the Texas Brigade marched from that place of Hell, at first in dust mixed with ashes, later in mud, as the rain started to fall. Matthew, still weak, led his horse and walked with the men, though they urged him to mount his beautiful mare, which he eventually did. The company's plunder wagon, which they had captured from the Yanks several battles before, followed up their rear, laden with their blanket rolls and gear, with Spur at the reins, Morley on the seat with him.

Big Lars was chortling as he strode along, happy because the cunning Troyer had finally found him a pair of boots that would cover his huge feet. They fit just fine and felt wonderful as he marched along, matching the shorter strides of his smaller comrades. There was no place else he would rather be, particularly not at sea on some brutal ship. He was happy with his friends in the company. He (usually) had enough food and the men treated him with respect and affection. It was all he asked.

Troyer, the little ferret, was missing as usual, off on one of his long forays. Frank didn't worry about him. He could and would take care of himself. Josh Batton, the young man from Austin, was limping from a stone bruise that had gotten infected, but he wouldn't ride the wagon, too proud. He was a youngster of some education and upbringing, always willing to write letters for the rest who had little schooling, always ready to listen and sympathize with them in their problems. He was noncom or officer material but Frank hated to let him go. For his part, Batton had rather stay with the 'boys', as he said, when Frank had brought it up. So he remained in the ranks, though Frank thought uneasily that he probably should insist that he get his stripes and take a clerk's job with the staff. He could get it for him—he should get it for him. He was a young man with much potential—the kind that would be sorely needed by Texas after the war.

The little corporal, Luke Millett, was a feisty little rooster who would fight at the drop of a hat and usually win. He, like Frank, had grown up on the frontier and fought Indians from the time he was big enough to raise up a rifle and shoot it. He was better than good with a knife and carried an old Bowie nearly as long as his arm. Frank had seen him kill more than one bluebelly with it and he was deadly. Several times, he had faced off against men with bayonets and come off the winner. He was quick as a snake and yet the men all liked him, because at heart he was a good man, and didn't bully them more than he had to. And he would never ask them, any of them, to do anything he wouldn't do himself, the mark of a sound noncom. He doted on Frank, for some reason Frank didn't know, and was, to his embarrassment, always bragging him up to the men.

Frank had grown up on the Texas border, could use a knife himself, but always preferred the short gun. Colt Army .44's. He was a two-pistol man when he could be, because there had just been too many times in the heat of battle when there wasn't time to slip in another cylinder, let alone reload one. So, he carried one on his hip and another, short barreled one, in a holster at his back, where he could reach it with either hand. One of the guns, the long barreled, had been a gift from his old Daddy, gone under in the battle of Gaine's Mill.

They had journeyed together to Austin at the call to arms and enlisted in the Texas Brigade. His father had bought them both new pistols there, trading in the bulky old Pattersons they both had carried. Frank had chosen a long barreled .44, his father the shorter barreled version.

* * *

The old man had gone under fighting to the last, his hand grasping the guidon he'd so proudly carried into battle. The Yanks had thought for a time that they had captured it, but Frank had cleared a path with his rifle, then his pistol, and finally his knife, to his father's body and taking up his old man's weapon from his hand, had shot two more bluebellies coming at him before his men caught up to him and covered the bloody knoll with gray uniforms.

Hood had seen the action from the adjacent hill and calling to an aide, had summoned Frank and the remains of his company to him after the battle. He had made him a sergeant on the spot. And whenever their paths crossed, Hood always made time to talk with him. Frank had kept his father's short barreled Colt through all the skirmishes and battles since then.

Over his shoulder, he carried his 1859 New Model Sharps rifle, caliber .52. He had taken the rifle from a dead sharpshooter of Colonel Berdan's regiment after the battle of Gaine's Mill. The weapon was a prize among the Confederates, as the Berdan regiment's Sharpshooters were well known and more than a little feared, for their remarkable accuracy and volume of fire, due mainly, most thought, to the highly vaunted rifle they carried. It had proven to be all that the men thought it was, and he had made several outstanding shots with it, since he had secured it. It was a reliable arm, clearly superior to the Enfield most carried and much more accurate.

Jack Luther, striding along by him, was a cotton farmer from over by Crockett, between there and Madisonville, Texas. All he wanted to talk about were his crops, his hogs and his wife and kids, Frank was never completely sure which it was he had in mind at the time, because he had names for his hogs, too. He was continually asking his friend, Josh, to write him another letter home, and if Frank had been him, he had to think that he might have gone over the hill to see his family once more. But he hadn't, though he did complain more than most. With all that, he was a good soldier, keeping up, handy with his musket, solid in the face of the enemy. His coal black hair was long. Like the rest, it needed cutting, and his feet were coming through yet another pair of boots. Maybe Troyer could find him a pair, too.

The other men of the company were all solid, tried soldiers, with the exceptions of the few new recruits. Mike

O'Hara, that red haired laughing Irishman, was telling his companions another joke—always he was good for a laugh, even during the worst of times, like now, slogging in the mud. He fought like a demon and drank like one, too, when he could. And gray bearded "Old Man' Herrick, the oldest in the company, who yet could most likely out-march them all, and whistle while he did it. He always had a song going, either a whistle or a rousing march tune. And he had a good deep voice, one that was easy to listen to and sing along with. Right now it was "When Johnny Goes Marching Home Again", his favorite. He was singing out, the rain dripping off his beard, the others joining in, O'Hara with his fine tenor carrying the high notes way up there. And little Jimmy, the drummer boy, not so small now, though he had only been thirteen when he had joined up three years ago. Now he was a man, though still so much younger than the rest of them. He was a veteran, been wounded twice and had killed his share of bluebellies. Like Herrick and O'Hara, he loved music and was always good for a song or a dance.

Frank thought he heard something. From far back in the column came the distant sound of cheering. It steadily came nearer and the men, looking back in the rain, could faintly see a group of riders approaching along the line of march. The cheering grew louder as the men rode closer. In the van, Frank saw the light gray horse, Traveler, with its famous rider, Robert E. Lee, cloaked against the downpour. Like the others in the strung out column, he started to cheer the man they all so loved. Lee, his left hand waving, rode by in a slow lope, his five aides following after.

"Keep up your spirits, you Texans, we'll stop him at the river. . . at the river!" he shouted as he went by.

Little Jimmy looked at Frank. "Whar we goin,' Sarge?"

"Why, to the Chickahominy to stop Grant from takin' Richmond, is my guess, sonny." Frank didn't have to be a strategist to figure that one out. Grant had to be stopped from achieving what every soldier in both armies knew was his goal: taking the Rebel Capitol. Lee had sparred with him on the North Anna River and bloodied his nose. Now, it would be another fierce engagement on the banks of the Chickahominy, if they could get there in time to get themselves set in to stem the northern tide. A place called Cold Harbor.

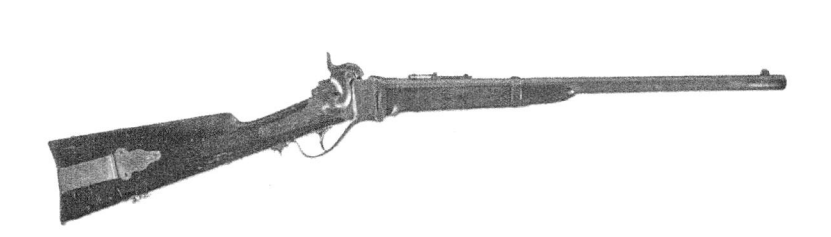

Chapter 9

Cold Harbor, May, 1864

The rain had stopped and now, hours later, in the dark, they were back in dust again, caking on them. It was hot and humid from the rain before, and the fireflies were out in swarms, lighting the night in a crazy, random way. The "Old man" was telling Jimmy that "the fireflies were 'GeeJums', the ghosts of old niggers, justa flyin' 'roun' in the dark lookin' for they's famblies." The boy's eyes were a little round, half believing, the others were snickering. Frank was just tired, his shoulder aching, the Sharps and the rest of his weapons and gear weighing him down. Four years now, he'd been riding and marching up and down the damn country, following the flag. He'd seen his share of the boys desert, just go over 'the hill.' He'd seen them shoot themselves to get out of duty. He'd seen them buy themselves out of service, if their folks sent them the money, a practice he'd thought was idiotic, because they were just conscripted again, later on. He'd seen them commit suicide, one even slitting his wrists and quietly bleeding to death one night, after Chickamauga. He'd seen them flogged for stealing and malingering. He'd seen them shot, when they were caught for desertion, even had to form up a squad several times and be a reluctant part of the proceedings, himself. In short, he'd seen about everything in this war that he thought he might ever see and much that he didn't ever think he would.

One time, right after Chickamauga, at Savage Station, he and the company had marched by half a battalion of bluebellies, who were lying in double ranks, all dead. It was hard to fathom. How had they all died so quick and so fast and without a quiver, so that all were in place, just so? He still shivered, thinking about it. And the battles he'd been in!! Since he'd lost his father at Gaines Mill, he'd been in a plenty more, too many really, to count. He didn't want to count them, couldn't, because then he had to think about them.

And he'd been wounded before—once in the leg, once in the same arm, the right one. But nothing to keep him from service, not that he would have used an excuse to get out of serving. No, he wasn't that way. Like most of the other Texans, he had that stubbornness deep in his bones that wouldn't admit defeat. But Lord, he was tired of this war.

The bluecoats were wearing them down, and the man they had now for a leader of the Army of the Potomac would finish the job. Grant. He'd keep throwing his big army at them until there were no Rebels left to fight. He could do it because he was getting three times the recruits that they were, maybe more, despite all their losses. He'd heard in this last battle in the Wilderness tangles that nearly 40,000 bluebellies had been killed or wounded. That was nearly equal to the Reb army!! And yet, Grant hadn't quit. No, Sir. He'd just hunkered down, gobbled up another 40,000 recruits and started in again toward Richmond, his main objective. The man was a plodding mule but he had no end of bottom.

Now, they were going to try to stop him again at Cold Harbor, a scant five miles from Richmond, another spot where there had already been one battle that the South had won, the year before. Battles on battles on battles.

He'd say one thing for old Lee, though, as long as he was General and asked them to go forward, they would, until there wasn't none of them left. Himself included, he guessed, for he loved the old man, too. Maybe if they killed another 40,000 Bluecoats, their moms and dads would rise up back home and just say, "Enough!!" But he wouldn't bet on it. Too much blood had been shed for one or the other to back off now until the bitter end.

* * *

The column shifted its lines as they came to the old fortifications and trenches of Cold Harbor and deployed wearily into their specified areas. They rested in place that night. The din of a battle off towards the crossroads woke them the next morning, a cavalry battle, from the sounds of it, moving back and forth. The officers got the men up and going, beginning the work of restoring and strengthening the lines. What was curious about it was that this time they were in the old Federal breastworks and the bluecoats were, or would be in their old ones.

At noon, they took a break and had a meal. The Company mess, thanks to Troyer, usually had something in it. Spur, by now a pretty decent cook, helped the detail told off by Frank to put a hot dinner together, a big stew, complete with coffee. For some reason, the black's daffy, smiling face as he poured out tin cup after cup of coffee helped raise the men's spirits a little. They knew that many of the men in the army had gotten little or nothing to eat the last two days, and were thankful for their bounty. Some of the men, Frank noticed, prayed over their meal.

Matthew and Frank, after eating, walked the line, surveying their work thus far, and decided to extend their trench line a little farther left, to intersect the 2nd Tennessee's line to the east.

"It stretches us out a ways farther than I like, but at least there's no break between us." Frank said. Matthew nodded. Frank put the men to work, using some shovels from the wagon, their big bayonets, even their dinner ware, to move the dirt. To the men's disgust and horror, they dug into a place where skeletons from the last battle started cropping up, skulls, ribs, leg bones, and cloth remnants: mostly blue.

That afternoon, Confederate reinforcements began streaming in from Richmond and Lee and his generals began inserting them into the fortifications, working to try to make an impregnable wall that Grant's army would beat against in vain. The lines were extended from Bethesda Church to the Chickahominy River, comprising a five mile front, a labyrinth of intricate, intersecting lines. By now, about every veteran in Lee's army knew how to build and defend fortifications that would make a military engineer in Europe envious.

* * *

Dawn, June 3rd
"Here they come, boys!"

It was 4:30 a.m. when the yell went up and the men gave up their efforts to sleep and running to their stacked arms, grabbed their weapons and headed back to the trenches. Spur came up to Matthew, nearly gibbering in his fear, his big eyes rolling until the whites were about all you could see in the coal black face. Matthew gave him the mare's halter rope and told him to get her back, deep in the trees and under cover, if possible.

"Stay there until I come for you or the line breaks. If that happens, save yourself. Get going. . . now!" he exclaimed, as the whistle of artillery began coming over their heads. Spur needed no second order as he scuttled for safety with the horse trotting behind him.

Matthew turned back and saw, by the twilight of the rising sun, the massed numbers coming out of the trees all along their front, squaring their lines, the officers and the noncoms dressing the ranks and urging their men forward. The soldiers, their rifles tipped already with bayonets, walking at the half-step until the order to charge was given.

He looked along their own lines and saw the entrenched men ready and waiting, the tension evident in their tight, anxious faces. For some reason, the bluecoats had given them an extra day to get ready, and they had made the most of it. The battlements were deep and formidable.

He was, had been, a cavalry officer himself, but knew his place during a defensive battle was behind his troops, making sure of their readiness, their placement, and their steadiness. He stayed upright, though he wanted to scramble into the trench himself, and bury his face in the welcome dirt. He didn't, he couldn't, but he admitted to himself that he wanted to. He steadied up. The blue colossus was moving nearer. They were about 350 yards out. Too far, but he could hear a few shots going off in the Tennessee regiment off left of them. And as he looked, men went to the ground in the blue multitude facing that unit. 'Good shooting,' he thought, that far away, but too soon. To his right then, came a volley, then the profuse din of men yelling and scores, hundreds, of rifles being fired.

"Wait, men!" he called. "Wait until they are in range. Then fire by platoon. First platoonnn. . . .ready!!"

The blue ranks lowered their rifles and charged. Matthew called "Fire!" and the first platoon let loose. Then the second platoon. He had them firing by unit, as they should, but it wasn't enough to stem the tide about to lap up on them.

"Fire when ready!"

He jumped in the trench close at hand and leveled the revolver, felt it buck in his hand as forty yards out, a big sergeant, his head turned back to shout encouragement to his troops, was hit by the bullet and went down, tried to rise and fell forward. The men rushed by him, yelling, screaming, and the wave swept up to the battlements. A volley by the first platoon, who had reloaded, pushed them back an instant. Then it was a general melee and it went on for what seemed long minutes to Matthew, who had emptied his pistols and was using his sword, until suddenly, the Federals, like a receding wave, fell back. They left a blue carpet of dead and dying men, moaning, screaming, crying for help, for release from pain.

"Reload! Reload!"

He heard his sergeant, Sergeant Shannon hollering down the line. He echoed the refrain. They were hurt, he had some men down, men dead, but the line hadn't broken. On his left, face down in the dirt of the trench, the youngster, Josh Batton, lay dead, his head lying a foot from the head of the dead bluecoat who'd killed him. Matthew fumbled with his Colt and dropped out his empty cylinder, replaced it with a fresh one. He holstered it and started laboriously reloading his other pistol, wishing he had taken the time to find an extra cylinder for it. He'd fired all twelve shots—knew with certainty he had killed more than half that number of Union soldiers. They were sprawled in front of the trench, some so close that now, in the risen sun, he could see their open eyes. But there were others out there who weren't dead, and they were already asking for water, for help, and they couldn't leave the trenches to give it to them. Despite the fact that the cannon were now ranging at will among them, the bluecoats were forming again in the tree line. He could see the twinkle of the bayonets.

"Get ready, men! Do as you did!! Fire by platoon."

From out of the woods came the blue horde again, their ranks dressed as before. This time, when they got half way, the officers had them kneel down by rank and volley fire. Seeing their intention, the entrenched veterans hunkered in their diggings, behind their earth mounds and let the dirt soak up the thrown lead. Very few, if any, were hit by the fruitless volley, but the firing of it heartened the attackers and they came on again. Matthew called out his orders and the volleys crashed home on the advancing line. Big gaps were blown in the ranks, but as before, the torrent came up and lapped against the bulwarks, to be thrown back yet again, with frightful losses. This time, the carpet of blue nearly covered the ground to their front. As before, Matthew found that he had fired a full load from both pistols. He had done execution with them and looking down the line, saw his sergeant, Shannon, still erect, with both of his weapons in his hands. He stuck one in its holster and did as Matthew was doing, reloading both. Matthew had seen him shoot and knew that he too, must have dealt sure death out to the assaulting onslaught.

Now, as he watched, the man took up a rifle, his Sharps, and leveled it carefully at an officer out at the tree line trying to rally his troops, seeking to stop the retreat and form them up again. He heard the rifle go off and watched as out near the trees, the officer spun and fell. Matthew's mouth opened. It was not according the rules of gentlemanly warfare to pick out the officers and kill them. not fair, not. . . he shut his mouth. War wasn't fair. not this war, anyway, and not the war he'd known in India. Shoot the officers, he thought, if that would save the men of their command. But it wouldn't. They would just be replaced by other officers who would do their duty and order them forward. From the trench came the sound of congratulatory yells, the men had seen the effects of the long shot. He turned away. The incident had heartened his men. Maybe for that reason, it was good. He didn't know.

"Reload, men, get ready for them. They'll be coming again!"

They did, unbelievably twice more, then it grew quiet. or would have, but for the screams, groans, curses and whispers of beseechment of the wounded to their front. And it was much the same along the whole five miles of Rebel lines. Only in one place had it been breached, by Barlow's Division, who had swamped Early's line at the center and been speedily, bloodily repulsed by Hoke's reinforcing brigades. The Union had lost another twelve thousand men in a morning's fighting. With these two battles, that of the Wilderness and Cold Harbor, the Union Army had losses that numbered as many as Lee's army totaled: fifty thousand men.

And hundreds of wounded men died in the killing fields in front of the gray lines while the two Generals exchanged polite messages concerning the amenities of a truce to take care of the injured. Grant's pride would not allow him to ask for a truce, thinking it would be an admission that he had lost the battle, of defeat, which it was.

It was an incredible three days before this was effected and many, well over half, had died by then, from blood loss, from their wounds, heat exposure and lack of attention. Many of the men in the trenches went of their own volition to give what aid and water they could. Since they had no means or medicine, most of the wounded died anyway. It made most of them sick, to see the ghastly result of their work, and there was not a man but wasn't changed in some way by the butchering of thousands of their fellow men. The rumor swept the lines that the bluecoats had refused the order by their General and their officers to continue the assault. They had stood quietly in their lines and wouldn't move when ordered. Grant had been forced to give up the attack. The Confederates had won a great victory!!

* * *

Matthew had succumbed to the entreaties of his men and the piteous sounds from the wounded and let his men go cautiously out to give what aid they could to those lying to their front. That afternoon, a pompous major came riding down the line and pulled up in front of Matthew as he stood at his ease in back of the trench.

"Why aren't you making your men work on the fortifications, Captain? And, sir, get those soldiers back from the wounded out there. They have no business helping the enemy!"

He was, Matthew knew, one of Hood's aides. He had met the man quite a few times around the headquarters but the Major showed no evidence of recognizing him—not that he cared. Suddenly he was blazing angry. He came erect. His right hand touched his holstered Colt. He was nearly incoherent, and slurred his words, which made him the madder.

"Major Williams, I am responding to a higher authority than you. Namely, that the good Lord has said that we should be merciful to those in need!"

He pointed out at the field with so many injured lying there. "And if those poor men out there don't need some help, I don't know who does! <u>My men will continue to do what they can to give them aid</u>!"

Sergeant Shannon came up as he finished and stood beside him in what the major, describing the incident later to his superior, General Hood, said was an "extremely insolent manner." The Major left, fuming.

The General said nothing. He was a religious man, and abhorred the slaughter. Privately, he applauded Captain Ground's action. The man complaining about him was not only an insufferable pompous ass, he was dangerously stupid, and couldn't be relied upon to command even a company. But he was his sister's husband's brother, and so he had to tolerate the fool.

"Major, I intend to talk with the Captain when I get the time. In the meanwhile, why don't you deliver this message to Lee's headquarters for me?"

He scribbled a message to the Commander, a message entreating him to hurry with the truce, in the name of a merciful God who surely would censor them for their procrastination in helping those poor souls out there who were beseeching their aid. He folded it and sent the pretentious lack-wit on his way. When and if he saw Grounds, he would congratulate him on his compassionate deed.

Dead Confederate Soldier
Courtesy of Library of Congress

Chapter 10

Petersburg, July, 1864

They had won a great battle but Grant, like a bulldog, refused to release his grip. If Lee had flexibility and daring, he at least had nerve and fierce determination. His objective was still Richmond and now Lee was forced into a defensive effort to deny him, fighting vainly against tremendous odds. All along, Lee had been afraid of this: being forced into a siege position which would contain him and strangle him, while in other parts of the South, Generals like Sherman had their way with the countryside, raping, burning and pillaging. It had to be, however, and pushed by Meade on the one side and Grant on the other, he went into the Petersburg fortifications reluctantly.

Petersburg was strategically essential to the South, being the rail link that Richmond and Lee's army depended upon for food and supplies. If it was taken, then the Confederacy's days would be numbered, which in reality, they were, anyway. Lee's army was late getting into Petersburg and the town was nearly lost—would, have been—if one of Grant's generals hadn't been so stupid.

Petersburg had been stripped of its defenders by Lee earlier and only 2,500 men were left, under Beauregard. William Smith's XVIII Corps, with nearly 20,000 men reached the town on June 15th, and attacked at dusk, taking some of the defenses, but then holding up. They were waiting for Hancock's troops, another whole corps, but then, inexplicably, took no action when he did arrive. Hancock's men champed at the bit. The old veterans in his corps scented a victory and were enraged when no attack orders came. In the meantime, Beauregard reinforced his lines and repulsed the feeble sorties until Lee came. Then the lines were strengthened and the Army of Virginia dug in. Smith had lost his chance to end the war.

Petersburg at the start, was a mecca for the company. Troyer was out day and night. He and another scavenging detail made up of men just like him found all manner of food, equipment and supplies. They grew fat on the bounty. They settled in and built bombproofs against artillery and mortar fire. Artillery duels were frequent and irregular, and sharpshooting was incessant.

Later, the food supplies began to fade away and it grew ever harder to find anything to satisfy a hungry belly. The Union army, on the other hand, had a profusion of supplies, as it was said that eighteen laden trains a day were coming the twenty miles from the coast to the front lines around the city on a railroad line his engineers had built.

Troyer started making nighttime forays through the lines to steal what he could no longer find in the town. Frank considered trying to curb him but decided the little thief knew better than he just how dangerous it was. He left it alone.

For six weeks, it was so dry one had to work to get enough saliva to spit. Then it rained—too much rain. The trenches and bombproofs turned to mud and filled with water. Men stood in it day after day. The water, except for some deeper wells far back in the metropolis, were becoming tainted with filth and the poor sanitation. Sickness and desertion began to take its toll on the Confederate army.

Five hundred yards down from the company's central bombproof, was South Carolina's 7th Infantry Brigade, situated right near the center of the lines facing the Union forces of the 48th Pennsylvania, a distance of about 130 yards separating them. On July 30th, in the early morning, a huge explosion rocked the ground, blowing a hole several hundred feet wide in the South Carolina redoubt. Dirt, timbers, equipment, and body parts rained down in all directions from the blast, including on the company. One heavy piece of oak came crashing down, smashing and killing a man lying near Frank. All were hit by the mud and dirt, some injured by other wood, rocks or even the pieces of corpses. A head with an arm attached landed in the wagon.

The concussion was so deafening that for some minutes, the men were not able to hear and no one immediately connected it with a bomb from the other side. Nor did they at first understand what was occurring—-the bluecoats were attacking. Evidently, the 48th Pennsylvania had mined a tunnel under the defenses and filling it with gunpowder, had blown it that morning. Now they were rushing through the gap, trying their best to capitalize on their ploy. But they were met with a scathing barrage from an alert Artillery commander, Lt. Colonel Haskell, who trained his guns on the approach to the gap and started pouring in broadside after broadside on the assault, charging his guns with grape to scourge the onrushing attackers.

The break, instead of being a portal to a Union victory, became a bottleneck that rapidly turned into a Union slaughter as the men on the receiving end of the cannon fire were blown away. But still they funneled into the opening and soon, just by their numbers, were making headway, as others darted through and gained a foothold in the gap.

"Come on, Texans, we've got to stop 'em!" This call from Matthew came as he shook off the explosion and threw his gun belt around his waist. The cry was echoed by the others as they grabbed their rifles and bayonets and headed over to where some of the surviving South Carolina men were grappling with the Yanks, mixing it up so that the guns behind them fell silent, lest they kill their own soldiers. More Rebs came running from other units nearby and the struggle in the crater became a mad mix of savage hand-to hand fighting. The blue and the gray were so closely intermingled with each other that it was hard to distinguish friend from foe with any certainty. Men used their pistols, if they had them, their bayonets and knives, rocks, clubs, their hands and even their teeth, to kill or put their foe out of the battle. Men went down and were trampled upon by others trying to keep their feet in the mess. Big Lars was roaring and wielding an Enfield rifle like a club, laying about him indiscriminately, knocking down friend and foe alike. The rest of the company, knowing how he fought, stayed well away from him.

Matthew fired at a bluecoat coming at him with a berserk look upon his face, his bayonet at the ready. The man went backwards and down, to be stepped on by another who came at him with a similar crazed look on his countenance, rifle forward, his bayonet seeking Matthew's middle.

Matthew fired. The man fell, to be replaced by two others who charged together and went down, like the others. A respite and he looked around, holstered his pistol and drew another from his waist. Then he was grappled from behind by a bluecoat who clutched him and stabbed with a bayonet. The knife went through his side as he twisted away, a sharp fiery stroke that galvanized him to swing his arm around and fire with the pistol tucked in the man's chest.

The man slumped, shot through the heart and Matthew got dizzily to his feet, his hand coming away bloody from where he'd been stabbed. Above the roar of combat, he heard a scream and looked up, saw the red headed O'Hara falling away from a stocky bluecoat officer who was engaged in pulling his saber from the Irishman's stomach. Little Jimmy, with a yell, jumped forward, his bayonet in hand, only to be skewered through the throat by the officer, who with a fiendish grin, twisted his weapon so that Jimmy's head nearly fell from his shoulders.

Matthew snapped a shot that missed as the officer crouched, then threw himself sideways with a graceful move as Frank tried to run him through with his bayonet. The swordsman swung his saber in a back cut that Frank countered agilely with the butt of his rifle, only to fall as the man hit him a savage blow to the face with the heavy hilt. He raised his blade for a thrust and fell then, with a hole in his forehead, as Matthew's second shot connected.

Then Matthew himself fell from a heavy blow from behind. From the ground, he turned his head and glimpsed a dark figure above him with a rifle, the bayonet raised for the final blow. Somehow, he got his hand around and up, the pistol in it. He fired and the man, hit in the stomach, screamed and dropped his weapon.

Then Millett was there, helping him to his feet, where he swayed dizzily from the buttstroke. Overhead, canister shot screamed, the artillery keeping the Union forces from reinforcement of their men in the crater. He watched almost dreamily as Frank and the rest of the Confederate force gained the upper hand and the Union troops were subdued and disarmed, then shuffled away, prisoners.

Big Lars came up, then Frank with some of the other men. They got him back to the bivouac area, laid him down and dressed his wounds as best they could. The wound in his side had sliced flesh deeply but fortunately hadn't entered the stomach cavity. They pulled its edges together and Frank did a credible job of stitching the lips of the wound, putting stitch after stitch in it. Then he poured the last of Matthew's whiskey over it, after taking a big drink from the bottle, then passing it around. He himself was bleeding still from a smashed nose, which he straightened by the simple expedient of pulling and reshaping it with his fingers. Matthew, right by him, clearly heard the bones pop together. Frank's eyes were already turning black from the hard blow.

All the men had wounds of some sort, mainly cuts and stabs, and for a while, Frank's crude sewing skills were in demand. Herrick came limping up, cursing the bluebelly who had killed O'Hara and Little Jimmy. He'd been shot in the leg. Jack Luther had been shot in the body, through the stomach, and bayoneted. Both seemed death wounds, but he continued to breathe so they finally decided reluctantly to take him to the battalion doctor, though they had little confidence in him. The man was weird—he believed in some little invisible things called 'germs.' At Frank's direction, some of the men went back then, and sorted out the company's dead and wounded. The Battle of the Crater was over.

* * *

Later they learned the Pennsylvania coal miners had tunneled for several hundred feet toward and under the Rebel lines, then packed the end of the hole with 8,000 pounds, four tons, of gunpowder to make the tremendous explosion which had taken the lives of 200 Rebels and wounded and maimed several hundred more. However, that was more than offset by the two thousand Blues killed as they attempted to secure the breach and after, in the crater fighting.

    Big Lars went at Matthew's request and found the saber the man had been wielding. It was a fine German blade and Matthew decided he would keep it for a souvenir. The man had been a master swordsman, Matthew knew, from the little fencing he had done in school. Lars had searched the body, but it had been looted already, the scavengers targeting the Union officers as soon as a battle was over. His name was, for the time, unknown.

Zouave – Courtesy of the Library of Congress

Chapter 11

Petersburg, 1864

Grant's force had been virtually replaced with new men: fully 60 percent of his force were casualties. Lee's forces had been deleted by only about fifteen percent. However, these men were almost impossible to replace. On the other hand, he had lost nearly half of his general officers. Men who couldn't be replaced: Stonewall Jackson, his mighty right arm, J.E.B. Stuart, his dashing cavalry cavalier, Gregg, Jenkins, Ashby killed at Harrisburg, Longstreet, badly wounded by his own men at the Wilderness and out of the fight, for now.

Three weeks passed. During this time, Grant extended his right flank to further encircle the fortified town and tighten the noose. Two other rail lines were threatened and after some hard fighting, finally cut off. Only one, the Danville, was left, the lifeline to the capitol, twenty miles away. This one could not be allowed to be cut. But, Grant, with his greater resources, kept drawing the line out, stretching the two forces ever longer, until the Confederate line of defense extended from the Chickahominy to Petersburg, a distance of thirty-five miles. Less than a thousand men a mile defended this line against four times their number of enemies. To maintain it in the face of such a force demanded a remarkable military genius, and few men could have done it, but Lee did. Not once during the campaign did Grant manage to take the Grand Old Man unawares and he was stopped at every point he probed, Lee rushing reserves up, always ready to meet attacks as they came.

During the remainder of the summer and into the fall, the face-off at Petersburg continued, while Early's force tried in vain to break the siege and bring some relief to Lee. In Tennessee, Johnston had been fencing successfully with two Union armies, Thomas and Sherman, keeping them from advancing south by a series of delaying moves, only to be replaced by a desperate Confederate government, who wanted him to stand and fight. Hood, the new commander of Johnston's army, was a hard charger, despite his crippling wounds. "Hit 'em hard!" was the only way he knew to fight. He didn't understand the tactics of delay and attacked. It was exactly what the Union generals had hoped for. He was badly defeated and his loss allowed a blue locust cloud to descend on the rich valleys of Tennessee, into Georgia and finally South Carolina, the breadbasket of the South.

Wilmington was the last open seaport to the outer world, the funnel through which the munitions and supplies had been largely obtained by the daring blockade-runners threading their way through the vigilance of the blockading Union fleet. Fort Fisher was the formidable defensive work which commanded the Cape Fear River mouth, keeping the northern ships at bay. In January, 1865, Grant ordered a massive expedition under General Terry to take the fort. Under a welcome fog, this force was landed and the fleet began a furious bombardment. Terry worked his troops up to the fortifications, and as soon as the naval attack lifted, shot home an assault that overran the defenders. The last open harbor to the sea was lost to the South.

Back at Petersburg, things had been heating up. Grant had sent a powerful force to Reams Station to seize the Weldon Railroad yards. Lee sent A.P. Hill to drive them back, which he did, though with a heavy loss, some of them Texas Brigade. The Federals, though, out of a force of 8,000 men, had 2,400 killed or wounded, with 1,700 more taken prisoner. Yet the Union army persistently kept up the pressure, extending their works, probing, constantly attacking, trying to find a weak spot. And men died on both sides.

On September 8th, The Union General, Butler, made a sudden attack on the right flank, at a place called Fort Harrison, which he captured, along with fifteen artillery pieces. Despite a heavy counterattack, he held on to it. In October, a turning movement against the town was attempted, Grant threw a large column across Hatcher's Run, which advanced to Burgess's Mill on the Boyden Road, an avenue to Richmond that was even more important since the Weldon Railroad had fallen to the Federals.

That was the last large effort attempted by Grant that winter, except for a movement on the 5th of February with the same purpose: to cut the routes to the Capitol. It didn't succeed: the advancing column was hit hard and driven back. The Blues lost 2,000 men to the Gray's 1,000 who advanced too far when they had routed the enemy, and were swept with a withering fire from entrenched Federals. Young John Pegram, one of the South's most gallant young Generals, died in the fire at the front of his troops. The news caused General Lee to weep. The young man had been a particular friend of his and he felt the loss deeply. He had just been married and Lee knew both families well.

The Confederate government, hearing of Hood's defeat and seeing their mistake in relieving Johnston, now bestowed an empty honor upon General Lee. He was made Commander in Chief of all the southern forces. It was empty and fruitless because now his hands were tied. He was engaged in the last moves of a tactical chess game, with nearly all his most valuable pieces lost to him. Had he been given that authority two years before, he might have pulled the South's chestnuts from the fire. Now it was too little, too late. His army had dwindled to less than 35,000 men. Too many of his good generals had been killed.

* * *

Early, who had caused a mighty diversion aimed at taking the pressure off Lee, had actually carved a path right through his adversaries until he was in sight of Washington, to the consternation of the North. Unfortunately, with his little 8,000 man army, he knew that he might take the capitol, but would speedily lose it again, his force surrounded and wiped out. He elected instead, to turn back and occupy Maryland, trying to keep alive the diversion. In Maryland, he was confronted by Sheridan and Hunter, who had been dispatched by Grant, along with 40,000 men, to clip Early's wings. Early was an extremely smart, experienced fighter and he made a series of brilliant stands wherever he could find the tactical high ground, defeating Sheridan time after time. However, Sheridan was reinforced by Wallace, with another 10,000 men, and Averill was coming from the east with a large force to gather Early into a pincers movement.

Early instead turned and at Kernstown, defeated Averill and his fellow general, Crook, driving them before him and capturing their supply trains. Then he went on and crossed the Potomac at Williamsport, stopping at Sharpsburg. Sheridan finally brought him to bay at Winchester, where, through overwhelming numbers he was defeated, though the Rebs had contested the field successfully until the end of the day, when a portion of Early's men turned tail and caused a panic which spread to the rest of the army. Troops which had never before turned their backs on the enemy fled the field. The artillery alone remained firm, and covered the disorderly retreat until Early, Gordon, Ramseur and Rodes, his Division commanders, could reform them and get them to fight. They did, and Early made a unified retreat to Fisher's Hill, where Sheridan finally caught him.

    Early was defeated and finally pulled himself out of the Federal vice with a few thousand men and his best remaining general, the intrepid Gordon. Sheridan left the field triumphant, moving leisurely down the valley to Strasburg, where he went into camp to regroup and rest. Instead of leaving the country with his tail dragging, Early and Gordon followed Sheridan and surprised the Union force resting on its laurels, at daybreak. The Rebels swept into the sleeping camp, shooting and screaming their Rebel yell, the surprise complete and devastating. It was the Blues turn to take to their heels, which they did, leaving artillery, baggage, tents, equipage, arms, supplies, and everything to the Confederates. The camp plunder was too much for the Grays, who were broken down, hungry and ragged. The stores held them like magnets and the fleeing army made their getaway.

    If the Rebels had followed their shocked enemy, they would have most likely been able to annihilate them, so complete was the rout. But after running for miles without pursuit, the discipline of an army returned at the same time that their commander, Sheridan arrived on the scene. He had been gone to find a telegraph and send the news to Grant of his victory and had returned to find his grand army a terrorized mob. He hurriedly restored order, reformed them and headed them back toward the enemy.

At the camp, the Confederates themselves were speedily defeated and set on the road, minus much of the loot they had gathered. Sheridan's cavalry, coming up, had hours of slaughter, their saber arms actually too tired to lift, finally, before the Rebels disappeared from their front. Early's force was no longer a threat, though he continued to harass the Union forces in the area for weeks afterward, with the few men he had left. Meanwhile, Lee was struggling to make headway at Petersburg.

Chapter 12

Fort Steadman

Had Lee been earlier given permission to withdraw over the Staunton River, he would have had the mountains at his back and could have drawn in all those detached pieces of the game such as Early, Johnston, maybe even Kirby Smith out in the West, making a respectable army with which likely he could again have assumed the offensive. Now, with Hood gone, and Early no longer a force to be reckoned with, he was, by March of 1865, at the end of his rope. Longstreet alone, was still in the field and fighting, attempting futilely to contain Sherman's advance.

Sheridan rejoined Grant and Sherman was advancing up through Georgia, while Thomas was coming too, through Tennessee. What was Lee to do? He could have fallen back on Richmond and defended that city to the end, which would not have been very long, and resulted in much loss of life before the inevitable occurred. He elected instead, to try a desperate measure, attacking straight through the enemy's middle, hoping thereby to roll up the left wing and throw the enemy into confusion.

* * *

The company had suffered like the other units all through the siege. Troyer had disappeared, along with a fourth of the pool money he had for the purchase of supplies. Morley had deserted with Matthew's mare and the stallion. Somehow he made it through the lines in the dark night, successfully traversing no-man's land leading the two horses. That had infuriated the company and had they somehow caught up to him, he would have been killed, slowly. 'Old Man' Herrick died of gangrene, refusing to the last to have the battalion doctor cut off his leg. Luther, as badly as he had been shot, pulled through, to the men's amazement. Spur, who had never been sick a day in his life, caught the cholera from the bad water and without Matthew's constant nursing, would have died. The men were amazed that an officer should bother with a 'nigger' but took it philosophically, saying the "Captain sure had a 'mort of mercy' in 'im." Matthew, with Frank helping, pulled his servant through, the two men forming a tighter bond as they watched at the delirious black's cot through several sleepless nights.

* * *

On March 25th, the attack force was drawn up in the dark of night before dawn, under General Gordon, who had regained Lee's army with a small ragtag group after Early's defeat. The Texas Brigade was to have a signal honor: spearheading the attack column. This unit would invest the fort to their front, the second would come up and complete the thrust.

General Gordon moved the first column out silently, towards the looming works of Fort Steadman and Fort Hascall.

The few sleepy guards were surprised and killed and the fort invested. The garrisons were hustled away as prisoners and Matthew ordered his men to turn the guns around and fired them on the neighboring redoubts on the right. Gordon, in Hascall, did the same on the left. Several batteries on either side were thus blown clear of their defenders in short order and those too, were occupied by Gordon's stormers.

Now was the time for the supporting column to come up and advance through the opening of the two forts, to fall on the troops now starting to form on their front, to be supported by the guns of the forts. A seizure of the hill in the rear of Fort Steadman would have effectually cut the Federal army in two at its center and Lee could then have rolled up the left wing, pouring his waiting divisions into the gap. But the support column didn't advance.

For whatever reason—misconception of orders, confusion, even treason or dereliction of duty—for whatever reason, a critical moment in the war, in the battle, which hinged greatly on the smooth execution of orders, was doomed because of the failure of the commander of the reserve force to attack.

Now the Federals were lapping at the forts, the defenders firing as fast as they could, the cannon blowing holes in the oncoming attackers. Matthew, seeing that the reserve column wasn't coming from the earthworks, raged along the fort's wall, directing fire, encouraging his men, trying to figure out a way to withdraw without being cut to pieces. Fort Hascall, to his left, fell silent, overrun, the few men left taken prisoner, but Gordon, as usual, finding some way to regain the Confederate lines. Matthew bitterly admitted that the battle was useless without the supporting column's arrival. And he was damned if he'd sacrifice the rest of his men for nothing.

"Cease fire, boys! It's done, it's over! He quelled the fire from the fort's guns and the Union soldiers came swarming up and over the walls, yelling their triumph. A big private came at Matthew, slowed, then picked the pistol up from where Matthew had dropped it when he'd raised his hands. Out of the corner of his eye, he saw Frank knocked to the ground by a rifle wielding bluebelly sergeant, who stooped and stuck Frank's pistols in his belt. Then they were hustled down and to the rear lines, the Federals taking over the guns and swinging them back to menace the Confederate line. They were prisoners.

Artillery near Fairoaks, Virginia -
taken in 1862 by James F. Gibson, (b. 1828)
courtesy of Library of Congress

Chapter 13

Prisoners

They had been taken well behind the lines. As they went, Matthew could hear the firing die down and finally quit. The guards had ordered Frank to be carried. He was still out from the hard blow to the head at the last of the fight, and just now coming to. Matthew looked up. The sky was blue, it was early morning. In the battered trees, birds were warbling and chirping. It was early spring and the thought struck Matthew that they should all be home, getting ready for planting. But here they were.

Was he relieved that the fighting was over? The Cause was lost, had been lost for more than a year. But it was defeatism to admit it aloud. He had never done so, but he had heard the men talking, and there'd been growing gaps in the ranks. Many more men of the Texas Brigade had been lost during the siege. General Gregg had been killed, Colonel Bass of the 1st Texas had been badly wounded, as had Polley, of the 4th, along with scores more, disabled and out of it. Some few had deserted, also. He thought of Morley, who didn't surprise him. He had often caught the man looking at his guns, his horses. But he wondered about Troyer. Had the man been caught, or had he actually deserted his friends? Frank didn't think so. But Matthew wasn't sure. The little thief was too aware of the situation and he was not one to continue until all were killed or wounded. The others who were gone—he wished them well. Had he been in their place, he might have taken off, too. But, like the rest of the veterans who had stuck, it was always Lee. They couldn't desert that old man. He cared for them and respected them. They could hardly do less for him. Maybe this was best, to go down fighting, but captured, not killed.

He went to Frank's side. knelt down and took a close look at the wound. He had nothing, not even water, to aid him, but maybe he could talk a guard into some. Instinctively, he picked one of the younger ones and went over. The man, a youngster, really, raised his rifle nervously. Matthew spoke in a low tone.

"Say, Private, my friend is hurt. Could you be so kind as to get us some water?"

The boy backed away.

"I'll ask the Sergeant." He trotted over to a man reclining on the ground, his rifle beside him, his head against the tree. Matthew saw it was the same man who had knocked Frank to the ground earlier, and thought that he was probably going to be told 'to go to hell.'

Surprisingly, the man got up and came over. Matthew saw that he had a kind eye and was reassured when the sergeant gave him his canteen off his belt. He shook it and found it was nearly full. He pulled a dirty handkerchief from his pocket and moistened it, then bathed Frank's swollen face with it. He sputtered and came around, his eyes jerking open wildly. He felt of his face, wincing as he felt the cheekbone and jaw.

"He really fetched me a good one." he mumbled. He took the canteen from Matthew's hand and tipped it up, then rinsed his mouth. There was blood in his spit. Matthew took the canteen then, and after a healthy swallow, handed it back to the waiting sergeant. He thanked him and the man nodded, then went back to his tree.

Matthew stood for a while, looking back through trees at the Confederate lines, which now were quiet. He remembered, for some reason, a trip he had taken a year or so before the war on a Mississippi riverboat, buying some horses. The boat had left him at a landing and backing out, had gotten up steam and glided downstream, leaving him standing there on the dock watching it go. He somehow had the same feeling. He was standing there watching the war leave him while it moved on down the river of time to its next stop, another battle, which he would not participate in, being a prisoner. . . .a prisoner.

He knew men in the Army of Virginia who would not have succumbed to that humiliation, preferring instead to fight to the death rather than have their honor sullied by giving up. He honored them. He was practical, he saw now, about life. Not an idealist any more, if he ever was. He had surrendered when he saw the situation was hopeless, to save lives that would have been wasted otherwise. And that was the state of the war itself, he now knew. It should be ended, with honor if possible, to save the lives of those on both sides who would otherwise die in this war whose outcome was already decided.

Matthew looked around. Sitting, sprawled or standing, there was, on about a half-acre, about 500 Confederates, some of them, like Frank, wounded. He went among them, trying to find a senior officer. He came upon several lieutenants, one wounded badly through the lungs and coughing his life away in the arms of a friend, blood streaming from his mouth. Nowhere, though, did he find an officer of greater rank than his. He gathered some sergeants, and told them to begin organizing the men in their respective units. Besides, his company, Company 'A' from the Texas Brigade had spearheaded the attack, plus an under strength South Carolina regiment. Evidently these groups had lost their commanding officers, so Matthew assumed command. He wondered idly if Siderus had been killed. He sent a sergeant to importune the guards to get some medical attention for the wounded, who were gathered now in a designated spot under some shade. He sent other men to check among the prisoners to find out if any had some skills to offer the injured. He did have some success here, as several, like Frank, had experience in their units with wounds and giving aid. The problem was lack of material, bandages, medicine and instruments to remove bullets. But a couple of the men had kept little packets of needles and thread, and these came into use now to stitch up some of the wounds. Water was at a premium, but those who had canteens gave them up to the wounded, and the sergeant who had given Frank some water led a party out to the creek where they were able to refill their own canteens.

    About that time, orders came down for them to be moved back farther away from the front line and Matthew directed the men to shed their heavier shirts or coats and thread sticks through them for stretchers for those who had to be carried. The guards mostly were sympathetic and gathered the stacked surrendered rifles also to be used for litters. First, though, the men were searched again for weapons and ammunition, and this second, more intensive search found quite a few knives and packets of ammo that had been overlooked before. A couple of small pocket revolvers were added to the pile. As the ranking officer, the guard sergeant, the same man he'd asked for water, queried him as to whether he had any weapons, rather than subject him to a body search. He gave him his word that he had none, thinking that he might be able to keep his money belt secret for a while yet. Then the prisoners were formed up and marched off, a sad, forlorn, slow moving column, many limping.

Chapter 14

Fort Delaware

They were put on a train returning to City Point on the ocean, at Grant's immense supply depot. There, a mile or more of wharves lined the tracks and food and war materiel of every sort poured ashore from transport ships and barges, which, when one looked out at the bay, carpeted the water like a flock of ducks on a pond. The detraining Confederates were awed by the immensity of the supply operation. Here also, Confederate prisoners were assembled for transportation back to the northern prison camps. They were heavily guarded and shepherded like sheep from the train to the dock and then onto a barge which took them out to a ship. There, they were herded down into the hold and the hatch covers battened down by jeering sailors. Water and navy ships biscuits were waiting in the hold and though it was dark, some light filtered down, enough for them to settle in.

    The ship got underway some hours later and they endured a pitching, sickening ride up the coast that went on for five days, as the vessel was working against a northeast wind. The hold's bilges became a mire of puke, shit and urine, with blood from the injured adding to the unholy stinking mix. Once at sea, though, to give the navy some credit, groups of prisoners in rotation were allowed on deck to take on some drinking water and food and try to wash themselves with sea water from over the side. The ship's doctor tended to the wounded in a desultory fashion and effected some measure of relief, though many died, despite his ministrations.

Then, when they were sure they could abide no more, they landed at Delaware City where they were given opportunity to clean themselves and given hot food, set up by charitable groups at this later period in the war. Matthew and Frank went with their unit and were given some soap to wash their clothes in tubs provided them. Thankfully, they did so, sitting around half naked until they dried. In the middle of the afternoon, they were formed up and marched to barges which took them to the infamous Fort Delaware, out on Pea Patch Island.

* * *

Fort Delaware was one of the most powerful and massive forts in the world, built on a marshy mosquito-infested island to guard the approach to the Delaware River. Construction had begun in 1849 and was completed ten years later. Its walls were thirty-two feet high and seven to thirty feet thick, of granite block and brick—25 million of them. Its hundred plus guns, heavy siege cannon, were stacked in three tiered layers. The moat was over thirty feet wide all around it, with one main sally port on the southwest side. The whole pentagon-shaped structure covered over six acres of the seventy acre island and its prison compound, overflowing outside the walls, covered another twelve acres. Thirteen thousand prisoners already were housed there, in the fort and outside in wooden barracks and tents, surrounded by water filled ditches, under the grape-shotted guns and the watchful eyes of the guards at the walls.

The Pennsylvania Artillery Regiment was stationed there and served the guns all through the war, while guard duty devolved on the 201st Pennsylvania Infantry and the 5th Delaware Infantry Regiments at that late period of the conflict. Other units had come and gone, completing their assignment and leaving the unhealthy place with unabashed delight to see the last of it.

As the long procession of prisoners stumbled out up on the wharf, the universal thought seemed to be one of despair, as the reputation of the place was already familiar to them. The massive high walls, the moat, the ditches, the high fences and the scores of sentries pacing their beats in all directions seemed to quell any thoughts of escape.

The prisoners were forced to stand in line while they were searched, even the officers and the wounded. Matthew had so far been able to keep his money belt hidden but now it was found and taken from him, along with his watch. However, a receipt was given him and he, like the others, entered the prison with nothing. It was April 1st.

The prison fort was well organized by now, under the methodical command of General Albin Schoepf, a man hated by the prisoners, called General "Terror." Due to the overwhelming numbers, or possibly the poisonous hatred of the Union commanders billeted there, conditions were atrocious. Water was contaminated and therefore typhoid, cholera, dysentery and diarrhea were common. But to go to the hospital, which all the wounded were directed into, was tantamount to a death sentence from which few returned. Prisoner exchange had dwindled with the years of war, since the Union strategy now was to win by attrition and so the camps on both sides were overflowing.

Both northern and southern camps were hellholes and Fort Delaware was no exception, though it could have been. Food was not scarce but too little got to the prisoners. The fort's quarters were divided into divisions with 150 men each in them, constructed of white pine planks nailed up vertically. Each division had three rows of bunks running the length of the division on either side, with a large stove in the center. There were no floors. The bottom bunks touched the ground and were damp and cold, so all tried to avoid those. Each man got one blanket, which, during the winter there, along the coast, with its freezing rains and wind, was not nearly sufficient to keep the body warm, so that men continually were getting up and crowding the stove. Nights were dreaded times.

The officers were separated from the enlisted men and Matthew found himself in Division 11, with many of the officers from Virginia or Georgia, most of whom had been in Jackson's division and captured at Gettysburg or later. He was assigned a lower bunk by a cadaverous major, in charge of the billeting for 11. The man hinted that he could be assigned one off the ground if he 'anted up a little gift.'

Matthew, upon asking, found that the guards were for the most part, decent and would remit any money confiscated to him as needed, in the fashion of a weekly allowance, if he but asked. Since some of the men were well dressed and pretty fit, considering conditions in the compound, more questions asked elicited the information that a majority of these men were getting help from friends or home, via mail, or had come into the prison with money on them. Those who were ragged and suffering in health and from the spring cold didn't have those advantages. The larger number of enlisted prisoners were in the suffering category and too many who had been there long looked like corpses from the shortage of rationed food. Rats were a delicacy and regularly eaten by both officers and enlisted men. After a cold, sleepless night, Matthew got up and stood in line to talk with the Union sergeant responsible for his division. His name was Williams and he had Matthew fill out a form requesting his money, over $2,400, be doled out to him $20 at a time, weekly. This was the most he could withdraw at a time.

"You'll receive your allowance on Monday."

"What day is it?" Matthew asked.

"Wednesday." That meant he had several days before he would be in funds. However, the sutler in his area was well stocked and had no problem giving credit—once. Matthew left and went to the store, where he, after negotiating with the sutler, was able to purchase another blanket, a coat, extra socks and some underwear and a felt hat. He also bought some hard rolls of wheat bread and took his booty back to his bunk, where he found the major and told him he was about to be in funds.

"Fine. when you want to move up, find me and give me a dollar." the major told him, turning to leave.

"Why don't you let me move now and I'll pay you two dollars when I get the money?"

The major reluctantly let himself be persuaded. Matthew had all he could do to keep from striking him. He was now about as comfortable as he could be, and in funds the next week, when he was given his money. He paid the sutler and the major, then went to the division sergeant and gave him $5.00 to hand over to Frank. thereafter, he divided his funds down the middle, sending Frank half. $10.00 a week kept them in relatively good shape, and they were even able to help some others, less fortunate.

After a week, Matthew had gotten paper, envelopes and stamps and sent letters home, telling them of his capture and where he was being held. He heard nothing back. Emmy, he knew, had been sent to England to school, and to be gone during the war years. No letters would be forthcoming from her. He knew Sherman had steamrollered through the Georgia countryside and could only conclude that they had fallen onto hard times at home. During the time they were held, he sent three more letters but never received a reply. Thinking of home increasingly made him apprehensive, so he stopped writing. His funds were adequate for now. Hopefully, they had gotten his letters letting them know he was alive and well.

* * *

Meanwhile, Lee had broken out at night from the Petersburg noose in a nighttime flanking maneuver that left the Federals confused and dazed. His evacuation columns had been aided by Longstreet's Corps feinting an attack that had drawn off the Union forces and opened the door. Behind them, the blowing of the magazine of Fort Drewry and the capitol city burning lighted the sky with a lurid red light.

Lee's columns had made it safely to Chesterfield Courthouse and rested there for a time, happy to be released from the defensive lines and back in the open. The warm April sun lighted their march and the army's morale rose. The odors of spring were in the air and the greening fields and the budding trees were a balm on their spirits and bodies until they began to think, remembering former victories and the fact that they still had their noble Leader at their head, that they were yet the equal to their powerful adversary. Behind them, though, the city of Richmond was surrendered to General Weitzel, in Grant's name. And ahead of them was another blow: the provision train which was to have met them at Amelia Courthouse, on the last rail line usable to the South, the Richmond and Danville, somehow got its orders mixed up and pulled on through for Richmond, leaving not one item for the starving and weary troops.

It was a telling blow. Grant was hot on his trail. The necessity for speed now was derailed by the fact that his men and horses badly needed food. Foragers were sent out as the army continued on. Some supplies, not nearly enough, were brought in. Each man got a handful of corn or wheat. No one complained, at least not in Lee's hearing.

Sheridan's cavalry was on the flank and rear of the army now, harrying them, with the Union infantry coming fast behind. Ewell's Corps, serving as rear guard, were finally heavily engaged at Sailor's Creek, a small tributary of the Appomattox River. When Anderson and Pickett's men came back to help, all three divisions were surrounded and finally surrendered. Thus, ten thousand Confederates, a third of the army, was taken. Along the way, another ten thousand dropped out from exhaustion and hunger—or deserted. Lee was left with a core of veterans whose courage had never failed and would fight now to the death, the last and the best.

The wagon and artillery teams were weak from lack of forage and the hard winter, and their progress was slow. Additionally, some of the road had gotten rain and was muddy. Soon, behind them, came the Federal columns, and Mahone's division, with some artillery, was ordered back to check their advance. At some cost, they did so, even making it back to the rear of the army without being cut off. The evening of the eighth, Lee reached Appomattox and learned that <u>those</u> stores cached there for their retreat had been just captured by Federal cavalry.

His army was surrounded, in fact, by faster moving cavalry, and he called a council of his remaining generals: Longstreet, Gordon and Fitz Lee. The consensus was that they could still reach the mountains *if* they could cut through the cavalry, and *if* the Union infantry hadn't come up to reinforce them. Once in the mountains, they could hold the Federals at a steep pass they had been aiming for while the rest of the army got through and away. It was a desperate last chance.

At 3:00 a.m. then, on the morning of the 9th of April, General Gordon took his Second Corps silently forward. On the heights above Appomattox, supported by General Long's artillery, and Fitz Lee's cavalry on the left, he started forward. Long's fire and Fitz Lee's charging cavalry dispersed the Union cavalry in disorder to their front, but it wakened a greatly superior force of infantry behind, which had come up in the night. They rapidly formed up and came forward, stopping Gordon, who sent back to General Lee, a dispatch saying that in order to advance, he would need immediate reinforcement from Longstreet's Corps. It was not available. Longstreet at that time was fighting to hold Meade back in their rear.

Lee rode up on a height sited by one of Long's batteries and ordered it to cease firing while he looked at the situation. Sheridan somehow had managed to get his brigades forward and in front of Lee's slower army, blocking his retreat. Lee saw it was hopeless and turned to his aide, Colonel C.S. Venable, and said, "There is nothing left for me but to go and see General Grant. I would rather die a thousand deaths."

So ended the Confederate cause, with the surrender of the Army of Virginia at Appomattox courthouse, though some tag ends remained to be tied up. Johnston's and Beauregard's army was still at Greensboro, North Carolina, trying to impede Sherman and Jefferson Davis had gone there right before Richmond fell, with the idea of setting up a new Confederate government.

Davis wanted to fight to the last man but this was no longer a popular concept and his followers fell away from him until he was captured finally, trying to make it to Kirby Smith's army still fighting west of the Mississippi. Johnston surrendered to Sherman on April 17th, seeing the hopelessness of continuing the war. Kirby Smith was reluctant, too, to end the conflict but finally came to the same conclusion and surrendered his forces on May 26th.

By that time, Lincoln had been assassinated and the North was enraged and seeking revenge for the long bloody war and the loss of their President, whom many had denigrated with their every breath, but who now, in death was exalted to a saintly status. His loss was another catastrophe for the South, as he had previously stated to his generals that he "intended to let 'em up easy." Now that was not to be. No less a person than Secretary of War Stanton had informed the nation right after Lincoln's death, that it had "been a Southern conspiracy and the President had been murdered by Jefferson Davis' agents. He reported erroneously that the whole tragedy was a part of the dying Confederate war effort.

That he was never able to prove this—as it soon became clear that no one in Richmond had anything to do with the murder—made no difference whatever. The basis of Lincoln's approach to reconstruction had been the belief that the broken halves could be fitted back together without bitterness and in a spirit of mutual understanding and good will. The war was over and they now had to go on. But that concept died with Lincoln and was not to be. The damage had been done and few people in the North now bothered to speak out for the sort of peace Lincoln had envisioned—one of "letting them up easy". Vice President Johnson, Stanton and the rest of the Radicals in the government, wanted the South to bleed and bleed and bleed. And it did.

Sherman and Lee
Courtesy of Library of Congress

Chapter 15
Freedom

Fort Delaware's portal opened and the prisoners were released on June 17th. Each was filtered through the inner gate and remanded back his belongings, whatever they were. With a longing eye, the same sergeant who had taken his money when he'd come in, gave him back his watch and money belt, when he finally got through the line and presented himself at the table. Then he walked down the drawbridge with the other men, where he found Frank already waiting for him. They had not gotten a chance in the two months of incarceration to talk or see each other.

    Matthew saw that his friend was thinner but fit, and that his head injury seemed to be healed. He was erect and clear eyed. Frank saw a man who had weathered as much or more than he had, his cheeks deeply dimpled on either side of his face by the bullet wound, but otherwise seeming in good health. They shook hands and smiled, neither saying much. Later would be time enough to talk. They both were seized with an overwhelming desire to put a great deal of distance between this place of gloom and death and themselves. The barge came and they got on, neither looking back. At Delaware City, they walked off the wharf and up into town. They were free.

* * *

The town had a cafe and Matthew led them there, where they found the place was already full. Likewise, they found that the town's stores were sold out of merchandise such as new clothes and food. They got mostly black looks and sullen service from the northern people and it didn't take long to know that their money wasn't much good nor their persons wanted around the town. They walked down to the train depot and got tickets on a train that would take them south. They sat outside the depot on the grass with others waiting, eating some bread and cheese Matthew had bought for them and listening for the train.

Presently Matthew said, "I've got to get home to Georgia. I've sent letters and haven't gotten answers back. I'm afraid Sherman has destroyed everything down there." He felt of his belt to reassure himself. "I've got money yet. I want to share it with you. Will you please take it?"

Frank shrugged. "I've saved some of what you gave me already. Don't need much, but I guess if you don't want me along, I could take a loan to buy a horse and an outfit." He paused and looked at Matthew. "I mean to pay you back when I can."

Matthew looked back into gray eyes. He liked this man.

"I never said I didn't want you along, Serg—Frank. If you want to come with me, I'd like to have you. The way back down into Georgia is bound to be dangerous now. I hope to take some wagons with supplies and as many good men as I can find."

"I think I'll trail along, then. Don't have much family left in Texas but I damn sure want to shake the dust of these eastern states and git back west. Too much hate and poison against a southern man here. There'll be some lynchings directly."

The train whistle got them to their feet. The cars were already crowded but they found seats together and sat down, Frank on the inside. Looking out the window, he could see the road near the tracks filled with former prisoners heading south by shank's mare. All over the north, released prisoners were flooding the countryside and it was inevitable that some real difficulties would arise, as these men, already in dire straits, began foraging for food and transportation. The train presently got up steam and with a jerk, started out.

"Probably would have bin better if they had sent us home aboard ship—but maybe not— I damn sure don't want another ride like the one that got us up here," he remarked to Matthew as they sat and watched the shattered countryside go by. Everywhere there were signs of the recent war. Even the car itself showed the effects—numerous bullet holes let shafts of daylight through its walls and the seats were torn and dirty. A little boy came down the aisle and offered them some cigars. Matthew bought a handful and gave half to Frank. They lit up and savored their smokes with deep satisfaction. Matthew had always been partial to a good hand-rolled cigar and Frank, who usually chewed, took his nicotine in any form.

Soon, another lad came by, offering some sandwiches, and Matthew was again an easy touch. They ate and smoked and the miles went by, the train quickly outdistancing the walkers following the track. Every once in a while, the conductor would call a town, the train would slow and with a hiss of steam, come to a shuddering stop. Mail, milk and cream cans were the usual freight, while passengers got off or on. The two, along with many of the others, endured the black looks of the northerners silently. They slept in their seats and finally the conductor hollered "Getttysssburrgg, all up and out for Gettttysssburrgg."

As the train pulled up to the platform, Frank looked out the window and said, "Uh oh. Looks like trouble brewin' out there."

Matthew leaned over him and peered out. There on the platform was a crowd carrying signs with various imprecations directed at the Southerners printed on them. "GO TO HELL REBELS" was one of the nicer ones. Some of the men in the car started muttering to each other. It was obvious that they had had a bellyful of being pushed around, and even in their weakened condition, were spoiling for a fight. Matthew stood up and addressed them.

"Men, what they <u>want</u> is trouble. Then you won't get home like you want. You'll be sitting in another one of their jails. Stay put in your seats. Frank, take a couple men and guard that exit. A few of you men at the end do the same there. Don't let anyone come in. Stand fast and steady."

The men heard the voice of command, and being the seasoned veterans they were, it was a compelling force. They remained seated, and though there was some commotion on the platform, the train pulled out with no one managing to get in the car, though several had tried and been rebuffed. Just as the train left the station, a rock came through a window and shattered glass over the men seated on that side. Frank came back and took his seat again.

They made it to Frederick, finally, in early morning, and got off to stretch their cramped legs. When they got back on, two Northerners had taken their seats and Matthew had to physically pull Frank away from what promised to be a fight, which both knew the others wanted. Matthew had the more sense. With them as debilitated as they were, neither were a match for any healthy rough-and-tumblers at that time, as those men looked to be.

They found separate seats toward the rear of the car and took them. Late that afternoon, the train pulled into Washington and they got off, cramped, dusty and dirty from the coal smoke that had been eddying around them for hours. The two men hustled to a waiting hansom cab, the driver waiting for just two more fares before pulling away from the curb. One by one the others inside got out at various destinations and finally the driver leaned back and asked Matthew in a surly voice, "Where's it to be, gennelmen?"

"The Stratford, please."

The man raised his eyebrows but flicked his whip and the cab rumbled a little faster over the cobblestones, toward the better part of town. He pulled up and Matthew paid the fare and left him a tip, to his surprise.

The hotel, Frank saw, had to be one of the better ones in Washington, though he was not one to be the judge. The big doorman gave them a decidedly cold look and started to block their way but a glare from Matthew got them past and in. At the counter, Matthew pulled a double eagle from his pocket and tapped it on the counter. The sound of the gold coin brought the clerk hurrying.

Soon they were in a nice suite, though without luggage, to the bellboy's disgust. However, he got a tip for answering a few questions and receiving some orders. Presently, baths had been prepared and the two luxuriated in the first hot water their skin had touched for months. The water was so dirty that they had to take another before they felt clean. By that time, a tailor had arrived and the two men were measured and more orders given by Matthew. The man left and the bellboy came in, laden with a large platter from which came enticing smells. The men sat and ate, wrapped in sheets provided by the now obliging bellboy. They were into their second drink and cigar when the tailor came back, triumphantly carrying clothes and followed by two helpers, both laden also.

Frank was shooting the cuffs on his new corduroy coat, examining himself in the hall mirror with some satisfaction, when Matthew announced, "Don't know about you, but I feel damn naked without a gun on me, especially carrying some money. Let's say we stroll down the street to a place I remember and see if we can find us some protection."

Frank turned and looked at his friend, now nattily dressed in a white shirt, tie and nice fitting coat, with shining boots on his small rider's feet that peeked from under a sharply creased pair of doeskin pants.

"By God, we look like a pair of damn swells! But it sure feels good to have some new clean clothes on again! Thank you!"

"Don't mention it. It's my treat. I know you'd do the same for me." He waved a hand. "I mean it, Frank, I don't want you to feel beholden. Let's go, if you're ready."

They strode together out the hotel door past a gawking doorman, the same that had seen the two ragamuffins come in, thinking that he would be shortly called to throw them out. He shook his head.

The store was farther down than a couple blocks, as Matthew had remembered, but they came finally to a sign that advertised "Sporting Arms and Accouterments". They went in and Frank was impressed by the weapons displayed in the shining cases and in rows of rifle and shotgun racks. An elderly smiling clerk came toward them.

"I say, may I help you?" An Englishman, from the sound of him.

"We'd like to see some Colt's pistols, if we may." Matthew answered.

The clerk led them over to a case full of new Colts, with every model represented, from the small Pocket .31 to the massive .44 Walker. Frank pointed to a steel framed Army .44 and gave a sigh of satisfaction when the clerk handed it over. Matthew selected a Navy Civilian in the same caliber. They traded the revolvers between them to heft but both came back to their original choice. Matthew responded to Frank's nod.

"We'll take these, along with two extra cylinders apiece, holsters for the right side, powder flasks, bullets, the works twice . . . and what are these? He gestured to an array of small snubnose revolvers nestled at the end of the case, and at his urging, the clerk brought them out.

"Colt's makes these for a gentleman's concealment if they should encounter an establishment where regular pistols at their side may be. . . .embarrassing and they still desire to be armed." he explained loftily.

The two had never seen such small sidearms as these, light and concealable, lacking the loading lever and with only about three inches of barrel. Matthew, seeing they were .44 caliber, was not to be deterred, and bought them each one also, along with an extra cylinder. They fit neatly in a wood box that carried a rammer, wads, powder flask, nipple wrench, extra nipples, percussion caps, a capper, and one hundred .44 balls.

Then they went to the rifle racks. Matthew favored the expensive English guns, Purdeys and the like, but his money was dwindling fast and he turned from them with a sigh. Frank was looking at some used rifles and pulled a Sharps rifle from the rack that was identical to the 1859 New Model that he had left behind during the last battle. This gun was in better shape, .52 caliber, and a set trigger model, also. The price was a little inflated, $27.00, but Matthew insisted that he take it. For himself, he chose a New Model Sharps sporting rifle in the same caliber, set triggered, 30 inch blued barrel and forearm cap of German silver. Again, the price ($38.00) was inflated but he decided to indulge himself and bought it, along with cases for them, cleaning equipment, rifle powder, caps, wads and balls.

A few more items remained to buy, such as knives and camp equipment, but the prices were too high there, so they bundled their purchases and burdened, walked back to the hotel. This time the doorman was helpful, yelling inside for bellboys as he saw them approach, who came and relieved them of their loads. Both were tired from the short loaded walk, their condition still way below normal.

In their room, they busied themselves with their new weapons, expertly cleaning and charging them. Both reveled in the feel of having a gun back in their hands, as neither felt comfortable after four hazardous years, being unarmed. Afterwards, they went down to the dining room and exulted in a heavy meal. Back upstairs again, they sat at their ease with cigars and a nightcap. Matthew's curiosity got the best of him and he asked about his friend's home in Texas.

Frank smiled and took another drink. He had a slight buzz on and his normal reticence had diminished with the whiskey.

"Not much to tell, really. My folks had a stage stop in the hill country on the Old San Antonio Trail, right by the Guadalupe River. Dad worked for the Bridgecock and Columbus line, the old 'B & C.' We always had plenty of horses around the place, he was forever buyin' and sellin'. Ma and my older sister, Marcie, kept the rooms and cooked the meals. I mainly just got underfoot 'til I was old enuf to help with the horses. Started in, though, when I was a little feller, running for stuff, swampin' out the stalls, curryin' teams, waterin' 'em and such. I was ridin' near 'fore I was walkin' And usin' a gun." He paused and took a drink.

"Daddy'd been a scout fer the army when they was down in Mexico. Taught me young how to hold a pistol and shoot a rifle. 'Paches was always raidin' back and forth along the trail, comin' up from Mexico. We had a few brushes with 'em."

He paused, to think. "'Member once, we got hit, lost most of our horses. I was near ten, I guess. Had an old man name of Whiskey Walt who h'eped out around the place. He was a boozer but I liked him. Been a scout with Dad somewheres down there, limped from a bullet in his hip. He was in the stable when they came. He shot one that was trying to git the gate open. 'Near blew his head off with an old singleshot shotgun we kept in the stables. The other ones swarmed in and got 'im, though he put up a fight with the pistol and the Bowie he carried, for a time. Filled him so full of arrers, he looked like a porkypine. I remember those being the first men I ever saw killed." He stopped and took a healthy swallow, his eyes half glazed, remembering back. Then he sighed.

"I was in the stable, too, hunkered down. My pa was shootin' from the house, along with a couple of drummers who were there that day, and a cowboy name of 'Pickles' Perdue. He and the drummers couldn't hit the broad side of a hill, just flung lead in the air. But Dad was a sure shot and dropped two of 'em. I made a lucky shot from the stables as they was pullin' out and put down another."

His cigar had gone out and he struck a match and relit it.

"Always bothered me that I didn't shoot when they was killin' pore ole Walt, but I was so scared, I shit my pants." He looked at Matthew, who got up and poured him another.

113

"Never tole anyone that before." He took a sip and a puff.

"Had a couple other brushes with 'em after that, and once with a bunch of C'manches, but we was always ready for 'em and they usually left us alone. Oh, they'd hit the stages once in a while, lookin' for horses and scalps, and the box and the horses'd come in with arrers in 'em. Then Ma took sick and died. and Dad, he started in drinkin'. Marcie and me pretty well ran the place after that, 'til the war started. Then Dad an' me took an' went in to Austin and joined up. Marcie'd married that damn cowboy, Perdue. Dad made the mistake of hirin' him after Walt got killed and he made up to her. Never liked him, so the war was a good excuse to git shut of the place.

Dad was a fighter. Couldn't never turn one down. He killed a lot of bluebellies, but he got killed himself at Gaines Mill. I got his Colt pistol—that and the one he'd bought me at Austin 'fore I went in, 'til we had that last fight at Petersburg. That sergeant that slammed me upside the head got 'em both." He looked at his ash and dropped the dead cigar in the ashtray.

"And that's my story. Marcie and her husband're still runnin' the place on the Guadalupe, I s'pose, if the 'Paches didn't wipe 'em out. Heard they was raisin' hell down there during the war. Still are, I reckon." He got up and made another drink for them, handed one to Matthew.

"I need to make a call tomorrow on one of my father's banks." Matthew said, blowing a smoke ring and taking a sip of bourbon. He felt the need to respond though Frank didn't ask any questions, deciding to let his friend either explain himself or not, as he preferred.

"My father, his name is Danforth, owns—did own, anyway, extensive holdings in Georgia, Virginia and Maryland. When war seemed inevitable, he, like a good southerner, transferred a majority of his money to Richmond, to help support the government. But he told me in confidence that he had left nest eggs here in Washington that I could draw on if necessary. We're on our way to being equipped for our trip home but the country is in a state of unrest and it won't get any better as we head into Virginia and through the states that damn Sherman swept through. We're going to need horses, camp gear and some good men to come along.

I'll go see about additional funds, but I wonder if you might see about scaring us up some horses and gear, maybe keep your eye peeled for some men we might get to tag along with us. They have to be men we can trust and ones that'll do in a fight, if it comes to that." Frank agreed and they left the subject and headed for bed.

The next morning, after a big breakfast, for both men were still trying to gain back some lost weight and were ravenously hungry at every meal, they went their separate ways, agreeing to meet back at the hotel for dinner.

Matthew took a cab that the obliging doorman hailed for him and went down to the Preston Merchants bank, on the corner of 11th and West Main. He entered and after a wait, was shown in to the office of the Vice President, a Mr. Birmstein. He was elderly and dry and his handshake was like taking hold of a snake, Matthew thought. But he greeted him courteously and called for coffee, which Matthew thought was more than generous, in light of what he had seen of northern hospitality for Southerners, so far. The coffee came and Matthew sipped and listened. Birmstein knew his father personally, it turned out.

"I know your father on a first name basis, Matthew. . . .Might I call you by your first name? Yes, I *know* him, though not well, of course. He left a *considerable* amount of funds in our bank, after drawing much more out to do his share to help fund the Rebellion. An *extremely* unwise move, but understandable, in the circumstances. How much? Oh, how much did he leave here with us? I would have to check the figures again, after interest added and so forth, but in excess of $50,000 dollars. However. . ." He paused uncomfortably. "Yes, he did leave instructions that you might withdraw funds from the account but. . . I am sorry to have to tell you that at present, the funds are *frozen*, by order of the Federal government, who most likely will seize the assets of all known Confederates to help pay for the war." He spread his hands in a helpless gesture.

"We can only comply with the order, but. . . I know that your father would wish that I help you and I am prepared to do that, since the money has been here during the war years and has accrued *considerably*." He made the same gesture.

"We were obliged to report the principal figure but deliberately deflated the interest rate, as he wisely instructed, and deposited those accrued funds in another account. Those would be available without a problem. Let me go see just how much that account has in it." He rose and was gone for several minutes, then returned, looking at a slip of paper. He handed it over to Matthew. The slip read $3,087.67. He dropped it on his desk.

"Thank you, Mr. Birmstein. I'd like to withdraw the full amount. I am heading home and intend to take a couple wagon loads of supplies with me for my family and their retainers. When I get there, I will tell my father of your kindness and honesty, you can be sure." The man was flustered by the gratitude and emotion Matthew showed.

"I might say that it is considered in some legal circles that the freezing of assets in such a way by the government is no longer legal now that the war is concluded. It may be that soon your family will again have the principal restored to them. It is only right, after all, since the money is *yours*."

He rose from behind his desk, a little aging man, but firm in his principles and deeply honest, Matthew felt. He wouldn't have had to do what he had done. His father had chosen well. There were some Northerners who still had some milk of human kindness left in them, despite the war.

"How would you prefer the funds? Currency? or gold?"

Matthew told him and the man left, then returned a short time later with the amount, which he insisted upon counting out on the desk for Matthew. Matthew put the gold away in his worn money belt, reflecting that it was about time that he replaced it with a new one, and for security, buy one for Frank to pack, also. He stuffed the currency in his coat pocket wallet, making it bulge. Then he shook hands with Birmstein, took his card and left.

He was satisfied. His father had told him earlier of the arrangements he had made but Matthew had been dubious they would hold water, so to speak. At least at this bank, they had. He also felt that the money left there would sooner or later return to the family, although there might be considerable time before they could access it. He hailed a cab at the street and proceeded on his way.

* * *

Frank, meanwhile, had taken a cab, too. While in it, he asked the cabbie about horses. The man was helpful, some money changed hands and they headed off to the outskirts of the city. Matthew was in the hotel dining room, looking at a menu when Frank walked in and took a seat at the table. He looked somewhat smug.

Matthew asked, as the waiter brought him a menu, "So, how was your day, pardner?'

The easy use of the word threw Frank for a second, then he grinned. "Had some luck. Got in with a cabbie who knew what I wanted and he took me out to a livery on the south outskirts that had some damn fine animals. Jesus, it was good to see some horses that hadn't been abused, were well fed and ready to take on the trail! He's got what we want, Matthew. You'all mentioned you liked Arabian horses, old son. Well, I saw one or two that'll most likely satisfy your craving. I put some money, $200, down on four I liked, for them to hold until tomorrow, and maybe, if you had any luck, there's a couple more we could pick up that would fill the bill. Damn, it was fine to get in that stable and just smell HORSE again!"

He looked up when the waiter came and said carelessly,

"Just bring me the biggest steak you got, with all the fixin's."

He took a drink of his water, looked around and caught the eye of another waiter hovering around the tables and ordered a drink, made it two when Matthew nodded.

"So how was your day. . . Pard?"

"Well, we're in funds. I visited both banks and both were very helpful. I deposited our money belts in the hotel safe. There's a good sum in each of them." He leaned over the table and whispered, "There's over four thousand dollars in each." He leaned back as Frank exploded.

"Jesus, four. . . .that's more money than I've ever seen!" He began to sputter and Matthew laughed, a good laugh that had been months, years, coming. It was a rich laugh, that drew attention and had such humor in it that waiters and customers, hearing it, chuckled themselves.

Frank was astounded. His friend had never, in his memory, laughed like that. The fact was, he had more than once thought him as absent of humor, and wondered if it was really something he wanted to do, partnering with a man who saw life as only a burden to be endured, not enjoyed. The laughter reassured him, and he reciprocated. They finished the meal in high good humor and went upstairs for their drinks and smokes.

* * *

The next day, they enjoyed a leisurely breakfast, took their money belts from the hotel safe and journeyed out to the livery stables Frank had visited the day before. His friend knew horses, Matthew decided, looking at the animals the livery man brought forth for their inspection. The two part-Arabians, one a bay, the other a dark chestnut, immediately took his eye and though he insisted upon riding them, he knew his choices would include these two. For his part, Frank tended to the larger, longer Standardbreds, in solid colors, mostly dark bay or brown. The two he selected were representative of that breed, long backed but balanced, clean legged and clear eyed. They each also picked another two animals to take along.

Frank, like Matthew, insisted on a black hoof, claiming it was harder than a pale hoof. Neither liked a black horse, as both considered the color sunburned too bad, though Frank referred to something in his Texas country called "sand scald" that affected lighter colored horses, and so he shunned those, too, preferring the middle dark colors as more durable. He admitted a weakness for a grulla, though, if he could find one.

Matthew, from his experiences in the India desert regions, knew that it was hard to find a light colored horse there, such as a white, a palomino or a light chestnut, since over the years, they had virtually been bred out of existence. Evidently, the reason was that those horses couldn't take the hard use and the sun. But a gray like Palukan was prized, for good reason. Its coat was hard and resistant, reflecting the bright light.

The upshot was they bought horses and went back to the city jubilantly to get some horse tack and find some men to take along, as Matthew felt they needed at least a half dozen. Matthew had been reading the papers and they were full of the lawlessness, disorder, misery and privation rampant in the southern states. It was risky to head down into it unless one had a strong party, the more the better.

The cab dropped them at a 'horse equipage' establishment and they selected and bought team harnesses, saddles, blankets, bridles and halters and other gear they needed, some of it used but serviceable. The owner, thrilled at the large sale, offered to deliver the 'equipage' to the livery the next day and they left telling him they might be back for more.

Getting men would not be hard, Frank thought. Getting good, loyal ones would be the trick. More and more released prisoners were streaming into the Capitol. Frank went to a place the cabbie took him and entered the smoky, dim bar, with an air of excitement. He was armed and had three hundred dollars on him in currency to use as honey to catch some flies. The place was a known southern sympathizer's establishment and packed with men, some still wearing the colors of their regiments. He bellied up to the bar.

When he caught the burley bartender's eye, he announced with a Texas whoop, "Whooeee! Drinks are on me!" That caused a veritable rush to the mahogany and shortly he had men toasting his health from every direction.

As the crowd now looked kindly on him, He turned and hollered, "TEXAS BRIGADE—any Texas Brigade in this damn place???"

That caused another stir and several men edged forward, working their way up to him. He immediately recognized little Luke Millett, his old corporal. He hugged him when he came up, tears in both their eyes. Then he spied a hulking man behind Millett. Big Lars!!

The reunion was emotional and Frank endured another back-cracking hug from Big Lars. Together, the three edged their way out of the crowd and to a back table, where the others had been sitting before Frank had come in. When they got to the table, though, some others were there. Big Lars didn't hesitate, just took them by their collars and threw them into the crowd. They disappeared, preferring not to contest it with the huge fellow. Frank, on his part, was exultant finding two of his old crew so easily. The three, joined by a couple other Brigade men, drank and talked, Frank buying most of the drinks. Finally, though, he decided that he'd better return to the hotel, that Matthew would be worried. He put the proposition to them and they were eager to accept. Frank then drew money from his vest and gave some to each one.

"Here, you'all take this dinero and clean yourselves up some, buy some new duds, get some riding clothes and hunt us up at the hotel at nine. And if you see or hear of any others from the company, ask them if they want a part of this. We'll take as many as ten or twelve, if they want to come."

He got up then, staggering a little and went out, to the shouts of several men who had enjoyed his largesse. Outside, he stood in the gathering dusk for a little until a passing cab came along. Then he hailed it with a piercing whistle and headed on back to the hotel where Matthew, worried, welcomed him at the door with a smile. They sat for a while and Matthew listened as Frank told him of finding the men and that they were coming at nine, after they'd cleaned up a little. He also mentioned a tidbit they had told him, of Millett and Big Lars running into Morley on the road into Washington. In Luke's words, "His walkin' days were over after Lars got done with 'im."

The next morning, over breakfast, they decided they would check out of the hotel and camp over at the livery, using it as a headquarters to complete their outfitting. After buying so many horses from him, the livery man had gotten very friendly and offered them his place to stay, if they wanted.

Looking at the menu, Frank sputtered,"This place is too expensive, and I'm just gettin' tired of livin' like a swell. Doesn't fit me, I guess."

Matthew saw the wisdom in that. Their downtown business was done, now it would be better to be out where the men and horses were. They needed yet to buy three or four wagons. And they needed to buy supplies. He was sure it would be better to buy in the city than out in the war-torn countryside. But they could finish their business from the livery.

Their meal done, they headed back up to their room and packed, then called the bellboy, who had to summon help to bring their luggage down. They sat in the lobby reading the Washington papers—at least Matthew did, as Frank didn't seem to be able to sit still long enough to get any reading done. He paced back and forth in front of the big windows, looking out at the passing carriages, horsemen and pedestrians.

A little before nine, Millett showed up. Big Lars wasn't with him.

"What happened to Lars, Luke?" was Frank's question when he saw that the little man was alone. "Hope he didn't decide not to come with us."

Before he could answer, Matthew came over and Millett wrung Matthew's hand, smiling broadly, showing his pleasure at seeing this man again for whom he had so much respect. Luke looked presentable. Evidently, he had taken Frank's advice, bought clothes and cleaned up in the interval. He chuckled.

"Oh no. He was just too scared to come in the place, is all. Can you beat that? Big as he is, scared to come in a hotel." He waved a hand toward the entrance.

"He's waitin' for us outside, along with some others hopin' you might take them along."

They went out to a small crowd of men. Big Lars, of course, stood out head and shoulders above the rest of them. He waded through them and shook hands with Matthew excitedly. Frank saw Jack Luther in the bunch and went to him, smiling. Jack Luther was wan, looking ill and deeply emotional when he shook both their hands. Matthew thought, shaking his thin hand, that he was on his last legs. There were others whom he knew slightly, but no more from the old company. He counted heads and saw there was eleven in all. A nice turnout.

Frank was greatly pleased with Millett's choice, Matthew saw, and he took the men across the street, where they sat in the grass of the park in a circle around him as he told them of his plans. He told them then he would equip them, including guns, and feed them, with a $20 dollar gold piece for signing on, payable now, and give them another $20 when they reached their homes. That caused a murmur of appreciation and a few questions. One of them was what he expected down south.

"I expect trouble, men. We will be well armed and careful. We won't rush. We'll take our time and keep scouts out always. If any of you have homes along the way, we will stop and see what we can do to help out. If you want to stay when you get there, I will pay out a day rate for those days you've been with us. You'll be able to keep your weapons and the rest of your gear when you separate from us, except for the horses." He looked around and saw Frank.

"Anything you want to add, Frank?" Frank rose to his feet.

"Just this." He looked around the circle. "Men, you have a good leader here in Matthew Grounds. I back him <u>all</u> the way, as do Big Lars, Millett and Jack here. The rest of you know of him probably only by reputation or not, but when he gives you orders, they better be obeyed. If you can't go along with that, stay here." He stepped back. It was clear that none wanted to do that.

Matthew had his money out and as the men stepped up, he handed them a double eagle each. "Men, tomorrow we'll be at the livery stable. Come there. You'll need to outfit yourself with some good road clothes, including boots, hats and coats. Be there for sure by six and we'll put on a big feed for you." That got some smiles.

The men, most of them, drifted away to spend their new funds. Millett, Big Lars and Luther stayed there, along with another man whom Frank knew was a pretty good cook, though he had an unlikely name—"Stewberries." He had been a cook for the Richmond and Weldon railroads at different times, and knew his way around a stove. Frank, seeing him, immediately put him down for cook duty, which the man agreed to. Matthew gave him some money to get a good cook outfit. The man's eyes squeezed shut and tears came rolling down his cheeks. He'd been a prisoner for two years and more, and just wanted to get home to Richmond. This was a heaven-sent opportunity.

They went back to the hotel and gathered up Frank and Matthew's gear. The doorman, eying Big Lars, who stood above him, got them cabs and they pulled out to the livery. Frank took a horse from there and went to find some wagons. Stewberries went off to find an outfit and buy some supplies. The others settled in at a corner of the horse pasture. Matthew had the cab go back to a nearby hardware store he had seen in passing. He entered the long, dim building and was met by a young clerk with an eye missing. As soon as Matthew started to talk, he interrupted him with a harsh, "A damn Confederate! Get out!! We don't want your business!!"

Seething and on the edge of losing his temper, Matthew turned and made his way out of the store. As he started to step into the cab, an older man came out, the boy's father, and was profusely apologetic for his son's behavior.

"Please, sir, allow me to make amends for his lack of courtesy by waiting on you myself. I am sure we can satisfy your needs in the way of hardware and dry goods! We need to put this horrible war behind us. Please come back in." Matthew allowed himself to be led back into the building. The son had disappeared.

Hours later, he came back to the livery and the first person he saw was someone he had thought dead: Amos Troyer. He was sitting on a stump when Matthew's cab brought him to the gate of the horse pasture, chatting with some of the men around a fire where a coffee pot was perking and a big stew kettle was bubbling as it hung from a tripod. The men looked fed and rested and all got up to welcome him. Millett came up to help unload the blankets he had bought for bedding. At Matthew's direction, he began doling them out, two apiece to each man.

"Hello, Troyer, I fancied you were dead, but obviously not." Matthew met him as he came forward slowly, his hand out.

"Hello, Sir! No, like all of us, I came close, but no. They captured me at Petersburg and I thought for a while, they was goin' to hang me, 'cause they'd got me with the goods on me, a knapsack of biz'cuits from their supply wagons. The money I had on me saved my life." He'd had a noticeable limp, Matthew noticed.

"No, the big sergeant who'd collared me just used a rifle butt on my knee here so I wouldn't be able to do any more sneakin' through their lines. Nearly killed me," he said matter-of-factly.

"I 'uz in hospital a time, got the cholera there, got well, then got shipped up the line to Fort Meecham, 'til the war ended. Would've tried to escape but with this leg, wouldn't have been any good to you'uns, anyways. Wouldn't blame you if you didn't let me come along. I can't march." He said sadly.

"That's not going to happen, Amos," Matthew said kindly, remembering the man's first name. "We're glad to have you. I remember many times when you kept us from going hungry, found us more ammunition when we were about out, or boots and such when the men needed them. Frank mentioned you even found some more Laudanum for me when I was wounded. No, you are surely welcome to come along. We'll put you to work and if nothing else, you can still use a rifle, I bet." The man brightened.

"Yessir, I can do that, for sure. And maybe still do some good findin' things for you, if I can get horseback." He grinned, deeply pleased he was accepted.

Matthew turned to the rest as Stewberries came up with a plate and cup of coffee, "Frank didn't make it back yet, eh?"

Millett answered, "He came back at noon and ate a bite, then took three of the men with him somewhere. Found some wagons, I think."

Matthew dug into his meal—a delicious beef stew and well baked bread. The coffee likewise was tasty and Matthew was reassured that the man was a competent cook.

"Well, I bought a power of supplies today, and it's waiting for us to get the wagons to pick it up. Lars, I couldn't find you a saddle, so I guess you're going to have to drive a team. not many horses could pack you, anyway." Lars grinned at that. He preferred riding a wagon to being horseback, and all in the company knew it.

Matthew had decided on four wagons since they had the manpower now, and they had been able to buy teams at a discount, paying $65.00 a pair for them. Matthew had Frank pick out five teams, and a few more more saddle horses from those the livery owner had rounded up for them to look at.

At dusk, the men heard a rumble of wagons on the road and crowded the gate, which Millett opened to admit Frank and the men driving four new looking freight wagons. Matthew recognized the teams he had bought and correctly guessed the men had rode them to wherever Frank had bought the wagons. The others crowded around as Frank got down. He saw Troyer right away and went to him, giving the little man a bear hug reminiscent of those Lars was wont to give out.

After the teamsters had gotten a plate of food, Frank told Matthew that he had "had to go plumb to hell and gone the other side to the city to a big wagon park there, then haggle with a damn Vermonter who was tight as a tick, though the park was overflowing with wagons over 'near thirty acres." Frank snorted. "Got 'em cheap at that, though—paid the S.O.B. $47.00 apiece for 'em. He damn sure knew that I was 'bout to go somewheres else for 'em."

Together, the two men looked them over. They were stout Studebakers freight wagons, nearly new, with the canvas covers still white.

"We might want to paint out the U.S. on 'em, though." He chuckled. Matthew nodded.

"We'll do better than that. I'm going to replace those wagon covers with new ones. We'll cut these up for tents and flys for the men. I don't want to show up down there with wagons that shout U.S. on them." Matthew responded, "They look damn good, though, and you got a good deal on them."

Frank agreed, Millett, standing nearby and hearing them, nodded his head. The wagons were normally worth five times that and more. With the war's close, it was clearly a buyers' market.

"I had some luck, too. Found a merchant that had quite a store of goods backed up and got them cheap, also. Barrels of good flour—some pretty decent salt pork, some government biscuit he hadn't shipped yet when the war ended. Bacon, beans, coffee. I laid in a big supply, since we have the room. Tools, a plow for each wagon to haul, a bunch of goods and stores for you to pick up tomorrow. I thought we might put Troyer to work to find the men some weapons for them. We'll want them equipped with pistols of the same caliber, if possible, and the same for rifles. That way, we're not fighting different ammunition problems all the time. I thought Colt .44's like ours, and .52 calibers for the rifles, Sharps, if possible, too."

"He may luck on to some Springfields, but I doubt we'll be lucky enough to find any Sharps." Frank drawled. He sipped the last of his coffee and watched as the men worked, pulling harnesses off the teams and watering and feeding them. They'd bought an extra team, Frank thinking they might rotate it through the line so that one was resting all the time. Double teaming the wagons wouldn't be out of line, if the wagons were as filled as Matthew suspected they were going to be. He thought he might suggest it. They had the money.

That night, the men were filled with food and happy, the night was warm and the fire camaraderie sparked many a story. The men were late to bed but early the next morning, the smell of coffee and bacon frying got Matthew from his bedroll while it was still dark. Stewberries was an early riser. Soon, the others were up and at their ablutions at a nearby horse trough. By that time, Stewberries had breakfast ready and called, "Come and get it, you men!"

They didn't have to be asked twice. All of them were still catching up on lost meals. Their good mood continued with the hot meal and coffee. So far, booze didn't seem to be a problem with any of them. He had seen no bottles being passed around. Not that he was a teetotaler, but he felt that there was a time and place for alcohol, when the work was done, and in small quantities. He knew that didn't always go along with what Frank or most of the men might feel about drinking. He would take it slow with them—they all had a new lease on life and needed to unwind from the deep stress that war had placed on them—himself included.

Frank directed Millett to get the teams in and hitched up. When that chore was accomplished, the wagons rumbled out to wait for the store to open. Troyer saddled a horse that Frank pointed out to him, a little buckskin that Frank had thrown in to the string despite his color misgivings. The horse was small but athletic, and Frank had liked its looks. It was short enough that Troyer, small as he was, had little trouble even with his leg, getting aboard.

The saddle was one of several used ones that the livery man had shown from his extensive tack room. Since they were in good condition, Matthew had purchased all of them but one, a ladies. The men had spent the day before cleaning and soaping the leather gear they had so far, mainly to keep occupied.

The saddle fitted him pretty well and Matthew helped him adjust stirrups, then sent him on an errand to find weapons for the men. Matthew himself saddled up and went back to buying supplies. He also wanted to find a doctor. Not for himself—he felt pretty good, though the face still ached at times, especially at night. He wanted to have Luther and Troyer seen by a good physician before they left the city. Maybe they could get some help for their wounds. Neither were well. Luther especially, was sickly and frail.

He also had to attend to a family matter. A great-uncle lived in the city and Matthew wanted to see him before he left. He was old and at one time, Matthew had been a favorite of his, when the family had come up to the capitol. He lived not far from the White House, on Pennsylvania Avenue. He caught up his bay Arabian and saddled it, though some of the men offered to do it. He turned them down, saying he didn't need any help, letting them know that he wasn't expecting any special treatment, just because he was bankrolling the operation. Besides, like Frank, he was just enjoying messing with a horse again.

* * *

The house was unpretentious, but Matthew knew that the old man had been a prosperous merchant in the years before the war. However, the man had never been one to display his wealth. He lifted the large brass knocker and let it strike several times, as hard as he could. Samuel Greene had been very hard of hearing. Presently, Matthew heard a step at the door and it opened, a woman's round face peering out at him through thick glasses.

"Yesss?" She was Dutch, he decided. He didn't know her.

"Hello. My name is Matthew Grounds. I'm a nephew of Mr. Greene's. Is he in?"

She opened the door ushering him into a foyer, then asked him in broken English to wait while she got him up from his chair.

Presently a white haired elderly man hobbled in to the foyer, stopped and peered a moment at Matthew, then opened his arms wide and hugged him, crying unashamedly. Matthew, feeling emotions rising, hugged him back. The old man had long been a widower and thought of Danforth's son as his own.

He had been without news of him for years and had continually worried about his safety. He led Matthew back into the house and introduced him proudly to the housekeeper, Mrs. O'Fallon. not Dutch, but Irish. She gave a blimpish curtsey and asked if he wanted 'some refresssmens.' Her English was poor but it was plain that she took good care of her charge. The house was clean, the dishes were spotless, the coffee was excellent.

Hours later, after a fine midday meal, Matthew, promising to write and let him know of the conditions at home, took his leave. The old man had tears running down his face again at Matthew's departure. Matthew was uncomfortable with the fact that most likely they wouldn't see each other again. In Matthew's wallet was a check from him for another five thousand dollars, an amount Samuel had insisted on pressing upon him, for his welfare and that of his family at home, when he had found out his intentions. He rode to the bank the check had been written on and cashed it. He now had so much money on his person that he was concerned about carrying it around, yet he needed to have it readily available on the trip. He would, he decided, keep a couple men with him from now on.

He turned the horse, which he decided to name Stonewall, back towards the livery, hoping that Troyer had been able to find some arms for the men. As he went by an alley, a big gray, gaunt dog came out from behind some refuse and began following him. He went several blocks and the dog was still back there when he looked. At the livery, he turned to get down at the gate to the pasture and the dog was right there, watching him. He pulled his horse through and the dog looked at him. Some impulse made him give a low whistle and the dog, taking its cue, shot through the opening, startling the horse. He settled him down and it followed him docilely to the wagons, which were parked in a semicircle by the fire, where the men were. He off-saddled and threw his gear up on the tongue of the near one. The dog was there, sitting and watching him, its tongue lolling out.

Frank came over as he was currying Stonewall, who was eating a ration of oats from a feed bag, and said, "Looks like you acquired a friend."

"Yes, he followed me from town."

"If we feed him, he'll be sticking around. 'Course, it would be good to have a watch dog or two around the camp."

"I vote we feed him. He looks like he'd make a good watch dog to me." He finished currying and turned the animal out by pulling the nose bag off and shooing him away. The horse moved a few feet, then went to the water trough. Matthew walked over to Stewberries and asked for some meat scraps, which the cook obligingly cut off for him from a covered quarter of beef hung in a tree close by. He went back to the dog and laid them on the ground. The dog came forward and ravenously ate the meat down, then looked hopefully for more. Matthew took a closer look at the animal. Its size and appearance suggested wolfhound to him, though he'd only seen them a few times in England and India, where an officer or two had brought them from Europe. It was rough coated, with a long nose and ears that drooped.

"Odds are it'll be gone in the morning.' he thought. 'Headed back home.' But it wasn't. The dog stayed, knowing a good thing, as the men spoiled it and fed it all their scraps. It was Stewberries, who had a bright wit, who named it 'Grant.'

And later a few other dogs showed up, looking for handouts, too. Jack Luther made friends with a small brown and white terrier that showed up, looking starved. He soon had it sleeping on his bedroll.

Matthew had inquired and learned the name of an excellent doctor from his uncle. He rented a buggy from the livery and when Troyer returned, took both Josh and Amos with him. On the way, Troyer mentioned he had made a contact with a man who had some used weapons for sale. He had been a Union sutler in the war and had come home with all kinds of loot. Troyer had heard of him and going to his home, had found the man to be at first very secretive about what he could furnish them. Some of the money that Matthew had given him spread on the table had loosened him up and soon, Troyer said, he had taken him down in his basement. There, he had opened boxes and crates and shown him Colts and even some Sharps, along with cases and cases of Enfields. Some were new and still in grease preservative. He was sorry, but he had no Henrys. The Colts would cost $30.00 apiece, complete with all accouterments like molds and powder flasks, with an extra cylinder thrown in. Troyer had specified .44 caliber, as Matthew had told him. The rifles, and Troyer thought he would be able to get all Sharps rifles, would be more—$34.00. And the flasks and molds would be extra.

"He knew I wanted the Sharps and they're new—I think they'd come straight from the factory, from the looks of 'em. We can get Enfields, though, if you think that's too much to pay?"

"No. I want you to take the Colts and the Sharps, for that price. And Amos, buy a half dozen extra of each, along with all the ammunition, balls, bullets, powder, caps, you can. I don't want to be short, and maybe some of my people might need them."

They drew up at a two story brownstone a half mile or more from his uncle's house. This residence, though, was prosperous looking, with a beautiful carved walnut front door, complete with some inner chimes that sounded when Matthew pulled a brass handle. A small brass plaque pronounced that "*Mattheus F. Holden, M.D.*" resided there.

A muscular looking black man answered the door and hesitantly ushered them in. Matthew figured that the majority of the good doctor's patients were well-to-do and well-dressed when they visited their physician, not such as these rough looking men.

They waited in a sumptuous anteroom, the other men fidgeting and uncomfortable, feeling out-of-place. Matthew found a newspaper dated that same day and read it voraciously. The top story was about the plague of southern soldiers and released prisoners who were infesting the city and causing trouble. Another had to do with the recent hanging of the Lincoln conspirators, with some implications about the 'southern conspiracy.' Presently, the doctor came out, a portly older man with a set of neatly brushed long side burns that were turning white. He bent a piercing eye on the three men and coming to a conclusion quickly, addressed Matthew.

"Now, sirs, what might I do for you?"

Matthew said, "These two men need your ministrations, Sir. They're recent soldiers of the Army of Virginia and both have survived serious wounds. I hope you won't be like some of your Northern compatriots and refuse to see them because we fought against the Union. I'm prepared to pay for your services. " The doctor gave him a hard look.

"I'm faithful to my Hippocratic Oath, Sir, and have no qualms about administering relief as it is needed." He smiled.

"Of course, had you come during the War, I might have had to turn you away for fear of aiding the enemy. Who's to be first?"

Troyer looked at Luther and got clumsily out of his chair, then hobbled into the exam room, acting a little like a man on his condemned walk to the gallows. Matthew felt a tinge of pity for him.

The exam took some time and finally Doctor Holden came to the door.

"Would you come in, please, Sir?' Matthew came in to the room and saw Troyer sitting on a table, his pants off, the leg on a stool. Holden walked over to him and gestured to Matthew, who came near.

"The man has a crushed knee, caused as he said, by some repeated blows from a rifle butt. The knee joint is demolished but could benefit from some extensive surgery to clean out the bone fragments and restructure some of the joint so that it can be straightened somewhat. Additionally, the cleaning of the wound will reduce the constant swelling and much of the pain, thereby allowing a return of some limited mobility." He looked up from peering at the leg in front of him.

"The cost of the operation, which I would perform here in my surgery room, would be $200. Can your wallet stand such an expense?"

"Yes sir. But how long would it be until he could ride in a wagon or sit a saddle?"

The doctor pursed his lips in thought. "I would say possibly a week before he could undertake limited travel in a wagon lying down, with the leg elevated. It would, of course, depend upon his speed of recovery."

"And what do you think, Amos.? Do you want to undergo an operation? It may help you considerably." Matthew asked him. Troyer looked dubious.

"I dunno, sir. Do you really think it would help my old leg?"

"My uncle says this man is the best doctor and surgeon in the city. He's lived here all his life. That's all I can say except that if it was my leg, I would want to have it be the best I could."

"Then, sir, if you don't mind payin' for it, I'll go through with it. It pains me so, every day, it's all I can do to stand it. I'll make every effort to pay you back, yes I will."

"Never mind that, Amos. You more than did that already. You found that Laudanum for me when I was nearly out of my mind from my own wound.

"The doctor looked at Matthew's puckered face. "I see you've suffered also, because of this war. That wound had to be the sort that could well have driven a man crazy with the pain. I've seen it. I could examine you, also, while you're here."

"That's kind of you. I'll surely avail myself, after these men are taken care of, Dr. Holden."

They set the operation for the next day at 9:30. Then the doctor ushered them out and called in a white faced Luther.

Almost an hour later, the doctor came out and motioned Matthew into another room, his office. Holden gestured to a chair and Matthew took his ease while the doctor sat for a minute, marshaling his thoughts.

"This one is evidently one of the miracles that I have seen come from this war. He was shot through the body here." He indicated a spot nearly in the middle of his stomach. "He was bayoneted here." He indicated another spot in the right side of the chest. "Either or both wounds usually are fatal to those who receive them. He took both of these injuries and survived, but

136

he is not going to live much longer, I fear, unless another miracle occurs. The stomach wound has done some extensive damage to that organ and it cannot adequately process the food it ingests. The chest wound cleaved the right lung and it alternately collapses and re-inflates. It does him little good in that condition and I will need to operate on him also, permanently collapsing the lung so that he will be able to breathe more normally through proper inflation of the left. This is not so complicated, just cutting a nerve that goes to the lung, but I fear for his being able to take any such surgery, in his condition. The stomach wound is such that I can do nothing other than to advise him of what to eat and not eat." His bushy eyebrows went up, indicating to Matthew that he was leaving the call to him.

"He's an intelligent young man. I suggest we put it to him and let him decide. I will pay for the operation, though, if that's what he decides, doctor. And here is the payment for Troyer's right now." He took his fat wallet from his coat and paid Holden $200 from it, laying the money on the open desk.

"And how much do I owe you for the exams, including my own?"

"Another $20 will cover them, sir." Matthew took out some more greenbacks, laid them on the others.

Luther's response was much the same as Troyer's had been. Any cessation of the pain and misery would be much preferable to the way he was living now. And he said the same to Matthew, that he wanted to pay him back.

Matthew's exam was shorter. Holden took a small magnifying glass to the interior of the mouth and peered intently around in it. Presently, he laid it down and asked,

"Who did the surgical work? It is very nearly what I would have attempted, and nicely done."

"A German doctor named Klindt, attached to the 18th Georgia. He gave me considerable relief."

"I see only one ulcer on the left side that I want to open. Most likely I will find a bone fragment that has worked its way down from above, one that wasn't evident when the good German doctor was operating on you. We can do it now, if you' like."

Matthew was reluctant to have a renewal of pain but he knew the doctor was right and it needed to be done, so told him to go ahead. The operation was surprisingly swift and relatively painless. Ten minutes later, he came out, dabbling his mouth, the kerchief bloody. The doctor had decided to do Luther's operation in the afternoon, following Troyer's, and told them he would see them in the morning.

Back at camp, Matthew told Frank of what had transpired.

"We're going to be delayed a week. Troyer, and most likely Luther also, won't be fit for travel until then. It bothers me to wait that long, but it can't be helped. I'm not going to leave them behind."

They discussed the implications of a week's delay, neither happy about the prospect of staying any longer in northern territory.

"Tomorrow, follow me with some of the men and a wagon, we'll take Troyer to his meeting with the arms man and pick up the weapons, then I'll go on with Amos and Jack, to take them to the doctor. I want Millett to come with me while I'm carrying all this money. And while you have a belt full, I want you to take Big Lars along with you wherever you go, to watch your back. The last thing we need to do right now is lose our stake." Frank readily agreed. The money made him nervous.

The next morning, they harnessed two of the teams and hitching one to a wagon driven by Big Lars, pulled the road into town, another wagon following with Troyer and Luther in it, driven by Millett. Matthew and Frank rode their horses, along with one of the other men, a hard faced Kentuckian named Lee Puckett. He had a deep knife scar that ran the length of his face, from right eyebrow across his nose, down to his chin. Two of his fingers curled awkwardly on his left hand, from he said, grabbing the bluecoat's big Bowie with his hand and getting the tendons cut.

"But it saved my life, it did, because I had time then, to get'im with mine." He always gave a lopsided leer and drew his own great bone gripped Bowie, razor sharp, when he told the story. He didn't tell it often. He was quiet, morose, black whiskered, with piercing eyes, a lean man of indeterminate age, about middle thirties, Frank judged. The two men took to each other instantly and Frank had asked him to come along for the day. In his own way, he was as intimidating as Big Lars. He had somehow kept his sidearm at the surrender, a Colt Navy .36, well used and worn. He was anxious, though, he told Frank, to get one of the new Colts that Troyer had told the men he had found. "This ol' shooter's 'bout wore out, it's killed so many bluebellies." Frank thought longingly of his father's gun and his own he had lost, and silently vowed that never again would any man take his guns.

* * *

The two wagons stopped at the arms dealer's and he opened the door and motioned them around the back of the place, where he had stacked some of the crates containing their weapons and other materiel. Matthew and Frank had him open each one, though the man acted nervous doing it outside. Satisfied that the equipment was as Troyer had described it, and that it was all there, the other men started loading it while Frank paid him.

    Millett followed Frank into town to the doctor's residence and the two escorted the nervous men into the waiting room, where Holden met them. Both men were resigned and facing the surgery pretty bravely, Matthew thought. The muscular black man came in and asked Amos to come back to the operating room and he shuffled back with him. Matthew followed them and found the doctor there readying his instruments, along with another man, who evidently was going to assist, with the black man. Troyer was directed to undress and Holden asked Matthew if he wanted to stay to watch the operation. Matthew wasn't queasy, but decided that he wasn't needed and elected to stay out with Luther and Millett.

    By the time it was Luther's turn, he had worked himself into a state of emotional turmoil so that Matthew was sorry that he hadn't asked that Luther go first. Hours later, the doctor came out to say that he felt it would be better if both stayed the night before being moved, maybe longer on Luther's part. Millett and Matthew took the wagon back to the camp.

* * *

    Had they left in a day or two, they might have gotten away without any problems. Staying the extra week, though, brought several to their door. Without enough to do, the men started to find excuses to filter away from camp during the day after finding out that Matthew intended to wait for Luther and Troyer to recuperate.

    After finding the men were bringing whiskey back to camp, Matthew put his foot down and told them if they expected to go along, they would have to stay out of town and keep off the booze. Some of the men were a little cranky about that, especially Puckett. Frank, though, settled him down. Instead, they began some all day poker games. Next, other Southerners from town started gathering at the camp, at first just visiting the men there, then, finding they intended to travel south soon, clamoring to go along. The third day after the operations had been performed, Matthew and Frank were dismayed to find over fifty men gathered around the camp, causing the livery man to finally declare they had to move, that they were scaring away business, and that the dogs were starting to bother the horses.

They were trying to decide what to do, since Troyer and Luther were both unable to move yet, Luther especially being in serious condition, when from the city, they saw a detachment of soldiers riding towards them. The men started bunching up, when Matthew, sensing what might be wrong, told Frank to get them to sit back down around the fire, and to conceal their weapons, which had been issued to them the day before.

The detachment, a strong contingent of thirty soldiers, armed and led by a captain, stopped at the gate, dismounted at the order and remained by their horses, while the captain came over to them. Matthew met him, noticing that he was an older man, heavily mustached, with a limp.

"Hello. I'm Captain Selden. Are you the leader of this group?" He had instinctively picked Matthew out.

"I guess that's right, sir. The name is Grounds, Matthew Grounds. Might I be of service?" He stuck his hand out, determined to be friendly, knowing, he thought, what the trouble might be. After a slight hesitation, the officer shook with him, throwing him a piercing look.

"You might begin by telling me what you and these men are doing here—and what is in the wagons?"

"I gathered these men together—at least I recruited a dozen of them—to accompany me and my goods down to my home in Georgia, in the hope that they would help protect the supplies intended for my family back there. What has happened is that these other men have found out where we are going and want to come along." The captain looked carefully about him at the wagons, the lounging men, the horses and gear, and came back to Matthew.

"Well, that doesn't sound like another plot to kill someone in our government or an attempt to take over the halls of Congress. That wouldn't be your intent, would it, sir?" He asked shrewdly.

Matthew sensed that this man would be very hard to lie to and had no intention of doing so.

"I can assure you that all we want to do is go home. I had some funds and decided that it would be better to buy the supplies and wagons here than to try to find any in Virginia or the other southern states so—unstable. I have two men who needed medical attention and Doctor Holden, who operated on them three days ago, insisted that they needed to recover for a week or two before they went. Come with me, I'll show you."

He led the officer to where a wagon cover had been staked between two wagons to cover the beds of Luther and Troyer. They were both being tended by Stewberries and the others, and Seldon went to them and examined them, when Matthew asked both to show the captain the proof of their recent ordeal with the knife. He got up satisfied that Matthew wasn't lying, at least, about operations the two had just gone through. Then he asked to look in the wagons and Matthew told him to go ahead. He was satisfied with what he found, though he looked questioningly at the extra arms that were stored there.

Matthew told him that they were just discussing what to do, as the livery men had said that they must leave.

"I'll let you go right now, if you promise me you'll get on the road and put some distance between you and the city limits before dark. Otherwise, I'll be forced to detain you, and it may go hard on you for gathering armed men—Southerners—within the city here. I don't want to do that, but I have my orders, too. You'll have to take all these men—including the skulkers outside your camp."

He waved aside the objections that Matthew started to raise about that. His voice hardened.

"No sir. My instructions were that I either put you on the road today, headed out of the city, or detain you at Fort Lincoln Prison for an undetermined length of time. You and <u>all</u> your men. Oh, we know about you already. I've had men watching you for days. This city, sir, is on absolute edge, since the President's assassination."

Matthew, seeing the futility of any more argument, turned and told Frank and Millett to get ready to move out.

"Luke, put all the bedding in one wagon and spread it out. Get Amos and Jack up in it. There's at least five men with injuries out there around camp who can ride in the wagon, too. Throw saddles on all the horses we can. Our men will ride those, or drive." He turned to Selden. "Those men out there need boots. Might I send a couple men to try and see if they can find some for them?"

"No. You must get on the road. Maybe you can find them south of here. I told you the truth, sir, when I said that you need to move immediately. Right now, the city police and the army are engaged in scouring the city clean of all Confederates. By this time tomorrow, any found in the city limits will be sent to the jails or prison again, for vagrancy. You don't have much time." He stuck out his hand. "I fought against you, and you were a valiant foe. But I have my orders, sir."

* * *

By midday, they were outside the city limits, miles down the Potomac Road. The wagons were rolling easily, the horses all at the walk. Strung out behind them were hundreds of men, all likewise evicted from the city, some horseback like themselves, but most walking. Many were barefoot. Few had bedrolls, and most were without knapsacks and food. Strangely, though, after the first miles had passed, the men's spirits had lightened. They were, after all, headed home. Some were even singing.

Captured Confederate guns at Roanoke
Courtesy of the Library of Congress

PART II

HOMECOMING

Chapter 16
Virginia

The Exodus, as Matthew had come to think of it, had grown to about a thousand men before they had reached Alexandria, back on Virginia soil, in the shank of the afternoon. The townspeople there, accustomed to seeing large bodies of men on the road, and finding these to be southern prisoners of war returning home, were sympathetic to their plight and came from their homes with coats, blankets, boots, food of all kinds—the outpouring of sympathy was an emotional catharsis for many of the men, and their emotion was touching. Riding beside the front wagon, with Millett working the lines, he directed his band to travel on through the town and to go into camp on the other side, by a flowing creek.

Matthew waited by the road and directed the wagons into the pasture and the horseback riders followed, then the walkers came straggling in, a mob of men that had been through hundreds of bivouacs over the years and now, with literally nothing to camp with, laid down where they were after getting a drink at the creek alongside the horses.

He rode on a little farther to find out if he could get permission from the farmer who owned the land, after learning where he lived from a townsman. He found the old man, Hawkins by name, sitting placidly on his porch. He was deaf as a post and fitted a bullhorn to his ear when Matthew shouted out his question. Then, finally deciphering what he wanted, nodded his old white head vigorously and said, "To be sure, to be sure, yawl kin set up just thar by the crickside there. No chicken thievin', though, hear me?"

Matthew assured him that the men would leave his chickens alone, or, if he suffered some loss, would pay him for them before he left next morning. The old man looked at him and nodded his head again.

"Lawdy, b'lieve yawl would, at that." His bright, sparrow-like eyes remained on Matthew as he remounted and turned his horse away.

When he got back, Matthew's men had a fire going and Stewberries had supper on. Matthew watched the hungry men gathering and decided he couldn't eat if they couldn't.

"Millett, get men up in Big Lars' wagon and roll down some barrels of hard tack and salt pork and open them up."

He got up on a wagon box and addressed the crowd.

"We've enough to feed you tonight and I am going into town to see what else we might get for you. I'll need some sergeants among you to help out. Every sergeant here please step forward." A number of those present came up to the wagon.

"Men, we need to keep some order. Sergeant Shannon will tell you your duties and you must establish some messes so that all can get something to eat tonight. It can only be done through your helping us. Sergeant?"

Frank came up and with the sergeants helping, got the men in line to receive their portions. The men, though some were ravenous, were orderly, accustomed to queues and discipline. With the prospect of food, there was some good natured jawing among them.

Matthew saw that the sergeants had them in hand and mounted his horse, Early, the chestnut that he'd ridden that day. He rode into town, where some of the men had stayed, taking in the townspeople's hospitality. There was a store at the corner and he dismounted and went in. The store owner was glad to sell him all the blankets, pots and frying pans he had. Matthew had him pile them out on the sidewalk and said he'd send some men for them. He rode to the next store, two blocks down and did the same thing. Then the next.

That night, many of the messes had some form of cooking utensil, most bought by Matthew, some given by the townsfolk. But all had eaten something, for Matthew had found and bought some cattle and the men, expert butchers all, had quickly turned them into rations. The meat, much of it charred on sticks over a fire, along with the hard tack and salt pork, had filled their bellies. And many of them now had blankets.

* * *

He checked on Troyer and Luther that evening and found them both in constant pain and becoming feverish. Holden had sold him Laudanum and some fever pills. He gave them both a dose of each and was gratified to see the pain ease from their faces. Two of the other men were in need of the painkiller also and he gave them a dose apiece. He then went and found Frank, who was visiting at one of the messes.

"We're going to hold up here for some days. This is a good spot. Good water and not many mosquitoes. I'm going to ask the old owner if we might stay. Our hospital crew need rest from the wagon for a while—maybe three or four days, we'll see. One thing, some of the other men here are ready now to move on and maybe they will, without us." Frank nodded his agreement.

Matthew was walking toward the house when he met the old man coming toward him, walking bent over with his cane but making pretty good time. Matthew fell in beside him and they went together into the camp area. Hawkins moved among the messes, looking at the men reclining around the fires, cheery and talking together after their meal. The old man beamed when they waved and greeted him. Matthew managed to lead him over to the hospital wagon and give him a look at their plight. A couple of the men waved at them, fed and feeling better, now that the wagon was still.

He shouted in the man's ear, "We need to stay for a few days and let these men recover. Will you let us?"

The old man stared at him and then nodded his head, "Stay? Stay as long as you need to. I wasn't using this pasture anyway. And say, I have some pigs I want to give these men to butcher. Do you want 'em?"

"We certainly would take them. The men would be glad to have them, but I'll pay you for them, and rent the pasture,too, if you prefer." He had to shout several times to get that message across. The old man shook his head.

"Won't take any pay. Wouldn't hear of it. Now get some men and come with me. I'll show ya the pigs."

Matthew rounded up Frank, who yelled up his sergeants. After he told them what was up, Frank got some small rope from the wagons. They followed the man up the creek to a low concealed stable and tight pen where a dozen pigs were laying or rooting in the mud at the creek shore.

"You can take half of these. Just go ahead and cut 'em out and take 'em a ways away 'fore you kill 'em, so the others don't get all upset. Smellin' their own pig blood puts 'em off their feed."

Matthew gave it over to Frank, who, with the other sergeants, cut out the hogs and shooed them out the gate, securing them as they went. The men were past experts by now in slaughter of stock and made sure that each hog was flipped and tied securely, then dragged away. Soon, hog carcasses were hanging from the nearby trees. Stewberries and some of the messes had gathered pans and pots and saved most of the blood, to make blood pudding, a prized delicacy.

The men had several good feeds but by the second day, Matthew saw a lessening of numbers around the fires—some of the men who had gained their strength were going on home. Another two days passed before Matthew ordered them back on the road. By that time, a little more than half of the original number, about four hundred, were still camped there at Alexandria. A few stayed when the wagons swung out onto the road again, headed south, but most followed them, stringing behind them as the wagons pulled ahead.

* * *

With some minor variations, this was the course followed each day by the home marchers, or 'Homers', as Stewberries called them. Matthew would go ahead and try to buy utensils, blankets and food, often on the hoof. However, he didn't always have to use his wallet, as many of the towns gave freely to the returning marchers, and soon, all the messes were adequately supplied with cooking utensils, every man had at least one blanket, and many of them had shoes or boots on their feet.

As they had marched, it became normal that the men formed back into their units as they were during the war, some of them large, some small, as in the Texas Brigade people. Incredibly, some guidons even appeared, fluttering in the breeze ahead of the companies as they went forward, deeper into familiar territory. At each town, some of the men found themselves at home or just dropped out for some reason or another. Woodbridge went by, and Fredericksburg, until they were less than thirty miles from Richmond.

There, by the burnt ruins of that city, quite a few of the men filtered off to try to find families and loved ones. The remainder, Carolinians, Georgians, and men of the other states, a much smaller number, kept on, bypassing the shelled out and devastated Southern Capitol, all carrying an ache in their hearts.

Petersburg was next down the line and here the men, seeing the deserted fortifications, the devastation and the stark visages of the few remaining residents, quickened their step to get away from the place with all its horrible memories. Matthew led them forward at a fast pace until past dark, before Frank finally went up and asked him to stop. They were up early the next day and on the road, to put as many miles as they could between themselves and the memories this part of the country evoked.

Chapter 17
North Carolina

Emporia came up and Matthew stopped again for a time, to rest his patients. Troyer was getting better by the day. Several times, he'd swung himself out of the wagon and walked a few steps, using a crutch. The leg was healing. Luther, too, was coming around, breathing better, eating a little. Matthew was hopeful that both would improve even more, as time went by. Frank was not so sure, but he kept his outlook positive when he visited with them.

Emporia was a town of 2500, about twenty five miles from the North Carolina boundary, in flat farm country that showed the effects of the recent war. Most of the houses and outbuilding had been torched. People had returned and were living in tents and hastily thrown up sheds. Few livestock—cattle, sheep, pigs—were visible, nor were any ducks, geese or chickens seen. Both armies had scoured the country repeatedly and little was left but some scanty volunteer crops coming up. Matthew fed the men, about two hundred, from the wagons, which were showing some heavy depletion. At each town,

Matthew had tried, but was unable to do much toward replenishing his stock, as the merchants were more interested in restocking their own shelves than selling what they didn't have. When he could, he bought on the hoof and let the men slaughter for themselves.

They rode through Roanoke Rapids, a small town whose ruins proclaimed the far-reaching hands of Sherman's pillagers, set up against rolling foothills. Here Troyer proclaimed himself well and asked to be allowed to ride a part of the day. Matthew was dubious but he let him take the buckskin. Its usual rider, Peter Balsom, an old sergeant from the 18th Georgia, he directed as a turnabout driver for Millett. Balsom was willing. He, too, had an old leg wound that bothered him and it was easier to ride a wagon than a saddle.

The hospital wagon was down to ten men now, the rest having made it to their homes, except for one, whom they buried along the road. He had quietly passed away in the night at the camp before Roanoke Rapids. Matthew had said the few words over his last resting place. It was now mid-July.

At Goldsboro, where Sherman had stopped his northern advance for several weeks, they were appraised of just how terrible the Union Army's advance through the country had been. Hardly a building was left standing, the town completely razed, and there were many new graves overflowing the cemetery. People there, both black and white, were clearly starving. Matthew, seeing the destruction, and knowing that his wagons would attract attention, decided to go on through and try to avoid the towns thereafter, as much as possible. It was as he had feared—total desolation. He couldn't keep his mind off what he might find at Pendemere.

Out of Fayetteville, Frank rode up and fell in alongside Matthew. "We're being shadowed. Troyer just came in and reported that he's seen groups of men out west of us. I'm afeared that they're just waiting to get us in the right position to try us."

Matthew looked back. He could see nothing, but Troyer and his outriders were able scouts and he took them at their word. He looked forward. There was water coming up, and the horses needed it.

"All right. We'll water up ahead. While the wagons are bunched up, get out the extra weapons and arm your sergeants. Try to do it on the sly, if you can. Alert the men. Fill the water barrels. Make sure we're loaded for a skirmish. We're not stopping and we may not get to choose our ground."

A mile or more farther down the road toward Lumberton, a large body of men, some mounted, some not, came from the trees out of a low coulee and spread across the road. Matthew could see they were all armed. He didn't count, but his practiced eye told him maybe a hundred and fifty men were out there. He waved an arm back and Millett, in the front wagon, swung off immediately to the right, followed by the others, who made a tight little enclave. The followers behind, seeing the prospect of a battle, and being unarmed, spread out behind a ways from the excitement. Some few, though, came on forward, and Matthew saw them talking with Frank. Evidently, they were asking for weapons, too. He wished now he had them to give.

Three men rode forward from the mass of men to their front, signaling that they wanted a parley. Frank started to mount his horse. Matthew waved him back to the wagons and went forward himself, walking his horse towards them. The three were hard bitten, bearded men, wolf-like—and heavily armed. He stopped and waited for them to approach, hitching his belt so that he could easily reach his weapon.

"That'll do," he said in his quiet voice, when they had gotten near. But it carried to the men, and that, along with his quiet, confident demeanor, stopped them.

"What can we do for you gentlemen? The bigger man, a tall long haired, black bearded man, looked at his men with a smile at their being called 'gentlemen'.

He replied in a deep voice,"Wal, we'uns is right curious as to what you got in them wagons."

"Wounded and exhausted men—Southerners like yourself who fought the Union, were captured and just want to get home."

"Thet so? Then you won't mind if we jist take a look, then? This hereabouts is our country and we like to know who'se usin' our road."

Matthew shifted his body in the saddle a little. "Sounds to me like you don't believe me, that you're calling me a liar, sir!" He saw their gaze shift then, and Frank came sliding to a stop beside him.

One of the men confronting them started to swing his rifle towards Frank, and Matthew drew his pistol and shot the man from his saddle. Frank was in action then, too, firing into the man on the other side of the leader as he tried to bring his weapon up. The big leader, seeing he was about to be shot, dropped his rifle to the ground, spooking his horse for an instant.

The man Frank had shot groaned, "Asa, he'p me. . . ." and fell from his horse.

"Now, sir. Pull that pistol in your belt—very slowly—out and throw it in back of you." Matthew directed him. The man carefully complied.

"Take his reins and bring him along."

Frank grinned and reaching over, scooped up the man's reins from him, then pulled him along, following Matthew. They left the two men lying there on the ground. The leader, his face white and strained, said nothing beyond a muttered curse, as he was led up to the wagons. The men were armed and ready, waiting to see if an attack was coming, after seeing the shooting of the two men on either side of the bandit leader.

"Pull him off his horse and tie him up tight."

Big Lars grabbed the man by his arms and literally lifted him from his horse, the man looking like a child in the hulking man's grasp. Millett ran to help tie him up. Running his hands over the man, Millett came up with a narrow bladed dagger. He stuck it in his own belt. Matthew dismounted then, and came to stand in front of him.

"Now, sir. All we want is safe passage through this country, but we are not going to be stopped or threatened by every damned outlaw band we might encounter. You're going to come along with us until we get to Florence. We might let you go then, or, if you give us too much trouble, or your men decide to try to get you back, we'll just decorate a tree with your damned carcass. Throw him in a wagon and watch him."

Big Lars grinned and gathering him up, tossed him high into one of the wagons.

Matthew carefully reloaded his pistol and holstered it again. Frank was doing the same, watching the men milling around the bodies lying out on the flat. A gun went off out there, the ball whistling through the camp, then several, a couple smacking into the wagons with thuds that brought memories back to all the men present. All of them, including Frank and Matthew, took cover, then Matthew climbed into the wagon where their leader was and grabbing him up, held him so that the men out beyond them could see him and know that he was their prisoner. The men, recognizing him, quit firing. Matthew threw him down again. He jumped down from the box.

"All right, saddle up and get the wagons moving. Keep bunched up."

Outside of Florence, into South Carolina, Matthew had Big Lars toss the man out on the road. They left him tied and lying there.

Chapter 18

South Carolina

Columbia lay in the sun like a raped, beaten and savaged woman, as indeed, many of her female inhabitants had been, not by the regular Union army, in most instances, but by the 'bummers" who had collected in the wake of the long column as the march through the heart of the South's bread-basket progressed.

For the most part, these men, deserters of both armies, freed Negroes, the flotsam of the conflict, were the wolves circling the herd, always looking for their own gain. Gangs of these men ran rampant as law and order gave way to anarchy. It was a moot question as to whether Sherman and his officers condoned the actions of all their men and the 'bummer' mob who followed them. The multiplicity of incidents occurred throughout the South as the armies of Johnston and Hood were defeated and local legal authority there was overrun. In Georgia, Sherman's officers had managed to keep their men under some restraint, but in the state which most Northerners saw as the prime mover of the rebellion and the first to secede, those restraints were tacitly removed. Columbia, like Petersburg, was another city to pass by as hurriedly as the group could.

Two days later, Frank and Millett were visiting while they rode along next to the wagons. Out on either side, Puckett and Balsom were on the scout for now, while Matthew was a ways up ahead, followed as usual by the dog, Grant. A hundred or more men were marching in their rear, holding back a couple hundred yards to let the wagons dust settle. Most of these men were Georgians and Texans from the Brigade, and Troyer had somehow found Enfields around Columbia for about half of them, bought with Matthew's funds. The sergeants had distributed them to the most steady and loyal men, and in that way, their rear was secured. The followers were in considerably better shape than they had been when they'd come out of Washington. They were no longer scarecrow ragbags, but, for the most part, hale and hardy men who strode along the road as if they were conquerors instead of the conquered. Their clothing had improved, they had blanket rolls around their shoulders, and most of them wore boots of some kind, another improvement from the searchings of Troyer, whom most just called "The Forager.

"Millett turned back and looked forward again. He spit a brown stream. As they rode along in the warm summer sun, they gossiped idly.

"The Captain was pretty damn sudden back there by Lumberton. I think he's mighty worried about what he'd goin' to find when he gits home, and it's workin' on 'im."

Frank worked his jaw and relieved himself of a large cud of tobacco, another fruit of Troyer's constant exploring. He'd turned up a barrel of chew tobacco that a farmer had earlier hidden and now offered for sale. Matthew had thought that the weed might lift the spirits of those men who longed for it, so had given Troyer the money to bring it back. Consequently, all the men who wanted it were able to partake, including the little corporal and Frank.

"He almost started the ball before I got there. I'm not so sure, though, he needed me. He was that quick."

"He's spent a lot of money to get us this far. Most of it, he wouldn'a had to mess with, buyin' clothes and boots an' all for the bunch back there. And throwin' the feeds he's been givin' us."

"He's a generous man. A good man. We've gotten to be close friends, but he's never told me yet what's made him . . . sour on life. My guess is he lost a sweetheart, but he's never said. I know he don't have much to do with women. But he dearly loves a good horse."

"He's sure sold on them A-rab horses. Me, I like a good Standardbred, myself, like you."

"Have to admit, he makes a fine figure on a horse, makes me think of what General Lee must of looked like when he was his age. They say he was the best horseman in that West Point school."

"Yeah, he sits that high-stepper like an Englishman. He told me he went to school over there, and I know for sure he was in India with a British regiment. He's got some scars, you know, to show for it."

"I remember when we bandaged him up at Petersburg, I wondered about 'em, then. Looked like saber cuts."

"He was in some battles over in India, he told me. Didn't say much else."

"His folks musta been pretty rich?"

"His dad was one of the heavy dealers up in Richmond, sounds like. One of the "One Hundred" that financed the war."

"What do you think we're goin' to find down in Georgia?"

"Most likely about what we're seein' 'round here."

What they were seeing in South Carolina was devastation unending. The houses and outbuildings were blackened ruins. The fields showed the effects of burning, too. Nowhere was there livestock. And there were people, starving people, who seemed listless and unable to restart their lives. They had seen very few who were working their land. Those who were attempting to, were usually scratching the ground by hitching themselves to the plow, their womenfolk trying to work the handles. It was heartrending to see the change in the country, once so fruitful and blooming, prosperous, with the people hale and well fed, even the slaves, singing in the fields. Had that all been an illusion?

* * *

At a downed bridge that had once spanned the Savannah River southwest of Waterloo, they were brought to a halt. The river was up. Rains upstream had come down and had made the stream temporarily impassable. They pulled up alongside a copse of trees and made camp.

The trip through South Carolina had not been without strife. The man Asa, had regained his band and stalked them for some time, before, thinking they had let their guard down, he had struck them at dawn in a light thunderstorm that had blanketed the countryside with rain.

One of the scouts, a man named Tom Britton, had alerted them the night before, when he had been working the back trail, as Frank had instructed. Britton, a sandy haired, hatchet faced young man with a prominent adam's apple that worked its way up and down the man's neck as he talked, told them he had seen skulkers hiding in the bushes about a mile back, but had acted as if he hadn't spotted them. As the man had arguably the best eyes in camp, Frank believed he had certainly <u>seen</u> something. So, talking with Matthew, they decided to double the night guards and get everyone up before dawn and ready for an attack. That had been done, and with the first rays of light, through the rain and the breaking clouds, Britton and Millett, another man with the sharpest of eyes, called low warnings to the others. They had pulled in the followers that were armed, after dark, warning the others to be ready to get out of the line of fire. Now, a wall of rifles pointed out from the camp.

    The outlaw band was working its way in, the men bent over and coming towards them, trying to shield their rifles from the rain. Matthew whispered to the men near him to let them come on, get closer. Frank, on his side, and Millett, did the same. The men, all seasoned veterans, well knew the importance of waiting for the foe to get close. They had waited.

    When the men were fifty yards from the wagons, Grant and some of the other dogs set up a row, and Matthew had seen that the attackers, feeling that surprise was lost, had begun sprinting toward. He fired at a shaggy, bearded man who was just raising up to pull the trigger himself. The man had gone over backward, shot high in the chest. Immediately, a volley had blasted out at the incoming men, leveling many. Then the men in the enclave had pulled their pistols and for a time, the battle sound was deafening. The conclusion, though, was foreordained, with the first shocking volley that had killed so many of the band. At that range, nearly every shot had gone home. The remaining outlaws had either fallen by pistol shot or had scrambled away, wounded. Few had escaped the carnage.

    It was over in a few minutes, and Matthew and Frank, walking the ground afterward, had seen the leader, Asa, shot through the head and lying on his rifle, near the forefront of the other men who lay dead. Thirty-three men had died that morning in the wet grass, and the bloody marks at other places showed that some had been hard hit and still had dragged themselves off.

    Matthew hadn't let the men go after them, saying they weren't killers, just defending themselves. Frank grinned at that, but was careful not to let his friend see it. They had cleaned the battleground of weapons and like all soldiers, had rifled the pockets of the dead. They hadn't gotten much.

Chapter 19

Georgia

The river was down after a day and a half of waiting, and they forded it below the ruined bridge, Frank on his big dark Chestnut, Grabby, testing the water first, and making it over with little trouble, the horse swimming like a duck, high in the water. He waved and Millett slapped the lines and his teams hit the water on the run. They had doubled up for the crossing. The wagon wheels hit a soft spot near the middle that threatened to bog them down but the little corporal never let his horses slow down. They made it out and up the bank with a rattle of chains and popping hocks, and Frank motioned for the next one.

  The last to come across was Big Lars and instead of urging his teams on when they hit the middle, he let them slow down and the rushing river threatened to drag them downstream. Frank, though, had his rope down and hitting the water with a big splash, Grabby took him close to the front team and he threw his loop over the near horse's head. As he turned for the bank, he hollered at big Lars to "Git 'em goin', slap 'em up." He did and the teams straightened out and got underway again for the bank, which they reached without the wagon tipping over, though it was a close thing for a second. Then they were up and over the bank, safe on solid ground. The men on horseback made it safely also, the tails of their mounts pulling some of the men behind, but the rest of the followers were stranded there unless they wanted to swim it. Some of them, determined to come across, too, had put their weapons and clothes in the wagons, and now about thirty men went into the water. Frank had the men with horses be ready to help, their ropes ready. More than one man was helped from the water by a loop from one of the helpers.

Three men, though, poor swimmers, were swept downstream, and Frank spurred Grabby along the bank, Balsom and Puckett following him closely. Once again, Grabby made a diving entry in the water ahead of the struggling men and Frank's glistening loop whirled once and out across the water, settling over a head. The man slipped his arm through the rope and Frank reined the big horse around and headed for the bank, as Puckett, on a big dun, took to the water behind him. Balsom ran past them and spurred his horse into the river farther down, whirling his loop to throw, but the man slipped under the water and wasn't seen again. He reined his horse around and repeated the run downstream, but it was wasted effort, the man was gone.

"What was his name?" Matthew asked after the men had returned. He and the others had watched helplessly as the drama played out below them

"Calvin Talbert. The men called him 'Callie.'" Frank said, dismounting wearily. He was drenched to his hat. Balsom came up and flung himself off his horse.

"I tried, Captain. . . .he just wasn't there. Never came up," he said, apologetically.

165

"Don't blame yourself, Pete, you did all you could. We'll carve his name in that tree there before we go on." Matthew pointed to a large beech close by the river. Millett pulled his Bowie and going to the tree, began working a flat spot on its face.

"How do you spell "Talbert?" he called to the men, looking at Frank. He was silent. Matthew responded, "T-A-L-B-E-R-T."

Chapter 20
Savannah

Matthew was encouraged. The city was largely untouched, though its dockside warehouses had been burned, along with its docks, right down to the water. Those were being rebuilt and the town had an air of recovery about it, a purpose that had been missing throughout the march from Washington, through Virginia and the Carolinas. Here, men were generally busy and there were some ships in the harbor that looked like they were in the process of being unloaded. His mind, which had been in a perpetual state of depression from the constant thought of war and witnessing the ruin of the South, began to recover a little. The sun was bright and the smell of magnolias pervaded the air as he walked Stonewall down the bustling main street toward the Savannah Bank of Commerce, at the corner of fifth and Main, the institution where his family had banked for many years. He dismounted and looped the reins in the steel ring of an elaborate hitching post and went in. The pretentious interior, once somewhat intimidating to him, now looked a little shabby, and cushions were protruding from a couple of the horsehair chairs in the lobby. Yet, there was a teller behind the cage, old

Mr. Keely, who remembered him immediately, and came from behind the low wall and shook his hand warmly. Their conversation brought Mr. Allyson, the portly owner and manager, to the door of his office, and seeing who it was, he too, came forward with his hand out.

"Matthew Grounds!!! I do swear!!! I am so pleased to see you!!! Please, sir, come inside and sit down." The banker called for coffee and an old black man brought it in, in two porcelain cups instead of the usual sparkling silver set, saying nothing, and shuffling out again silently. They sipped the brown liquid for a little, then Allyson said, "I won't ask about yoah war experiences, Matthew, we've heard too much of that lately, and every family has been so'ely hurt by it. You knew, maybe, that Gilbert, who served in the 18th, was killed at Antietam? Lord, it's nearly been the death of me and Emily. Hester, his sister, was took sick and we thought for a while, we were going to lose her, too." He drew out a handkerchief and blew his nose, then wiped his eyes, shaking his shaggy white head.

"Changin' the subject, I will say that Savannah is on its way to making a commercial recovery that will be the example for the rest of the southern states. We're rebuilding. Ouah harbor is filling with ships clamoring for cotton and bringin' in a plentiful variety of products and supplies for our city, this being one of them." He raised his cup, then hesitated. "I expect that you have just returned from the no'th and haven't heard anythin' 'bout yoah fatha' or Mistress Ma'tha?"

Matthew felt a tremor of apprehension. "I just made it out of South Carolina this mornin'. The river was up and the bridge was down. We lost a man at the crossing, a Talbert boy from Macon. He was almost home." He steeled himself, took a sip of coffee. "What about my father?"

"Son, brace yourself for bad news. Your father was, as you know, one of the "One Hundred" who mainly financed the majority of the rebellion. He was a known figure, Matthew, marked by the Union, and Sherman had him on his list. Pendemere was one of the first holdings visited by Sherman's troops and it was burned, every building, every field, all the stock confiscated and the Negroes dispersed. Nothing is left, son.

Danforth and your aunt, along with some others in the area, fled before they arrived, on the blockade runner *Swordfish*, which was one of the last ships owned by him and his partners still afloat. After a chase out to sea, they were caught by the *Monroe*. Your father's ship was almost away free, when it was hit in the magazine by a lucky bow shot. It blew up, Matthew, with a loss of all hands, and the end had to be swift, if that's any consolation." He wiped another tear away. "Yoah fatha was a dear friend."

Matthew sat stunned.

"Sherman dallied here for a couple weeks, then continued his march no'th. Of course, when every Federal unit was across the river, they destroyed the bridge, as they did the warehouses and the docks here." His rheumy eyes wavered over the cup, as he raised it to his lips and sipped.

"I'm sorry to have to be the one to tell you. Have you heard yet from yoah sister, Emmy? I heerd from yoah father that she was in London, visitin' yoah late wife's family."

"No, Sir. I've heard nothin' from anyone for years. I know her address, I think. I'll need to write."

He sat silent. It was hard to take in, but he had known in his heart since Fort Delaware, that with no response to his letters, something had to be badly wrong. He leaned back. What to do now?

"I guess I'll ride out to the place and see for myself." He thought of his money. "I had some money, in case they...."

"You can certainly deposit it here, Matthew." The old man offered.

"I guess I will, some of it.....I'll...."

He got up and pulled off the money belt. It was still heavy, despite the demands on it the last month. Frank had complained about his belt enough, its weight, its responsibility, so that when they had spent, it had mostly come out of that one, rather than his. He counted out five thousand dollars, all the gold and much of the greenbacks, on the desk and Allyson made out a deposit clip for him, then gave him a sheaf of counter checks to use. They shook hands and Matthew, still numb, the old man teary eyed again, went out to the sun and the distinct smell of roses and magnolias, neither of which had much impact on him. The ride back was a blur.

* * *

Back at the camp, close by the river, the men knew immediately, by his blank, numb look, that Matthew had gotten bad news, and all were sympathetic. Balsom took his horse, loosened the saddle and slipped the bridle so it could graze. It was noon and Stewberries had made another fine Dutch stew, complete with some vegetables Troyer had brought in from a farmer's market downtown. Millett brought him a plate full and he gathered himself enough to eat some, then gave the rest of it to Grant, who, seeming to know something was wrong, had been hovering by him. He gestured to Frank, who was waiting to visit with him and the two walked off a ways. Matthew told him in short, terse sentences what had transpired. Frank said nothing, just put a hand on his shoulder briefly. Neither man was much on open display of their emotion, however, their feelings ran deep.

"I guess I'll have to ride out there, at least see for myself," Matthew concluded. Frank turned and called to Big Lars to bring in Grabby from the rope corral. He started gathering his gear.

"I'm goin' out there with you. Don't want you to be alone." Matthew didn't argue.

When they mounted, Millett and Lee Puckett swung in beside them. Matthew said nothing. A wan Jack Luther, who had finally gotten up out of the hospital wagon, but was still wobbly and weak, stood with his hand on Grant as they rode out. His little terrier, Goober, sat by his side. More of the men had since left, after getting across the river, but there was still a core of them, including those who had signed on to drive and guard, who were left in camp.

They passed several large plantations, Matthew's old neighbors, whose houses and outbuildings were intact, but also some whose farms were leveled. Matthew, forewarned, still was shocked when he saw the place. It was a blackened ruin, the house, barns and stables burnt to the ground, the fields still showing scorch marks from the fires. Some of the woods back of the house had also burned, but Matthew, gazing around dazedly, saw some lean-tos hiding in the shade there, not too far from the family cemetery. That was one place he couldn't stand to gaze on. He dismounted and sat on an old hitching stone, Frank coming to stand beside him. Presently, an old man came stumbling out from the bushes, Spur's old daddy, Marcus. He came closer and recognized Matthew as he sat there. Then he came forward at a shambling run, yelling, "Massa, Massa Matt'ewww!"

Matthew opened his arms and they embraced, the old man crying incoherently. From the woods, came a few others, older men, women and kids. Matthew recognized all but a couple of the youngest children, born during the war. Lastly, holding back fearfully, was Spur.

* * *

Spur was thin to the point of emaciation, and afraid—afraid Matthew was mad at him for losing all of the Captain's belongings, even his clothes and toilet kit. After Matthew had been captured, he said, that 'Cap'n had come and taken everything to he's tent.' Questioning from them had finally determined that it was Siderus, that he had claimed Matthew owed him for the horse that he had gotten from him, and had used that lie to garner his remaining horses, his weapons, tent and everything it had in it, even Spur. But Spur had run away and somehow, after many misadventures, had made it home.

"You did fine, Spur. It's not your fault. You did fine." Matthew repeated. He was just glad to see his childhood friend again. What had been stolen could be replaced. But what to do with these old retainers who had stayed on the land?

Saying that they would bring food and some other supplies they needed, Matthew and the others rode back to the camp. Spur watched him go with tears running down his cheeks. Whatever happened, Matthew was determined that his people would not suffer any more.

Back at camp, evening was setting in and the other men had just finished eating supper. Stewberries had kept some warm for them and they ate gratefully. Matthew spent a sleepless night trying to come up with some answers and finally decided to go back in to Allyson and ask him his advice.

Next morning, after a good breakfast, he and Millett went through the wagons and made a quick inventory. Half their stores were consumed, the wagons rolling light compared to their weight at the start of their journey in Washington. It had come to him in the night that he wanted to go west, to see Frank's state, and experience some fresh, new land, some towns that were not razed to the ground, some people who weren't starving and beaten down. One thing he was sure of—at this point, anyway, he couldn't stand to stay here and tackle the work of rebuilding Pendemere. He needed a year at least, to clear his mind and decide the course of the rest of his life. He had always had a yen to see the frontier, the herds of buffalo, the huge open country beyond the Missouri that men talked of all the time. He would go with Frank to Texas. Maybe his friend's homecoming would be better than his own.

They had found gold in California while he had been in England. And then, throughout the war, people had been talking about strikes in the Rocky Mountains in Montana Territory at Alder Gulch and Helena, in Idaho in the Boise Basin and the big strike at Leadville, in Colorado. Like all the other men, Matthew had listened and dreamed someday of going to see those far-flung places, but always, he had admitted to himself that his obligations at home would come first. Now, the obligations had mostly been wiped out. But, he had to find some honorable way to care for his people, who depended upon him. Maybe Allyson would have an answer for him.

He did. The Baptist minister was an honest, upstanding man, Matthew might remember him, Pastor William Rainey, who had taken many of the homeless darkies under his wing. They trusted him and were being cared for. As for the land, if he would sign a letter authorizing the bank to act as signatory for the lease of the property, the rent funds would be put in his account and the taxes and other expenses that might accrue paid from it. He could leave some money in his account for a buffer.

"We would, of course, have to charge a small fee for this—2% of the rental." Allyson told him, folding his hands over his ample stomach.

"I am just going to take you up on that, Mr. Allyson." Matthew offered his hand and the fat man rose from his chair and shook it.

Next was to find the minister, which didn't prove to be hard. He was at the church. He proved to be a mild-visaged older man, one whom Matthew trusted immediately. He told the Pastor of his dilemma and explained that he would like to leave some money for their care and welfare. The man assented and Matthew pressed a large sum in his hands, saying that he would write and find out if he needed more, or, if there was an emergency, he could get some through Mr. Allyson, at the bank. The man was grateful. Few of the owners had done so much for their retainers.

That afternoon, he went back to Pendemere, a wagon following him, Millett driving. He left in the late evening, having spent the time with his people, after having given them the contents of the wagon, supplies, seeds, tools, the wagon itself and the team. He had also visited the cemetery.

Spur had wanted to go with him, had insisted, but Matthew had told him that he was needed there, that he would come home later and get him. Spur had thought he was punishing him for losing his gear, but Matthew had tried his best to disabuse him of that notion. He didn't know if he'd succeeded. He wasn't easy in his mind, but what else he could do, he wasn't sure. He had left 'Bills of Sale' for both the wagons and the team of horses, trying to explain their importance. But to them, the most important thing he had brought were the garden seeds and the tools. All of them knew how to use those. The rest, they were sure, the horses, the wagon, maybe most of the supplies, would just be stolen by white men who coveted them. But, they decided after Matthew and Millett left, that maybe they should do their best to get everything hidden.

* * *

"Gather 'round, men. I told you when you began this trip, that I would pay you at the end, and that you'd get to keep your gear. Well, today's payday. Come up and I'll give you your wages." He spread his money and his notes on a wagon end gate and the men trooped forward. To each man's wages, he added a double eagle, shaking his hand afterward. The followers, he had decided, could keep their Enfields, too. They had given him good service. There were twenty or so of them left, and he gave them a five dollar gold coin. Luther, Puckett, Stewberries, Millett and Big Lars, he told to stick around, that he had something to visit with them about. The others having gone, Matthew and Frank drank coffee with the men that were left.

Then Matthew told them, "I'm going on with Frank and see some of this Texas country he's been telling us about. Jack, you're from over by Crockett, so you probably would like to travel with us. You others, I don't know what you have in mind. But you're welcome to come with us. Day pay, as usual, if you do. I only plan to take two wagons. Frank wants to bring some supplies to his sister. You might know she runs a stage station out there and he's sure she probably needs some things. That's one. The other will be for us."

He held out his cup for Stewberries to replenish. "What about you, Stewberries? We'll need a good cook."

"Hell, boss, I guess so. I don't have much kin left, and they're in Austin, anyway." He'd been unable to find anyone in Richmond.

"Millett, Big Lars?"

"We're with you, boss. Neither of us have any kin anywhere. Might as well trail along with friends." Millett spoke for both of them but Big Lars nodded his agreement.

Puckett said nothing, just nodded his head also.

"Then we'll keep the best wagons and teams. Frank, you pick. Then take the rest to the market tomorrow and sell them for us. Same with what we don't need. Sell it. Stew, you tell us what you don't need or want.

We'll keep the weapons, and see what the market for them is like out there. Frank says it should be good.

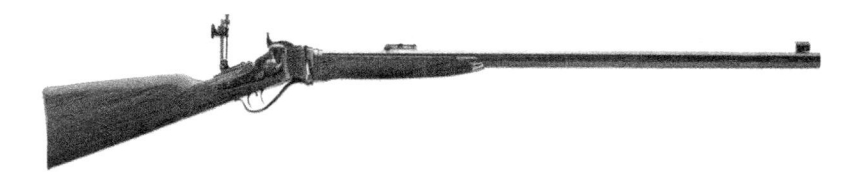

PART III

TEXAS

Courtesy of the Library of Congress

Chapter 21

Austin

Frank pulled his saddle off with a groan that was echoed by his horse, who'd been ridden hard but wouldn't be put away wet, as Frank was always careful to take good care of his horses.

He'd been in the leather almost continuously since Abilene. He turned and dropped the saddle over the stall rail, slapped the horse on the butt and urged him into it, where he brushed the sweat foam and dirt off him with a currycomb he found hung on a peg by the door. Then he filled a gourd with some oats from a barrel in the tack room and spreading it in the trough in front of the horse, he pulled off its bridle so it could eat. He stretched his back to its limit, hands behind him, trying to ease the ache, waiting for the horse to finish. Then he opened the stable door to the corral and grabbing him by the mane, urged him through it and shut it behind him.

He pulled his Henry from its scabbard and checked the loads, filling the 15 shot tube magazine again. Then, he drew his pistol and carefully checked the loads. He never wanted to get in the fix he'd found himself a year ago, walking out on the street and having his Colt light three loads, after a running battle with some Comanche. There were two men, cowboys from Fort Stockton, who had been on his trail because he'd killed their brother, when he resisted arrest. They'd started firing as soon as he appeared and he'd shot back, wounding one, killing the other. Then, as he started forward, he'd remembered his pistol was light some loads, how many he didn't remember. He kept walking, wishing for his back-up gun, but that one had been dropped when he was trying to replace a cylinder in it during the run from the Comanches.

The wounded man had raised up, propping himself up from the ground on his left hand, aiming his pistol at him, as Frank had pulled the trigger. The weapon had snapped on an empty cylinder and Frank had stared death in the face—but the man had died before he could fire. He'd had the shakes so bad he needed about a quart of redeye to get them to quit. And he'd gone and bought another back-up pistol, like the one Matthew had gotten for him in Washington those years ago—a snub nose .44 that he packed in a chaps pocket on his left side or at the back of his belt, if he wasn't riding.

He dearly liked those new cartridge guns they were coming out with and he guessed he would either trade in his Colts or get them converted over, if he could ever get the money together. It seemed like he was always broke—either he'd get to gambling and drinking, or he'd find a cute little senorita to spend it on. Didn't matter. He was always broke. Matthew, he knew, would loan him the money, if he wasn't mad at him, which he often was. But he had too much pride to ask for it. He knew he drank too much, damn it. Just like his daddy. But the booze helped keep him from dreaming, and that was good. He hated to dream, because it was usually about Cold Harbor, the bluebellies attacking, and them firing and firing, just layin' em down. He'd wake up in a cold sweat, shaking. —Piss on it. He didn't even like to think about it.

He walked over to the Ranger barracks and through the door. The men there, a dozen or more, were in their bunks or at the table, playing penny-ante. McAllen spoke for them when he asked,

"What the hell, Frank, we didn't expect you back until tomorrow. You come all the way from Abilene? Did you find 'em?" Mackey McAllen was the talkative one, always full of questions and chatter, even when they were setting up an ambush or on a night trail. He couldn't keep still or silent.

For answer, Frank threw two pairs of ears on the table, startling the card players, who stared at them.

"Yeah, I found em. Said they won't be usin' their ears any more. Said I could have 'em. I brought 'em back for you, Mackey, so you'd have some ears to talk into when nobody else was 'round to listen."

Then he laughed. It was a grim laugh that brought more than one weak chuckle from these hardened men. Frank was the acknowledged hardest of the bunch. not that any of the men were afraid of anything—least of all other men. They had all of them proven their courage on many occasions. Two or three were nearly as old as Frank, maybe. But none had seen the action with the hostiles before the war like he had, none had fought the war battles, none had the tenacity, the damn-all wildness, and the streak of mean that, when he was drunk, nobody wanted to mess with, guns or knives. When he was drunk.

When he was sober, which, thanks to the Lieutenant, was most of the time, he was a man to be with and back up. A man that was fun-loving and humorous, willing to help out at whatever needed doing. A generous man, who had loaned money to each of them at one time or another. There wasn't a better man to ride the river with—when he was sober. And all of them freely acknowledged it. He was the best of them, Oh, Mackey was maybe a better rifle shot, Bucky Albright maybe a better bronc stomper, Gaines Campbell better with a rope, Tracks Stephans better on a trail—but with a pistol, there was probably no argument—it was Frank who could take their money when it came to splitting cards, throwing rocks, driving nails, just doing anything with a pistol, either hand. And all around, he was a damn close second.

Long Henry Lowery, the horse thief, a noted gun hand, a killer, had found out the hard way that Frank Shannon was his better. That had happened on the streets of Goliad, when Lowery had issued his challenge to the Rangers and the rest of the men had wanted to take him without a face-off, from ambush. Frank wouldn't hear of it, though the L.T. had issued strict orders that there would be no grandstanding, no more single combat, that the job was to apprehend those breaking the law without hazard to themselves, if it could be done. Frank had said to hell with that. A Ranger was better than a damn horse thief. He walked out on the street and faced the man and killed him. The boys that saw it said you could cover the two holes in his vest with a silver dollar.

And he could use a knife, as the big Mexican had found out, there on the Brazos, that night in the Mex cantina, when he had found Frank messing with his woman. He'd been a greaser with a reputation for being a killer with his blade. They'd gone at it in the crowded cantina, and Frank had taken a cut or two, just little ones, but had carved the Mexican a new mouth and a couple belly buttons before it was done. The men had been petrified that they might have to bring him in on a murder charge but they had persuaded the Lieutenant that the Mexican had pulled first and cut Frank first. All of them were prepared to testify to that, they'd said.

At that, the Lieutenant had fined him a month's pay. "For tarnishing the Ranger reputation," the Lieutenant had said. Huh, as if it mattered that they cut up a few cow—thievin' greasers. Actually, it had helped their reputation, if anything, because the Greaser bastards were always talking about their knives, braggin' and such, about what great hands at cutters they were, and Frank had shown 'em how a Ranger could use whatever weapon they wanted, and do it better!! And he'd been half drunk at the time.

That, they knew, was what had really pissed the Lieutenant off. He hated for Frank to get drunk. Oh, he didn't mind them drinking —a little—but Frank couldn't do that. He couldn't just drink a little. When he drank, he had to drink a lot—so he wouldn't dream, he said. And the Lieutenant, who had been with Frank from the first, practically, couldn't abide that. Couldn't and wouldn't. He had drummed other men out of the Rangers for drinking. He kept telling Frank he was going to have to do it to him, but he never did, because, usually something would come up, like the recent killings down at Abilene.

A freighter on the road had been robbed and killed, and it looked like Apaches. But some sharp-eyed old coot there had found the boot marks and spread a tarp over them. When Tracks had seen them, he had snooped around and cut trail, then had followed them to a range shack forty miles from the road, where he'd seen the two men holed up, snuck in and checked their boot tracks, then had hightailed it back. A shoot-out alone with a couple killers wasn't Tracks bent. He was a tracker, not a shooter, unless he damn well had to. The Lieutenant had sent Frank down there alone because the rest of them were headed out on the trail of a bunch of rustlers down on the San Antonio River, which they hadn't caught, to the Lieutenant's disgust.

Now he was back, and Tracks, there in his bunk, just rolled over and pretended that nothing was wrong. Not that it was. The men didn't really fault Tracks. He was half-Cherokee and they knew why he didn't want to get into the killing of white men. It seemed to be resented on the frontier and usually got the Indian dead. Grounds had told him he was hired to track, and that was all. And he would do that, best he could. But he left the shooting to the white men. Mexicans, of course, were excluded. They were open game for anybody.

Frank took to his bunk after he'd washed up, and he'd no more than laid down when the dinner bell gonged. That got them all moving, because one thing none of them missed, if they could help it, was a meal in-barracks. On the trail was something else, and they missed plenty of those. Here, though, they pretty much lived from meal to meal.

As they trooped into the long mess hall and went through the chow line, they observed that the Lieutenant had, for once, beat them in. He was sitting with two other men at the head of the table, where he always sat. The one gent had a head that was outsized for his body, which was small, gnarly and undernourished looking, like a windswept cedar on a ridge. The other was a tall gent who sported a calfskin vest with a watch chain lined with nuggets and had a bloody bandage wrapped around his head.

Both were stuffing their faces with the hot barbecue and bread that the Mexican cook was forever making for them, but which, being Texans, all had to admit, was pretty good, better than straight beef and beans, any time. The Lieutenant, who never seemed to care much for Mex cooking, was finished already and drinking his coffee. He was a stern visaged man of medium height, sandy haired, going a little gray, with a square face that seldom smiled and eyes that pierced you.

A bullet had smashed its way through both sides of his face at some time, and left large, sunken puckers in both cheeks. Stories circulated about how he had gotten the ugly wound, but none knew the whole truth. All the men knew about him was that he and Frank and some others had come west after the war and run into a band of Comanches, marauding and killing, over on the Trinity. They had not only stood them off, but had taken their trail and wiped them out in a pitched battle, though they'd lost a couple men themselves. The Ranger Captain, McNelly, had caught up to them just after the big fight. He and a company had chased the Comanches for a hundred miles, to come up late after the battle. When the men had explained how they had chased and caught the band, McNelly had offered them all Ranger badges. Shannon and Grounds had politely declined that time, saying they had other things to do. A man named Lee Puckett had taken him up. But then the Captain had seen them again at a stage station over on the Guadalupe that Frank's sister ran, and always a persuasive man, had persuaded the Lieutenant to come work for him. Frank had followed later.

His sister, it was said, was a widow, and one of the men with them, a little corporal, had taken after her and she had caught him. They had married up and a big fellow that was friends with the corporal had stayed with them there at the station. The others with them had separated and gone their various ways. Lee Puckett had been discharged by the Captain after Puckett had carved up a fellow Ranger in a dispute over a woman in Austin. It was too bad, as Puckett was another one to ride the river with, and the Lieutenant had protested, but to no avail. The Captain made it plain at the start of any man's stint with the organization that they could fight with outlaws and civilians and maybe, just maybe, get away with it, but never with each other. They had to be close as brothers and watch each other's backs, without grudges burning or problems among them. He wouldn't abide it.

Frank gave his report, the two outsiders listening intently. He omitted the part about the ears, which was a good thing. Killing killers was one thing, mutilating the dead was another thing that was no longer abided by the Captain, who they said, was getting too damn civilized. Afterwards, the little gent got to talking with the Lieutenant.

"This man sounds like what we need to handle our little problem, Lieutenant."

"This Ranger has just gotten in from a hard assignment. He deserves some rest."

"This job wouldn't be much for a man like he is. After it gets done, he could rest up for a while at the Bar 7, if he wanted."

Frank's ears were perked up. "What's the job, Matthew?"

He seldom called the Lieutenant by his rank, just Matthew, which the Lieutenant took without comment. The others gave him due respect, as he was himself a man that no one of them wanted to mess with. He was strict and he was straight with them. He'd never ask them to do anything, take any trail, or face any odds, that he wouldn't, himself. And he was no slouch as a shooter, either, being maybe as good as MacAllen with a rifle and, if Frank was believed, as good or better than he was, with a pistol. The men discounted that, just ascribed it to Frank's staunch defense of his friend. He'd never shot in their competitions. They'd never seen him do any practice. He'd never even had any face-offs during his sojourn as a Ranger, though they'd had to admit, they'd seen evidence of his prowess in the tangles they'd had with the 'Paches, the

Kiowas, Comanches and the numerous Mexican and Texican cow and horse thieves they'd chased, and he had never come up short.

What they did know was that he had plenty of sand and was damn smart. Somehow, his forays against the outlaw bands continually crossing the Rio Grande from Mexico were more successful than the other Ranger companies. He just got the job done—better than most.

But he was a solitary man who preferred his own company for the most part, though he and the Captain got along well and they always had a chess game going when the Captain happened by. Otherwise, he kept to himself—him, his dog and his black man, a daffy crippled Negro named Spur who kept his little casa for him, did some of his cooking and his clothes. The story was that the black had come from the old Grounds family's plantation, but no one knew for sure.

He wasn't a womanizer, either, going to Gertie's only once in a while. Gertie, a striking redhead, ran a reputable whorehouse on East Street and it was said that she was gone on the Lieutenant. Whenever he came in, the lovely madam dropped everything and anybody and hustled to accommodate him, always taking the chore on herself.

Several times, he had stayed all night, something she never allowed the other men who visited her establishment to ever do. She was all business and the men could never understand just what she saw in Grounds. He damn sure wasn't good looking, not with ugly twin puckers on his face from a bullet wound. He wasn't bigger or stronger, or funnier, or —whatever, she liked him, and it was apparent to anyone who saw them together.

She had, herself, come from some southern family of good name, it was said, in Richmond. It was even mentioned that she had known him before the war, but that was probably not true.

What he did like, they all knew, was a damn good horse, and he had several that were top of the line—some animals Frank called <u>A</u>-rabs. They'd brought them from way back east. To the Texans, they just didn't look like a normal horse, having small heads and ears, arched necks, a little deeper chests and shorter backs than the usual Standardbreds or native stock of Texas.

They stood up well, though, against the other horses, taking all the riding they gave the rest of the horses and more. But the Lieutenant certainly babied them, talking to them, giving them a little extra feed. They were pets of his, that and the big dog, Grant, that stayed in his quarters now that he couldn't keep up on the chase any more.

The Lieutenant couldn't abide a man who abused his horses, had even fired a man from the force for the way he treated his mounts. Then, they remembered, he'd called him out when the man had protested and cussed him, saying he'd kill him, if he wasn't a Ranger. The man had backed down when the L.T. had taken his badge off and come off the porch. Nothing had come of it, though the man, Siller, was a cousin of the Governor.

The two men at the table were buffalo hunters. Ole Wiegand and Earl Stratford had been working a large herd over on the plains between the Colorado and the Brazos River, and had done well last winter, filling heavy freight wagons with hides, and taking them into town to sell. They had gotten an unprecedented price for their skins—$3.00 for a regular bull hide, $2.75 for a cow hide. The sales had netted them several thousand dollars and they had paid off their men and were partaking of a few well-earned drinks at the El Diablo, when one of their skinners had come in the saloon and told them that another skinner named Del Meade, a towering, intimidating bear of a man when he was drunk, a fighter they'd heard had killed a couple men with his knife, was on the prod because he felt they had cheated the men, not paying them enough, considering the big prices they had gained from their skins. They were in their cups and didn't bother worrying about it. After all, they had paid the men what they'd said they would, a dollar a day and found, and even given them a bonus, a $20 dollar gold piece, each, when they were paid off.

But when they had come out of the saloon that evening, headed for another cantina down the block, they'd been held up. The street was dim, no street lamps lit, but the light from the bar they'd just left was enough for them to be pretty sure that the big masked man who'd held a gun on them and taken their pokes was Meade. Stratford had said something to him, gotten belligerent, and the man had hit him a powerful blow with his pistol, knocking him down, cutting his head.

They had gone to the sheriff there but he, a crook himself in their estimation, had done nothing. What was their evidence? he'd asked. Who else had seen it? How could they prove it? And they'd admitted they couldn't, but were still sure who it was. He'd shook his head and told them to come back when they had some proof.

'Now what?' they'd asked themselves. And had come to Austin to the Rangers, hoping they could do something.

Matthew had thought about it. He turned to Frank.

"You want to tackle it? Go take a look at this hombre and tag around with him, see if in fact, he might be a thief? You could take your time, but try not to get drunk again."

Frank shrugged. "Wouldn't hurt, I guess. How much did he steal?"

Wiegand answered for them. "I think it was close to $3,800. We had the rest of our money on us, too. And we hadn't paid our bill yet at the store." He looked at Stratford, who nodded his head dolefully.

"We'd pay a reward, Ranger, if we could recover most of our money."

Matthew responded. "Rangers are paid a salary to keep the state's laws. We don't take rewards." He looked at his watch. "It's your call, Frank. If you don't want it, I'll have MacAllen do it."

MacAllen, hearing his name, showed his enthusiasm for the job, grinning and nodding his head.

"No, I'll take a run at it. But I'm getting tired of this duty, Matthew, when a couple buff hunters can make that kind of money in one winter and a Ranger is making only $45 a month and has to wear out his own horses and damn gear!"

He got up and stalked out of the room, back to the barracks to get his rifle and saddle a horse. Wiegand and Stratford thanked Matthew and followed him out. They caught him at the stable, leading a fresh horse in from the corral. While he saddled it, they told him what they could about Meade, describing him as a tall man, bearded, brown eyed, with a cut above his left eyebrow that went deep into the brow, skewing the eyebrow just a little with the scar, wearing a big Bowie and a Remington pistol, and most likely wearing a gold sailor's ring in his right ear.

"Ranger, no matter what your Lieutenant said, if you can get our money back for us, we will damn sure give you some of it. That you can be certain of!!" Wiegand told him forcefully.

Frank grunted. "Better wait until we see what comes off."

He pulled the cinch tight and tucked it in. Then he swung into the saddle and asked Stratford, standing nearby, to hand him up his rifle.

"Pretty good gun, Ranger. Make a good Buff gun. Ole uses a Sharps himself. I like the Remington."

"I'm partial to Colt pistols and Sharps rifles. Now, if I get the job done for you, where can I look you up?"

"Come out to the Bar 7. It's down on the Brazos River, by San Felipe. If you ask in town there, they'll tell you how to get out to us. We might's well go on home, no money or credit left, anyhow. Damn. We'us havin' fun for a while."

"I'll ride out there when I have something to tell you. Adios 'til then."

He pulled his horse around and headed for Washington. there were twenty or more bars and cantinas in the town, he knew, and he had the job of finding a man, this Meade, who might be at any of them. That meant visiting quite a few of them, maybe. Damn, a tough job but somebody had to do it.

He grinned. Sometimes the job had its good side. Not often.

Chapter 22

Washington, Texas

Del Meade was drunk. And so were his friends. All of them. And all the bar were his friends, now he had some money. What they didn't know was he had a lot of money. Those two old skinflints, Wiegand and Stratford had held out on their hands, giving them a few dollars for a whole winter's hard, dirty cold work, when they had gotten thousands off their labor. Seldom had they stooped themselves to doing any of the skinning, just lording it over them, plowing the big animals down, then riding off to find some others, or doing their constant reloading at the coffee fire. He'd had no trouble with them when he'd taken their pokes, just a little guff from the taller one, Stratford, which he'd cooled off with a tap from his pistol on the head. The little piss-ant, Wiegand, had trembled in his boots, afraid he was going to kill him or hit him, too. He'd lifted his mask and spit on the little shit's boots before he'd left. He should have just killed them. Couldn't say why he hadn't. The heavy money belts had distracted him.

At that, both of them were lucky he hadn't carved them a new asshole, like he'd done with the two down in Galveston, the big sailor and his buddy. The big bosun from the sloop, the *Calais*, had knocked him down with a heavy fist after they'd had words about Kitty, the little bar girl who worked the floor of the Crow's Nest Bar, there on the waterfront. He'd surprised them, had come up with his knife and cut the big sailor across the throat, taking out his windpipe, and the blood had flown across him and the room. The friend, another man as big as he was, had grabbed him by the arm, spun him around, and thrown a swing that would have taken his head off, but he'd gone under it and zup, zup, had stabbed the man twice in the belly, the last time dragging the razor sharp blade around and under his ribs, spilling his guts half out of him. The man had gone down, to quiver by his now dead friend, and Meade had scrambled out of the bar, automatically wiping his knife clean on his pant leg as he went. He'd stolen a horse and taken out, headed north. Last fall, he'd met the two hunters in a bar in Austin, and fearing the law would be on his trail, had signed on to skin for the winter. It was something he'd done before, but as a butcher's mate aboard ship, slaughtering and skinning beeves for days at a time, quartering them, cutting them up.

    He knew a knife as well as he knew his own arm. His favorites were the English made Wilkensons, though Russells could hold an edge, too. And he'd had a few German made knives that he liked, also. His favorite, though, for carrying, was the big Bowie that some blacksmith down in Arkansas had made for him, before he'd joined the Confederacy. It seemed to hold an edge longer and fit his big paw of a hand better than most all the others. He didn't use this one for skinning. He kept it back for fighting, taking it wherever he went, like his big Remington pistol, a heavy damn thing that he could hit something with, if he held it just so. He was poor with a rifle, his eyes weren't good enough at long distances, though it hadn't always been that way. Time was, he could shoot with the best of them. He'd proved it at Bull Run and Chickamauga, before he'd decided the war might be the death of him and had deserted, finding his way out west to Galveston, where he'd shipped out for Europe aboard one of the last blockade runners to make it out of the Union net. He'd jumped ship in London, and had been one hop ahead of the bobbies there, after him for a little problem he'd had concerning a cutting in a water front tavern, when he'd gone and signed on with a schooner bound for America's west coast.

In California, he had participated in enough shady deals in the gold fields that the Vigilance Committee there had put him on their list. He had narrowly escaped the noose, by shipping out again on a fast ship bound for Shanghai. He'd killed the Second Mate when they'd gotten ashore, something he'd sworn to do, when the man had used his starter on him once too often.

He'd made up to him after the ship had anchored and they'd all gone ashore. Once there, he'd gotten him drunk and quarreled with him about who was paying, then killed him with his Bowie. He'd cut him a few times, before he'd put him under. No, the big knife was his best friend, his only true friend. It never let him down. He took another drink, the best Tequila the cantina here had. Then called for another drink for the house. Damn, it was good to have some money in his pocket. And that little Maria, she was a luscious looking handful!! Small, but with big tits. Tonight, she would be his plaything, if he could just tickle her fancy a little more.

A drunk cowboy came jingling in the door, a lean man with his hat thrown back. A drinker, Meade could tell, who loved the booze and couldn't wait to get to the bar. He was deep in his cups, had had a plenty, but didn't stagger, just leaned on the bar and called for whiskey. "No damn Tequila," he said. But the bartender could only give him the cactus juice, all he had, which he grudgingly took. Like most of the Texas cowboys, he wore a Colt pistol low on his right side. Meade snorted drunkenly. Most of them couldn't hit a bull in the ass with their little pistolas. He'd seen them firing away at each other on the streets and the bystanders and the street dogs were more at risk than the drunken stiffs standing off trying to kill each other. A couple of times, as he'd watched, they had emptied their guns, then had gone back in together and started drinking again. A knife and close-in was the best sure way. A knife never ran out of bullets.

The cowboy drank his drink up and lurched out, undoubtedly headed for another cantina where there maybe was whiskey, not the tequila, which was all most of the bars in Washington could offer.

* * *

The night with his Maria was about all he could have wished for, though she had to get up early and go home to get breakfast for her kids and a husband. So he finally rolled out of the rope bed behind the cantina and splashing some water on his face, checked his poke. He still had a wallet stuffed with bills and a money belt that was full of gold, double eagles, that made the damn thing weighty. Maria had complained about it, but he'd kept it on throughout their exertions on the squeaking bed, that protested against their wild panting gyrations.

He was sated. She was a willing female who had taken all he could offer and given him a good deal of satisfaction. In return, before she'd left, he'd pulled out a five dollar piece from his pants and presented it to her, laughing at her shining eyes and eager thanks. It was twice the going rate for a poke, but what the hell. She'd earned it.

He ambled down to a cafe on the corner, the owner just taking some corn tortillas and some grits out of the brasada, which, along with the coffee, had the makings of a good breakfast. He ate and contemplated his next move. He needed to buy a good horse or two, get on the trail away from here, though so far, no law had come snooping around, bothering about the hold-up. But they would, he was sure.

He went down to the livery. The old man there, a one-legged man who pegged himself around the place, cleaning stalls as he talked to him, said he might have "some ho'ses foah sale. Yawl'll go on out back an' tell me if yaw'll are in'trested in any of 'em."

The corral had about fifteen horses. A couple good ones. There was one though, that particularly took his eye. He was a big Standardbred, dark bay, with a bright eye and a set of straight legs that looked like they could run forever. He prided himself on being a good judge of horses, having grown up in a livery. His old man back in Arkansas had been in the horse business and a sharp damn dealer he'd been. Del had stolen the best horse he'd had in the stable when he'd left, after the old man had taken a stick to him for running off and getting drunk the night before, leaving two of the horses tied in their stalls all night. Oh, he knew his horses, and this was a good one. He went back inside.

"See the one I might want, that big dark bay back there. What do you want for him?"

The old man paused and spit, just missing a fly inching its way on the threshold, then grinned. "Tell yu, I'd like to sell 'im but I cain't. . . . He b'longs to a cowboy came in yesterday." He spit again, the juice getting the fly this time, covering the insect with brown liquid, which struggled under its burden for a bit, then lay still.

"Tall bastard? Wears a gun low? Brown vest?"

"Tha's him. He was drunk when he came in last night, but he made sure his horse had a feed befoah he settled in for the night up in the loft. Still there, I think. Haven't heard 'im rustlin' around up there yet."

Meade looked at the ladder going up in the loft and taking hold of the rung above his head, pulled himself up and looked over the edge. The loft was half full of horse hay, and there was a form rolled in a blanket over by the wall.

"Hey there, bud. Want to have some coffee, do you?"

The figure stirred a little, then groaned. It turned over and he saw that it was the same man he'd seen in the bar last night.

"How 'bout some coffee—and maybe some grits?"

The man groaned and sat up. Looked for his boots, then pulled them on, with an effort. He looked out the loft door at the sun, which was well up. Then back at Meade.

"Sure, might's well. Damn, I could use some coffee. My mouth tastes like a skunk took a shit in it." He hawked and spit and got up, then reached down and grasping his gunbelt, threw it around him and buckled it. Meade noticed that there was a Bowie, smaller than his, scabbarded and on the belt, also.

He climbed back down, and after a moment, the man came down it, reached the floor and offered his hand. "Frank..Davis. From over San Antonio way."

"Del M..Majors." I just came from a cafe that has some pretty good tortillas and coffee, why don't we head down that way?"

"Sounds good, at least the coffee." Frank returned.

Together, they headed down the street, the old man looking after them from the door of the livery.

At the cafe, they sat down and Frank slurped up a couple cups of coffee, then had a breakfast, then some more coffee.

They sat in the morning sunshine, on an outside patio, served by the owner's oldest girl. Their conversation got around to the war, somehow, a certain topic among veterans, and they discovered that they had been in some of the same battles, including Chickamauga, where the creek had run red with blood. Then, they visited about Lee, whom both had seen frequently. And his horses. That got them talking about horses they'd had or seen, and Meade, a great talker, felt dry from all the conversation, so they adjourned to the bar, after Meade generously paid for the coffee and Frank's meal.

The bar was open and serving by late morning. Meade made sure he chose one where he knew whiskey was served and they both imbibed the hair of the dog, washing down the coffee and grits with several large shots of rye. Finally, Meade got around to what he'd been angling for—buying a horse.

"Say, saw a dark bay in the livery corral this morning, would that be yores? Looked like he could run some."

"That horse? He's one of the best I've ever flopped a leg over. Tough, smart, knows cows and how to work 'em. Can outrun a jackrabbit. Quick. Won't b'lieve it, but I've even run down and roped a few baby antelope off 'im. Great horse." He took another drink, called to the bartender, who refilled his glass and that of his companions.

"Want to sell'im? I'm lookin' for a good horse that can eat some distance. I'd give you a good price. What's he worth to you?"

"Wal. . . now. I sell _him_, I got to buy 'nother to get back to the ranch on. . . .But, come to think on it, Old Pegleg had a grulla in his pen that I kind of liked. Wondered what he wanted for 'im. I always liked a grulla. Don't know why. A bay like

Concho is 'bout the toughest damn horse, to me. No sun scald, no saddle sores. Never quits on you."

"How 'bout a price?" Meade prodded. "Wal. . . I'd have to have . . . . $140." An astronomical price in those days, in that horse country, for a using horse. Horses typically were selling for $35-$85. Or less. Seldom more. Both knew it. But sometimes a man, with money and a yen, would pay more for something he really desired. Meade considered it. He knew he could go down and buy the grulla for at most, $75. On the other hand, the bay was the better horse. And it could be the difference to keeping breath in his body if he was well horsed and it came to a long chase. Maybe he'd buy both of them, if the cowboy didn't beat him to the grulla, if he got him drunk after he paid him and then slipped out, went down to the livery. He ordered another round of drinks.

"How 'bout $100?"

"Nope, sorry, but I don't really want to sell him, anyway."

Meade looked at the cowboy, seeing a slouching casual looking man, not young, a long brick-like face, with a strong jaw, and a wide thin lipped mouth. Gray eyes that had seen maybe too much, as most veterans had. Hair that peeped from under his weather-beaten hat, clothes that had seen a lot of work and dust, a worn leather vest that didn't sport a watch, which meant probably that the man had either hocked it or had no money to buy one, for a watch was a lone piece of jewelry every man wore, usually, besides his weapons. Lean, long rider legs and worn boots that sported spurs, silver Mexican ones with big sharp rowels. Meade ordered another drink, paid for it with the change from the double eagle he'd slapped on the bar earlier. The cowboy thanked him and sipped his thoughtfully.

"No, I think I'd have to have the $140. Gold. No less."

Meade thought about it, and what he might do, then came to a conclusion and decided he'd buy a horse. He opened his shirt and dug into his money belt, the cowboy watching him, a slight grin creasing his face. He grabbed out some eagles, put them on the bar and counted them. Seven gold eagles. He had three too many, and slipped them back. Then the cowboy did a strange thing. He took a badge from his shirt pocket and flipped it on the bar, like a piece of money.

"Texas Ranger, Meade. Just slip off that money belt slow and put it on the bar. I b'lieve you stole it." He looked at Meade through those gray eyes, and the wide mouth turned stern.

Meade pushed back off his bar stool and drawing his big Bowie, told Frank, "Not in a minute, you sunuvabitching law dog!! I'm keepin' it. It's mine~~!!"

He made a quick thrust at the cowboy, who slipped away from the knife, kicked back, and drawing his own blade, slashed Meade's arm as he drew back for another thrust. Del howled at the sting of the cut and then got set, as Frank weaved forward, slashing at Del's face. He missed, and Del got in a vicious swipe himself at Frank, which cut him across his right shoulder as he gracefully dodged away. The cowboy was quick, Del admitted. The two men, both bloody, were both grinning now, for they were in their element and one wasn't going to walk away from this little set-to. Neither bothered with his pistol. It was to be knives and Frank had accepted the weapons when he'd drawn his own. If now he would have pulled his gun, it would have been an acknowledged show of yellow and he'd not been able to hold his head up among his peers.

Now it was a slashing attack on the bigger man's part, with Frank coming away from it with an arm dripping blood, like Meade's. Neither seemed to get slower as the fight continued, but faster, as their blood heated and their muscles loosened.

Now it was Frank who feinted, drawing the man out, then swift as a snake, brought his knife around and across the bigger man's chest, a deep line which spouted blood as the keen blade did its work. Meade, then, was ferocious in his anger, and leaping forward, wrapped Frank in his great arms, edging his knife toward Frank's throat, Frank straining to keep it away.

Frank, in the bigger man's iron grasp, struggled for an instant, then lifted his left boot and stabbed the spur on his heel deep in Meade's calf, causing him to holler in Frank's ear and loosen his grip. Frank rowelled him again, raking the wound, then worked his arm free and brought his knife in under the man's armpit, burying to the hilt. Meade broke free and dropping his own weapon, reached for the knife, tried to pull it out. He fell to his knees. The knife came slipping out, with a big spurt of blood following it, which drenched him. Looking at Frank, he fell forward, on his Bowie lying on the floor.

Frank was bleeding, himself. Cut deeply on his shoulder and arm, he slipped down and sat, leaning against the bar.

* * *

Five days later, he kneed the bay away from the creek, after it had drank nearly its fill, and walked it up to a large casa on a slight rise above the flood plain. He dismounted somewhat stiffly, the shoulder bothering him, and threw the reins over a hitching post in front of the door. Coming up on the porch, he rapped on the open door, and a voice in the back of the place yelled at him to 'come on in.' He did, stepping through an arched doorway and into a low, long room with Navaho rugs on the floor, and rifles and riatas hanging on the wall. Wiegand stood up from a low chair, a drink in his hand.

"Ranger! You made it back. How did it go?" Frank pulled off the heavy money belt from around his waist and threw it on a table, then pulled a fat wallet out of his chaps pocket. He threw that on the table, too. Wiegand's eyes bulged and he jumped for the money, then remembered his manners and picking a bottle up from the floor, handed it to Frank, who looked at it, then took a long pull. The little man emptied all the money on the table and began counting it.

"Damn, Ranger. There's more'n $3400 still here!"

"Didn't count it myself." Frank rejoined wryly, rubbing his bandaged arm.

"Jesus. You're. . . you got cut some, huh?"

"The man liked a knife. He wasn't goin' to let it go without a fight." Frank took another pull, shuddered a little.

"Sit down, man, sit down!" Wiegand pulled a chair away from the table for him and Frank sat gratefully. Stratford came through the door and stopped in amaze, seeing the money scattered on the table.

"Earl, damn it, the Ranger brought back nearly all our money! $3400!"

"The Hell you say!!" He sat down with a thump on the chair he'd pulled out, took the bottle as Frank offered it and chugged a heavy pull on it.

Under serious urging and another bottle, Frank was persuaded to tell the story. He told them about wearing a pair of spurs he'd borrowed from another Ranger, how he'd roostered the man with them, and caused him to loosen Meade's grip when he was about ready to cut his throat. Then he had to go get the spurs, Meade's Bowie and his pistol from his saddle bags. The men looked at the spurs, fondled the knife, handled the gun, and wanted to hear the story, complete with the smallest details, again. Stratford couldn't put the knife down. Wiegand kept aiming the Remington.

Finally, after the second bottle was history, Wiegand suggested a trip into town, to the Double Barrel Bar. Frank agreed. He was agreeable to about anything at that point.

"Shay, Frank, I want that S.O.B.'s knife. Now, I know you Rangers can't take any reward, but think you could sell me this big damn Bowie—for $250?" Stratford's words were slurred but his mind had been working.

"An. . . Frank, I want this big pistola—how 'bout another $250 for it?"

The men were big hearted and generous and wanted to do something for this man who'd gotten their money back for them when the law had just shrugged its shoulders. And he'd gotten cut up and killed the big S.O.B. doing it!! With a knife, by God!! The big skinner had gotten a dose of his own medicine. Surely Frank deserved more than just a parsimonious feeble thank you!!

Finally, Frank, in his clouded, alcoholic mind, seemed to come to grips with the fact that, *'Hell, he wasn't taking any reward, he was just selling the arms he'd gotten in a fair fight. And anyone could do that,'* he reasoned. But he was a little uneasy when he thought of Matthew. Therefore, taking another drink, he didn't—that is, he didn't think of Matthew again.

* * *

He was deep in a whiskey fog there in the bar at Bastrop. Wiegand and his partner, Stratford, had gone back to the ranch a day before, having drank about all they could handle and more. Frank had remained. He had drank that night for hours. The next day, they had gotten up there at the hotel and he'd gone down and had breakfast and then bought a new outfit, boots, hat and all. Then he'd gone back to the bar.

Now, he looked at the door swinging back and forth, and Matthew stood there. "Come on, Frank, Drink up and let's go."

"How'd you find me?" The words came out slurred.

"Wasn't easy."

The ride back to Austin was quiet, and Frank had some time to sober up. Matthew had left him at the stable and after supper, Matthew had sent Spur for him.

"Tell me what happened. Give me your report."

Frank had told him what had transpired, how he'd had to kill Meade. How he'd taken the money back to the two buffalo hunters at their ranch. Matthew had taken it all in.

"Where'd you get the money for the drinking and the new outfit, the clothes and all?" he asked quietly.

Frank squirmed in the chair.

"Wal. . . I brung back the pistol and the knife that Meade had on 'im and the two ole boys wanted them. So they bought 'em off me."

"For enough to keep boozing two or three days, and buy a new outfit? How much did you soak them?"

"Wal. . . .$500."

"$500?"

"Yep."

Silence.

"So you took $500 for a $20 pistol and a $10 knife?"

Silence.

"What you did was take a reward from them. You took money from civilians for doing a job you were being paid to do. I'm sorry. I'm goin' to have to have your badge."

Frank sighed, got up and flipped the badge on to Matthew's desk. Turned and walked out.

Matthew sat. He'd just fired a friend. He had few friends. He could count them on practically one hand. And none of the others had saved his life, as this one had, more than once. Since they had started this job, it had been coming between them. There was just too much difference in the way that each approached it. And who could say which one was right? He scribbled a note, got up, and undoing the Ranger badge from his vest, dropped it beside Frank's, and walked out.

He entered the stable and saw Frank glumly tying his bedroll and gear to a pack saddle on Concho. His saddle was on Grabby, and he had turned out his other four horses.

Matthew got his bridle down and went out into the corral and caught up Early. He brought him back in, the other horses in his string following behind, wanting attention. He let them all in the stable and gave each a little oats while he threw his saddle on Early. Then he pulled another saddle off a saddle tree in the tack room and saddled Grant, for Spur. By then, Frank was curious.

"What are you doing?"

"Couldn't let my pardner go alone, so I fired myself, too. I was getting tired of Rangerin' anyway."

Frank experienced a thrill of emotion that traveled up and back down his spine. He turned away.

"Glad to have you," he mumbled.

Matthew turned and gave him a straight look.

"I tell you, Frank, I'm goin' to come with you, but on one condition. You have to let me buy the drinks for you from now on."

"Hell, Matthew, you don't need to buy me. . . ."

"No—what I mean is, you don't drink anything but what I buy you." He turned and looked Frank in the eye.

"You're killin' yourself with booze, Frank. Just like you told me your father did." He did something uncharacteristic for him. He put his hand on Frank's shoulder. "Now, you're my friend, about the only one I have, and I don't want you to die that way. If the booze doesn't get you, some sonofabitch who wants your head, will just wait until you're so far gone in the redeye that you can't take him, and you'll end up goin' that way. I don't want that to happen. Now, is it a deal?"

Frank swallowed and said, "I want you along, Pard, but I don't know if I can handle not drinkin'."

"Then we'll just have to take it a day at a time. A drink or two isn't goin' to hurt either one of us, I'll just have to see that we quit it at that."

"As long as I know that I can have a drink or two . . . pretty regular, why, I'd say it's a good deal for me. I don't know about you, though."

"I'm not complainin'. . . .Pard."

PART IV

KANSAS

Chapter 23

Dodge City, Kansas

James Siller, the man some called "Killer" Siller, or "Killin' Jim" was puzzled. He was sitting at his ease in the Variety Saloon, downing a few shots and water, waiting for the big card game to get going, when two men had walked in, avoiding a fist fight going on just outside. Buffalo hunters, by the look of them. And he was sure that he'd seen them before. The taller one was a lean man who had the Texan look about him, despite his greasy buckskins and slouch hat.

    He wore a pistol low on his right side. His pale gray eyes had darted around the smoky room as he'd stepped through the batwings, as had those of the other, a shorter, stocky man with a strong, stern, deeply tanned face and. . . he had it! The man had turned just so, and he'd seen the scar puckers in the face. The sonofabitch!! He'd fired him from the Rangers!! It was that damn Lieutenant. . . Grounds. And the other one was Frank. . . Shannon.

    He took another drink. He'd always wanted to go back and get Grounds, the Lieutenant, they'd called him. It was a little piece of unfinished business, among others, like the killing of Sheriff Whaley over in La Grange, that he liked to clear up when he could, just to keep his life tidy. Whaley had died from a shot in the night, when he'd been making his rounds. And the deputy, who'd laughed at him when he'd asked for a smoke. He had died, too, coming home in the early morning.

A lazy man who would rather kill than work for a living, Siller fancied himself a professional gambler. And he prided himself on being a neat man, one who dressed well and kept up appearances, even when his money belt was low. An empty money belt just meant that he needed to find someone who had a full one and then relieve them of it. If they had to die, so be it. It was something he'd done so many times, in so many places, that by now, the incidents were blurred in his memory.

He reached and felt of his gun—a Smith and Wesson .44 Rimfire that he'd had a gunsmith in Topeka cut down to 4 inches. The gun had no notches on its white bone handled butt, but they could have been there, an even half dozen. The gun was a good one—he'd taken it off a man in Topeka, a card game, actually, and the man had drawn to a pair of aces, gotten another and was sure he had the pot. So sure, he had raised Siller with the pistol when everyone was all in. Siller had grinned and put his own gun up, a heavy old 1860 Colt Thuer conversion .44. The man's face had crumbled when he'd proudly laid his aces down and Siller had topped them with four kings. He loved a hand like that—it stayed in his mind for days, years, the great feeling when the other players saw they had been beaten. The man had tried to buy the pistol back but Siller had refused to sell it.

The pistol had proven to be a great gun and he'd sold the Colt, which was loose and a little out of time. Too bad, the old gun had accounted for three or four men, if he remembered right. But the Smith and Wesson, after he'd gotten the gunsmith to shorten the barrel so he could better conceal it, had been his killing gun since that game. It was compact and he'd had a saddle maker craft a nice hidey holster that fit under his arm.

He'd shot the gun quite a bit. Whenever he had some time and nothing to do, he'd go out back of the saloons and kill some bottles. It was a usual practice in the towns, throwing their empties out back where they could be used for target practice at some later date. Some of the saloons that had been in operation a while, like the Variety, had a small mountain of trash and bottles behind it. Most men, though, didn't want to spend money on ammo for practicing with a belt gun when they could buy a drink with it. He was an exception and so the gun had gotten enough use that he was familiar with it, and knew how it would shoot. And he'd practiced pulling it until he could get it in action with a blur of motion. He had to think about this. He had nothing against Shannon. It was Grounds he wanted. He had thrown him out of the Rangers and humiliated him when he had objected. As he watched them at the bar, the thought of it brought a rush of anger. *'Oh, yes, he had some unfinished business with Grounds!!'*

* * *

Frank and Matthew had been working the buffalo herds on the Arkansas, both using the long barreled New Model Sharps in .44/77. These were beautiful guns, good dark walnut stocked, with real silver forend caps and the long range tang sights, though these, with the abundance of the buffalo, were usually unnecessary. They had gotten them a few months ago in Oklahoma City from an old friend who was now a prosperous merchant—Amos Troyer. They had been riding down the street, just in from Fort Gibson, looking to re-outfit, when Matthew had seen the sign "Troyer's Hardware, Amos Troyer, Prop." They had gone in asking for him, and the clerk had told them that the proprietor was busy, could he help them? Matthew had gone to the racks of guns and pulled the very ones they now had off the wall, lying them on the counter. Then Troyer had come limping from his office, having heard their voices. The little man had been delirious with joy at seeing them. The reunion had been emotional and they had gone home to meet his wife and three children, one a boy named Matthew. His wife, Ellie, was a dark haired little sparrow of a woman, who nonetheless, seemed to rule the roost. She seemed hospitable though, especially after Matthew turned on a little southern charm. They had visited into the night and Matthew had let Frank drink several drinks, never saying anything to him about it, even partaking himself, as they basked in the friendship of the man who'd gone through so much with them.

When asked about it, Troyer had shown them his leg, which, while not normal, was still much better than it had been, and served to get him around without crutches. What's more, he had told them that the guns they had picked out were on him, as part payback on the operation Matthew had financed, way back in Washington. He'd insisted, and Matthew, seeing it was a matter of his pride, let him give them to him.

Next day, they had gone back to the store, a big building filled with all manner of merchandise, and outfitted themselves again, practically having to force their money on the man. At that, he had charged them nearly wholesale prices. They had bought cases of the new cartridge ammo, also bullet moulds, 350 pounds of St. Louis shot tower lead, which was premium quality, four 25 pound kegs of DuPont powder and 5,000 primers. They had also purchased a couple serviceable extra guns of the same caliber, for back-up weapons. Their old guns had gone on the shelf. They were about done, being shot out from all the killing they had done in Oklahoma, the fall and winter before. They'd kept their Henrys, though.

Of course, they had to buy a new camp outfit, too, bedding, clothes, a medium and a large dutch oven, pothooks, three frying pans, tin plates and cups, knives forks and spoons, a meat broiler, a grindstone, skinning knives, two coffee pots, coffee mill, shovels, spades and axes. They had loaded up their purchases in two new light wagons, the skinners, Happy Jack and Slim, along with Spur, helping. Slim, the best teamster, drove a four horse team pulling their heavy new freight wagon, which would haul the hides. Everything was new, to replace all that they had lost to the Kiowas.

They'd had some trouble in Oklahoma, down on the Canadian, with the Indians on the rampage, and had to fort up with some other hunters at a place called the Buffalo Wallows. Not content with running off their horses and destroying their wagons, they'd come after the hunters and skinners, intent on killing the men who were destroying their meat supply. Twenty some hunters and skinners had stood off over three hundred Indians, killing some every time they came within range, after their first initial charge, which had resulted in a pileup of dead and wounded Indians in front of the wallow. Three men had been wounded, one who later died, in that first furious charge of the whooping savages, that had nearly overrun them. At that, they would have been if it hadn't been for Matthew and Frank's quick shooting with their .44 Henrys, guns which some of the others had derided when they first seen them, as 'rabbit guns.' They were no good for buffalo hunting, maybe, but in a fray like this, up close, they had been priceless.

The war party had been led by a big brave on a peculiarly spotted pony, brown, white and black colored, which was very quick and agile. A couple of the men had fired at him and missed, when Matthew caught him as he was turning and hit him in the side, the Henry .44 bullet smashing him from his horse. He lay to their front for the rest of the fight, which lasted almost until dark, then the Indians pulled out, after trying to retrieve their dead and wounded. Another Indian had been killed in trying to get the leader up on a horse and away, but they finally were successful in retrieving the body when the others swept around behind them and feinted a charge.

Then the men stood and watched helplessly as the mob of retreating bucks lit out for the horizon, the hunters horses, all the teams and riding mounts, spread out in front of them. The wagons, their contents, including their water barrels, had been pillaged and burned, along with the bales of hides they had worked so hard to accumulate.

It had been a long walk back to civilization, the wounded on the four horses they had kept away from the Kiowa, one being Stonewall, Matthew's horse. All the others, Frank's included, had gone into the sunset with the Indians. They had gleaned some flour and a couple frying pans from the smoking wagons, along with a sack full of cups, plates, knives and other paraphernalia, a few scorched cans of food.

Spur had a bad leg he'd sustained back in Arkansas, when he'd been shot while trying to steal a chicken from a farmer who'd objected by unleashing a wad of heavy bird shot. He was unable to keep up as they made the walk out, and Matthew had finally put him on Stonewall, along with the wounded man, to keep him from being left behind. This had caused some heavy grumbling among the other footsore hunters and skinners, most of whom were southerners, and felt Negroes should never be treated special above whites. Matthew had turned on them and made it plain that it was his horse, the wounded white skinner was on it, as was the next man who was unable to walk—Spur. If any of them wanted to do anything about it, he should step away in the prairie and they would have it out. None did. But the hard feelings remained.

When Charlie Grove, the badly wounded man, had finally died, they'd put the next worst-off man horseback, an elderly skinner named Williamson who should by rights have been home in a rocker, had he a home to go to. Most of the hunters and skinners were like Frank and Matthew, displaced southerners who'd lost it all during the war, or never had much to begin with.

They walked until dark and made camp, surrounded by buffalo on all sides. They had traveled northeast, taking direction by the sun, parting the herd on either side of them as they went. The constant argument between the hunters was always whether they were killing the primary herd off, many saying that they were just killing the natural increase, and not making a dent in the overall buffalo population, as the Indians feared. It was a question whose answer was years coming, and at the time, none of them could guess of such a virtual annihilation of a species. They slept, never out of the sound of lowing cows, the blat of calves and bawling bulls, but a sound they were used to. Since Grant and the other dogs had been killed by the Kiowa when they'd taken the camp, they had no guard animals, so a vigilant watch was kept.

They'd run into some other hunters after three days of hiking, who helped them out with loaned horses, and finally they had made it into Fort Gibson. There, at heavy expense, they had purchased some new mounts. Matthew had managed to salvage his money belt from the smoking ruins of one of the wagons. It was lean now, after spending a year's earning at Troyer's, and buying new teams and wagons.

The money had mainly come from his earnings as a Ranger and later, their hunting. The Federal government back east had not only succeeded in withholding the accounts of the "One Hundred," prominent Confederates, but, diligently tracking down the real property of each family in the respective Confederate states, had confiscated that, also. The accounts in Washington had vanished, along with the money at the Merchants Bank in Savannah. Pendemere was gone also, sold by the carpetbagger "Reconstructionists" who'd come swooping in like vultures to grasp up everything they could, in the name of "Justice." It was Northern revenge, but little could be done about it.

The retainers were displaced from their ancestral home. Spur had made his way to Texas, to Matthew, the last survivor of the little band who'd gone to find their master. When he'd come to Austin, finally, he'd been like a lost, starving dog who'd just made it home, when he had seen Matthew walking back from the stables that morning. It had taken weeks of recuperation to get his health back. The leg, filled with suppurating sores, infected from the shot, some of which was still in it, despite several visits to the best doctor in Austin, was never going to be very strong. But he had been content, because he was back with Matthew, his "fambly."

* * *

They'd started again, after Oklahoma City, and their new guns had wreaked destruction among the buffalo. "Happy Jack" King and "Slim" Haines, the two skinners, were kept busy all the day, while Spur kept the camp for them. Four times, they had packed their hides and headed in to sell them. Their big hide wagon could hold at the most 200 hides, the others only about 75. Three times, a buyer from Rath and Wright had made his way out among the hunters and bought their hides at camp, his big wagons trailing behind him. Frank, never good with his money, had handed it over to Matthew for safekeeping and to keep the partnership going.

They'd pooled their earnings in the hope that some time, somehow, they might find a place and a way to establish a horse ranch, one where Matthew might achieve his dream of raising Arabians crossed with Standardbreds, to bring a new type of horse to the West, one that would be sought after by the army and all those who wanted and needed that better type of horse. It was a dream that sustained both of them. Now, after a winter's hunt, following the herds, they were in Dodge City, and a filthier, more wide open town, they had never seen.

Fort Dodge had been established on the Santa Fe Trail to try to offer some protection to the wagon trains and mail crossing the Plains. Later, when the Indian Wars had gained in ferocity, it had served as a supply base for troops who were fighting the tribes. It was natural that a town spring up there, becoming a trade center and a watering hole for all. Now the little burg had a hotel, twelve saloons, two grocery and general merchandise stores, a couple blacksmiths and restaurants, three or four whore houses—and a growing cemetery. There was no law enforcement and like the towns located off the military reservations, no military jurisdiction. The railroad was advancing over the wide country and now railhead was at Wichita, coming west at a rapid clip. Hide buyers, drifters, traders, whiskey peddlers, and salesmen of all types, even a few stockmen and cowboys mingled freely with the off-duty soldiers and hunters in the saloons and other businesses.

Matthew had found a buyer, G.W. Baldwin, from Rath and Wright, who had been more than glad to buy their hides, knowing them to be good shots, so that the animals weren't perforated, and their skinners, men who took pride in their skinning, hadn't gashed holes in the leather. He also knew that the hides would have been properly stretched and dried, then pressed and packed away, the bull hides separated from the cow hides, and none of the smaller kip hides. So he was willing to give top dollar and did: $3.35 apiece for 347 hides. The money flowed from his voluminous belt into that of Matthew's, which again, after a long year of hunting, had a satisfying heavy weight to it. G.W. had his men transfer the skins from the hunter's wagons into his, Happy Jack and Slim were paid for their months of work, and Spur given some money to pamper his sweet tooth and to do a little carousing at a place that would serve Indians and others of dark complexion.

Leaving Slim, a Temperance Christian, to watch the camp, Frank and Matthew rode into the town and into the Variety, a little nicer saloon, from the looks of it, than the others on the short main street. They stood up to the bar. Matthew was out of loose pocket change and had to get into his belt to get some money to pay for the drinks. They stood relaxed, savoring the first drink they'd had for weeks. It had been a long, tough, work filled winter.

"Hungry, Pard?" They'd had several drinks and now Matthew wanted to get him away from the bar and stuff some food into him before he lit off like a fire that had been doused with lamp oil. He knew that once Frank got going, there was little stopping him. Best to quit now.

"Guess so, sure you won't have one more?"

"Let's drink up and go. I'm hungry for a restaurant meal."

Reluctantly, Frank threw his head back and drained the last drops, and they went through the swinging doors.

Outside, the night had descended and for an instant, they were blinded.

At that instant, a shot came from the side of the building and they both whirled, then hit the ground. Another shot came flaming out of the darkness. Matthew grunted.

"You hit?" Frank whispered urgently.

"Believe he touched me with that first shot. . . in the arm."

"Cover me!" Matthew, on the ground fired twice. Frank got to his knees, then his feet, and scrambled for the building, reaching its corner. His gun drawn, he peered around, and another shot bellowed from the darkness. Matthew returned the fire. Frank, racing to get around the other side of the building, ran square into a figure emerging from the batwings, who grunted and fell, with a curse. He didn't stop, but charged around the building as fast as his long legs would take him, to just see, with his night sight getting better, a figure running away, crouched low. Frank kicked a can as he came on, and the form in front of him whirled and fired. The bullet whipped by his head and Frank stopped and fired twice, then again. The figure dropped. He came up cautiously, approaching the man with his gun aimed. The gun lay by his outstretched hand and Frank picked it up. It had an odd feel. He turned the body over as Matthew came up, then behind him, some others. The man was dead, hit by all three bullets, but it wasn't until a lantern was brought, that a bystander recognized who it was.

"That there is "Killer" Siller." Siller. Both men remembered then.

"He was after your hide, Matthew. You remember callin' him out, that time in Austin? He wouldn't face you. A damn backshooter."

"I remember."

"You okay?" The lantern light picked up a dripping of blood off Matthew's left hand. With an effort, Matthew holstered his pistol. "No. I need some doctorin'. Let's get in to the light."

A drunken man came up then. "Which one of you bastid's ran over me when I 'uz comin' out of the damn bar just now?" He stood swaying belligerently, a hand on his gun. Frank pointed.

"That'd be him right there. I got 'im for you."

The man stared at the dead body. "Whoee. . . "

Matthew's arm was deeply grooved and bleeding freely.

Frank found a drunken doctor in one of the bars, finally, and brought him back into the Variety, to the table where Matthew was sitting, his arm wrapped in semi-clean bar towels and still bleeding. The man had thought to grab his ever present bag when Frank had taken him from his evening's drinking and now he opened it, and taking up needle and thread, attempted to thread the needle. After a couple clumsy tries, Frank lost his temper.

"Give me that, you sonuvabitch!" He grabbed it and with a fluid motion, threaded it and handed it back. "Now, do yure best job on 'im or I'll take that damn thing and thread your eyes with it."

The doc looked at the man confronting him and rapidly began sobering up. For a drunken doctor who'd been drummed out of his practice in Illinois, he proceeded to do a very creditable job, stitching the wound its length after cleansing it with carbolic acid. The bullet had passed between the arm and chest, ripping his shirt as it went through his sleeve and cut a path through the inside of the arm. Siller's gun was lying on the table, and Matthew picked it up curiously while the doctor was working on the torn path of the bullet, making him wince. It was a Smith and Wesson .44. six shot revolver, short barreled, with four cartridges expended. He handed it to Frank, who tucked it into his belt after taking another look at it himself.

"I asked around. Siller wasn't liked. He was a gambler and a thief, and some thought he was a murderer, too. He even liked people callin' him "Killer." I don't think anyone is goin' to lose any sleep over his passing. And there's no law in this dump."

"Self defense, anyway, with no witnesses."

Later, seated in the restaurant and taking on a big buffalo steak and some welcome spuds and coffee, Matthew, his arm bandaged and slinged, had to have Frank cut his meat for him.

"You see, Frank, if I'd let you drink yourself into a daze, you might not have made those dead center shots. I saw where you hit him. He was a dead man twice over.

Frank snorted. "I've shot better with a load on, but at that, I might have fallen down a couple times gettin's so I could shoot 'im." He grinned and waved a hand. "You're right, I guess. You sure never know when you're about to git blindsided."

"I think he was mainly after the money, Frank. He'd seen me open my belt at the bar. He was sitting in the back , a little out of the light, or I may have recognized him. 'Course, he had a mustache and side burns, and when he was Rangerin', he was clean shaven." He picked up a forkful of meat, not really hungry after the fight, and a little dizzy from the wound and blood loss. He looked around the busy place, a little uneasy and at a loss to know why, unless it was just all the people around. He brought up a subject they'd chewed on many times at night around the campfire.

"Frank, I'm getting tired of this hunting business. . . but what else to do. . . .I don't have a glimmer."

"Yo're tired! My damn shoulder hurts all the time. But, you got it, Pard. What else to do. . . .I don't know. I can't see us goin' back east. . . or south, being happy merchants like Amos, or stage station hands like Millett and Lars. I still like the horse ranch idee. I was thinkin', though. What about headin' for the gold fields up in Montana? They say there's some pretty country up there, even if it's full of Indians. Big game country and not so damn hot. We've got some money now. We could head to Wichita, trade off our two light wagons for a couple heavy ones, and haul some goods to the gold camps. That'd pay our way up there. Maybe even pick up a couple, three passengers to take along. Lots of 'em, they say, lookin' for rides at the rail head back there. We could knock off the hide hunting for a while, see if maybe the mining districts up there have somethin' for us. And check out the grass possibilities for a ranch."

They finished their meal and headed back to camp.

Chapter 24

The night was crystal clear and the millions of stars made a sparkling display above their heads as they walked their horses back toward a distant fire's glow. Slim, a man who needed very little sleep, was keeping the fire stoked with dried buffalo chips and had the coffee on for them. When he saw Matthew's arm in a sling, he asked questions that had to be answered, so despite the fact that Matthew was deathly tired, they stayed up and jawed for a time. Then Matthew looked around and asked, "Spur make it back yet?'

"Nope. Thought he'd be the first one. You know how he likes his bed." Spur was a man who slept hard and was hard to awaken in the morning. He wouldn't sleep on the ground, because of his fear of snakes, so he usually threw his buffalo robes and blankets up on a wagon.

"Strange." Matthew said. His mind was already in bed and he was about to go out like a light, despite the coffee.

"Guess maybe he met up with a gal over there." Frank wisely thought.

They headed for their own robes. Next morning, Spur was still gone. Matthew was slow coming awake and Frank, after drinking a couple cups, and eating the plate of bacon and leftover stew Happy Jack had given him, thought he'd mosey into town and see if he could find him. He saddled his new dun, Aces, and threw a leg over the leather.

The town was roistering along, Frank thought, as he rode in. A piano was tinkling in the Variety, and the Trail's End had some kind of argument going on, as there was loud voices shouting in there. Frank heard scraps and pieces as he went by, something about the war, which was a topic revisited time after time. Then two figures came rolling out the door, followed by an angry bartender, who stood over them with a club, threatening mayhem if they started anything again "inside." The men ignored him as they clubbed at each other with slow swinging fists. Frank rode on.

The bar, Smith's Emporium that he was aiming for, was one that catered to the colored folks—mainly because the man who ran it, "Nigger" Smith, was of decidedly dark complexion himself. A little outside of town, it was like the others, in nearly full swing. Frank draped his reins over the hitching post, by half a dozen other horses, and entered the place. It was, even in the early morning, smoky, with just about every habitué either smoking a cigar or pipe, or lighting one. There was also a hanging odor of spilled beer and whiskey, along with the pungent odor of unwashed men, all of which made it a place in which Frank was in his element.

He sauntered to the bar and for an instant, was at a loss, thinking of his promise to Matthew. He covered it by asking for coffee, which, at that time of the morning, was something each bar served as a matter of course. There wasn't hardly a man on the frontier who wasn't addicted to his chew or smoke and his coffee. The bartender, a burly older Negro who, Frank found, was the owner, served it up in a surprising clean mug for him. Frank dug and found a quarter. The man took it and gave him back a couple dimes. Frank sipped the coffee and gazed around the place, which was about like the others up and down the dusty street—raw plank floorboards and walls, with lanterns hung high in the tall ceiling, which were pulled down, filled and relit when needed. Over each of the two gaming tables, a lower lantern also hung, which illuminated the players and cards through a smoky haze. Most within were of either Mexican or Negro descent, though there were a few whites.

Frank looked keenly about, his eyes searching for Spur. There was no sign of him. He turned back to the busy bartender, who was making another pot of coffee on a beat up stove at the end of the bar. "Say, barkeep, I'm lookin' for our cook, a man called Spur. He's a nigger with a limp. Bad right leg. Goin' gray 'round the ears. A little feeble minded. Seen 'im?"

The man turned at the sound of 'nigger', but saw that Frank, a southerner by his talk, didn't mean anything by it. It was a common term, like 'greaser' or 'mex.' or injun, and to take offense at a white man's saying it, could mean trouble. He decided to be gracious and came down to where Frank was standing. Frank realized what he'd said, and tried to placate the man by commenting in a friendly manner,

"Good coffee, 'nother cup?"

Smith filled it without answering, then looked up. Into eyes that brought forth an answer. "I was busier 'n hell last night. Come to think on it, I did see a black man come in that had a pretty good limp, older man. But he had a few drinks and went on out, and I didn't see him again last night. He likely went on over to Sally's. Want me to send somebody over to see if he's around there?"

"Would you do that? His name's Spur. Here's a dollar for the one who goes."

"Sure thing." Smith summoned a wizened little Mexican, who took the buck and went out the door. Frank sipped his coffee and went over and watched the table play for a while.

Presently the batwings flipped and the Mexican came back, shaking his head. "Nada, the negrito warn't there."

Frank was frustrated and hated to go back to camp and Matthew without Spur. He felt in his pocket. He had a ten dollar gold piece there, along with some other change, and he dropped the gold on the bar. "I'd 'preciate it if you'd keep yore eye out for 'im. I'll be back in, or my pardner, maybe later. His name, like I said, is Spur." The man took it without comment, just nodded. Frank walked out. He reported his failure to Matthew, who was up, looking peaked. He shook his head in puzzlement. Evidently, he had expected Frank to return with the errant Spur. Later, they both went back and combed the town, asking more than a few people about Spur. Finally, they went into the Variety and asked for the proprietor, Ham Bell, who came out and talked with them. He was a handsome dapper man, jet black hair slicked back, who affected silk vest and a big gold nugget watch fob. He also, Frank noticed, packed a smaller gun, in a shoulder holster that bulged his suitcoat on the left side. He advised offering a small reward and Matthew put it up: fifty dollars. Bell said he'd post it up on his board by the door right away. They did the same at Smith's, adding the forty to Frank's ten, then drifted back to camp.

The rest of the morning was spent getting ready and sorting out. Happy Jack wanted to stay with them and see the gold camps. Slim wanted to head back to civilization now that he had a decent stake, but would go with them to Wichita and catch the train there. Matthew kept looking back at the town, thinking that Spur might appear at any moment. But he didn't.

They made a short start on the 150 miles to Wichita and camped in a low draw where there was a drying pond of water for the horses, about ten miles from Dodge, heading east. That night, all missed Spur's cooking and chatter. Matthew went to bed in ill humor. One by one, it seemed, every tie to his past life was being cast off.

* * *

A week and a day later, they rode into Wichita, a bustling town no longer at the head of track, as they had encountered the track laying crews thirty miles this side of the city. They had all pulled up to watch the crew hard at work, the teams pulling scrapers that were working ahead of the crew laying the ties and the two crews busy laying rails. A half mile down the track, they encountered the tent city which catered to the enterprise, mess halls, bars and brothels, mixed together and yet apart. Matthew, seeing nothing there to interest them, went on through, but was stopped a half dozen times by men asking to buy his team or to cadge a ride back to Wichita, having been sacked by the foremen, who wouldn't abide a man who wouldn't or couldn't work. Finally, Matthew, stopped by a prosperous looking man asking about the teams, told him he might sell the teams, with the light wagons, for a price, if he would quote him a good one. The man, a contractor for the railroad desperate for big working horses, quoted him two hundred fifty a team, which almost made Matthew gasp.

"The wagons aren't any good to me without the teams. They'd have to go along, and not for nothing." The man didn't blink. "Another hundred apiece for the wagons." he said. They made a deal right there and transferred the contents of the two into the big freight wagon, with room left over. Slim left them here, to go to work for this man, Gentry Gimble, one of the contractors who had the dirt working in front of the track crews. Gimble had asked if any of them wanted to work as teamsters and when Slim found that he was paying four dollars a day and found, he signed on. They said goodbye to him on the street. Their saddle horses, they kept, though again, they were propositioned on them more than once before they cleared the tent city. The road followed the track, for the most part, and by the time they made it to Wichita, the horses and the men were used to the smelly, coal and wood burning locomotives clanking up and down the rail line, pulling the rattling flat work cars and a few passenger ones.

 Wichita was a merchant town, smelly with the hide piles that paralleled the tracks on either side for a quarter mile, waiting for delivery back east, the property of the two great hide buying firms in the area, Rath and Wright, of Dodge City, and Loganstein and Co., in Leavenworth. From the east, many of the hides would be processed and sent on to Europe, where such entities as the English and German Armies would use the leather for accoutrements, being a softer, more pliant product than cowhide. The wool was used for stuffing cushions and making fiber, the robe hides of better quality used for buggy robes, coats and other garments. Robe hides were prime only in the winter, while leather hides were obtained all year around, even summer. In summer, the hides had to be treated with poison, to stop the hide bugs, which would eat and destroy the hide.

 Many hides were lost because of poor skinning and poor care taken after the skinning. Some estimates, probably accurate, said that for every hide taken, a hide was lost. It was a monumental waste of a great animal, and many moral men, would have little to do with it. Colorado and a couple of the other states, including Kansas, had passed ordinances against the killing, but there was little enforcement.

At Wichita, Matthew found to his dismay, that he had sold the teams and wagons too cheap. He was rueful and apologized to Frank, who merely shrugged. "Don't worry about it, Pard, let's go see if we can buy a couple big, heavy duty wagons and fill them with supplies. Then it's "Ho for the gold fields!" He laughed, happy to be out of the hunting for a while.

After some industrious prying on Frank's part, they came up with two more wagons, sturdy but not new, by any means. After a lot of talking on the trail to Wichita, they had decided that oxen teams were the way to go. They were cheaper, could pull better, even if slower, and took less care, where horses needed grain while they were working hard. Regretfully, they sold Dick and Dan, Pete and Pauly, and their favorite team of big Belgians, Sam and Stan, and bought oxen for the long haul to the mountains. Neither Frank nor Matthew wanted to work them, so they looked hard to find some gold seekers who could work the teams west for a passage. Happy Jack came up with one man, a friend he'd known back east, who was, he claimed, a good "bullwhacker." His name was "Wrong Wheel" Bender, a man of dubious intelligence who reminded Frank of Big Lars. When asked about his friend's monicker, Happy replied that it came from him working on a wheel on the off side, when he had a spare one on board his wagon. When asked why he just didn't replace the bad one with his spare, he'd said that, "that wheel fits t'other side." For all that, he was good with the stock, being of close to the same temperament and mentality.

Frank found another man by accident. Standing in a bar called the Long Branch Saloon on Front Street, he heard a voice that sounded familiar. He turned and beheld a hatchet faced individual just pouring a drink down his lean mouth. Lee Puckett!! The man was drawn down like a coyote and even more mean looking, if possible.

When the backslapping and howdies were done, Frank asked him what he was doing.

"Not a damn thing, right now. Was workin' for McLeaf and Burns, guarding their payroll to the head of track, but they just lost the contract and let us go. What're you men up to?"

"We're gatherin' some supplies to fill our wagons and headin' west to the mines up in the Rockies. Lookin' for men to go along."

"I'm not a damn bull whacker, Frank. No damn good at it. Don't think I'd be much help to you. But I do know a man, friend of mine from the company, who's a damn good teamster and ox man. Benson Greene. You'd like him. He was an 18th Georgia man and told me several times he'd like to see the western mountains and the gold fields there." He took another drink of the one that Matthew had bought him.

"Hell, thinkin' about it, I might trail along with you, if you'd have me."

"We damn sure will, Lee, can always use a good gun hand on the trail. It's Indian country up there, Cheyenne, 'Rikaree and Sioux. Be good to have you come along." Matthew concurred, and bought them all another drink. In due course, they met Greene and added him to the party. Now they were about ready, but Frank, telling Lee about Spur, and missing his cooking, prompted that worthy to say,

"Say, Frank, Stewberries is at the Head of Track. He's workin' for the railroad, cookin' in their mess. Making lots of money, but it wouldn't hurt to visit with him. He said he was wantin' to get back on the trail again, that he missed it."

*　*　*

They loaded up with pure staples—flour, sugar, molasses, coffee and salt, one wagon full of flour alone. The others with the rest of the staples and their camp outfit. Frank thought of tobacco and at his insistence, Matthew bought it in bulk, a couple large containers of cigars and another of tobacco 'chaw.' Matthew drew the line at whiskey, though the men were pretty insistent about how it would command a premium price at the gold fields. He wasn't a prude, just didn't want the trouble of having it along. On the sly, though, he threw a couple cases of bottles in his own gear, for medicinal purposes. He was also able to find some other medicines that he thought might be valuable on the trail or at the mining camps.

At Head of Track, it didn't take any convincing to get Stewberries to throw down his job and come along. When they made it back to Dodge finally, slower because of the oxen, Matthew peeled off to stop at the Variety, to see if there was any news of Spur. Bell confessed that he had nothing, so Matthew swung out and trotted Stonewall down to Smith's and went in. Frank caught up with him as the doors swung and followed him. Smith was, as usual, behind the bar and the place was working up a head of steam. Smith saw them right away as they came in and gestured to them to come down to the end of the bar.

"Well, I've got news but you're not going to like it. My swamper found him yesterday morning. Saw the crows and ravens circling down in the coulee, then a couple coyotes came up. He went down there thinking maybe it was a dead deer or something, I guess. He found him. I covered him with a tarp, waiting for you to get back. Left him just as he was, to show you."

He turned the bar over to another Negro, who went behind it to start serving drinks. They walked out of the back door, around empty bottles and trash and down into a coulee a couple hundred yards across the prairie. A smell came up from it that both recognized from the war. A tarp lay on the ground, weighted down with rocks, but partly rooted up. When they came up and pulled the tarp away, a bloody mouthed coyote came charging out, almost running into Frank's legs as he scooted away. Matthew's shot sounded an instant later, and the coyote crumpled, dead, just yards away. Smith's eyes widened.

Spur lay half buried, face up, his upper torso uncovered and a swarm of flies and maggots working on his face. Despite that, it was evident that he'd been shot in the head. Matthew turned away. Smith and Frank threw the cover back on the body and rocked it down.

Smith said, "I can get him buried for you. We started a Boothill of our own, out a ways to the west of the other one."

"Is there an undertaker in town?"

"Yeah, but he may not want to have any truck with a black man. If he does, he'll charge you plenty for a coffin and a service." Smith rejoined, with a grimace.

"Money isn't a problem." Frank said, as Matthew went back toward the saloon. They followed him through the bar and out the door. They mounted and rode down the street. Near the middle of town, they came to a small building with a sign on it that said, 'Dodge City Mortuary, Angus Smallbridge, Prop.' They dismounted and went in. Inside, they heard the sound of sawing in the back, then, after ringing a little bell at the invitation of a sign on the counter, a fat man came puffing from behind a curtain, bald and round-faced, with a wide, expressive mouth that curiously turned up in repose, so that he always seemed to be smiling.

"What might I do for you gentlemen?" he asked in a Scottish brogue that rolled off his tongue.

"I have... a friend who has died. I'd like a proper burial for him." Matthew answered woodenly.

"Certainly, sir. Unfortunately, my deluxe caskets haven't arrived just yet, and I am forced to say that I have only one style for consideration—pine. I can let you have one in a regular size for...." Here he took a moment to mentally measure the size of the purse of the man standing before him.

"... 20 dollars," he finished. "A discreet service at the graveside will be five dollars extra. Singing will be another five dollars. I can do a small headstone out of native rock for another five dollars."

"Yes, yes, that will be fine. I want the works.... But I want one of the songs to be "Dixie, and the other "Rock of Ages. Does your singer know those?"

"Oh....certainly, sir. Certainly... 'Dixie and Rock of Ages' it will be." He paused in his bill writing. "And where is your friend? Outside?"

"He's under a tarp out behind Smith's Emporium." Matthew answered.

"Smith's....he's not a nigger or a mex., is he?" Matthew's voice turned dangerous. "And if he is a colored man?"

The man began to bluster. "Well, sir, I don't do the colored people. Bad for my white business, you know..." His voice got a little quavery at the end when he saw what was in Matthew's face and eyes, and he swallowed when Matthew brought his pistol up as Frank murmured, "Easy now, Pard!"

"But for you, sir, I will make an exception, yessir, I will!" The man stuttered. '*This damn frontier!! Everyone out here had a gun in their hands. A'course that made for more business,* he thought. The man had money and he'd charge him an extra ten dollars for the livery.'

The funeral came off at dusk. The coffin was necessarily closed but the mortician did it up well, at that, Frank thought. One of the soiled doves over at Gertie's, a blonde girl named Dolly, did the singing. She had a golden clear, throaty tone that throbbed out the two songs after and during the service that made many in the throng which had attended from Smith's and around the town, weep. The words of "Dixie" came out as a lament over the grave and made Matthew think again of the fun he and Spur had as kids, running through the stables and playing in the fields.

"I wish I was in de land of cotton,
Old times there are not forgotten,
Look away, look away, look away, Dixie Land!
In Dixie Land where I was born,
Early on one frosty morn,
Look away, look away, look away, Dixie Land!
Den I wish I was in Dixie
Hooray, hooray!

In Dixie land I'll take my stand!
to live and die in Dixie Away, away,
Away down south in Dixie Away, away,
Away down south in Dixie."

'Poor Spur. Poor, poor little daffy darky friend of mine. The rest of the service was a blur.

"Sir, Sir!" It was Dolly, the singer, plucking at his arm as he walked with Frank back to their horses. Did she want more money? She'd done well and deserved something more. He was digging in his belt for it when she said,

"I heard 'em talking about it, I think, Sir. One of 'em asked the other why he'd shot the nigger and the man said,"Because he would have told that damn Grounds he'd seen me."

Matthew turned and looked at her. "What else did they say, girl?"

Big eyes looked at him. She was really a pretty little thing. How did these girls end up in those houses? he thought idly. Probably a damn trick of fate, just as had happened to Spur.

"Well, the one asked him something I didn't hear. They were in the parlor and it was noisy, but then the bigger man, he said, "He'd most likely have some questions about his gear and his horses. Questions I'd just as soon not answer. The man is a deadly pistol shot."

Matthew was still dazed but it was Frank who put it together. "That sounds like that damn Captain Siderus. Was that his name, honey?"

Dolly wasn't sure, but Gertie might know. Matthew and Frank went back to the whorehouse with her. There Gertie, the same Gertie who'd been in Austin, received them in her parlor. She was reserved and cool. Neither man had so much as said goodbye to her when they'd left Texas. Matthew, seeing she was offended and guessing the reason why, apologized for the oversight as gracefully as he could. She thawed a little. '*After all, she was just a whore,*' she thought bitterly. They hadn't come for pleasure, she found, when they asked her about what Dolly had heard, and who it might have been. She didn't have a name, but her description was on the mark and they left finally, sure that it had indeed been Siderus. Who the other was, was anybody's guess. They hadn't been back in the time intervening.

233

"Give this to the girl, will you?" Matthew handed her $20. "She'll just drink it away, but yes, I'll give it to her." She took the heavy coin, intentionally brushing his hand as she did. A tingle ran through her. He'd hurt her but she still. . . had fond secret thoughts of him. He existed in her mind as the southern gentleman and she built her fantasies around their being together in a South where no war had ever come. She swallowed.

"Where do you go next, Matthew?"

"Frank and I are freighting up to the gold fields. We had enough killin' for a . . . .lifetime. I want. . . .some peace, if it exists." he said, looking at her. Perceptive, he could tell she was emotionally upset but concealing it well. He patted her hand and squeezed it a little. She responded, looking at him. He turned and left. She looked down at the coin in her hand. And sobbed.

courtesy of Library of Congress

PART V

THE TRAIL

Chapter 25

The trail to Laramie was a long hard one, with blow sand, steep banked coulees and not much water. They'd followed the Arkansas for a time, then angled north toward the Smoky Hill River and on up to the Republican. Matthew was glad they'd decided on oxen, they stood the trip better than horses. He'd taken along some grain anyway, for their mounts, and used it sparingly on the other stock, when grass was scarce. The trail was rutted from wagon trains before and much of the grass on either side was eaten off by the trains and the buffalo.

The country was desolate and barren, for the most part, though there were buffalo, pushed up from their normal grazing grounds by the relentless pressure of the hunters.

At the Republican, they were in the midst of miles of buffalo, and the men were wanting to stop and hunt, but the wagons were already well loaded and the heavy hides would have burdened them too much, and above taking meat, they didn't shoot much. It was Pawnee country and several times, they saw bands of Indians but they never came near. At one place, Sandy Creek, they came up to a government train that had passed them earlier and helped them pull their wagons over the crossing, then let them help get their wagons across.

Julesburg came up, on the old Fremont route, and they stopped for a while to rest their stock. Puckett and the others went into the town to wet their whistles and got drunk, but Matthew managed to keep Frank out of it. Finally, tired of Frank's crankiness at not being able to imbibe a few, he went in with him and they both had several drinks at the Lone Star, a saloon owned by an old Texan, who talked to them incessantly about his home state in a sirupy drunken drawl that even Frank had a little trouble understanding.

They went on to Fort Sedgwick, another lightly garrisoned little stockade, then up the trail to the north fork of the Platte River, which they followed to Fort Laramie, where they crossed the river on a cable ferry that had been built by 'Old' Jim Bridger in '65, after several emigrants had lost their lives trying to cross the treacherous river. They'd seen a few bands of Indians, probably Pawnee, but had been fortunate, not being bothered by them. Others had not been so lucky, as the Sioux and the Cheyenne, it was said, had been raiding everywhere, striking hunting camps, emigrant groups and even escorted government supply trains. As a result, Fort Laramie, in the midst of the Indian country, but a key point on the Oregon Trail and the route to the mining camps, had grown into a large military complex, with hundreds of soldiers stationed there. Prices were exorbitant, the Post sutler charging a dollar for a chew of tobacco. Frank was smug about their own supply of the stuff,

"We'll make a killin' on it, Matthew, when we get to the mines. Think of it—a dollar a chaw here, what'll it cost in the camps?"

Matthew, curious, asked for flour and the sullen trader charged him a dollar for a pint of it, about a half pound. Then _he_ got smug, thinking of the whole wagon load they had. If they could just get their wagons intact to the mines, they'd be rich. What worried him, though, was the dumping of so much excess baggage he'd seen along the Platte, stoves, furniture, and even food. In one spot, they'd seen what must have been tons of rotting bacon. Everything was worthless unless it could be gotten to its destination. But most of the dumping had occurred because of overloaded wagons and misuse of their stock. He'd favored their stock, shoeing them early on, and taken it easy, resting them often and graining them frequently. It had told, and they had reached the fort in good shape, not like some, who were camped beside the place, and would most likely stay there, their stock footsore and lame.

They pulled out a couple days later, after Matthew had gotten tired of enduring the pleas of emigrants desperate to buy their oxen, their horses, anything to get them over the trail. From somewhere, the Post sutler had learned of his wagon of flour and offered a price for it that Matthew had scorned, knowing what he was charging across the counter.

"Better to sell now, for a profit, than lose it all to the Indians up the trail," the man had retorted. Privately, Matthew had decided that before _he_ got it, he would give it away to the emigrants.

The trail from Fort Laramie west followed the north fork of the Platte River up into the very heart of the Indian country. It was sage brush covered, hilly country, interspersed with little creeks full of wild plum. Antelope and buffalo were seldom out of sight. Often they jumped flocks of prairie chickens and sage hens that numbered in the hundreds. There was no getting lost, as they followed a rutted trail that took them ever west and north. Fifteen miles a day was a good average, with the oxen grazing late in the morning and at night, to keep their strength up, and a cup or two of grain, when the haul had been long. The men existed well on Stewberries' cooking, never growing tired of his hump steaks, broiled ribs, stews and bread. And always there was coffee, Arbuckle's, hot and tasty. Once in a while, there were pies, when Stew had the time. The three freight wagons were stuffed with a cornucopia of foodstuffs that Matthew didn't begrudge his crew. Then, at night, the men were able to enjoy their smokes and the gabfest that always occurred around the fire. It was a time of content for all.

Three weeks out, they were in sight of the Red Buttes, the day a red letter one also, as they'd seen a small herd of elk. It was the first that any of the party had seen of these great animals, though they'd heard of them. Puckett was adamant that he would shoot one and so Matthew let him, reluctantly. The man was a daring rider astride a fast Texas pony, his favorite horse, Jigger. They were soon out of sight of the wagons, pursuing the band of fleet animals, who, without seeming to work at it, seemed to float over the uneven ground.

Abruptly, they heard a shot, then several, some of them pistol shots. Matthew, sensing danger, called to Stewberries, in the lead wagon, to start a circle. Up over the hill came Puckett, being closely chased by a war party of twenty or so Indians, whooping and shooting. The sight made the men whip up their teams and the three wagons made a tight little bunch-up, with the horses of the dismounted riders within.

"Set your brakes and chain the wheels, boys! Keep it closed up!" Frank hollered, as he uncased his Henry and checked its sights. Puckett's horse came leaping along, whipped hard by Lee, as he strove to keep ahead of the yelling riders behind him. He came up to the wagons, jumping his horse over a tongue and into the circle, as the men fired a volley that made the Indians pull up sharply, their number reduced by two, with another clinging to his horse's back, then slipping off to the ground. The others began circling, shooting and yelling, then, as another telling volley rang out, dropping yet another pair, and rolling a horse on its nose, the riders quirted their mounts away, out of range.

Then they began shooting at the circle, which was a mistake, as they hadn't backed off far enough. Matthew, Frank, Stewberries and the others were all marksmen, and after they got settled, made some shots that backed the Indians off even farther, leaving another couple dead on the ground. Stewberries was using his long range Sharps .50/70, and the others switched to their Sharps .44's. The two parties sniped at each other until dark, when the Indians were able to retrieve their dead and disappear.

Several oxen and one of the horses had been hit by their fire, and Frank worked hard to save the lives of those he deemed might recover. Puckett was also wounded, low in the back, a disabling wound that kept him down for some days. They journeyed carefully on to the nearest water, Red Springs Creek, three miles away, then laid up to let their wounded recover. All but one of the oxen, paunch shot, was able to recover, the clear desert air healing wounds in record time. Puckett, though, took some time to get over his painful injury. The bullet had gone in and lodged under the bottom rib at the back, on the left side, and after a big dose of Laudanum, Frank probed for the object. He was successful finally, and brought the lead blob out. However, the dose they had given Puckett had been too great and he was a day and a night coming to. Matthew privately thought maybe they'd killed him, but he eventually awakened. Carbolic Acid in the wound channel served to prevent suppuration and he was back riding in a week's time, though stiff and sore. They went on.

Pronghorn Antelope photo courtesy of Robert Cherry

Chapter 26

In another two weeks, they had crossed the head of the Powder River, skirting the edge of the Big Horns. Buffalo were in sight, antelope racing by, and elk came trotting out of every cut and out of each little grove of trees, it seemed. The country was a game paradise as they neared the mountains, and they often saw bear and cougars, the animals having little fear of humans, just standing curious as they went on by. But the trail showed many signs of other set-tos that the travelers had with the Indians—dead stock, burned wagons, and graves by the wayside.

A day away from the Powder, they came up on an emigrant train laboring up a slope, twenty wagons in all. The rear guard, five men, came riding back and their leader, a stocky little man on a big black horse, called out a hello in a booming voice.

Frank rode forward, followed up by Matthew and Puckett. When he reached them, the little man put his hand out and shook, saying,

"Damn glad you caught up with us, we've had some Indian trouble—they've hit twice now—killed three of our herders and ran some of our stock off. We've been short teamed for a week now." Matthew and the others had seen some freshly dumped goods on the trail, some burned trail wagons, and the graves, with crosses that were already rubbed down by the buffalo.

"I see you're well-armed. Can we travel together? Be for the best, we're thinkin.'" We've got womenfolk along, and I have to admit I've been scared at the numbers of Redskins I've been getting glimpses of along the trail. Have you had any mix-ups with them yet?"

"We got hit back a ways. Hurt a man and shot some livestock. We were able to run 'em off." Frank reported.

"We were hopin' to be to Fort Kearny by now, getting late and I'd hate to be caught out here in this damn country by an early winter's storm." The man, giving his name as Able Cass, handed Frank a chew, and he pulled off a piece with his teeth and handed it back, being neighborly.

"Many thanks. What say, Matthew? Want to join up with them into Kearny? Might be a good idea, more strength in numbers, I say." Matthew assented and they went on together.

The emigrant train, led by Cass, was a hardy band of thirty men and half that many women, all from Missouri and eastern Kansas. They were headed for the Bozeman gold camp and had been part of a larger train that had argued and split off, the bigger, faster wagons, pulled by horses, going on ahead.

"Don't have any doubt we'll find 'em up at Kearny, laid up, most likely, with their stock worn down. They was pushing too hard, and wouldn't listen. Slow and sure will get it done, I always say." He spit a tremendous gob of brown liquid. "At that, we'd been there, too, if we hadn't lost a third of our stock, damn it."

They traveled together, taking it easy, as Cass and Matthew concurred on that subject and by slow stages, they made it to Cantonment Reno. Like Fort Sedgwick, there was a little stockade there, with a detachment of soldiers from the 2d Battalion of the 18th Infantry, poorly equipped and armed and most of them rank recruits from the east. Matthew observed, too, that their uniforms and boots were poor goods, shoddy made and already falling apart. Less than a hundred soldiers to guard more than a hundred miles of trail against the Sioux and Cheyenne nations!

They were out of tobacco and coffee, so Matthew took pity on them and, to Frank's disgust, sold them some coffee and cigars for little more than he'd bought it for. Maybe he had given it to them, for the Lieutenant had to pay for it with army script, redeemable at the nearest Army paymaster. Who most likely, thought Frank, grumbling, wouldn't pay for enlisted men's tobacco or coffee.

He found it damn hard to do a good deed for bluecoats.

Sixty five hard miles north, in the middle of the fifth day, they came up over a last hill and saw the fort in the distance. Matthew had been told by the Lieutenant that they had built a big fortification and so they had. It was fully 1600 feet by 800 feet, though shaped more like an egg than a rectangle, and set between two creeks for an easy water supply, Big Piney and Little Piney. Eight and ten foot logs had been hewed on two sides and set touching each other three feet in the ground.

Inside were quarters for the men and officers, storerooms, a sutler's store, a stock corral and stables, a hospital and even a guardhouse. Around the walls, about four feet from the top of the logs, were firing platforms, accessed by steps. A large gate for wagons was set in its middle, with a smaller one, an officer's gate they called it, off on one side. On either side, were cannon bastions, and at each end, blockhouses set into the walls.

It was an imposing structure, set as it was, out in the wilderness, in the middle of Indian country. There were about 300 men at the fort, commanded by a Colonel named Carrington, a somewhat pompous, full-of-himself, officer of a type Matthew and Frank harbored many unpleasant memories of, from the war. Despite the extreme danger, Carrington had brought his wife and children to the fort, and let the other officers do the same. As a result, kids were running hither and yon around the big place. Matthew shook his head, aghast at the thought of what a war party who got inside the log structure might do to these helpless dependents. And there were several trains parked helter-skelter around the flats in front of the place, which Matthew, had he been in command, would have directed to be double circled in a more defensive attitude.

Cass came up, an agitated little man whose words tumbled over each other, "Damn it, Grounds. I'm hearing from these people that the commandant isn't letting *anybody* through! Says he can't give them protection and safe passage with an escort because he's short of men. Can you beat that? We're stuck here, sounds like. Let's us go see the man."

Matthew, despite himself, could see the officer's dilemma: short of men, with civilians that he couldn't protect on the trail, piling up here at his fort. What to do?"

They went through the open main gate, another thing that Matthew would have insisted be closed always. '*A determined sudden, swift mob of attackers could have forced their way into the fort before the gate was swung to,*' he thought. The big, heavy log gates were cumbersome and took a lot of manpower to drag closed and barred. Inside, they headed for the main post headquarters, though Matthew felt a futility taking over his consciousness, a doubt that said that anything he attempted in this life was for naught. He shook it off and entered the

Colonel's tidy small office, following Cass. They were announced by a burly old Irish Sergeant Major with a bass voice and a heavy drinker's face, florid, with broken veins and a twisted nose that bespoke plenty of fisticuffs in his past.

The Colonel, a sandy haired man with a short, trimmed mustache and tired eyes, rose to greet them. "I'm Colonel Carrington, men. . . .?"

"I'm Able Cass and he's Matthew Grounds. We just got in. We heard that the trail was closed. We need to be on our way. Winter's fast approaching."

"Right you are, but I can't let you pass, men. The Sioux, the Arapahoe and Cheyenne are all out and on the war path. Red Cloud has over five thousand warriors at his beck and call. I can't tell you how many times our details have been jumped and how many incidents on up the trail I've recorded, of civilians like yourself killed. For your own sakes, I can't let you through. You'll just have to wait for a government train and escort I'm expecting from Fort Laramie, and go on back there with them. They should be here soon. In fact, they're overdue."

He listened with some restraint, as Cass reiterated his determination, their need, to go on through. Matthew listened without comment. Carrington restated his position and they finally left, before the man had his sergeant throw them out.

They sat on their duffs for almost a week. The government train never showed itself, and it was no secret that the Commandant and his staff were all worried. They needed to be resupplied before winter, or they stood a good chance of starving, even in this land of plenty. As closely as they were enveloped by their foe, sending out small hunting parties was tantamount to sending them to their death, and large ones were not likely to get the amounts of game needed to sustain them for a long winter, as the Indians nearby had already spooked most of it out of the area. Nonetheless, parties did venture forth, to just as frequently be run back to the fort, by the ever present and alert Indians. Wood trains, heavily guarded, were coming and going.

The men were grouped about the fire at midday, sipping coffee and digesting their meal, when Carrington and one of his staff, his adjutant, Captain Murphy, came up to the group.

They both accepted a cup of coffee, and Matthew, seeing them drink, had the idle thought that they were in short supply of that commodity. Carrington's next words affirmed that suspicion.

"Grounds, I'm hearing that you have three wagons full of supplies. Is that so?" he asked.

"One wagon full of flour, one full of other staples, Colonel, coffee, sugar, tobacco, molasses, some salt, and such. The last is mostly our camp gear, plus some grain I had for the stock. I do have some medicines along, Ammonium Spirits, Laudanum, Liniment, Carbolic Acid, and clean bandages, and so on."

He saw a look pass between the two officers.

"A courier came in last night. He'd been riding at night, laying up in the day to get here. He tells me that the train I've been expecting was turned back by repeated attacks by the Sioux and Cheyenne, down at the Powder. Two thirds of their stock was stolen away and they just couldn't come on to us. We find ourselves in a predicament—ordered to hold out here but not sufficiently supplied to do so.

However, what you have on those wagons would allow us to carry out our mission through the winter. Now, I can't pay you what you'd expect to get at the mining camps but still, I can guarantee you that I will allow you a profit—more than you'd get from the post trader at Laramie. Would you be interested?"

The question was almost in the form of a command, and Matthew knew that if he said 'no,' they stood to lose the stores anyway, because the Colonel was in a bind.

"I'm stuck with empty wagons and useless teams, if I sell the contents, Colonel. Will you agree to buy them, too? I might keep one back for our gear. I'll have to talk with Cass."

The two officers looked at the small, closely guarded herd of oxen and Matthew knew the thought was in their minds that if they couldn't use them that winter, they could certainly eat them. Carrington nodded. "I'd take them, too."

Matthew looked at Frank, who nodded. "Then I'll bring my lists and let's go to your office, sir, and see what kind of deal we can make."

He sold it all by weight, item by item. Neither party was in a hurry. There was nothing else to do, so the scales were brought out by the sutler, the wagons hitched up and run through the big gate and up to the post storehouse. There, with the help of grinning and relieved soldiers, they unloaded first the big flour wagon, then the next one, down to the tobacco and the cases of whiskey. Matthew held back some small portions, a couple bottles of the whiskey and some tobacco for the men. The rest went into the big storehouse and Murphy saw that a double guard was placed on it. In return, Matthew got a strict accounting and army scrip that came close to paying him back for their venture—if they could get the government tender to some major post that would honor it. In the meantime, he had to be satisfied.

Cass had asked him before if he would consider selling any of his pulling stock, and Matthew had responded to that request after he'd talked with the Colonel, finally selling him five yokes of oxen for a little more than Carrington would allow, but payment rendered in gold. He also traded the one big wagon he'd held back for a lighter wagon, and harness. He had horses among his riding stock that would serve as a team for it. Now, he had a conveyance for his camp outfit and bedrolls. He was satisfied, had to be. That meant he wouldn't be taking from his belt to pay the men, anyway. He went back to Frank and explained what he'd done. Frank just shrugged and said,

"What else we gonna do, Matthew? It's my fault, I guess, for bringing this cock-brained idee up, to come up to the mines. We'd done better to head back east."

"Not true, Frank. I wanted to come just as bad as you. You didn't have to talk me into it. We're not broke, anyway."

Matthew paid the men, apologizing for getting them into the fix and to a man, they were philosophical about it, saying they'd known that it was going to be dangerous. While they were talking, they heard cattle lowing, and to their amaze, a herd of cattle came streaming over the hills, up from the trail, yelling cowboys hazing them along. While the herd was being held on the flat, kept some distance away from the emigrant and post animals, a rider that Matthew instinctively knew had to be the man in command came loping toward their fire. He drew up and dismounted, a tall young man, a stockman drawn down by days in the saddle. His horse looked as tired as he did. Stewberries poured him a cup of coffee and the man accepted it with thanks.

"How do, men, I'm Nelson Story. That's my herd out there. I've heard that the trail up ahead is closed, by orders of the Army. Is that so?" He sipped as Matthew explained the situation, listening without comment.

* * *

Two days later, they watched as the emigrant train pulled out for Laramie. Carrington had reluctantly sent a thirty man detachment with them, under Murphy. He'd given the others a spiel about how he couldn't feed them if they stayed on and winter caught them, that he wanted them to go, but Matthew and the rest had listened in silence. Matthew had the idea that the man felt he'd done his duty, that he knew those left behind were probably going to go on, whether he let them or no. But his main concern was the emigrant women and children.

Story's herd and men, most of them hard riding Texans, were tired from the long trail up from Laramie. They had gotten little rest, with several sharp engagements with first the Cheyenne, just below the Powder, then the Sioux, as they came on. Story, with he and his men all well-armed with Colt's revolvers and Remington rifles, fought back and somehow kept the herd intact. They were resting at Kearny, Story declining to answer directly when Matthew queried him as to his intentions. Story was an ambitious young man. He had already made his stake, a sizeable one, in the gold fields. Then he'd gone to Texas and bought a herd of cattle and hired the hardest riding, toughest crew he could find to bring them on North. He was not the kind of man to let anyone stand in his way.

Later, he came to the fire and asked Matthew to walk out with him a ways. In the dark of the evening, both men savored the cigars Matthew offered and presently Story asked, blowing smoke,

"What about you, Grounds? I didn't see you heading back down the trail with the train a couple days ago.?"

"No. I think we'll go on up to the camps. That's where we were headed to begin with. Be a long circle around to go back to Laramie and then over to Salt Lake and back through Idaho."

The other assented.

"Well, that's what I think, too. Guess we'll go on if I can manage to get the jump on the Colonel. He's having a party tomorrow night, plans to put some of those supplies you sold him to some good use, I guess. I'm invited, just like you. I think I'll go. And in the meanwhile, my men will ease the herd out on the trail. I'll catch up to them in the morning. Want to come along? We could help each other. I need your guns and maybe your good sense. It wouldn't hurt you to have some extra hands along, either, to do some fighting, if need be."

"I'll ask the others, Story, but for Frank and I, I'll say 'yes.'"

"I'll wait to hear what they have to say, Grounds."

"Call me 'Matthew." They shook hands."…And me, 'Nelson!" the other said with satisfaction. Having these men come along could just be the thing that would save his little enterprise. He was undermanned as it was, and under-gunned, if Carrington's gloomy assessment was correct as to the numbers of Indians they were up against.

Photo courtesy of Robert Cherry

Chapter 27

Story's plan worked. Matthew and he both attended the party and it was a gala affair. The fort women had used their allotment of flour and sugar to good effect and the cakes they'd made were superb, as was the punch and the coffee, which all present were addicted to, and had missed so much. Matthew, for his part in bringing the supplies up the trail in so timely a fashion, had been lionized by the women, who knew that they were a godsend, with the government train turned back. The men, too, received him with much courtesy and good will, though he was, they knew, a former Rebel. Some there had fought against the 18th Georgia and its brother outfit, the Texas Brigade, and knew of their effectiveness in the war. It was hard for them to be beholden to a Confederate. Story was lionized as a handsome, articulate and intelligent young man. Frank, who could have come had he wanted, said he felt out of place with all those bluecoats around, and would get their mounts and gear ready.

Story and Matthew danced their way through the women, not neglecting one dance card. They talked in between dances. The music was provided by a surprising good enlisted ensemble who seemed to know every song requested. Matthew, who hadn't danced in years, since the war, when the Brigade had been on leave in Richmond, felt the old moves returning with the music and was enjoying himself. His depressive mood was lifting. Mrs. Carrington was a statuesque blonde who loved to dance, and he found himself her partner several times. She, for her part, was fascinated by this Rebel, yet repelled, too. Her older brother had been killed at Petersburg, perhaps by this very man, as he had said when asked, that he had been there. He was the epitome, she thought, of the southern gentleman soldier, a courtly man of some elegance, even in clothes that were not meant for the ballroom. She sighed. The war had split the country down the middle and it would take a generation or more to heal the ugly wounds.

At twelve, the Colonel rose to give a toast. "To the United States, gentlemen. May her flag always wave over this great land of our's. . . and may the hearts of our countrymen soon heal from the disastrous conflict we so recently have experienced."

Everyone, including Matthew, raised their glasses and drank, the others seeing with satisfaction that this Rebel at least, had apparently put aside his differences and was content to be back in the fold. He felt no remorse, he realized. It <u>was</u> his country now. It was raining when they came out. Story was happy. This rain would cover the sound of their leaving and most likely keep the Indians under cover. When the two men got back to camp, there was none. Frank stood waiting, holding coats for both of them, their horses nearby, and they mounted without a word, and turned north.

* * *

The next morning saw them far up the trail. The going was good, the cattle and horses rested. They made good time, skirting the stands of timber and keeping as much as possible to the open. Story's men were outstanding young Texas cowboys and superb riders. They were also well mounted. Story told Matthew that he intended to use his crew like firemen—if a fight started, they would race to where they were needed.

"Your men are all well-armed and can handle themselves, Matthew. We'll take care of the cattle, as much as we can. You do most of the shooting. If things get too bad, some of us'll peel off and help all we can. Try not to get bogged down in a battle. The idea is to keep on going. Could we get one of your men to stay out ahead of our point and guide him? We don't want to find ourselves going up some blind canyon."

Matthew asked, "How about it, men? This is strictly volunteer duty now."

Puckett spoke up. "I'll take the job. Guess I've already been inoculated for Indians. I should be able to smell 'em now." The others laughed. With Puckett out in front on his fast horse, the way was assured.

* * *

So that was the way the drive went. The Sioux luckily never hit them in any strength, just little harassing groups that would snipe or make a run for the herd, to be beaten back by Matthew and the others, the flying squad, they called themselves, or the fire brigade, sometimes the cowboys getting in the act, if things started getting hairy. Talking around the fire about the light resistance they'd encountered, it was Frank's thought that the bulk of the Indians were off hunting, 'making meat for the winter', and the others staying in close to the fort, as Red Cloud wanted them to. It was probably a good assessment. Though they had a dozen encounters, the fire brigade was able to beat them off.

* * *

Two weeks later, they were working their way over a series of low, heavily grassed foothills west of a range of small mountains, the country gradually changing from broken scoria buttes and long stretches of sagebrush and greasewood coulees.

Buffalo were constantly in sight, as well as deer, antelope and occasionally, small herds of elk. The smaller species were underfoot as well—myriads of prairie chickens, huge flocks of sage hens, and little bunnies, along with their bigger cousins, the bounding jacks, starting to turn white now.

Puckett was still in front, leading the way. They'd had a couple sharp engagements with the Sioux—one at a perfect ambush site that had been foiled by the long range shooting of Stewberries and his counterpart, Hank Owens, who drove the light wagon for the Story outfit.

Owens was an older man, one eyed from an old war wound, and too old for the saddle, but, like Stew, he was a good cook and teamster, one who was always able to find a way to maneuver his wagon up and over or around the obstacles the trail offered. Stew trusted his judgment and often followed him when the trail got tough. He had been a hide hunter for years, until the life had soured on him, and he had met up with Story at Wichita, who'd taken him on. He kept a big Sharps on his wagon, and was as good with one eye as most were with two.

The flying squad was, that Morning, doing battle with a group of Indians that were trying to cut off the drags, off on the east side, when Stewberries, looking sharp, saw some braves skulking down to a vantage point on the west that would, had they made it, serve as a perfect shooting platform to sweep the entire left wing of the herd. Stewberries and Owens drew up and unlimbered their big guns, both .50 Sharps. They killed three Indians on that side before the rest broke cover and ran back into the timber. The drags were able to get by the spot with the loss of one man, Petey Snider, a young man from Ohio whose family had close ties to Story's. A lucky shot by one of the Indians had taken him in the neck, killing him instantly. They wrapped him in his blankets and buried him by the trail. Matthew spoke the words over him from his little Bible, then they had the herd cover the signs of his burial.

* * *

On this day, the fourteenth day from the fort, Puckett, then 'Pan' Skillet, Story's point man, broke over the rim, and the flowing herd of rangy longhorns followed, the animals closed in on either side by the ever present riders, the drag closed up by the camp wagon, Stewberries, and the rest of Matthew's group. Matthew had found that Story's cowboys had actually taken a vote back at the fort and elected to go on, just one man voting against it. He had been kept under guard until they left, then left behind.

The low pass through sandstone ridges stippled with scrub cedar and nut pine, opened into a great valley, called by some Indians, the Elk River. The French had named it the 'Roche Jaune,' the Yellow stone. Down below, maybe four miles away, it lay like a silver ribbon, threading the valley floor through great groves of cottonwoods and brush. The scene reminded Matthew of one from the Bible—multitudes of animals grazing in the meadows, and nowhere could be seen the evidence of man. Across the river, Matthew saw a brown, moving mass of buffalo, the Northern herd, which, he had heard, stretched far up into Canada.

Ahead, the trail broke to the left, under the bluffs, headed generally west now. They followed it, working toward a spot that would intersect the river and allow the herd to water, after nearly a day without drinking. As they approached the edge of the large river, Matthew saw up ahead, a finger of smoke rising to the horizon. He galloped forward to where Story was, gazing at the smudge.

"That isn't a village, I don't think. There'd be more smoke." Story surmised. Matthew pulled his English made binoculars from their case and put them to his eyes. The trees, though, hid the sight of anything on the ground from him.

"I can't see anything but trees. Let's get a little closer, then send out a party to take a gander."

After the cattle had all watered and they had choused them onto the trail again, they went on forward another couple miles, then Matthew took Frank, gathered up Puckett at the front, and they loped ahead, toward the smoke.

It proved to be a small train of eight wagons, apparently hit the day before, burned and one of them still smoldering. Coyotes and a pack of wolves ran from the coming of the men, but didn't show much fear. Crows hopped in the branches, cawing their defiance at the interlopers to their feast.

The burned wagons lay in a jagged line, evidence they'd been jumped too quick to maneuver into a defensive circle. Beside the wagons, on either side of the trail, lay bodies, and they weren't a pretty sight. The men had all been scalped and mutilated. The women lay half naked, with torn clothes. All had their heads caved in by crashing tomahawks, the death blow, and were scalped, too. The children, there were ten, Matthew counted, lay in various attitudes of death, with arrows sticking from their little bodies. The crows and scavengers had been at them. All the men showed evidence of fighting hard for their families, and none looked as if they'd gone peacefully to their reward. It was a grisly tableau of death that sickened even the veterans among the men, when the herd came up and the cowboys caught sight of the massacre.

* * *

They halted the herd and were digging graves, Stewberries and Hank making a late meal, Matthew, Frank, Pan and Lee Puckett on alert guard, when Matthew thought he heard something—a cry. Was it a baby? It came again, a soft wail. He looked intently at where he thought it came from, a low ledge of rock twenty yards away. Could someone, injured, have crawled off and hid there? Or was it perhaps an Indian trick? He signaled to Frank, who had heard it, too, and was signaling back. They headed cautiously toward the sound, both very ready to shoot, if need be, and keeping to cover. Puckett saw them edging toward the low rock wall and came over, to back them up, if needed.

A low growl, menacing, threatening, stopped them all in their tracks. Something was there, all right, but it didn't sound human. The men looked at each other. Matthew reached forward and parted the bushes slowly with the barrel of his rifle, finger on the trigger. Beyond, the rock came down into an overhang that formed a protective cavernous hollow. In it, was a dog, a big one, rust colored like a bear and with a head like one, lying on its side, an arrow sticking out high up on its back. The animal rolled on its stomach, and tried to get up but was too weak.

"Easy, boy. . . easy, now. Matthew set his gun down and came slowly forward, as the big animal tried again and failed to gain its feet. A pool of blood under it attested to its wound's seriousness. "Easy, boy."

"Want me to shoot it, Matthew?" Puckett, standing back, asked helpfully.

Matthew shook his head. "Easy, boy." He reached out and petted the big head, stroked it and the dog lay back on its side again, panting. The arrow was deep and he saw blood seeping from its mouth. The blood looked a little pink. The missile had maybe nicked or hit a lung. He grasped the shaft and the dog raised its head, growled. It was too deep. He'd need help. He backed away. Best to get Stewberries and Owens, he thought. Tie the dog, wrap its mouth so it couldn't bite. Laudanum?? It would work, but how much dose to use? He thought of Puckett. He'd given too much. Maybe a dose that would be about a third less. Maybe it would work.

"I want to get Stew and Hank and see if we can't do something for that animal." He hurried away and gathered those two men and, with bindings and medicines, they headed back to the rocks.

Chapter 28

Matthew eased himself in the saddle. The graves had been dug well by the men, deep and covered with flat rocks. But as for names on crosses, there were none. The wagons were too well burned and they couldn't come up with any clues of identity at all. Maybe, though, Story had thought, they might be able to send back to Fort Kearny and see if they had any insight on the matter.

"They maybe signed in there before they went on," he said. Matthew wasn't so sure. Why hadn't this train been held up like the others? More likely, they had skirted the fort at night, and come on undetected. It might have been Cass's forward train. He'd never seen it at Kearny.

The dog lay on the bedrolls piled on the wagon. They'd actually been able to use Laudanum on it after they'd got it to drink, mixing it with water. It had lost consciousness, and to be sure, they had bound the jaws and the feet before they had started to work, finally getting the arrow free after a struggle. It had lost a lot of blood and, after it had regained consciousness, hours later, Stew had made a thick broth of boiled buffalo liver and marrow bone and fed it sparingly. The dog had barely gotten any down, but that little had evidently done wonders. It was perking up some. It might live, Matthew thought. Puckett, like some of the others, was derisive about the effort they'd made for a "damn dog." But Matthew counted it time well spent. The dog had taken an arrow trying to protect its family. The least they could do was to try to save its life.

The herd was pointed upriver. They'd all expected to run into more Indian trouble, but so far, since the Yellowstone, none had transpired. To their left, over north it was, a big lump of rock jutted out of the river, a rock that was surely a landmark, though none knew what it was called. Miles farther on, they crossed into a part of the valley ringed on either side by tall sandstone cliffs, and in that grassy bowl, by the river there, was an Indian village. Matthew estimated forty some lodges erected in a double circular fashion, that was at once a way to help defend its inhabitants and perhaps had some religious context. A good sized village, and one that could give them a hard fight, without doubt. The men bunched the herd up and got in closer to one another, anticipating a battle. But Puckett was up ahead, conversing with some braves that were fronting him. And they weren't acting warlike. Matthew spurred Stonewall up there. Frank and Story were close behind.

Puckett was talking sign to them, and they were nodding and talking back.

"They're Crows. Say they didn't know about the emigrant train being hit, but I wonder. They do say that there's Sioux close. They blame the killin' on them. They're all snakes and hate the white man, so we best be careful of 'em."

He threw out some more sign and the head man, a tall, hook-nosed brave, threw some back at him. Puckett turned back to them.

"Quirt here says the way is good for the white man's buffalo to go on to the white man's village in the mountains. He says that weather is coming but we should make it before the big snow. He says the crickets tell him the late winter will be a bad one and we should hang much meat. That's what all of 'em are doin,' getting ready for an early, bad winter. He asks if we got any sugar? Has a sweet tooth, he does. And tobacco."

Story answered, "Tell him we'll give him some sugar and some molasses, if he wants it. And a little tobacco, for safe passage through his country. Tell him we will give him even more sugar if he will have his braves scout the Sioux out for us and tell us where they are." More sign was thrown back and forth.

"He says it is good. He will send scouts out to find the enemy." Puckett spat a gob of tobacco. "He's a good one, I believe. The Crows are generally the White man's friend, since we fight both against the Sioux and their kin."

They kept the herd going past the village, then bedded it down a half mile farther on, by the river. Matthew pooled some stores with Story and they, with Puckett, brought the bundle back to the village. There, they had to smoke and eat with Quirt, while warriors ducked in and out of the teepee, and squaws hurried back and forth, bringing food and drink to their honored visitors. It was late before they were able to leave the lodge and mount their horses for camp, the nearly full moon lighting their way.

When Matthew got back to the fire, he checked on the dog and was happy to find it better. Stew said, "He ate some food, Matthew. Took some water, too. Only thing is, he wet some of the beds he was laying on and the boys are upset with him. What should I do?"

Matthew replied. "Maybe we can get a slicker under him. He can't walk. He's going to have to ride." He went to the wagon and dug deep in his bag, bringing forth a bottle. He went up to the fire and handed the bottle to Benson Greene, who accepted it with pleasure, pulled the cork and took a good swig, then passed it on.

"I'm sorry, boys, that your bedrolls got pissed on. I'll wash 'em out for you myself at the river, if it'll help any. In the meantime, here's a bottle to help ease your mad. If I could figure another way to carry the dog along, I would."

The men were mad, but the bottle eased it. Matthew was as good as his word, and took the wetted bedrolls to the river and washed them off himself, then offered his roll and spare blankets they had along to the men whose beds were wet. Frank helped him get the dog onto Matthew's slicker. Matthew rolled in a horse blanket by the fire.

Chapter 29

Bozeman was a wide collection of shacks, tents and hovels clustered around a long main street, situated on the other side of the pass named for the man who'd found it, and not far from Fort Ellis, which effectively controlled the mountain passage. They drove to the edge of the town and Story located his herd on a nice piece of grass by the Gallatin River. They breathed a sigh of relief. They'd made it through after all. The weather the last two weeks had been tough on the stock and on the men. They all had coats and such, but it wasn't always enough. They'd piled all their clothes on and kept going, getting off to walk when their feet got so cold they couldn't feel them. Right now, the temperature was hovering at zero and every stove in every shack and building in town was going full blast.

    They headed for a saloon, the first one on the street, and the warmth and smell of unwashed bodies and stale alcohol and smoke rolled at them when they opened the heavy door. Matthew's men all bellied up to the bar and he bought them the first round. Several card games were going at the back and some of the men gravitated that direction, watching the play, warming themselves at the big wood stove heating the room. Some of them, like Puckett, were inveterate card players.

Frank and Matthew leaned on the bar. "We're here, Now what do we do, Matthew?"

"Well. . . .I've been thinking that what we need to do is buy a stove, if we can, and build ourselves a big cabin for us all to winter in. We'll go over to the fort later, and see if we can get paid on this scrip from Carrington. I don't hold much hope we can, but maybe. . . maybe. Then just sit tight, I guess, until spring. See what we want to do, then. But, we want to get settled in, first."

The next day, Matthew and Frank went to the fort, which was surrounded by another stockade like that of Fort Kearny. The buildings were unhewn lodgepole, plaster with mortar, but with rough sawn floors. The whole thing came from a big new sawmill run by a water turbine wheel, which fascinated Frank.

Colonel John Gibbon, Commander of the Seventh Infantry Regiment there, was a famous Union veteran, organizer of the Potomac's famed "Iron Brigade," during the war. Later, he'd risen to Corps Commander. The Indians called him the "One who limps" because of an old wound. Square shouldered and tall, he sported a large, bushy mustache. He was not a man who liked rebels, having fought them for five long years.

He was reluctant to pay on Carrington's scrip, though he knew if he didn't, his own scrip would become suspect, so he offered Matthew a deal: two thirds in gold, which the paymaster had right there, and the rest in supplies and such for the winter, discounted 10 percent.

"You throw a good stove in, and you have a deal, Colonel," Matthew retorted, after looking at Frank for an okay. It happened the Army had a barracks stove in storage and the deal was made. Matthew's belt gained some weight and substance again. He was relieved to get anything from the man.

They gathered the men, Benson Greene, Stewberries, Happy Jack, Bender, and Puckett and discussed the idea of building a big cabin to bunk in for the winter.

"We have the stove." Frank said. "Got it from the army, plus a bunch of supplies. We'll build the cabin and a store room, with a good stable and a corral for our mounts." The men, looking at a bleak alternative, readily assented, and they got the axes and crosscut saws out, Matthew buying what they needed, braces and bits and compasses, at exorbitant prices.

Happy Jack had been a carpenter and he directed the activity. They went out in the woods a ways from town, found a flat spot on a little rise and scratched out a large outline for the building, then started to work. Puckett found a stand of dead and dried lodgepole up one of the creeks and they began felling, limbing and hauling the logs out. Stewberries was the best with a team and he did the hauling, dragging the logs up to where the men were cutting the notches and rolling them up. In five days of grueling work, they had the walls up and had found a big long ridge pole to form the roof foundation. That in place, they slaved hard before another snowfall came, to cover the roof, using limbs and some wagon tarps they were able to get from the Army stores. The men built a jig to half—saw the logs and form a crude floor, which Happy Jack worked to get level. He wasn't completely successful, but the finished product, complete with a couple whiskey bottle windows and a strong door, looked pretty good to the cold men.

They set up the stove in the middle of the floor and erected the chimney, then stoked it up. Happy made some bunks along the walls and the men lined them with pine boughs and covered them with canvas. Throwing some buffalo robes on them, they declared themselves moved in.

The storeroom was a one day affair, complete with a heavy door. They waited for a blizzard to subside, then worked to build a stable close in. Matthew had gotten the Army to add some horse hay to the payoff and they made several trips with a sled, pulling it over and stacking it by the stable. They were set, it looked like, for the winter. Happy topped his efforts off with some pretty comfortable chairs, strung with buffalo hide, that the men again threw robes on. Those, and a couple tables close to the stove, made it a comfortable quarters.

Matthew was happy. He'd felt some responsibility for the men, them being there, facing a winter in the mountains, and he'd wanted them to have a haven. Now they did.

The problem now became boredom. Matthew went into town and to church, as did some of the others, like Greene and Happy Jack. Frank, never a church goer, was at loose ends. He took care of the horses. He braided some hackamores and halters. He worked on their leather equipment. He was a hands-on man, and not a deep thinker. He had to keep busy, or drink, and somehow, with Matthew's help, he managed to keep away from the saloons. The others, though, frequented them, especially Puckett, who was always after Frank, his friend, to come in with him and down a few and play a few hands. It was hard, but he resisted, with Matthew's help. He and Happy made some better windows, finding and buying window glass and making the sashes themselves. They planed the floor, working the wood down and taking some care with it. They made some more furniture, some wall cabinets for dishes, and a scrub basin, to wash up. Puckett derided their work, saying that next, they would be puttin' up curtains.

Somehow, the winter passed. Matthew, knowing Frank couldn't read, got in the habit of bringing books and other reading materials back to the cabin and reading them to him, Frank using the excuse his eyes were bad, from a spate of snow blindness he'd gotten during their work. Some of the others couldn't read, either, and nothing was said. But all listened when Matthew, in his quiet, but strong voice, read to them, the men whittling, working leather or lying on their bunks.

When Brother Van came to Bozeman, travelling in the dead of winter from Mission Valley, Matthew prevailed upon Frank and some of the others to come with him to church, for the man was a noted speaker and gave an excellent sermon.

Frank enjoyed himself and Brother Van, an old frontiersman, made the men feel at home. The singing was good and the potluck after was tasty, so Matthew got them to come to church several times thereafter. He particularly enjoyed it, as the ritual gave him some peace from his thoughts of the war.

Puckett had been doing a lot of gambling and was starting to run with a rougher crowd, if one could differentiate between the men in the rough camp. These men, though, were ones who seemed to have no means of making a living. Several times, he had asked either Frank or Matthew for money and it was hard to tell an old comrade 'no.' Usually, he got it.

He came to the cabin on an afternoon when Frank and Stewberries had gone hunting and the others had gone to Fort Ellis, to the sawmill there to buy some lumber to make a big sled to pull in firewood.

The weather was calm and fairly warm, though not thawing. When he came through the door and up to the stove, which was throwing out some good heat, he warmed his hands and glanced at Matthew, who was sitting in a comfortable chair reading, the big dog they had named 'Bear' lying by his feet.

Puckett, half drunk, ever disdainful of educated men, thought probably it was the Bible.

"Where's the boys, Matthew?"

Matthew looked up from his book, one of Shakespeare's plays that he'd borrowed from the Fort library.

"Hmmmm? Oh. Well, Frank and Stew are off hunting and the others went over to Fort Ellis to get some lumber from the mill." He turned a page. "They have it in mind to build a big sled and pull down some firewood to sell around town. Happy Jack says he can build a good one. He's made one before."

Puckett hesitated. He reached a conclusion in his mind and said, "I saw a man you been lookin' for —Siderus? He's down at the Full House, playin' cards."

Matthew came out of his chair. "You say he's at the Full House Saloon?"

"I heard a man there call him that. This man's black haired, wearing a mustache. Couldn't see that he was armed, though. He was doin' pretty well at the table when I was watching 'em." He went to his bunk and dug around there, looking for something. Matthew strode to his own bunk, threw off his money belt, which would weigh him down, and wrapped his gun belt around his waist. He pulled his pistol from its scabbard and checked the loads carefully, then holstered it again.

"You goin' down after him?'

"I am."

Puckett acted indecisive.

"You want me to come along?"

"It's my fight, Lee. Thanks just the same."

Puckett still acted dubious.

"Well. . . "

Matthew put his coat on and went out the door. He saddled Stonewall and rode the half mile to town. At the front of the bar, he dismounted and took his coat off, tied it on the back of his saddle. Then he adjusted his gun belt and walked in the saloon, the usual bar smog enveloping him.

He strode to the back where a card game was in progress.

Six players were seated around a table there—a couple drummers he knew slightly, one a firearms rep for Colt, the other a hardware salesman. Two, by their clothes, were miners. There was an older man he'd seen before, a hunter. And Siderus.

It was an older version of the man, gray around the temples, heavily mustached, with a dissipated sag to his face. He glanced up from his cards as Matthew approached and his face blanched. The others, sensing something, looked up also.

"Hello...Grounds...", the man, in his fear, stuttered a little, then fell silent. Matthew stood there, solid, his anger a tangible thing.

"You stole my horses and gear during the war, when I was captured at Petersburg. Then, you Sonovabitch, you killed Spur in Dodge, to keep him from telling me he'd seen you."

He was so mad, his voice was hoarse. "Come outside... now!"

"I'm not... I don't have a gun on me, Grounds!"

"Get one. I'm callin' you. . . ." He flung himself sideways as he saw Siderus's arm go under the table. A shot blasted and the bullet whipped by Matthew as he drew and fired twice. Siderus slumped, then slipped from his chair, a pistol clattering to the floor. Matthew kept his pistol out. He remembered that the girl had mentioned a friend. He turned to the bar as a scuffle broke out. 'Pan' Skillett and Tom Healey, another of Story's cowboys who'd known both Frank and Matthew back in Texas, had hold of a stranger, a red bearded individual wearing a long buffalo coat. A small revolver lay on the bar.

"He was fixin' to backshoot you, Matthew!" Healey said.

"Pan and me grabbed him and got his gun away." The man broke free from them. "You bastard! You shot my kin!"

"Who was Siderus to you? What's your name?" Matthew asked, holstering his weapon.

"My cousin. My name's Jim Carter. From Atlanta." the man replied sullenly. "Who're you?"

"Matthew Grounds. When I became a prisoner at Petersburg, Siderus took my horses and gear. Then he shot my man, Spur, at Dodge City, to keep him from telling me he'd seen him on the street. Now, do you want to take up his quarrel with me—face to face, right now?" The man thought an instant, then the fight went out of him.

"I guess not. He's dead now. I'm claiming his outfit, though."

"You didn't hear me. I said he stole my gear at Petersburg. Whatever he has will make up for that, maybe."

"Well. . . he owed me some money! "

"How much?"

"Well. . . a hundred dollars." The man stated it with a bravado that all who heard knew to be false. Healey emptied his pistol of its loads.

Matthew looked around the silent room. He raised his voice.

"I want it known that this man, Siderus, stole two horses and all my gear after I was captured at Petersburg. Then at Dodge, my servant, Spur, ran into him on the street, and I believe Siderus killed him to keep him from telling me that the sonovabitch was there in town." He gestured back at the body lying on the floor.

"He shot first, after lying about not being armed. I killed him and I'm claiming whatever he had here in town." He looked at the table and continued. "Including his poker hand and the money he had on the table."

He walked back and rolled the body aside with an ungentle foot, sat down and examined the cards the dead man had been holding. In front of him was a stack of money—three piles of double eagles and five dollar pieces, with a couple spilled piles of silver dollars.

"Gentlemen, what's the bid?"

The hunter, 'Stumblin" John Jacobs, spoke up. "'Fore the game was <u>interrupted</u>, Siderus was just calling. So I b'lieve the pot's light $30. An' you have cards comin' if'n you want 'em."

Matthew looked at the cards again and threw in an eagle and two five dollar pieces, from those on the table. The hardware salesman threw his cards in, as did the two others. It was between the Colt drummer and Matthew. The salesman called for cards and the hunter dealt him one. he looked at Matthew, questioningly.

"I'll play these." The salesman, a florid faced man who'd evidently seen much through small, piglike eyes, said, "I'll bid $10.00"

Matthew said, "I'll call that and raise $40.00"

The Colt man perused his cards, then threw them in, conceding the pot.

Matthew threw his cards in and raked the pot, then pocketed the money, saying, "Gentlemen, have a good evening. The drinks are on. . . Siderus."

He got up and went back to the bar and plopped $100 on the wood in front of Carter.

"Here. I don't believe the man owed it to you, but I'll pay the debt on your say-so. Now, here's my advice. Leave the country. I believe that you helped your cousin after he killed

Spur. You tried to back-shoot me. If I ever see you again, I am going to call you out."

The man looked into Matthew's eyes and grimaced sickly. Taking the money and the empty pistol, he turned and left the bar. The others crowded the bar and the barkeep obligingly set them up.

Jacobs turned the body over and went through the pockets in its clothes. He brought it up to the bar and dumped it in front of Matthew, a Remington .41 derringer, a wallet and a knife.

"Here's what he had on 'im, Matthew. Did you want his boots? Looks like they might fit me and I'm needin' a new pair." He raised his worn foot wear so Matthew could see their condition and Matthew nodded his okay.

"Good shootin', by the way. I thought he might have got you when he shot through the table like that. You hit 'im dead center." He grinned through jagged teeth.

Chapter 30

When Matthew approached the cabin, he saw that there was no smoke coming forth, which he thought was strange, because he'd left Puckett there. He unsaddled and turned Stonewall out, forking a little hay to them before he went in.

The cabin was dark and cold and he lit a lantern, then stirred some coals and adding a few slivers of kindling, got the fire going again. Bear whined at the door and he let him out, then thought of his money belt. He was a little upset with Puckett leaving. He'd left the belt because he'd thought that Lee would stay and thus it would be safe. He went to his bunk. The belt wasn't there. Alarmed, he searched around the bunk, then looked over the cabin. He must have decided to leave and hidden it before he'd gone, to keep it secure. Where could he have hidden it? Then he noticed that Puckett's bedroll was gone and all his stuff. He went back out and checked the stable. Puckett had gone, alright, and his other horse was missing, too. Could he have taken the belt? It contained nearly seven thousand dollars. Maybe he had intended to borrow some and seen just how much was there, and temptation had set in.

The realization that Puckett, a man they'd fought beside, could have turned out to be a thief, struck hard. The thought sickened him. He sat on his bunk and the lantern burned low. Bear whined, hungry. Finally, Matthew hunted him up a chunk of cold meat, which the dog devoured. About then, the door went back and Frank and Stew came in, blowing and headed for the stove.

"Brrr. Gettin' cold again out there. Below zero tonight, I s'pect. How's the Deacon?" Frank jibed. He'd started calling Matthew the "Deacon" because of his consistent church going. "Where's the boys?"

"Happy and Greene went to the sawmill to get some timbers to build their sled. I'm not sure about Puckett—yet."Something in his tone made Frank turn. He knew his partner and there was something wrong. "What's up?"

"Well. . . .I'm not certain." Questioned by Frank and Stewberries, he finally told them what he knew.

"Jesus, Pard! You went down and braced Siderus without me?" He sat down at the table and looked as if he needed a drink. "He's dead, huh? Yeah, he would be. So much for callin' you "Deacon." And the money—you surely don't think Lee took it? Hell, after all we bin through with him?"

The thought made him cringe, thinking of a friend's betrayal. Stewberries started getting supper and about that time, the others came in, all looked hard at Matthew, then tried equally hard to act as if nothing was wrong. Evidently, they'd already heard what had gone on downtown.

Presently, Bender asked where Puckett had gotten off to. Stewberries muttered, "We think maybe he took off with Matthew's money belt."

"What?? The Hell you say!! Why that sonuvabitch!! He owed me some money, too!!"

All the men but Greene grumbled at the news. Puckett had hit them all up for drinking and gambling money and they, like good friends, had loaned him their money freely. But to steal it!!

Greene, his best friend, stuck up for him.

"Aw, boys, Lee maybe just hid it here in the cabin when he left, because he didn't want to leave it lyin' around." With that, they all gave the cabin another once-over. No use. They found nothing. That and the fact that his bedroll and gear were gone, finally forced them to the conclusion Matthew had reached before. Puckett had turned thief. Matthew was drained from the day's events and hit his bunk early after the meal, leaving the men up to cuss and discuss the thing.

Next morning, after coffee and a little breakfast, Matthew motioned to Frank and they walked out to the stable.

Matthew opened the topic both had dreaded visiting about.

"Puckett about cleaned us out, Frank. There was 6,900 dollars in my belt." He choked up, thinking about what he'd done, losing not only his money, but Frank's as well.

"I blame myself. I lost my temper and took out when he told me about Siderus being downtown. I left it on the bunk because I knew I'd have to move fast and the belt was heavy. He must have seen it there and checked it out. And there was just too much for him to pass on it."

Frank was cool. "I see it different, Pard. Don't matter what there was in it. Five dollars or fifty thousand—he's still a damn thief. He stole from men who fought with him and for his worthless hide. I don't know what I saw in that damn skunk. Other men knew he was no good. You, for one. I knew you were never too high on him."

He bit off a chew and worked it around a little, then said, "Oh, hell, his time will come. In the meanwhile, we'll get along. We got our gear and the horses. We got this cabin. Sum'thin will come up this spring." He put his hand on Matthew's shoulder. "Don't fret about it, you know that with me, it's easy come, easy go."

Matthew said, "I did count what I took off Siderus. $485."

"Great! It'll get us by until spring."

Chapter 31

Spring came quickly. The middle of April, the mountain country was in full greenery. Happy Jack put his carpentry skills to work downtown, helping build a new bank for a group of investors. Benson Greene found a job with Waddell and Burns, driving stage between Bannack, Virginia City and Bozeman. "Wrong Wheel" Bender got a job at the saw mill, and being on the outs with Stewberries for some reason that Stewberries didn't know, moved out of the cabin the men had come to call "The Mansion on the Hill." That left two open bunks and Frank found a couple pilgrims to rent them to, for enough money to buy groceries, though flour and coffee were at a premium. Still, they got by, with the hunting bringing in meat all the time. Meat was bringing 25 cents a pound downtown.

In May, Matthew was restless and told Frank he had a yen to go to Alder Gulch, and around to the rest of the diggings, just to see them and find out what the opportunities were. Frank knew the truth of it but felt the same. *Puckett*!! They left the cabin in charge of Stewberries, who was cooking at a restaurant downtown. They saddled their horses and threw packs on the other ones, and headed west.

Travel between the camps was picking up, with people on the move. Indians, too, were on the trail. Sheridan, in the Pahsamoria Valley, or, as the white men called it, the Ruby, was a going mining camp, with the Wisconsin Mine, the Red Pine and others up all the little creeks being worked at a frenzied pace. Farther on, they hit Nevada City, another claim camp, with mining going on all over the surrounding hills of the Tobacco Roots and along the Ruby River. The setting was idyllic but the good claims were long taken up.

There was no sign of Puckett in the camps, though they searched each one. Virginia City, set back in the hills and higher in elevation at the head of Alder gulch, was a beehive of activity. They camped up on the ridge east above the town, close by the already occupied cemetery. As darkness fell, they walked to the edge of the hill and watched and listened as the camp tuned up, the hollering, screeching and pistol shots ripping the fabric of the hills' silence. Bear sat with them and showed some interest, his ears perked at the noise below.

"Damn!! She's quite a hummer!" Frank said, sitting down carefully to make sure there was no cactus. "Time was, I wouldn't be able to sit here and listen to all that goin' on without bein' right there in the middle of it."

Matthew, smoking a last cigar that they had gotten at Sheridan when they'd gone through that camp, said pensively,

"I guess I don't have the desire any more to 'see the elephant' or hear the wolf howl." He flicked the ash. "That all left me after my wife died—it seems a hundred years ago, before the war."

Frank was silent. In all their time together, Matthew had never mentioned that he'd lost a wife, that he'd even been married.

"What was her name, Pard?" he asked tentatively, trying to draw him out a little.

Matthew was silent for a time, and Frank thought maybe he wasn't going to answer. Then he sighed. "Her name was Melissa. She was a beautiful girl—still is, in my memory. She died of fever there at Pendemere. We'd only been married a few months. When she. . . I thought life was over for me. I think it was. What we've been through, Frank, the war, the Rangers, the Indians and all, it doesn't have much taste to it, really."

Frank was silent in his turn. "Well, Pard, you do have a couple pretty good friends—Old Bear here and me."

He patted the big dog's head. Matthew drew a long puff. "Yes, I do. I realized that the day down in Texas when you walked out of the office. I couldn't let you go, too, Frank. We've been through too much together to just walk away from one another." He drew another strong puff, let it out. "I guess that's why I was so upset when Puckett did that to us. A man shouldn't do things like that to his friends. We trusted him. . . and he let us down."

They sat on the hill and smoked a while longer, the noise from below, if anything, increasing, then hit their bedrolls.

* * *

They went on north to Bannock and that camp was like the others: a busy, crawling, repelling hive of people, all after the yellow metal, to the exclusion of most all else. Puckett wasn't there.

The Ruby Valley drew them back and they finished the summer teamstering for Cox and Cobb, a long haul outfit freighting between Salt Lake and the camps. Wherever they went, they looked for Puckett, but since now time had passed, they'd lost hope that he might still have any money on him, if they did find him. He was a boozer and a gambler. It would have left him like Fall leaves being blown from a tree.

With their winter's stake assured, they headed back to Bozeman to bunk in at their "Mansion on the Hill," hoping that Stewberries had been able to keep the place going while they been gone.

Bozeman seemed bigger, more town-like, not just a mining camp any longer. They rode on through, waving occasionally to men they knew, and on up to the cabin. It seemed like they were coming home. It had smoke coming from the chimney. Stewberries must have sensed they were coming, for he met them at the door with an apron on, then, after the howdies, went on down with them to the stable. They unsaddled and hobbled their horses, then staked them out to graze, with long halter ropes on. Going back to the cabin, Stew treated them to fresh baked bread and hot coffee. The place, as they looked around, was tidy and neat. Happy had built a couple more bunks in the far end, and they were all, with the exception of Frank and Matthew's, occupied. Stew and Happy had done a good job of keeping it up.

Stew poured another cup of coffee, then said, "You didn't hear, I guess, about ol' Wrong Wheel?"

"What about 'im" Frank asked."Well, a big damn log rolled on 'im over at the saw mill. Kilt him deader'n a bug."

"Why, that's a damn shame!" Frank said. They discussed Bender for a time and his fine burial.

Then Frank asked,"How's the others?"

"Well, Benson's doin' okay. Saw him at the restaurant one night. He mentioned it was about time for you men to show up. He'd like to bunk in with us again this winter, if it's okay with you." He got up to cut some more bread.

Matthew said, "I think that'd be fine. I like his company. How's Happy?"

"Oh, he's doin' good. Working hard and saving his money. They're putting up a new store, Lamson and Sons. Big general merchandise outfit. He wants to go back east, maybe next year, before snow flies."

He hesitated, then asked,"Did you ever meet up with Lee?"

"Nope. We never did. Went around to about every camp. Some of 'em, Stew, like Virginia City, are hell roarers, let me tell you." Frank said.

"What's this I bin hearin' about a lot of miners and others with rich pokes gettin' murdered over in that country? Sounds like California in the fifties, around San Francisco and Sacremento, when they had a big gang of cutthroats working the gold fields."

"That could be, alright. We did hear of it happenin' but never saw any ourselves, though we did see some pretty hard sights."

That late fall, the men worked at hauling firewood with the big sled Happy had built, and hunting. That, plus the rent paid by those men using the cabin, got them through most of the winter.

282

Chapter 32

The first part of January was open, and travel resumed between camps. One of the riders on the trail was Puckett. He knew it wasn't smart. He was toying with his life, going back to Bozeman. But he had his orders and it was certain death not to obey them. He thought, too, that this ride was punishment for the careless way he tackled his last job. He'd been drunk at the time, the young miner had been a camp favorite.

It might have gone off okay, if he'd hidden the body more carefully, but in his drunken state, he'd just heaved it over the bank of the river and it was found the next week. What was worse, the boy was a favorite of Plummer's and he'd been expressly ordered to leave him alone. But he'd been out of funds, as usual, and the kid had foolishly shown his fat poke at the bar that night. Puckett had seen it and gone out the back way, following him later back to his camp. Not wanting to wake another group of miners lying at their camp nearby, he decided he'd better do it quietly. He'd jumped him just as he was getting in his blankets and stabbed him with his Bowie. Unfortunately, he'd missed the heart and the boy had struggled for his life. Oh, yes, he'd put up a hell of a fight, even with his wound, but

Puckett had prevailed, finally slipping his knife deep in his vitals. That was the end.

The youngster's poke was full, as he'd thought, but Plummer, giving him hell later, was furious. Not that he was scared of Plummer, the sneaky bastard, but Boone Helm, Gallagher, Whiskey Bill and all the others made up too much of an overwhelming force for one man to go against. No, it was death to deny them. He wished now that he'd never got in with them. Taking the dispatch to the owner of the Arcade was his punishment, but if he was careful, it should go off alright. First of all, he'd enter the town at night and leave at night—deliver the message, get a bottle, then ride out again. He'd stashed a fresh horse at Three Forks. He had some jerky along and he'd make do with that. He never needed much food, just the whiskey. He just wished he had his little Texas pony, Jigger, under him. But this one would have to do. The other had gone in a poker game, along with much of the money in the belt he'd gotten from Grounds.

He'd really thought that matter would probably go his way. He'd seen Siderus and his pard at the saloon and thought that Grounds most likely would go down in a cross fire. If that happened, the matter of the money belt would have died with him, being as all the saloon vultures were always around. But it hadn't happened that way, worse luck. Grounds had downed Siderus, and Carter had not gotten a shot off. Skillett and Healey, damn them, had seen to that. Carter'd told him that Grounds was smooth and fast. He knew that. There was no doubt Grounds was damn good with a pistol—but <u>he</u> was, too, if it came to that. Ahead of him, the lights of the town showed up on the horizon, against the lowering sky. He spurred his bay on.

Frank was bored. He'd had a belly full of the same conversation with the boys and Matthew had run out of books to read him, except that damn Shakespeare, with all the 'thou's and thee's'. He just didn't find it that interesting. What he really wanted was a drink, several of them, but Matthew, in his obstinacy, wouldn't come down with him. He decided he'd go down anyway, and drink a cup of coffee with Stew, in the back of the kitchen. Stew was working nights again this month, so coffee with him would have to do.

But talking with him while he was working was hard. The kitchen was crowded and Stew was always having to bustle around. So he got his cup and sat back by the door. He'd finally decided to leave and happened to look out the door as he was washing his cup. A figure came riding by and it looked familiar. He ducked back, then watched it as it stopped back of the Arcade, dismounted and went in, after hammering on the door for a while. Frank slipped out and edged along the shadows until he found a place where he could watch when the man came out. After a few minutes, here he came. Damn!! It was Puckett, sure enough.

Wary as a coyote, the man looked around, then headed back down the alley, right past him. Frank, deep in the shadows, didn't move or make a sound. He waited until Puckett was almost out of view, then followed him. He headed west, out of town.

Frank sprinted back to the restaurant, then decided he'd better get a good horse, not the nag that Stew was riding to work. He tightened the cinch on it and headed up to the cabin.

At the stable, he dismounted and got the horse unsaddled and turned out. Stew would have to walk home tonight. He whistled up Stonewall, imitating Matthew's call. The horse came right to him and he slipped the bridle over his head.

Working fast in the dark, he quickly saddled him and was leading the animal out the of the stable when he heard the ominous click of a hammer coming back.

He said quickly, "Matthew, is that you?" The hammer eased back and Frank sighed his relief. It wasn't his time to get shot for a horse thief tonight.

"What the hell is going on?" Matthew asked, coming up to him. "I go out for a piss and hear a whistle, then find you easing Stonewall out of the stable. Where you goin' this time of the night? On Stonewall?"

"Matthew, I saw Puckett. He came into town, delivered something—a message, maybe, to the Arcade, then came back out and headed. . . " Frank was talking to thin air.

Matthew had gone in and taken down a bridle from its hook, then walked out into the little horse pasture. In a short time, he was saddling Frank's horse, Spades. Together, they went on up to the cabin and going in, took down their Henry rifles from their pegs, along with ammo, filling their pockets. The others, playing cards at the table, watched with their mouths open as the two men made their preparations.

"What the hell's goin' on, Frank?" Happy asked.

"Spotted Puckett. We're goin' after him." He grated. The men nodded. "Give 'im a bullet for me!" Greene, his estwhile friend said. The men picked up their cards. In their minds, Puckett was a dead man.

The two rode west. A half hour passed, the men in an easy, ground eating lope, the horses getting warmed up.

"You were goin' after him alone, <u>Pard</u>?" Matthew finally said. Frank could tell he was still mad.

"Yup. I admit it. I was goin' to get 'im. I was afraid I'd lose him if I took the time to come get you. We still might. Probably will. He's got a good start. Only thing is, he may not have had a fresh horse. Couldn't see real well, but it looked like it'd been running." Frank admitted.

"Well, Pard, if I hadn't caught you, I'd be damn mad at you. I am right now, but I can excuse the hurry, I guess. He most likely has a horse stashed somewhere along the way. He wanted to get in and get out, quick, the way it sounds. Now, what I want you to do, is trade horses with me and spur up, get on him hard. I'll follow and take him up after you've run him for a while. Don't kill Spades doin' it. Drop back when you have to. I'll go past and take him. I don't want any argument." he grated, beating down Frank's protest.

"He's my meat, Frank. If he gets me, you take him."

They pulled up and changed horses. Frank put the spurs to Spades and the horse, willing and a goer, jumped forward into a run.

A mile, two miles, then Frank, coming over a rise, saw in the waning moonlight, a rider ahead of him. The man was loping his horse easily. He urged Spades on, the horse working but still breathing well. Frank, back in Oklahoma City, had chosen the horse for its bottom and he was determined to beat Matthew to the bastard. It all depended on how Puckett was mounted. And that worried him. That Jigger horse of Puckett's was a damn good one, a swift and athletic horse, with plenty of bottom. The only thing was, how many miles had it gone already?

He was within a quarter mile when the rider ahead looked back, having heard something, maybe. Frank cursed his luck. He was skylighted on another rise and Puckett couldn't help but see him. He did. The pace quickened. Frank kept Spades to a steady gallop, not pushing, a ground eating run. At first, he was gaining, then Puckett pulled away and maintained the pace for a couple miles. They were coming up on the three forks. He looked back. He couldn't see Matthew, but he knew he was back there. It was now or never. He put the spurs to Spades and whipped him with the reins. The horse, willing, gave forth a burst of speed. The distance perceptibly shortened between the two riders. Spades was running hard.

With only several hundred yards separating them, Puckett disappeared from view, hidden by some alders along the river's edge. Spades leaped down the bank and Frank came upon a blown horse, head down, its sides heaving. It wasn't Jigger! Where was Puckett?

Frank pulled his gun, thinking that he'd ridden into an ambush. Then he heard hooves drumming away on the other side of the alder thicket. Damn! Matthew was right. Puckett had stashed a horse along his route. Probably Jigger. A fresh horse. He was going to get away, after all.

When Matthew came up, minutes later, Frank had the saddles off both horses and was rubbing them down.

"He took off that way, Pard!! He's got a fresh horse, just like you thought! Probably Jigger." Matthew didn't pause. He spurred Stonewall around the thicket and took up the chase.

Up on the flat, the sun was coming up. Ahead, over a mile away, Matthew saw Puckett. He was riding bareback, running his horse toward the foothills. Matthew cursed himself for not taking another horse with him. But looking down, he felt a little assured. Stonewall was still running strong, seemingly fresh yet. The horse was a good one, maybe great, and in its prime yet. It had never been tested. Matthew had no idea just how much heart it had. He did know it wasn't as fast as Palukan. That was a horse in ten thousand. What was this horse? Today would tell. He set a steady pace that the animal under him fell into naturally. He wasn't gaining, but he wasn't dropping behind, either. An hour passed. Amazingly, Stonewall seemed to be gaining strength, getting his second wind. Matthew subtly urged him on a little faster. The distance began to shorten.

Puckett looked back and cursed. '*If he'd been on Jigger. . . .*'

This horse just didn't have the bottom for a long race. But it was fresh. There was that much. The other's had been running since Bozeman, long miles back. Soon, it had to fade. It would fade. No horse could run that long and keep its feet. Unconsciously, he began to use his spurs.

Slowly, surely, Stonewall crept up on the horse and rider laboring in front of them. An hour went by and the distance was long rifle range. On the horizon, the sun was full up. A hundred yards, then another two hundred yards, and Matthew pulled his Henry from its scabbard. He levered a shell and threw it to his shoulder. The rifle went off over his horse's head. Stonewall didn't flinch, kept the rolling, pounding rhythm of its hooves steady. Matthew levered another shell in and strained to center his sights on the rider in front of him. He fired. Suddenly, the horse ahead stumbled, then rolled, nearly turning a summersault, flinging its rider away. Matthew pounded up, then made a flying dismount as Puckett, that wiry snake, came up off the ground. The two men paused for an instant, facing each other. Then their hands went down, Matthew's blurring as he brought his gun up and fired, all in one motion. Puckett, caught with his weapon coming up, was arrested in his draw by a powerful center blow. He fought to bring his gun up, then an eye blanked as Matthew fired again, throwing his head back. He went back and down, his pistol falling from a lifeless hand. It was over.

* * *

Puckett's horse was still kicking, shot in the spine. He went to it and put it down with a shot behind the ear. It lay back with a sigh that reminded him of Palukan. This horse hadn't the speed, the heart or the endurance, but it had given its all, just the same. He thought of the countless thousands of horses that had been sacrificed during the war —for what? They were dumb animals, loyal to men, who never deserved their fate. . . But then, who did? What had driven Puckett to throw away the ties and values he had all his life, to end up here? Life was a mystery he couldn't unravel.

He sat on the horse's rump and hunted in his pockets for a cigar, then lit up. He needed to get a smudge fire going to signal Frank, let him know that he should come on. But let it wait a while. He was feeling the strain now. He went over to Stonewall and loosened the saddle, patted that great horse, then hugged it, surprised at his emotion. It nickered and nuzzled him. He wished he had an apple or something for it. Was it hurting? He looked it over, felt of its legs, finally dropped the saddle off and rubbed it down with the wet blanket, just to make the animal feel like he was doing something for it. It seemed fine. He looked up and saw the sun well up on the horizon, a few clouds scudding across the sky. Wind up there, he thought. But not down here. It was calm and growing warmer. Still, he shivered a little.

* * *

Frank came up some time later, the smudge fire still smoking a little, but its embers putting out some good heat. Matthew was standing by it, warming himself. The horses were walking slowly, head down, spent. Looking at them though, Matthew thought that maybe their wind wasn't broken, that they'd be all right. They would stay here the night. He'd walked a little way into the willows and shot some sharptails with his pistol. He'd brought them back to the fire, where he'd plucked and gutted them. They were roasting on the coals and about ready to eat. There was water in the river nearby. They could keep a measure of warmth under the saddle blankets and by hugging the fire. But they had no coffee, which both greatly missed.

Chapter 33

The curious citizens of Bozeman saw something out of the ordinary come down the street—two men on very tired horses leading another worn horse carrying a body. The two, Frank Shannon and Matthew Grounds, rode on through town and out to Fort Ellis. There, they were admitted into the Commandant's office and got to speak with Colonel Gibbon. Matthew explained what had happened. Since Montana Territory was a military district administered by the U.S. Army, it fell on Gibbon's shoulders to dispense law and order, something he was loath to bother with, having enough on his plate with the Indian troubles. But the nearest civil law was at Salt Lake City and it was not able to deal with the lawlessness of the gold camps.

He gave out with a grunt, easing his butt on the hard chair
"Have your witness come in and give me depositions as to this man's thievery. Give yours to the clerk out there. As far as I can tell, he got what he deserved. Hmmm. . . Grounds . . . aren't you the man who shot and killed a gambler down town last fall?"

"Yes sir. That was thievery, too. And he had killed a friend of mine in Dodge City. Frank here can attest to that."

Frank nodded his head.

"Doubtless, doubtless he could." He looked at Matthew, then Frank, and made up his mind.

"Well, give your depositions. If I hear differently about either of the matters, I will have to issue a warrant and send you and the matter down to the authorities at Salt Lake. Otherwise, you are free to go." He got up and shook hands with them, a busy man.

As they headed back to town, Frank asked, "What about the body, pard?"

"We'll take it down to the undertaker, I guess."

It cost them forty dollars to see to the burial. However, Frank had found more than that on the body, so the horse, saddle and weapons they'd found—another Colt .44 in a saddle holster behind the cantle, and a Henry rifle—gave them some slight return on their lost funds.

"What about the note? You goin' to do somethin' with it?" Frank had found a note on the body. Opened, it read,

HP
C & C moving merchandise next wed.

Taking the low road.

K.

"What do you s'pose it means?"

"Off-hand, I'd guess it sounds like Cox and Cobb may be shipping a load of dust out next week and somebody wanted to know about it. I'm not sure what the low road means. Let's take it over to the office and let Major Cox look at it."

Cox and Cobb had freight offices on the corner of Wilson and Rouse. They were one of the major freight companies servicing the gold camps of Montana and Idaho. Major Cox was the manager on this end of the line and Cobb, his partner, was at Salt Lake. Cox was a large man of imposing stature, somewhat pompous, but when in good humor, very genial. He was also very shrewd.

Frank and Matthew were escorted into his office by a clerk. Frank turned and shut the door in the surprised man's face, making Cox, seated at his desk, raise his eyebrows.

"I take it you gentlemen don't just have freight to consign or want to hit me up for another job?" he asked, looking at them. They showed the effects of their recent hard run, their faces stubbled with whiskers. Matthew particularly, with his puckered face, looked hard and fierce. Cox knew these men already and his judgment was that they were not to be treated lightly.

Matthew handed him the note. Cox put a pair of spectacles on and read it, then looked up.

"Hmmm. Where did you get this?"

Frank spoke up. "Off Lee Puckett's dead body. Him not objecting at the time."

"Just who is Lee Puckett?"

Matthew explained. Cox sat a while in thought.

"Well, gentlemen, I want to tell you that I certainly am appreciative of your letting me have this. <u>Very</u> appreciative! And if I can ever do anything to repay you, just let me know. Yes sir. Just let me know! Jobs or anything."

They left without learning what the implications of the note might be, but satisfied that it had perhaps done some good.

* * *

In February, a man named Vernon came into Bozeman and got the miners all stirred up with talk of finding gold at the head of a creek down east. He showed some impressive gold dust and nuggets. Those knowledgeable miners who saw it, before the man spent it, said it hadn't come from any of the mines or claims they knew around the fields of that country. (gold has its own signature and can be identified by mine and the area it came from) The thought of a new camp, new claims and new country made the restless men's mouths water. The fact that it was in the middle of Indian country made little difference to them.

Red Cloud, by his relentless pressure on the Bozeman Trail, had finally forced the government to close its little forts, Reno, C.F. Smith and Fort Kearny. As soon is the soldiers had marched away, smoke began coming up from the stockades as his braves came in, looted and burned them. The Trail was closed and the only way to get supplies to the camps was by Fort Benton on the Missouri, then overland, or Salt Lake, up through the mountains. Both ways made supplies exorbitant. A new route from the east was essential to the camps survival and it made sense to go down the Yellowstone to the head of navigation there.

So an idea was born to push an expedition from Bozeman in the spring to check out Vernon's assertions and at the same time, to scout out a route for wagon travel along the Yellowstone. Since the Bozeman Trail was closed, some of the leaders talked Waddell and Burns out of their cannon, complete with some canister and round shot. All the men wanted in, to be among the first to stake out a new field. Swiftly, a formidable force built up to make the incursion into Sioux country. Fully a hundred and fifty men signed up, most war veterans who'd smelled powder many times before. Many who had fought Indians all their lives. They called their venture "The Yellowstone Wagon Road and Prospecting Expedition."

Then, the men were in a quandary as to who they should elect as their captain. They needed someone of great ability to take on such a job, someone who knew tactics and men, someone the men would respect and listen to, without arguing every order. They looked for a leader.

Chapter 34

Two days after the incident with Puckett, Frank was approached by Otis Koontz and young 'Doc' Wickershamm as he was going into the Weir Mercantile.
"Say, Mr. Shannon, do you have some time to talk with us?" Koontz rumbled. He was part-owner of the Dancing Lady Mine up Beaver Creek, a tall, thin darkly whiskered man that reminded Frank of pictures he'd seen of Lincoln. His features were craggy and cadaverous, and he had standout ears that looked like little wings under his hat. Unlike what he'd heard of the President, though, he had a deep, bell-like voice.

Frank turned from the door.

"Sure, what's up?"

The pharmacist, an educated young prig who Frank thought held himself above the rest of the populace because of his education, said, "We heard about you and your partner, Grounds, running down a robber last week, and Grounds killing him. Is it true you men were once Texas Rangers?"

"Wal, I'm not in the habit of blabbing our history around on every street corner, Doc. But to answer your question—yes, we was in the Rangers. Why?"

The chemist, whom they called 'Doc' in somewhat mocking allusion to his inflated demeanor, was set back a little, but went on bravely.

"We—that is—a group of us, including myself and Otis here, are interested in getting our expedition down to the Yellowstone started this spring. But the sticker is we haven't been able to find or agree on a leader."

"Wal. . . "Frank was prepared to be flattered about being asked when his own ego was deflated a little.

"What we were thinking, Shannon, was asking Grounds if he'd take it on. "Koontz interjected. "We knew how close you and he were and thought we'd approach you and find out if you could talk him into it?"

"Hrummph. Wal, I can't talk for my partner, and I sure don't try to do any persuadin' on him. I can tell you he operates best if you just come out straight at him and ask."

"Do you think he'd be interested? We need a man like him—an army officer, used to commanding men, and a Texas Ranger, a man who can handle himself, if it come to it. Not that we would overlook you, Shannon. If he'd take it on, we'd like you to function as his second in command. You two are used to working in tandem. We understand that you were an army sergeant yourself, a veteran of many battles, and a Ranger. How about it? Would you be willing to take the job on?"

Frank's feathers were smoothed a little by that and he replied, looking hard at the two."That's a tall proposition. We'd be traveling through the heart of the Sioux nation. The lower Yellowstone is their country. They'll fight. . . .hard!"

"We've assembled a tough outfit, too, Shannon. You know most of them. Hunters and trappers, miners, ranchers from the Gallatin here, merchants. . . .most of them are veterans. Some, like yourself, have fought Indians many times. We even have a couple artillery pieces, a twelve pound howitzer from Fort Ellis, donated by Colonel Gibbon. And we've got Waddell's Big Horn gun, the twelve pound Napoleon. We've got a hundred rounds for them. The men who've signed up are determined to go. Most of them you know, are Confederates. They wouldn't have a Union man over them. We've talked it over and we settled on Grounds and you. We're prepared to offer you and him 'first selection.'

"First selection" meant that Matthew and he would have first choice of the claims in the new field, a caveat that could make them rich, if the field was a good one.

"I don't know if he's interested, but I'll ask him. And if he says 'Yes,' I'll throw in with him, too." Frank said. The two men insisted on shaking hands.

Matthew, when the question was put to him, said 'no' at first, not wanting to be responsible for others' lives again. His answer didn't surprise Frank. Frank didn't argue, but when Otis and 'Doc' came and talked with him, he surprisingly came around to it. They were at loose ends and if there was gold down there, they would be in on the strike, with the best claims. That was a powerful incentive.

PART VI

DOWN THE YELLOWSTONE

Photograph courtesy of Library of Congress

Chapter 35

The meeting was a roistering one, rowdy and loud, which made some sense, as it was held at the largest building in town, the Arcade Saloon. Matthew stepped forward, and the gathering, some half drunk, slowly quieted.

Matthew looked around the assemblage. Frank stood behind him, part of the crowd. "Men, Frank and I have been asked to lead the expedition. If that's your choice, too, let me know right now."

The clamor turned into a united voice of 'yes, yes!!"

"All right. If that's your vote, then we'll take it on. Now that's settled, I have some orders for you. First, weapons. Every man will have at least one rifle and a pistol. Preferably more than one. As much ammo as we can get. We may have to fight every day. Running out of ammo would be the death of us." Weir stepped forward. He and the merchants, with the extremely high costs of transportation of their goods, were committed to finding a better route to bring in their goods.

"I'll donate every bullet I got in my store."

Cross did the same. Those two merchants together made for a wagon load of ammunition of every make and size. That subject was quickly taken care of. "

Next, stock. No oxen. For speed's sake, it will have to be horses. Every man should have a mount or a place on a wagon.

No walkers. They'd slow us down too much. Food. Rations for a month. We don't know that we'll be gone that long but we just can't depend on hunting to get us through. Fighting will likely scare the game out of the area and we could be on short rations quick. Also, our stock is weak right now, from the winter. We'll need to start building them up. That means hay and grain. Those with the feed will have to share. Frank and I have some left and we'll throw that in. Those with grain, like you, Harper, will have to pitch in. We'll all need to pitch in." At that, several of the other merchants came forward with offers for the rations or feed.

"Next, you miners. We'll need shovels and picks to dig fighting holes and trenches." He smiled at the groans. No one liked to dig. Most still thought of the expedition as a lark and they didn't like the thought of being put to work.

"Now, I know you men want to make this trip and maybe come back to your claims or your summer work. No claims will be jumped while we're gone, on penalty of death. That will have to be posted and understood by the whole country.

We'll go in a couple weeks or so. We should be ready by then and the weather should have broken. A month or so, and we'll be back. If you obey orders and do your part, we should <u>all</u> make it back. To do it, we'll have to fight the way that Indians don't like, with volley fire, trenches, fighting holes and the artillery to back us up, when they crowd us. That's the way we figure it. If anyone doesn't like it, step forward now and say your piece." The men all looked around. No one stepped forward.

"Okay. Bill Cameron, I hear that you were an artillery captain. You're in charge of the guns. Round up some gunners who have experience for your gun teams. Practice them but be careful not to use too many rounds.

Wray, you were a division adjutant during the war. You just volunteered again. You and Wickershamm work on getting the supply and ammo lists straightened out. Make sure that every man has his rifle and pistol and has contributed enough food for the month. Also, we'll need to draw up the stock lists and the wagons. We'll all have a lot of work to do before we leave."

Chief Red Cloud - Sioux Chief
courtesy of Library of Congress

* * *

Preparations went forward. Every store in Bozeman and a few in the other camps chipped in to help with provisioning the expedition. Wray allotted claim shares for every donation, as they did for all the other materials gathered, hay, stock feed, rations, ammo—everything that was needed.

Two weeks had passed and the train began to assemble outside of town. Twenty two wagons and teams were lined up, and at least a hundred pack horses. Stew had asked to come along, so he, Frank and Matthew had broken some of their horses to harness to their wagon. Carter, when he'd left town, had taken Siderus's horse. He had left his own, though, and another pack horse, and Matthew had appropriated them. No one had argued. They also had Puckett's second horse, a good one, though light for pulling. Stew contributed his, and between Frank and Matthew they had a couple more to hitch up. They'd left Happy with the cabin.

Matthew was in a quandary as to whether to take Stonewall.

"If I take him, the Indians may get him. If I leave him, he'll probably get stolen."

Thanks to Frank and Stew, Puckett's chase and death had become a legend around town and men had come up to the corral to gaze at Stonewall and discuss his qualities. He was a marked horse. Matthew had been approached half a dozen times by men who wanted to buy him and the extravagant offers made it hard to say 'no.' He had also heard, through Stew, (who heard all the gossip down at the restaurant) that the outlaw contingent was damned upset with Matthew and Frank and that they had promised to steal Stonewall at the first opportunity. Like anything of value, came the headache of trying to keep it.

Matthew decided to bring him and take extra pains to keep him safe.

Frank was taking Spades. Stew would drive the wagon.

He was a good teamster and soon had the teams used to hitching up by putting their nose bags on, leading them up to their places beside the chain and then had them ready for their bridles by the time they'd finished eating. He could drop the harness in seconds, just by releasing two buckles each and stripping the harness (attached to the chain) as they were urged forward.

They departed on a chilly morning, the men all complaining about the weather but excited to be on the trail. Matthew and Frank rode up and down the line, getting them started. Right away, they had trouble with Wickershamm and the rest of his young cohorts, who wanted to ride on ahead. They had to be confronted and detailed off in groups with the vets, some old hands with the contingent in front, some in back, with outriders on either side. Finally, the whole cavalcade was lined out and moving along. Frank and Matthew came back together and rode for a time beside Stew, in the lead wagon. He could be counted on to set the pace and go where Matthew told him.

"Things are goin' along now, looks like. But we're goin' to have trouble with them young bucks. They're hard to hold in. And some of 'em already said they'd be damned if they were doin' any diggin'." Frank reported. Matthew nodded without comment. He had a few ideas about bringing them to heel.

* * *

They moved slowly down through the country of the Crows, but on the north side of the river. The grass was still poor yet and they had to baby the stock, as the animals were still weak. In places, they had to help the animals pull through the drifts, first shoveling, then getting on ropes and heaving the wagons through, sometimes as many as fifty men on the ropes. Each night, Matthew made them dig fighting pits, to the men's disgust. Some of the young ones like Wickershamm rebelled and Matthew had some of the old heads go out on scout, then come running back, firing their rifles, yelling "Indians." That scare, coupled with a couple dark nights and pickets firing all night long, had the men edgy and there was no more grumbling about digging.

 The last of March, they crossed the Yellowstone on the ice, not far from the mouth of a big creek Stanley's survey party had named Porcupine. Then, due to finding better grass and the poor condition of the stock, they laid over for five days. While there, prospectors went out and checked that creek and the surrounding country. No gold was found, though buffalo were plentiful.

 The morning of the sixth day, they pulled out and headed across country, following an old Indian trail that pointed south, in the direction of the Rosebud. About eight miles from the river, two hunters who had gone ahead, Bill Hineman and Charlie Dryden, came running their horses into the train, closely followed by a pack of Sioux. They pulled their ponies to a halt when they saw the large outfit in front of them, then headed back over the hill when they came under fire from a number of men who got into fast action. One horse was rolled and another staggered as it was whipped along, but all of them made it over the crest, the horseless Indian picked up by a friend.

 Matthew pulled the train up on a high ridge for the night and water for cooking had to be brought from a gulch a half mile away. However, nobody grumbled. Even the youngsters could see the site was easily defensible.

The next day, another ten miles were made, and, as before, Matthew located them on a high point, again quite a ways from water. The following day, they made about eight miles, when they found a spot to fort up that was close to water, along the creek. The stock needed rest again, so they stopped there. As it was around noon, some men were detailed by Matthew to scout the course for tomorrow's jaunt.

About a mile from camp, going up a steep hill that had a thick growth of pines, George Herendeen, a little behind, looked up from the trail they were following and saw an Indian running through the timber. He raised his Sharps and fired, dropping the runner. It was an ambush, prematurely sprung, and the rest of the Indians started firing themselves, evidently using repeaters. The shooting was intense, but the party of whites didn't lose their composure, as most of the ten were old hands. Half would fire while the others would retreat, then hold up while the first party scrambled, covering them. The train heard the commotion and Matthew sent another group out to protect their retreat and the Indians were held back. In that way, all made it safely back, though a horse was killed.

While this was going on to the left of the train, a young man named Bostwick was stationed out as a picket on the right. Out about six hundred yards, on a point, a horse was standing, seemingly tied. Bostwick watched it, curious, then walked his horse toward it. As he crossed a little gulch which hid him for a moment, a half dozen Sioux, who'd been hiding, rushed over the hill and got within twenty yards of him before he saw them. He was packing a Winchester and raising it, fired and wheeled his horse, spurring him to full speed as the Indians began shooting. His horse was slow and the Indians caught up to him and shot him in four places, using up their ammo. Bostwick was swaying from side to side, about to fall from the running horse.

The Indians quirted him and struck him several times with their hands, counting coup. Coming up beside him, a Sioux had an arrow to his bow, about to skewer him, when Jack Bean, an exceptional shot, knocked the brave from his mount with a well-aimed bullet. He'd been on picket duty a quarter of a mile down the ridge from Bostwick and hearing the shooting, had jumped his horse into a run to Bostwick's aid. The wounded man rode just over the hill and fell, while Bean and Yates, another picket, spurred past him and charged the Sioux. Their shooting chased the Sioux off and Bostwick was saved. He was carried in more dead than alive but eventually recovered, thanks to Wickershamm and Frank's doctoring.

Bean had killed at least one of the Sioux, for the next morning, taking that same ridge as a path for the train, they found where a large amount of blood had been spilled by one or more of Bostwick's attackers.

Matthew had been stern about making a tight defensive circle with the wagons each night, using heavy chains between them to bridge the gap and make a corral for the stock. This night, though, the corral had been made too small and some of the stock had to be left outside. Matthew had detailed several herders as night guard, accordingly. Ten o'clock came, full dark, but Dick Robinson, who had an eagle eye, saw an Indian and took a shot, seeing him fall. That kept the camp up, and about eleven, a mounted group of Sioux charged right up to the wagons, trying to run off the horses, firing into the camp. The herd tried to stampede but were, with difficulty, kept together. The Indian Robinson had shot commenced yelling to his people, trying to get their attention for a rescue. Some braves rode up to him where he lay, but unknown to them, they came close to a rifle pit with five white men in it. These opened fire and the Sioux scattered, though their wounded one was saved.

Next day several blood spots were found but no bodies. All the men in the rifle pit claimed hits. That morning as they hitched up, Indians began sniping at the train, and this went on for most of the trip, but always, Matthew had picked men firing back, making it hot for them.

Next day, they made another ten miles and camped on a ridge that began the slope down to the Rosebud.

Matthew by now had a decent grasp on most of the men's abilities. He detailed the best ones for scouts to go check out the country side for Sioux before the stock was turned out to feed each morning.

Stewart Buchanan, an old trapper, went out with them and found sign that the Indians had divided, some going up the Rosebud and some down, evidently to bring up the big villages.

"We'll be hip-deep in Injuns in a day er so," he observed.

Matthew knew they would have to be ready for them. He had them cross the creek and pull onto a bench about four hundred yards from the water. Just above the camp was an Indian trail thirty feet wide, indicating a big village had recently passed. When Buchanan showed the men this, everyone, even the coffee coolers, grabbed shovels and picks and the dirt began to fly.

During the day, no Indians were seen. Just before dark, though, groups of Sioux could be seen in every direction.

"Hold fire, boys, until you are sure of your shot." Matthew extolled on the right. Frank did the same on the left.

At full dark, the Indians began hooting like owls and howling like coyotes. Then a flock of geese flew over and the Sioux changed their tune, making the night hideous with their imitations. No one slept. Late in the night, about one, a shot was fired by an Indian nearby and the camp dogs all went out barking. Only one came back, and he was shot through the body by an arrow, which was still in him. He had to be put down by his owner. Matthew was thankful then that he had left Bear back at Bozeman with Happy. The other dogs were eaten by the Sioux within a hundred yards of the corral, the white men smelling the fire and the cooking meat.

After the dogs had been eaten, the train all heard the deep sonorous voice of an Indian giving what was likely a speech. When he finished, a bell tinkled and a volley of fire in every direction came from the Indians. After that, a volley came at intervals, always heralded by the bell. As soon as the men heard the bell, they hunkered down and the bullets went high, doing no harm—except by one canny brave, who had occupied a rifle pit that had been dug earlier close in to the breastworks, not fifty yards away. He had dragged a piece of drift wood to the front of his hole and was firing from its cover. His weapon was a heavy muzzle loader and his pit was in full view of the horse corral. Though he fired slowly, nearly every shot was killing or wounding a horse.

Frank ran back to where Matthew was leaning on a wagon.

"Pard! That one is giving our stock hell! Can you get Bill to give him a round?"

Matthew called over to Cameron, who had his gun crew swivel the Big Horn gun around. He aimed it carefully, then cut a fuse extra short. He pulled the lanyard and the shell hit the piece of driftwood, exploding it into fragments. No more shooting came from that quarter the rest of the night.

"Give 'em a Rebel yell, boys!" Matthew shouted, and the men of the train all responded. Up to that time the Indians had been yelling and screeching, but when the gun discharged, it got suddenly quiet. After that, the Indians fought silently, for the most part.

Dawn came and then it was found that the heaviest firing was coming from an ash grove a little over a hundred yards out.

"Give that bunch over there a couple doses of canister, Bill!" Matthew directed, pointing. Cameron did so and that quieted the grove, the rounds spraying the trees and everything in them.

As soon as the sun came up, the men were able to see their gun sights and then the Indians were subjected to some fine shooting by the train members. As the Sioux raised up to shoot over the rim of a coulee out a hundred yards or more, they were shot in the forehead, the big bullets nearly taking their heads off. Nine or ten Indians died that way. That made the rest cautious, and they started holding pistols over the cutbank and firing without taking aim. Some of the train's sharpshooters hit their wrists at that range and the warriors grew more careful yet.

A little coulee on the left was about fifty yards out, which had sheltered the majority of the Sioux all night. Quite a steady firing came from this and some of the stock were getting hit. Frank ran down that way to see what was afoot and was aghast to see Stonewall down, along with half a dozen others. Either the Indian that Cameron had obliterated with a shell had shot him, or one of those in the coulee had done so. Matthew's pet was dead.

"Oh, damn, damn, damn." he said, chewing his lip. He went back to Matthew.

"Pard, bad news! Stonewall's been killed." He said, wiping his brow and agonizing at his friend's reaction.

"Stonewall. . . .You sure he's dead?" Matthew asked.

"'Afraid so. Just come from there. And they got another half dozen or more down. Either that brave in the pit got him last night or that bunch in the coulee over there to the left that's been doin' the shootin' into the corral."

'Stonewall'... Matthew unconsciously wiped his face. He felt a red fog coming over him. He turned and dug in the wagon, coming up with a bag from which he pulled another pistol, Puckett's gun. He checked the loads and Frank, knowing what was coming, dived in himself and pulled out Siller's Smith and Wesson. It was loaded and he stuck it in his belt.

"Listen up, men! I need twenty or thirty men over here—now. Pistol men!!" Matthew called. Men came from every direction, checking their weapons, stuffing loads in them.

"I want good pistol shots—get a couple of them, so you have at least a dozen rounds." The men, at least a third of the train, scrambled around, borrowing or cajoling their friends' weapons.

Matthew turned to Frank. "You stay here and take command if I go down." He said, laying a hand on Frank's shoulder.

That worthy felt a thrill go down his arm at the touch and he nodded, then thinking, exploded, "The Hell I will!! I'm comin', too!! We've watched each other's back all these years and I'm not stoppin' now." Matthew looked pained but nodding, turned away and called out to Cameron.

"Bill, just before we charge, you fire both guns to keep their heads down! And Bill, you're in command if we don't make it back." He turned back to the men and detailed off thirty men, dividing them into three teams of ten each.

"Buchanan, you take a crew—this one—to the mouth of the coulee, Frank, you take this one down around the bottom. I'm taking this outfit straight on and hit them in the middle. The rest of you men, shoot when the big guns fire, then hold up, and let us go in and do the job. Now, get ready!" He signaled to Cameron.

Both gun teams fired simultaneously, the signal for all the rest of the train to let off their weapons. The three crews lit out from the wagons in a run for their objective.

The center was reached first and the shooters were over the top and among the Sioux before they were aware, almost, of the attack. It was close work. Matthew fired, striking a brave who was coming at him with a tomahawk, in the base of the throat, dropping him. He turned slightly and fired again, breaking the arm of a Sioux drawing back an arrow. The man dropped the bow and started to run but was shot by another in the back as he fled. The Indians, probably fifty at least there in the coulee, broke and fled as the other parties came streaming in, shooting. Some stayed to fight and were killed, others were killed as they ran. The dead were scattered all over the flat, and nine dead ones were counted in the coulee. These were scalped by the young men of Wickershamm's group. The only injury to the pistoleers was the broken wrist of a youngster, Tom Woodward, who had been shot as he charged.

The attackers captured twenty three horses, rifles, a quantity of buffalo robes, blankets, moccasins and packets of leather wrapped pemmican and jerky. These horses replaced the stock killed by the Indian fire, but Frank knew Matthew was heartsick over Stonewall's loss.

Another party charged the opposite bluff later and killed two Indians and drove off the rest. Soon after this, An Indian mounted on a fine paint horse, wearing a beautiful war bonnet, came dashing out on a bravo ride. His course was across the length of the bench in front of the train. He was fired at by a dozen men and his horse was killed. The warrior was hit, too, but staggered to the coulee and made it out of sight. Later the horse was checked and they found nine bullet holes in the handsome animal.

Chapter 36

They laid over a day, thinking the Sioux might come back. Matthew had them dig a large rifle pit across the coulee, and thirty men were detailed to picket duty there that night.

That next day, around the morning coffee fires, some of the men started getting cold feet and talked of heading back. Matthew heard them and called for a meeting and a vote. A large majority, the miners, voted to advance, still wanting to prospect the head of the Rosebud. That was the course for now.

Some of them were fond of practical jokes and decided to play a trick or two on the Sioux. They poisoned some biscuits and some pemmican and left it lying about the camp. They also pulled some bullets from cartridges and pouring the powder out, substituted dynamite. These little tricks were deadly but they didn't hear of the results until later.

They headed out the next day and made nine miles, camping at the three forks of the Rosebud. Indians had been seen along the line of march all day, but wisely, none had ventured close enough to shoot at. Matthew had them dig pits as usual and they fully expected a fight, but none transpired. He then sent a strong party to go forward and select their route south towards the Big Horn Mountains. This group decided on the middle fork as the most likely and the next day they went up that fork to the divide between the Rosebud and the Little Horn River and swung into camp. Matthew sent Bean, Yates and Frank out and they managed to kill three buffalo, which were welcome, as the Indians had frightened the game away from the front of them for the last ten days. Prospectors working the river when they had time found little to excite them.

The next day, they made another ten miles and pitched camp on a fork of the Little Horn River. The grass was thick and they burned it off before them, then dug pits. That evening, one of the pickets saw a couple funny looking wolves and decided to give them a taste of lead. At his shot, the two wolves got up on their hind legs and ran off.

The stock was turned out to graze as usual, with a strong number of herders about them, taking it easy and laying about, holding their horses, when a picket on a hill began yelling "Injuns, Injuns!"

At this, some of the pickets and the herders ran in to the train. One of the herders, French Pete, was quietly taking his morning constitutional behind a sage brush when the cry went up. He had to leave his pistol and belt there on the ground. The Sioux came in sight, then, coming quickly in three groups, each about two hundred strong.

"Bill, have your gun teams give each of those groups a shot or two! The rest of you, get out there and protect the stock! Get that herd in here before we lose it! Frank, watch our backside."

The cannon boomed and the men advanced out from the wagons and knelt and gave out several volleys to the enemy that, with the devastating effect of the shells, made them lose interest, and they wheeled off before reaching the herd. As they retreated, one brave turned back and was making his horse rear

315

and caracole, showing off. Bean took careful aim and fired. The rider sagged, then fell, and the rider-less horse came running into the train's herd. The Indians began sniping from the nearby hills.

Some of the men, a small party, ran out to scalp the brave that Jack Bean had killed. They only got a hundred yards from the train when one, Zack Yates, was shot directly through the heart. He died instantly. The others lost interest in scalping and carried him back to the wagons, which were now corralled, with the stock enclosed within. Matthew and Frank distributed the men according to the lay of the land, but the site was not a good one, tactically.

"All right, boys! Look sharp now! Watch that hill over there!" A dozen braves had just then raced to the top of a little hill which commanded a position above them. They immediately started shooting and killed one horse, then another.

"Frank, take some men up there and root 'em out!"

Frank gathered ten men and as those in camp started some rapid firing, they headed on foot for the bottom of the hill, which shielded them from those above. They caught their breath and then ran up and over the top, gaining the crest not forty feet from the Sioux. The Indians were panic stricken and mounting, took off down the far side. Frank had packed his Henry along and now, resting it on a pine branch, fired and knocked a fat Indian from his horse. The others got into the act, then, and killed two more before the others got away. Some of the younger men, crazy for souvenirs, went down and scalped them.

"Bean! Come over here." Matthew yelled at their best shooter, who came to him. "Listen, son, see there where Pete left his pistol?" The young man nodded as Matthew pointed.

"Kill any Indian who comes near it. We don't want them to get any trophies, do we?"

He smiled and Bean, encouraged and flattered at being picked as a sharpshooter by this man they all admired, set up his sticks and laid his belt down by them. He fired several times in an hour and killed another three Indians who tried to gain the pistol and belt, lying there in plain sight.

The Sioux finally gave it up, seeing it as it was, a bait to get them shot. Five of the train members then started out to get Pete's pistol. As they got close, a warrior on a beautiful black horse came charging at them. The party fired and he went down. As he fell, his lariat rein became tangled and stopped the horse. The party coveted the animal, which was a good looking horse, but when they got up to it, the smell of white men became too much and it broke loose. They reluctantly shot it, rather than have it get back to the Sioux.

Then they turned their attention on the dead Indian, intending to scalp him, but the fire from the hills came thick and they laid up in a buffalo wallow, waiting their chance. John Anderson, one of Wickershamm's friends, was determined to get a scalp

What was his surprise, though, when he peeked over the edge, to see the Indian getting up. Anderson rose and ran at him as the brave tried to get his gun, a Winchester, around to shoot. He was dazed and too slow for Anderson, who hit him solidly in the face with his fist. Pulling his knife, he stabbed and killed him. Then he tried to scalp him but the bullets from the fast shooting Indians scared him off. He managed to whack off a piece of the scalp with a braid attached, then skedaddled. Wickershamm ran up then and tried, but his knife was too dull for the work, so he contented himself with cutting off the ears. Archie Campbell, another of the party, also ran over and managed to cut off another part of the scalp. Considering that almost three hundred Sioux were shooting at them from a distance around three hundred yards, it was an amazing spectacle of idiocy.

Matthew turned away, sure that all of them would be killed and furious that they had gone. Later, they all had sore butts from the chewing he gave them. Though the train started again, following the Little Horn, the Indians made it hot for them all afternoon, sniping from every ridge and vantage point. Camp was made on a flat, about half a mile from the Little Horn, where it would be hard for the Sioux to get an advantage. They were so harassed by the constant sniping the stock couldn't get out to graze.

Yates' body was carried along to this camp and then buried after dark by a rifle pit, so that when dug, its dirt covered the grave. In this way they kept the location a secret from the savages who would have dug it up and desecrated the body.

* * *

The next day was stormy and because the stock was again drooping, they lay over. In the forenoon, they tried to water the stock but the Indians kept running them in. While there, the coffee coolers again started talking and now there was some real dissension. Vernon had left the train early on, before they even crossed the Yellowstone, disappearing down the river, and many thought that he had been a shill for those trying to get a route established on the Yellowstone. They'd found no traces of gold and the country roundabout didn't have a look to it that signified gold bearing strata. Somehow, though, another gold story had gotten started among the men about a creek off the

Tongue River farther down east being rotten with the yellow metal, and now many of the miners wanted to go down there and check that possibility out. Matthew scratched his head but decided to take another vote. They took it and the clear majority, who were miners, voted to go on to the Tongue. At this, the older men, the experienced heads, decided to hell with it. They argued that the train would only be going deeper yet into the Sioux country, that they were already clearly outnumbered ten to one, and in another week, the Indians would have gathered their forces and by sheer force of numbers, sweep them off the earth. So they decided to go back, even if the others went the other way.

This cooled the others on the proposition of heading to the Tongue, as they all knew that dividing up would be their death. They re-voted and all determined to go back to Bozeman.

The following day, the train made a short march toward the Big Horn and camped on Lodge Grass creek. Just after Matthew put out the pickets, a large body of Sioux made a run and tried to cut them off, but they made it safely back to camp. The evening guards were doubled and, though several parties of Sioux came near and made the night vibrate with their yells and screeches, causing the pickets to fire and drive them off, no forceful attack was made. At this camp, the jokers in the train made another trap—a hole made up like a grave, complete with a headboard, concealing within it a howitzer shell that was fixed to explode if disturbed.

The next morning, the train had to cross Lodge Grass creek and to make the crossing secure, the howitzer was placed on a point that commanded the ford, until the wagons and men all got across, when the howitzer was rushed on over. Just above the ford was a thick grove of trees that Matthew, looking at it with his glass, could see was full of Indians. Across, the train struck out for the hills, trying to keep as far from the grove as possible. Some of the men, horseless now, were walking on either flank. What the expedition didn't know at the time, but learned later, was that a huge war party of Cheyenne, three hundred fifty braves, had joined the Sioux the night before and made their boast that they would ride over the train in the morning. They were the large group swarming in the grove. When the train came opposite the trees, the Cheyenne appeared, keeping a tight, formed line as they advanced.

"Good Christ!! They look like troops in uniform. What the hell are they?" Frank asked Matthew curiously.

"Damn if I know. They sure don't look or act like Sioux!! Get ready, Boys!"

The Cheyenne came sweeping out, an intimidating and menacing enemy force. The flankers came together and started toward the advancing Cheyenne, instead of running back to the train, stopping in an orderly fashion to stoop and shoot, then get up and advance again. This audacity bewildered the charging Cheyenne, who broke off and swung to the left, in front of the train, which corralled as quickly as they could.

In the rear of the train was a high sided coulee, which the Cheyenne swept into and then began a hot fire into the train. This couldn't be allowed to go on, and Matthew made up another charging party of about forty men.

They went fast, yipping and yelling their rebel yells, running out of the corralled train toward the coulee and the Cheyenne were amazed and shaken at the crazy white men's reckless bravery. They fled like sheep, some leaving their horses behind, as the men poured into the coulee, shooting and yelling. Though only a few Indians were downed, due to the trainmen being out of breath, and shooting poor, more were wounded. Several of the men captured horses and led them back to camp.

This battle broke the resolve of the Indians and they could be observed heading back to the last camp. Though some claimed they heard the buried shell explode, nothing was really known until years afterward, when a Cheyenne told someone that they had dug up the grave, that it had exploded and killed two Indians and wounded many more.

Chapter 37

At the next camp, two warriors came out on a promontory and fired at the train, the bullet striking just under a horse. Matthew had Jack Bean take a shot at them and that worthy, using his .45/120 Sharps and his sticks, took careful aim and fired. Matthew, using his Grubb-made English binoculars, and some others using their telescopes, watched, trying to discern the effects of the shot. Amazingly, the Indian who had shot at them fell to the ground, evidently hit.

Matthew gave out an exclamation. "By God, son, you hit him! You dropped him!"

Irving Hopkins, who had a marine single draw telescope, and Tom Rea, who had an old Army Signal Corps four draw telescope, agreed that the young shooter had hit his mark. The distance was argued and discussed and finally figured at nearly a mile.

"That shot surely equals Billy Dixon's down at Adobe Walls against the Kiowa and C'manche." Frank remarked, with a shake of his head.

Bean's long shot was the last one fired against the Indians on the trip, though Matthew made them take every precaution until they reached and crossed the Bighorn. Then, on Beauvais

Creek, a big party of Crows, Quirt's band and some Nez Perce came up to them. When they were shown the eleven scalps and the other trophies of their enemies, including Wickershamm's set of ears, they insisted on borrowing them and making a big medicine dance right there, celebrating the defeat of their enemies. They made a glorious night of it, though it kept the men up, with all the yelling and screeching.

Next morning, Matthew was washing up at the creek when Frank came up, trailed by Neil Gillis. Frank gestured to the young man. "Gillis here claims he saw a white kid running between the tipis. Think we should check it out?" Matthew thought on it.

"Yes, we're here and in their good graces right now. Let's see what's up."

The men got some coffee and walked over to the camp, which was crowded with sleeping bodies of the exhausted friendlies. They came up to Quirt's tipi and scratched on the cover, waiting respectfully until a squaw came and unlaced it. They stepped inside, trying to ignore the smell, which was soon dissipated as the squaw built up the fire and added some aromatic sagebrush to it. Quirt, his hairdo all messed up and showing the effects of a hard night, soon brightened up when Matthew offered him a big cup of coffee heavily laced with sugar and a little rum he'd brought along. He slurped appreciatively.

Frank signed and the talk opened. Quirt was obstinate and kept declaring ignorance about any white kids. Matthew finally lost his temper.

"Damn it, Frank. Tell him that we are heading in to the fort and unless we get any white kids turned over to us before we talk to Colonel Gibbon, he'll find himself in heap trouble with the Army!"

"I'm havin' trouble gettin' him to understand, I think. Gillis, would you run and get Buchanan? He talks some Crow."

Gillis left the tipi and soon returned with Buchanan.

"Tell him that we want any white kids turned over to us now. We know he has some. We saw them. I can't get it over to him myself." Frank said. Buchanan jabbered at Quirt, then turned back to Frank and Matthew.

"He says that they ain't his. The Nez Perce picked 'em up after the Sioux hit a wagon train down east. There was two of 'em, boy and a girl, but the Perce could only get the boy from 'em. The Sioux kept the girl. He says it was Bad Wound's bunch, A damned tough crowd of Uncpapas. The boy, he thinks he can get from 'em, if we want to trade for Sioux scalps." He scratched himself and yawned. He'd not been able to sleep much, with all the doings in the camps. The young men had gone over and danced and frolicked with the Indians most of the night, but he had found a willing squaw, which was more to his liking than dancing and raising hell around the medicine fire.

"Scalps." Matthew scratched his head. *'Who among the men would let their trophies go?'* "How many, ask him?" More jabber among the two.

"He says three. One for him, I guess, and two for the boy."

He listened. "And a horse. A good one."

"Tell him. . . they should give the boy up without any trade. He's our color, not theirs."

"He says the Nez Perce don't look at it like that, but traded for him with the Sioux and would expect to get paid back. Makes sense." he yawned.

"I want to see him." Matthew said.

"He says he might get them to bring him over." Quirt sent a squaw out of the tipi and she shortly returned with another squaw, a Nez Perce who was not happy at being brought to the white men. She left after a shouting harangue and sullenly came back with a scared little towheaded boy, three or four years old. He was naked except for a little breechclout and moccasins. His gray/blue eyes looked them over and Matthew felt a thrill and a chill run down his spine as he looked into the boy's big luminous orbs. His heart lurched within him. He glanced at Frank and noticed he seemed affected, too.

"Tell Quirt, tell him. . . .my people will talk it over."

Matthew gathered the train, some of them hung-over from the late evening festivities. They sat or lounged along the wagons, close up as Matthew spoke.

"Men, we've been through quite a trip. You asked Frank and I to lead you and we both tried to do our best. We're here today, and I wish that Yates was with us. He probably would be, if he had listened and stayed under cover. The fact is, we took on the Sioux and the Cheyenne and waded right through the best they could throw at us. Now, something's come up and I'm asking *your* help. This morning Gillis saw a little boy, a white boy, amongst the kids playing around the tipis. We went and asked Quirt about it and found out that his parents were part of a train that the Sioux had wiped out. They took him and his sister and the Nez Perce traded for him last summer. We think his sister is still with Bad Wound's band. But he's here right now. Quirt thinks the Nez Perce might trade for him,, but the problem is they want scalps. I want to trade for him, but to do it, I need your trophies, three of 'em. He also wants a horse, and we can do that. Frank and I have an extra or two, since we're this close to Bozeman. What about it, men? Are there any of you that will let loose your trophies for a little white boy?"

He looked around and the men were silent. He was disappointed. He'd hoped that they would give them up freely. He chewed his lip, as he was wont to do when he was getting upset. Frank, knowing his moods well by now, saw it. He stepped forward.

"Listen, boys, Matthew here stepped up when you-all wanted him to lead you. He did that, and the lot of you are here now with whole skins, most likely, because of him. He's not asking so much, some Indian scalps is all, for Christ's sake!! To save a little boy!! I've got some horses in the herd. I tell you what I'll do—a horse for a scalp!!"

At that, two men came forward, Archie Campbell and French Pete, and handed Frank two grisly objects—black haired scalps, one with a braid still on it.

"Hell, Frank, keep your horses! You can have 'em if that's what it takes to get a white kid back from a bunch of savages." Campbell said. Pete nodded, agreeing with him.

"Will a pair of ears equal a scalp?" This from Wickershamm, the young troublemaker, who had caused Matthew and Frank both so much grief during the trip. He stepped forward and handed Frank his trophies. Gillis came in to the group, leading a nice looking sorrel he had captured from the Sioux. He handed the halter rope to Matthew.

"Here, sir. I want to donate this cayuse to the cause. We all know you lost your pet this trip. This one here is the least we can do to make it up a little." The men yelled their thanks then, and another man, John Anderson, walked forward.

"How about half a scalp?" He handed it over to Frank.

Another came. "Oh hell, I didn't want the damn thing anyway. It's not Christian scalping people. I just did it because Rhea dared me to." He handed his over also.

"Thanks, men. We can damn sure trade them out of the boy now. I appreciate it." He turned away and Frank followed him with the trade goods.

The train stayed put until the trade was made, the squaw beaming now, with the enemy scalps in their possession. Quirt, too, was satisfied. He had the ears of one of his enemies, strong medicine, and a new horse, one of his enemy's war horses. Maybe the same brave who'd lost his ears had owned the horse. With a little imagination, he could picture the brave, earless and horseless, wandering desolately in the Shadow Land. He snorted contentedly and called for his pipe.

Chapter 38

The boy would only ride with Matthew. He seemed scared of everyone else, even Frank, who made up to him with tidbits of meat and other things he thought a boy might like, such as molasses on a stick to lick. The little towhead just scrunched back further into Matthew's belly as they sat on the horse, riding alongside Stew's wagon.

"What do you s'pose his name is?" Frank asked, walking Spades alongside. The day was a bright sunny one and the mountain air was exhilarating that morning, the sky clear as glass. Matthew had fed the boy and wrapped his chunky little body in a shirt, then put him on the horse, where he perched, hanging on to the horn, as Matthew mounted. They'd been riding for hours now and the boy had seemed content. *'No doubt he had ridden that way with his father,'* Matthew thought.

At noon, he dismounted and the boy still wanted to stay aboard, but Matthew shook his head and got him down. He followed him, then, stumbling as he tried to walk in the unraveling shirt. Matthew swept him up and carried him to the wagon, where Stew was bustling about, getting the coffee on and readying up a meal. They were about out of grub but Stewberries had managed to find some flour deep in one of the sacks, and there was bacon grease, saved each morning, that hadn't quite soured yet. They lunched on flour-rolled buffalo loin, cooked in the grease, last night's biscuits, and coffee. The boy tried the coffee and made a face, but drank water out of the wagon barrel. He ate like a little wolf, tearing at the meat and wiping it all over his face. Matthew was glad he had enough teeth to eat with. That would have been a problem, but they would have figured it out, somehow. After the meal, he took him down to the creek and washed him, despite his struggles.

That night, he snuggled in the bedroll with him and the close proximity of the squirming little body sleeping next to him kept Matthew awake for hours. He was strangely content, though, and hugged the boy close. Morning came too early.

Four days later, they pulled over the pass and came up to the fort. Matthew had been in a quandary the whole night, trying to decide if he should give the boy up. They had formed a close bond during the four days, and Matthew was thinking seriously of how he—they—might keep him. But the thought was preposterous, when viewed objectively. He and Frank were a couple wanderers, they had little or nothing to offer a boy. What he needed was a stable home and a mother, a female, to look after him. Later, he'd need to go to school. No, the thing now was to take him in to the Army so that they could sort his future out.

Frank, as usual, wouldn't go in the fort. Matthew took the child in himself and had to wait then, for the Colonel. He came in presently, in a temper over something one of his young officers had pulled the night before. The sight of the child made him curious and he wanted to know the whole story. Matthew took the time to explain, the child, still wrapped in an old shirt, sitting on his lap, big-eyed and silent at the strange surroundings.

"Sergeant, go find 'Mother' McCree and ask her to come in, please." He settled back and lit his pipe and wanted to hear about the expedition, and Matthew obliged.

"That little trip you men took through Sioux country upset the authorities back east, you know. They sent me word to stop you, but you had already pulled out. I decided I might as well let you go get yourselves killed, and maybe you might kill a few of them for us. Sounds like you did that, alright."

The sergeant appeared, "She's coming, Colonel."

"This woman has seven children. She works in our laundry and still manages to do a pretty good job raising them," he explained, blowing a cloud of smoke. "'Course, she has an older daughter that helps out." he added.

'Mother' McCree was Sergeant McCree's widow, who had been allowed to stay on at the fort after his death down by Fort Reno two years before, when a train he was escorting was attacked by Red Cloud. 'Mother' had a large brood and one more shouldn't matter, the Colonel said.

When she came, a heavy woman of massive proportions who reminded Matthew of a female grizzly, she scratched under her head scarf and allowed that 'she might take him along and see if the shoe fit, the poor little thing." The Colonel was relieved, as he had no funds to take care of orphans. However, he could divert a ration allotment or two to McCree and her family, he guessed, if necessary.

The boy howled and fought when she took him out of Matthew's arms. She was used to squalling kids and tucked him under her arm as she exited. The last Matthew saw of the boy was his crying face and pleading eyes. He shut his own, to get the sight out of his mind, and reminded himself that it was for the best. He said his goodbyes to the Colonel and came out into the sunlight. Somehow, the day didn't seem as bright as it had before. He felt a curious sense of desolation. Frank saw his mood when he came up and mounted. He wisely said nothing. He felt much the same.

Chapter 39

While Matthew and Frank had stopped at the fort, the train had passed on by the fort and through into the center of town, where men were standing, visiting, telling their stories, and getting thirsty doing it. The saloons were filling up and as they passed, the men all called and invited them for a drink. They declined with a wave, eager to get to the cabin and get unloaded and their horses cared for before they headed up town. Matthew had promised Frank a few drinks and both he and Stew a restaurant meal on him.

At the base of the hill, they saw with shock that the cabin was gone, burned. The stable, too. Only the corral was left.

"Looks like it happened a couple weeks ago. Been rained on since," Frank said grimly, gazing at the side of one of the walls that hadn't completely been consumed by the fire. He looked at Matthew.

"S'pose Happy or Greene let the fire get away somehow. Maybe a chimney fire?" They turned and retraced their steps back to town. Happy was looking for them and met them at the edge, talking almost before they hit the ground and gathered around him.

"I heard 'em talking outside and got up, then the cabin went up with a whoosh!" He threw up his hands, gesturing.

"I grabbed some stuff and my pistol and ran out. Bear come with me. They started shootin' and I fired back and took off, but Bear went after 'em, I guess, and they killed him." He shook his head nervously. "I heard 'em laughing about it."

"Who were they, did you hear?" Matthew asked.

"Yeah. It was Turner and Marks and some others. They hang out down at the Four Aces. It's the main stop for that crew, seems like. But, Matthew . . . that Turner, they say he's real quick with a gun. Killed a couple men over in Bannack and one in Nevada City, I heard. Marks ain't no slouch either, he's got some killings to his name."

"Good. Then no one can say it isn't fair." Matthew said, as he turned away. He put his rifle in the wagon and then pulled his pistol and checked its loads. Stew and Frank, seeing that, did the same.

Happy got nervous.". . . .I'm not a gun hand, Matthew. . . Oh what the hell. A man should stand by his friends." He pulled his weapon from its holster and made sure it was loaded. They mounted their horses. Happy jumped on the wagon and rode with Stew downtown. The bar was a long, low rough log affair, with horses tied to the hitch rack outside.

When they entered the smoky place, men looked around and the room quieted.

Matthew's voice rang in the silence. "I'm looking for a man named Turner."

From the back, a chair scraped and a man stood up, then the others from around the table. He was a longhaired and bearded individual in his middle thirties, burly, dressed a little better than the rest of those who came forward with him. He had a prominent forehead, eyes set back far in his square skull. His mouth was thin and set. His was a commanding presence, but there was an air of surprise that he was being called in his own lair.

"I'm Turner. Who's askin'?"

"Matthew Grounds. These are friends of mine. We owned a cabin up west of town that was torched by some two-bit night crawlers—sneaks that can't face a man in the light of day. They also killed a dog of mine. I'm hearin' your name connected with that little piece of shitwork. So I'm asking—did you do it?"

Turner snorted. "Puckett was a friend of mine. I figure you killed him by shootin' him in the back. He was too good a man for you to take him in a standup. So whatever you got, you had comin'." This was said in a sneering way, his words and the delivery of it helping the men with him steady up to the confrontation.

"Yes. Lee was a friend of ours, too, until he stole from us. And then went off and joined up with a bunch of cowards that sneak around in the night and light off a cabin when the owners are gone."

Turner's face twisted and his hand streaked down, coming up with his pistol as Matthew also drew. He moved sideways as Turner's gun blasted. Matthew felt the bullet pull at his side as he in turn, let off his shot. The bullet took Turner in the chest, blowing him back as he tried to raise his gun for another shot. Matthew fired again and the bullet took Turner in the face. He went down as Frank and then Stew, fired into the man beside Turner. Marks had drawn but his gun went off into the floor as falling, he pulled the trigger. The others threw up their hands when their leaders fell. Happy gasped in a whisper, "I'm hit, Stew!" Stewberries turned and held him up as he slumped.

"Take their guns, Frank. We don't want 'em shooting us in the back when we leave." Matthew held his pistol ready, menacing the crowd. Frank complied, holstering his own and grabbing weapons from holsters and up off the floor. He had an armload and they backed out of the bar, Stew helping Happy through the door.

Outside, Matthew said, "Give those guns the water treatment. Throw 'em in the puddle there—except for Turner's and the others. We'll take them along. Happy, how bad is it?"

Stew answered. "He's hit in the side—Frank, can you grab his other arm?" Together, the two men buoyed Happy along to the horses and got him, gasping, into the wagon. Matthew had watched the door of the bar and as it opened, threw a shot close into it. The door slammed again. They all got astride and away.

Frank said, concerned, "He *was* quick, pard. He beat you to the draw, I thought. Did he hit you?"

"I felt it pull at my coat—imagine there's a hole in it. I moved just as he shot. Happy took the bullet behind me. We better get him to the doctor." The men rode uptown and stopped at a sign that said, 'Silas Whitby, Doctor of Medicine'

They bundled Happy in, leaking blood, and the doctor, sitting in his chair at a desk, reading a newspaper, got up. Seeing the drooping, injured man, he hustled them into a back room, where they laid him on a couch. Stew and Matthew went back out, leaving Frank to help the doctor.

They waited, Matthew using the time to carefully reload his pistol and to check his coat, which did have a bullet hole through it. Stew went out to tend the horses. After an hour, Frank came out, followed by the doctor, scrubbing his hands.

"He'll be all right, I think, unless blood poisoning sets in. The bullet went on through and didn't cut any arteries or hit any intestines, as I can tell. Some blood loss, of course."

Matthew breathed a sigh of relief. "Can he stay here for a while, doctor?"

"I'm not set up to keep any one overnight but I usually make arrangements with Wickershamm. He has an extra room over his establishment. We'll get him fixed up there."

They headed for the Bailey Hotel and got rooms for the night. Then Matthew kept his word and took them out for drinks and a meal, in that order. Men, some of them who'd been on the expedition, had already heard what had gone on at the Four Aces, and wanted to talk to them about it.

As they visited at the bar, a deputation came over to them, composed of Wickershamm, Weir, Cox and Koontz and a couple others. They insisted on buying Matthew and his friends a drink, then asked if they might talk with them, in private.

The Arcade had a back office which the owner obligingly let them use and they all draped themselves around the small room, keeping their drinks handy.

Cox said, "Grounds, we heard what went on down at the Four Aces and we're here to tell you that the town is growing tired of this lawless element and their shenanigans. They're getting out of hand and we intend to do something about it. We talked around to the townspeople and we're in accord that we would like you and Frank to take on the job as town Marshals. The pay would be $200 a month for each of you. Additionally, you could pick another two deputies. Maybe Stew here would like to sign on, too?" The others nodded.

Stew burst out laughing. "Men, I'm just a cook, nothing more. Sure, I can use a gun. But, that was just to back up my friends here. I use a frying pan better. I'm not fool enough to think I could match up against some of the outlaw element like that of Turner or Marks. I'd be getting buried up at Boot Hill so fast that I'd never get to collect my first month's salary. Thanks, but no thanks, boys."

Matthew looked at Frank, then shook his head. "Frank and I tried lawing down in Texas and we didn't take to it. Neither of us would be interested, but thanks just the same, men." The others tried their best to persuade them, but finally saw that they were not getting anywhere. They had a couple more drinks, then left, dejected.

At the restaurant later, over a tremendous meal, Stew asked them. "What now, Matthew? Are you going to build another cabin? What's in the cards now?"

Matthew stirred some milk into his coffee and looked at Frank. "I'm thinking I'm real tired of the camps and the hustle after gold. Except for the killing, I liked being out after the buffalo. What do you think, Frank? Maybe go out and do some meat hunting and such, stay with Quirt or the Nez Perce for a while—live in a tipi for winter or two. I just want to get away for a time."

Frank didn't hesitate. "That would suit me fine! We still got a few bucks and maybe we could talk Stew here into goin' with us. Then we'd have a cook and a wagon man."

"Sure, if you'd give me a part share. I'm tired of full-time cookin', anyway." He liked and respected these men and had no qualms about throwing in with them. Wanted to, in fact. He was tired of the camps, too, and had a hefty little nest egg to fall back on.

Frank continued. "We're marked men. We stay here and we're goin' to be fighting and killin' 'til we finally go down ourselves. Now, I'm not scared and I don't think either of you are, either, but I don't see much future in it. Let's us gather up some grub and more ammo and head out of this burg."

"We'd better stay and see if Happy wants to come along. He's marked, too, since he showed with us." That got them up from the table and they went out to buy supplies at the mercantile.

The next day, they went by Wickershamm's to see Happy. He was awake and feeling better. After visiting a while, they asked him, "Happy, we're going to go off and do some meat hunting for the camps and get away for a time. We'd like to have you come along. Want to throw in with us?" Matthew asked.

Happy looked troubled. "I'd like to go with you but I got enough money saved up to head back east. Been wanting to do that—my folks been writing me and trying to get me home. So I guess not. I'm going to miss you all, though." He shook hands all around. Matthew visited the doctor and paid Happy's bill. The man had stood by them and had taken the bullet meant for him. It was the least he could do, Matthew felt.

* * *

They were passing the fort when from out of a little group of kids playing by the gate, came a small figure running after them. He was dressed in cast-off clothes too big for him and he had to keep pausing and pulling his pants up to run, but it didn't stop him. He kept on, and Matthew, seeing him, pulled his horse up and got down, opening his arms to the little figure that ran into them. He swung him up on his horse's saddle and climbed aboard after him. The boy settled back into Matthew and the horse walked on.

END

LLOYD'S MONTANA SAGA

BOOK ONE – THE REBELS

Two confederates meet on the battlefield and become friends during the Civil War. After the conflict is over, the men go west to make a new start. War-weary and restless, they find it hard to settle down.

Their journey takes them to Texas where they find work as rangers, then to Kansas, hunting buffalo, and finally to Montana, to see and experience the gold camps there.

BOOK TWO – PARDNERS

The early 1880's finds Frank and Matthew, with their adopted son, Toby, working to make a stake hunting buffalo on the Montana Plains. They run afoul of Stringer Jack's band of horse thieves as they attempt to start a horse ranch on the Yellowstone River, hoping to sell mounts to Fort Keogh's cavalry.

BOOK THREE – T.S. GROUNDS

Toby Grounds, the adopted boy, starts out on his own. He finds work with Theodore Roosevelt on his ranch in North Dakota, and follows him to Cuba into the maelstrom of the Spanish-American War. Later, he participates in the Philippines Campaign, battling the fierce Insurrectos.

Home again, a bitter love affair causes him to respond to Roosevelt's request for help with the plight of American missionaries in China, as they become engulfed in the Boxer Rebellion.

Toby comes home to take up ranching again, only to succumb to his need for money, which drives him into a bounty chase for outlaws in Montana's south country.

BOOK FOUR – HOME RANCH

Last in the series, this book continues the family saga into the 1960s where Toby's son, Matthew, struggles to build a ranch, pursuing his father's dream. He passes on his love of the land and strong will to survive to his son, Gable, who endures the Korean War to find his own destiny.

Throughout the entire series, the reader will anxiously turn pages until the very end.

ABOUT THE AUTHOR

Dave Lloyd is a fourth generation Montanan whose great-grandmother traveled up the Yellowstone on a steamboat to the head-of-track outside Miles City. She knew and told her family stories of the men and the women who lived at the time. Dave grew up listening to her and his grandmother, the first white baby born in the county, as they reminisced of that era's rowdy times.

Later, Dave was a working cowboy and became assistant ranch-manager on one of the largest ranches in the state.

Western Cattle Company, with hundreds of sections of land and cattle numbering in the thousands. He researches his books, and tries to make them historically accurate with their characters true to the times.

Lloyd has always been a gun, hunting and shooting enthusiast, and his readers are delighted by the old Sharps, Winchesters and other vintage rifles and pistols throughout Lloyd's novels.

The author lives in Helena, Montana with his wife, Donna, and continues to write of the early beginnings of the state he loves.

For more about the author visit www.lloydsbooks.com

CPSIA information can be obtained at www.ICGtesting.com
Printed in the USA
LVOW03s1916090415

433939LV00005B/147/P